THE
REPTILIAN
FACTOR

ReadersMagnet, LLC
10620 Treena Street, Suite 230 | San Diego, California, 92131 USA
1.619. 354. 2643 | www.readersmagnet.com

Book design copyright © 2021 by ReadersMagnet, LLC. All rights reserved.

Cover design by Ericka Obando
Interior design by Mary Mae Romero

THE REPTILIAN FACTOR

KERRY L. MARZOCK

Dedications

I am dedicating this novel to several people
who shared major parts of my life.
Two men who I loved dearly and who I think
about each and every day.
Both of whom have passed on,
but who remain in my heart forever.

My father, Eugene H. Marzock, passed away on 4/1/2013,
April Fool's Day, which truly was not much of a day for jokes.
My father was a wonderful man who met
my mother Wanda in May, 1944
at a skating rink while home on leave from the United States Navy
during a very deadly and tumultuous time - World War II.
He was eighteen and she was seventeen.
They would marry on July 14, 1945.
My dad was a very special and unique man who loved
his family dearly and who was always a devoted husband,
the best father, and a loving grandfather.
Without a doubt I truly idolized him and in my eyes,
my father could never do anything wrong.
Dad, I think of you every day and
will forever love you.

My husband and partner, Richard P. Clarke,
passed away on 4/27/2015.

We first met on 7/1/1976. My car,
an old black 1962 VW had broken down.
He arrived in a tow truck to pick me up so that we could
drive to where my car had been pulled off the road.
He always referred to me as his Independence Baby.
In turn, I always said that my knight in
shining armor road up in a tow truck
wearing dirty coveralls with a train cap cocked
at an angle on his head, a crooked smile
with a touch of mischief, and a twinkle in his eye.
He was thin as a rail, but extremely handsome
in a most wild and crazy way and immediately reminded
me of Rowdy Yates on the old "Rawhide" TV show.
On that particular day he stole my heart and then it broke thirty
nine years later with his passing. I held his hand to the end.
Richard came into my life when I desperately needed someone
special after going through a difficult period. We accepted each
other's good and bad qualities, but never did we fail to say, "I love
you", each and every day together.
Richard, I think of you every day and will forever love you.

....

Acknowledgements

I would like to acknowledge all my coworkers
in the Lockbox Department at AmeriGas Propane.
All very special people who I love dearly and
who were so extremely supportive when I went through
a very difficult period from the beginning of 2013 through 2015.
They were my second family and I'm not sure what I would've
done without them and their support.
They will always remain my dearest friends.
Yo Mama!!!!!!!!!!!!!!
Waaassss Happenin'!!!!!!!!!

I would also like to toss a treat to my fantastic cat, Gomer.
He was my parent's cat which I adopted in early 2013
because they both got very sick in early January of that year.
He thus adopted me and moved from Lancaster,
PA to become a Philly cat.
He literally sits either beside me, or on my lap,
each and every day that I write at my desk.
He truly is my biggest fan and
brings joy to each and every day of my life.
He is easily the best gift I ever received.
Purr away Gomer, purr away!!!!!!

Night Of The Sphinx

Bewitching time is but the sweet breath of night,
feral whispers wafting from a silvering moon
awaiting the explosion of a vibrant sunrise.
She is called forth to defile the beguiled,
sweet demonic daughter of the Chimera,
intoxicating Mistress of Evil's delight.

Moving to the swirl of biting sands
with the sway of haunting palm fronds,
she dances ~ she twirls ~ she spins to evil madness ~
pounding heart of a lion surging to come alive,
bathed in moonlight before pre-dawn's awakening,
nighttime breezes singing loudly for beasts to thrive.

Listen closely to the crackling winds.
Can you hear the lion's ravenous roar?
The moan and groan of hunger to be appeased,
carnal need to touch just one more sacrifice desired
by the feral beast who is now part woman born,
with the wings of an angry bird and lizard's lashing tail.

She slides with silent grace throughout the dark of night
selecting another victim walking upon the trail of shadows.
The she-beast whispers into the prey's unsuspecting ear,
"Which creature in the morning goes on four feet,
at noon on two, and in the evening upon three?"
The riddle left unanswered, his heart now belonged to her.

KERRY L. MARZOCK

Soft fingers lovingly caress like silken threads,
hands of a strangler flexed with brutish strength,
she revels in the power of one more conquest met.
Her magical beauty used to mesmerize and enchant,
demonic appetite once again sated with but one more
devoured soul, fresh taste of blood upon her sweet lips.

Within twitching ears a fading beat from yon dying heart,
forever consumed by human frailties, deceit and lies.
Roaring at a resplendent moon she unfurled her wings,
to soar high into darkened sky towards a beckoning morn
of an approaching resplendent blood-red, tangerine sunrise,
her urgent desires satisfied, monstrous hungers now subdued.

Gliding upon angry thermals, long wings spread wide,
sinister shadows brushed upon a quivering earth below.
Night after night her lion roared as death begets
more death, souls once wasted upon the living now
swaying within her chanting song of everlasting life,
for she is the Queen of Darkness, Demon of Destruction.

Then came that fateful night when she asked the question,
"Which creature in the morning goes on four feet,
at noon on two, and in the evening upon three?"
Oedipus smiled for he knew the answer to destroy her.
His reply, "It is but man - who crawls on all fours as a baby,
then walks upon two feet as an adult, and a cane in his old age."

With a painful growl that rumbled across the ground below
she emits an angry roar that thunders through the heavens,
a shrill shriek arose that stilled all human heartbeats.
This she-beast flung her body from the ragged cliff,
a demon now devoured by lost souls within her,
terrifying night of the Sphinx to be no more.
~ * ~ * ~ * ~
But still, when yon silvered moon hangs high
as the dark breath of night caresses me,
a growl starts low within my breasts.
For now this wild lion craves to stalk the streets
while angry raptor shrieks to flee the nest.
The demonic beast will rule once more
for unsuspecting prey will surely die.
^ ~ * ^ ~ * ^

©*Kerry L. Marzock*
July 22, 2006

Prologue

Josh Cranston decided it was high time to flag himself. His buddies from the office had departed the Silver Saddle around midnight. Glancing down at his wrist watch he realized it was now just a little past midnight. He silently berated himself for not leaving when they did, but that had seemed to be a major problem in his life going back to college. Always staying for one too many and then it was an adventure just getting home. He already had one DUI on his record and certainly didn't need another. It might end up costing him a really great job. His best friend, Craig Latham, tried persuading him to give up his keys and leave together, then return early in the morning to get his car.

Of course, Josh just laughed him off saying he was okay to drive and would leave as soon as he finished off the drink in front of him. That was an hour ago and two more gin and tonics later. Glancing at his watch once more he noticed how the minute and hour hands wavered so he decided it was definitely time. It actually looked as if the bartender was getting ready to flag him anyway. Or, take his car keys and call a friend.

He laid a fifty dollar bill on the bar, much more than the actual amount of his tab. However, he came here often because he loved the steaks. They were actually the best in and around Tucson. At least in his opinion anyway. He wanted to show Mark, his favorite bartender, how much he appreciated not being hassled about his drinking limit.

The lounge was somewhat dark so he tried walking as straight as possible, staggering against empty tables and chairs anyway. When he finally got outside he inhaled deeply in order to get some fresh air inside his lungs. Looking around the parking lot which was nearly empty he didn't see his vehicle. Then he mumbled *'shit'*, remembering that he had arrived late because of a meeting with an important client so he had to park in the rear of the restaurant since the place was packed as usual.

Nearly falling several times he stumbled and staggered to where his truck was parked. It was the only vehicle behind the building. While fumbling with his keys so he could unlock the door he suddenly heard a noise behind him. Dizzy, he spun around too fast, stumbled back against the vehicle and then slid roughly to the ground.

"Damn it, what the hell is that?" he muttered, laughing at the same time.

Then that noise erupted again, louder this time. It sounded like a sharp hiss, then was followed by a deep, menacing growl. Josh stared hard into the darkness, his vision extremely blurry. There was not as much light behind the building as there was out in the front lot. In fact, there was only a light bulb above the back door, plus just one light pole.

Suddenly Josh's eyes grew huge. He didn't know if what he saw was real, or just one of those famous pink elephant stories you always hear about. Charging straight towards him was the largest damn lizard he had ever seen. Before he even had a chance to yell, the hideous creature took Josh's head in its huge mouth and crunched down.

Chapter 1

Have I mentioned before that I hate snakes? Absolutely, positively despise the creepy-crawly critters. The cold-blooded, scaly, slithering, fork tongued, venom injecting, hissing creatures have no place in my life. Anything without legs and needs to squirm upon the ground is taboo for me. I honestly don't like lizards either, but at least they have legs. I suppose reptiles in general give me the creepy crawlies and there is definitely no love lost for spiders in my world either. Generally speaking, if it doesn't have a tail with fur, which quickly omits rats and mice, then I don't need to be within striking distance. Okay, then sue me! It's not my problem I hate anything that slithers, has more than four legs, buzzes around my head, bites, squeaks, or has a stinger. Huh, kind of reminds me of a few discarded, creepy old boyfriends I've had in my life.

So then you would think one of the last places I might decide to live would be good old Tucson, Arizona. Surrounded by dirt, sand, cactus, sagebrush, lizards, toads, scorpions, tarantulas, and snakes galore, especially rattlers, one would think I'd run away screaming 'no way Jose'. Well, guess again. That's exactly where I ended up due to a brand new job opportunity. I've always been a Pennsylvania girl born in a small western coal town with short coffee-stops in Florida and Virginia. Difficult teen years spent in Amish country of all places. Finally I ended up in Philadelphia, City of Brotherly Love, where a certain low-life part of society takes pride in breaking murder records annually.

However, after being a police officer for ten years in various departments and finally completing my Masters in Criminal Justice, I felt too much time would be spent getting into the Detective Division on the Philadelphia PD. So I started searching around for other opportunities. Presto, Tucson was looking for someone on their Night Detective Detail, recent grads welcome. Figuring I had nothing to lose I submitted an application. Shockingly a month later I received an e-mail requesting me to contact a Sergeant Denise McConnell which I promptly did. She set up a phone interview the next day with Det. Paul Robertson. Two weeks later I took a vacation, flew to Tucson and had what I thought was a pretty decent interview with five different law enforcement personnel. I stuck around three more days in order to scour the area and found for the most part I really liked it even though it was hotter than Hades on one of those days.

Then I headed on up to Scottsdale outside of Phoenix to visit my aunt Sis and uncle Sparky since I hadn't seen them in over five years. Sparky's formal name is Ray, but due to years as a volunteer fireman and a veteran of World War II he was bequeathed with the nickname of Sparky, which was pretty fitting considering his life.

My interview must've gone well because five weeks later they called and made me an offer I couldn't refuse. That night I decided to joyfully drink myself to sleep with Tequila Sunrises which certainly seemed appropriate enough. Actually, only two large ones put me flat on my butt followed by a nasty headache the next day.

So then, Amelia, (I prefer being called Amy) Stephenson strolled into the precinct the following morning with an awesome hangover and gave my sergeant the normal two week notice. They were disappointed that I was leaving, saying how much they valued my work and service, that I had a good future there if I could just hold on and bide my time. But what the hell, I'm 38 and certainly not getting any younger. It was tough leaving Edward J. McKnight, my partner of almost five years, as well as a number of other cops I had gotten friendly with. Yet it was time to move on since I had been in the proverbial Philly rut for the last year, or so. I'm not talking about the numerous pot holes scarring numerous city streets, either. Hey listen, a girls gotta' do what a girls gotta' do, ya' know?

I didn't have to report for duty in Tucson for one entire month so it gave me plenty of time to pack, get a mover and pray they wouldn't screw up my delivery. It would also provide enough leeway so I could take my time since I was driving there. Five years previously I had driven straight through to Scottsdale with my sister Irene after our uncle had a heart attack. No way was I going to kill myself doing that again.

Driving my Toyota Rav-4, what really struck me as I entered Arizona through the glorious State of Texas was all the emptiness, dirt, cactus, and sagebrush. It was literally everywhere! When I visited for the interview I mainly stayed in town with a side trip to the ski lodge atop Mt. Lemon. The terrain of Tucson compared to the Phoenix/Scottsdale area in the north is somewhat different. I actually wondered if I had made a huge mistake being a Philly girl and always surrounded by trees and changes of seasons like falling leaves, snow, and spring flowers. Admittedly, I won't miss the snow and ice.

Not to worry for within a month I was thrilled with my new surroundings, as well as the night shift to which I was now a full time member. I was now Detective Amelia Stephenson, thank you very much. I had taken the next step up the law enforcement ladder of success. Sometimes I still had to pinch myself hard.

The night shift crew welcomed me warmly for the most part. The chief, captain, and lieutenant seemed like forward thinking, give-a-girl-a-break guys, so I was anxious to prove they had not made a mistake in selecting me out of probably hundreds of potential candidates. There were, however, a few older detectives that still existed in those bleak dark ages. You know the type. Miserable jerk-offs who always feel that women should never be detectives, or even be part of the police force other than hold down desk duty, type forms, and handle pencils instead of guns. Oh, and run for coffee.

Thankfully my new partner was not one of those creeps. Detective Manuel Corroda (Manny for short) was of Mexican descent, dark skinned, about five feet, eleven inches in heels *'cause he was a good ole' boy,'* and wore cowboy boots all the time. Oh, and I suppose it didn't hurt too much that he was also as handsome as a runway model. First time I saw him my blood pressure soared at least ten points and I had to fan myself with a folder clutched in my hand, mumbling to myself, *'down girl, hold it together'.*

Early on the second Monday morning of my new tenure Lt. Anthony Reese called me into his office where I was to find hunky Manuel leaning casually against a bookcase in the far corner. After a few minutes of light banter I was then introduced to my new partner. OMG, how can I confirm my excitement other than declare my legs became wobbly and I had some difficulty putting more than two sensible words together. I quickly found out he was happily married with two children which was a good thing. That made it somewhat easier for me to digest because it could've been rather impossible for me to perform my duty when I might've been in constant *'heat'*. Still, what can I say other than I'm a single woman and just like the guys it sure doesn't hurt to just once in a while take a little look-see and admire the flesh. Know what I mean?

I don't know what Mr. Runway Model thought about me, but I'm not half bad in an attractive/athletic sort of way. Not short, not tall, just kind of in between for a woman at five foot, seven and a half inches. I rarely wear heels over an inch and a half unless I'm lucky enough to have a date with a guy over six feet. I concentrate very hard on my weight trying to maintain between one twenty-one thirty. I have dark brown hair, rather long which hangs down past my shoulders in the back that I often have done up in a ponytail and normally curled around my ears. Facial features are a mix of Irish and German. So, I'm certainly not beautiful, but I've been described as being pretty and attractive with a good figure. I suppose that's all in the eyes of the beholder anyway.

That was exactly one year ago almost to the day. By this time I had now been absorbed into the department as just one of the 'guys'. I had won over two of the three departmental dinosaurs to my side. The only one left was an old codger ready for the retirement heap, Carl Most. He sure as hell wasn't the 'most' likeable guy for sure. Manny told me Carl really didn't like anybody, especially wetbacks, anyway. Now don't worry because Manny didn't mind being called that, at least by me anyway. He had extremely thick skin and we bounced sharp barbs off each other all the time. Taking incoming flack and ribbing by your partner was part of the job.

Women and minorities in law enforcement learn to be tough from the beginning, or you simply didn't last long. He was just as apt to call me a slut quite often because of my dirty thoughts and comments. Seriously though, my philosophy in life has always been, 'if thou giveth', then thy must taketh' in return'. Especially being a cop which was difficult at best even on the easiest of days. There was no room in law enforcement for anybody that possessed a thin skin. You just took too much crap from fellow cops, as well as criminals, all the time.

Acquiring a real taste for Mexican food was another matter entirely. Back in Philly my primary Mexican cuisine was from Taco Bell, plus chili from Wendy's. I didn't realize you needed a fire hose when you ate a real, honest to goodness taco, burrito, tamale, or anything else from south of the border. Manny got a charge out of taking me to only the 'original' places where the food was genuine and the ingredients put hair on your chest. That aspect I informed him I could totally do without since it would look a little strange when I wore something low cut to show cleavage which rarely happened anyway. I stuck to it though, finally creating a toughened palate so that the full taste of food could be savored. Sadly, I could not figure out how to toughen the other end. What goes in as fire generally has to come out the same way, but normally as flames. Followed then by somewhat gooey ashes. Okay, okay, I know that's disgusting, but I really can get that way sometimes. Sorry, you'll simply have to live with it.

Upon arriving in Tucson one year ago I rented a small apartment figuring that there was no reason to go hog wild in the beginning. All I needed anyway was a place to hang my clothes, throw my bra over the shower rod, consume fast food, hopefully sleep without the aid of pills, and take a peaceful crap in private.

Over the past six months I was feeling itchy to have a more solid home structure. I started looking around with the aid of Vanessa Allenson, a very cool realtor, in order to locate a decent size house. I had come to like it here a lot and felt it was now my home. Moving into a house of my own would make things pretty much complete. I didn't need a white picket fence because in Tucson there was no grass to speak of anyway, only colored sand and rocks, so the small white fence would've looked totally out of place.

The house would mean some security, but I still looked forward to sharing it with somebody, especially a doggie and/or kitty rather than ugly lizards, scorpions, and black widows. If a nice guy happened to come along then I surely wouldn't mind sharing that part of my life with him either, that is as long as he wasn't some low-life, scum-sucking leech. I had more than my share of those creeps back in Philly.

After a few weeks of getting together when my schedule permitted, Vanessa showed me a cute little rancher near the edge of town heading towards Mt. Lemon. I was still within the city limits and had the Catalina Mountains outside my back door. How cool was that? The price was right too, falling nicely into my budget. I took my first week of vacation and moved in little over a month ago. Boxes still littered the floor in different rooms because my job left little free time to eat, bathe, and sleep as it was.

Hopefully a dog would come soon enough, maybe a black lab. I had to really consider my work schedule and how much the poor pooch would be home alone. Since I work nights, I often have to toil longer depending on whatever case I was lucky (or unlucky enough) to be assigned. As a result, I would need to find somebody good and trustworthy within my new neighborhood to check on the critter during daylight hours. A cat obviously was not a problem so I was considering that route first. After all, change the litter box daily, put down fresh food and water, then you could actually go away for several days even though the little bugger might be angry as hell when you returned. I have always loved the Siamese breed after spending an earlier part of my life with two wonderful little guys, Loki and Ming, who are now meowing loudly in feline heaven. My very special companions here on earth, they would at certain times simply not be quiet. So I found myself asking them constantly to just please shut up. Didn't matter though because they still continued to yammer away unless asleep, purring loudly.

For the time being I decided to just get used to my new abode. Get the house as spider and lizard proof as humanly possible considering where I now hung my bras. I carefully placed my shoes off the floor because they were great havens for tarantulas and scorpions. Not the bras, unless I left them lie scattered upon the floor during my lack of housekeeping skills from time to time. I truly can be a slob sometimes.

I also looked forward to making friends within the neighborhood. Several very nice neighbors had already welcomed me with small house warming gifts. As you can well imagine, my work shift makes it somewhat difficult to meet people. Plus, there were times when the pressure of my profession became so intense that I really wanted no contact with human beings at all when off duty. Possibly I would be lucky enough to meet my eventual pet sitter soon. If he just so happened to be extremely cute with a hot bod, well then I would suffer through that pain and agony easily enough, trust me.

However now, as I slowly stretched to wake up, I glanced over at the alarm clock which glowed 5:30 p.m. in big green letters. Rolling over I hit the switch for the beeper to remain silent. One of the things I've had to try and get used to with working the night detail was sleeping during the day. I'm somewhat better at it now though. I was lucky enough to have a friendly neighbor, an electrician, who hooked up convenient timers so that my two air conditioning units, plus lights, would pop on at exactly midnight. When I got home from a long night of pursuing hardened criminals then at least the house would be fairly cool. My shift usually ended around 6:00 a.m. so with traffic normally sparse at that time of the morning I could arrive home in less than fifteen-twenty minutes.

When I had rented the apartment I really hated running the A/C all the time. But then upon arriving home I found the place to be way too hot for sleeping if I didn't keep it running. When a dog or cat enters my life I will most probably have central air installed. I had been saving for just that contingency, but wasn't near that point yet.

Moaning like an angry wolf who had just awoke from a dream of hunting with the pack, I stretched one last time. Slowly sliding out of bed I stumbled half naked to the bathroom because I definitely had to pee. Sitting down on the toilet I reached for the half-read newspaper from yesterday. The big headline still screamed out at me:

Another Strange Death Occurs In City Of Tucson
Police Are Clueless While Bodies Continue Piling Up

Closing my eyes I groaned. Not in relief from sitting on the toilet, either.

The article droned on and on about another innocent victim being totally mauled and horribly half-devoured behind a very good steak restaurant and bar out along Benson Highway. Apparently his pick-up truck, which I found most cowboys drove, was parked around back of the building. Nobody had noticed it there until Mark the bartender left around 2:30 a.m. after cleaning up. Finding it rather strange, he grabbed a flashlight from the trunk of his car to poke around a little. He noticed a brownish looking stain on the ground that led about thirty yards to a line of sagebrush. Before getting there he started holding his nose and swatting at nasty insects buzzing around his head.

After vomiting up a late dinner, then with a quivering voice, he called the police to report a torn apart body behind the bar. Law enforcement quickly responded and began documenting the fourth mangled victim discovered within a two week time span. The brownish color had in fact been blood. Quite a bit actually leading from the driver's side door to the edge of the parking area. There were no foot prints to speak of, at least not of the shod variety. Any prints located by the CSI team seemed to be from something alive and definitely not wearing any footwear. Certainly not completely human, either.

So, just take a wild guess which detective team was fortunate enough to catch this case two weeks ago? Yep, only one hour before our shift ended, too. You get the prize if you said Detectives Manuel

Corroda and Amelia Stephenson. Over a two week period there were four hideous deaths somewhat connected that we knew of. A nurse getting off her shift, a teacher out walking her dog which was also missing, a newspaper delivery guy dropping off his last bundles at a convenience store, and now the unlucky drunk behind the bar. Like the headline screamed, bodies were piling up much too rapidly and it did seem like the police were totally clueless. It was apparent to Manny and myself that the deaths were the result of some type of animal. God only knew what kind and not sure if I even wanted to know.

Tossing the paper into the trash can I lowered my head and wondered how soon I would be getting a phone call from my steamy hot partner. As if I possessed telepathic powers, thirty seconds later my cell phone began playing the song 'Home on the Range'. Quickly wiping myself clean, I stumbled into the bedroom, jumped onto the bed, and reached for the singing phone to shut off the crooning voice of Gene Autry.

"Yeah Manny, I was waiting for your call. Where are you honey bunny?"

"About three minutes from your house. Figured you probably just woke up so I have coffee. Are you decent enough for me to venture into that evil sex lair of yours?"

"Hey partner, you know I'm never decent and maybe I don't want to be either with Mr. Hunk-a-chunk approaching my doorstep," grinning slyly since I really knew how embarrassed he got when I talked dirty, which was honestly most of the time.

"Amy, you're such a slut, you know that? I'm a very devoted father, happily married man, and a devout Catholic. Why do you want to corrupt me so much?"

"That's not what your wife told me the other night," I shot back, knowing this playful jabbing was about to end quickly.

He laughed. "Okay, down girl. I'll be there in five minutes so get dressed. We have things to do, people to interview, evidence to accumulate, and a killer to catch."

"You're no fun partner. I'll be in the shower when you get here so just come on inside. You have a key," I said, sliding off the bed and heading for the bathroom, "and *(pausing for effect)* if you want to scrub my back just let me know before you barge into the bathroom. I'm not about to act out Janet Leigh's role from the movie *'Pyscho'.*"

The phone went dead. I obviously had reached the end of what playful joking he would take. I tossed the phone onto the bed, grabbed a towel from the closet and turned on the faucets. In no mood for a hot shower, I tested the water until it was just tepid at best. I stepped under the spray and sighed. It felt so damn refreshing and woke me up fairly quickly. I then felt a slight breeze stir the shower curtain so I knew Manuel had entered the house. Sadly, I knew the back scrub would have to wait.

I yelled anyway, "Hey baby, I miss you. I'm in here and the water's so warm."

After washing and drying my hair I pulled on a pair of black slacks and a short sleeve white blouse. It was just see through enough that I could definitely hold the attention of any male I had to interview, sometimes a female as well depending on her sexual persuasion. Slipping on a pair of black canvass shoes which were extremely comfortable, especially since I had been on my feet quite a bit lately, I headed out the bedroom door and down the hallway towards the kitchen. Manny stood nonchalantly against the sink sipping his large black coffee. Christ all mighty, but he was freaking handsome. Sometimes a girl just had to toil under terrible work conditions.

"Why do you continue doing that?" I murmured, shouldering past him.

"Do what? I'm just standing here drinking coffee minding my own business."

"Are you aware just how much you always look like you're posing for the cover of GQ magazine? Or, do you simply love teasing the hell out of a single girl in heat?"

He just shook his head at my playful banter. Stepping towards the table he swung a chair around backwards and then straddled the seat. "Amy, you're just too damn intense sometimes. Let's put the sex remarks inside the slut box for now, okay? But I must admit, I like teasing you as well," he added, chuckling mischievously.

I walked towards the fridge, punching him lightly on the right arm as I passed.

"Ouch, what the hell was that for?" he whined, just like a little baby.

Clutching the other coffee cup I grabbed a carton of skim milk, poured enough to make the coffee look almost white, and dumped in about three heaping teaspoons of sugar. My Grandma Gable taught me how to drink coffee all doctored up, sweeter the better. As a result, I could never in a lifetime get used to it being bitter and black.

"You know I'm only kidding so don't get your panties in an uproar. Quit being a sissy because you could kick my sweet butt anytime you wanted to, Mr. Macho Guy."

He figured not answering would put an abrupt end to that line of conversation. It did for a little while anyway. Opening the newspaper he had brought in from outside he jabbed angrily at the headlines at the top of the first page with his right index finger.

"Amy, we need to come up with answers quick. I mean like today. This is the fourth person slaughtered by something monstrous and obviously very deadly. Quite frankly, the *something* is becoming more of a viable option every day," he growled, finishing his coffee and angrily tossing the empty cup into the trash can.

Walking past him I squeezed his shoulder lightly and moved to the opposite end of the table. He's about five years older than I am and it was easy to see these killings had been taking their toll. Hell, there were a few times during the last few weeks that I was beginning to judge whether I was really cut out for this detective crap myself.

"We will partner. I can feel something's going to open up soon. Most likely explode when it does. Hey, let's take a run out to the bar where the latest victim got killed. We can get a closer look now that the techies are gone. Maybe we can come up with something they missed. I've been trying to find a common thread between the other three victims and hitting a brick wall. Apparently, these are all just random killings, being in the proverbial wrong place at the wrong time. It appears there's just something really nasty out there slaughtering innocent civilians when the opportunity arises."

"Dammit Amy, we're a couple bad asses ourselves. Let's find this monster, or whatever the hell it is. Either arrest it, or make sure the thing is officially destroyed. We'll be unemployed cops if we don't solve this case soon."

I allowed him to drive so I could finish my coffee and allow scrambled thoughts to tumble around in my brain. We were both quiet, obviously thinking about the case. After working together for just over a year we had gotten to know each other quite well, discovering we really needed to chew on things, like a dog with a juicy bone. Then merge our thoughts which for the most part brought us to the same conclusions.

There happened to be two troublesome clues which continued to bother me. One was the amount of scales littering the ground around the crime scenes. I'm talking scales like from a snake, but much larger than normal. Either the killer was spreading them around in order to confuse us. Or, we were looking for a big ass alligator that shed them accidentally which was quite a freaky thought.

The other point was that at each of the first three killings, around the crime scene and then trailing off to eventually fade away, appeared to be wide, swirly tracks in the ground. Like somebody was dragging something heavy behind them. These tracks were not straight either, appearing to curve back and forth. Almost like a sidewinder would make when squirming across the desert floor. It gave me the willies just to think what that might be. Especially considering my abject hatred of all creepy crawly critters.

Night was beginning to descend as we pulled onto Catalina Highway. Suddenly, Manny's cell phone rang bringing me out of my deep reverie. I can get totally lost when chewing on facts or clues, trying to make something out of possibly nothing. Sometimes it worked and sometimes not. That was at least eighty percent of being a good detective.

I listened to him mumble, "Right...right...uh huh...you're shitting me! Sweet Jesus! Okay, we'll turn around and head straight over there."

Turning my head I stared at him, waiting for a response. None came.

"What's up partner?" I asked, definitely annoyed, but not really sure I wanted to know the answer considering how quiet he had suddenly gotten.

Slipping the phone back into his shirt pocket he shook his head. "Amy, it just continues to get worse. That was Cooper. Apparently another body was discovered behind a shed at Sabino High School on Bowes Road. They're not certain, but it may be a young female student reported missing by her parents when she failed to come home last night. I gather the body is not in very good condition, either. So what else is new?"

"What's happening around these here parts partner?" I asked. "What the hell are we dealing with? A damn psycho serial killer, or some out of this world creature?"

"Damn if I know, Amy. I'm not even sure this is being done by one person. Like you said earlier, this killer may not even be human. Hell girl, this is freaking Arizona. I will admit a lot of weird crap happens around here, especially out in the desert. But this is quite frankly overkill. I don't mean that to be a funny remark either."

Turning quickly to look straight ahead my eyes got huge. I yelled, "Watch out Manny, there's something on the road."

The squealing of brakes screamed through the air, as did the burning rubber of tires. Not only from Manny's car, but two vehicles in front of him, as well as at least one in the rear. It was a miracle nobody crashed, but the incident did result in obviously frayed nerves. As the car slid roughly onto the gravel shoulder I opened the door before we came to a complete stop and leaped out, reaching for my gun at the same time.

Glancing back at the road, whatever had been rushing across the pavement had now completely vanished. But what the hell had it been? I realized it was quite large and ugly, definitely some kind of animal. I hate to say that it clearly looked like a huge lizard of some kind, yet that's the closest image I could think of. I know there are plenty of lizards, snakes, and gross spiders in and around Tucson because I've seen them, but nothing even remotely that large.

Okay then, give a girl a break. Maybe some type of really large, rabid armadillo? I shook my head because it couldn't have been that. Possibly a huge dog, coyote, or a wolf? Nah, it definitely looked reptilian, low and long, very ugly. I felt Manny quickly move up beside me. I tried not to appear startled. That didn't work too well, though.

"See anything partner? What the hell was it anyway? Scared the living shit out of me," he half whispered, displaying more fractured nerves than I had witnessed since being his partner.

I shook my head and laughed, more to ease my own tenseness. "You're not alone, that's for damn sure. It looked like a huge lizard, or some really scary creature anyway. There's nothing that large around here that I know of. You've lived around these parts much longer than I have. Ever see anything like that before?"

"Nope, nothing of that size, or that creepy, either. Where do you think it went?"

I walked off the pavement, venturing about five feet onto the desert floor staring down at the ground until I found what I was looking for...prints. Kneeling down I pressed my hand inside one to try and gauge the size. I grunted, feeling it just didn't seem possible. It was larger than my hand. Too damn big for any lizard that I was knowledgeable about.

"Find something Amy?" Manny inquired, still gazing nervously over the long expanse of sagebrush and cactus.

"Large prints, pretty far apart. That's about it. Oh well, it's gone now," I sighed heavily, standing and nervously holstering my firearm. "We'd better getting going partner. There are no crushed cars to report, just a bunch of fractured nerves. Whatever that thing was, in no freaking way do I want to meet up with it again."

However, somehow I got the very strange premonition that wouldn't be the case. We quickly climbed back into the car as Manny sped off towards another murder scene. My keen intuition, both female and detective, told me I didn't want to investigate this death simply because it apparently could very well be the most emotional and youngest victim yet. As we flew down the highway in the opposite direction I kept thinking how the murderous streets of Philadelphia just might be easier to take than all this eeriness.

Chapter 2

Two hostile eyes observed the scattered vehicles drive away. Especially the two humans holding weapons. The creature's gaze centered entirely on the female. Even though the male was taller and broader, definitely stronger, the other one appeared to be the more tantalizing. Whether it would meet her again was unknown, but it might be worth the risk. Too much time had been spent locked away in a cement room being studied, prodded, examined, and tested. However, time was immaterial to the beast. There was no concept of days, weeks, months, years, even eons. All it knew for sure was that it was free and the body now used as a conveyance was rather slow and ponderous. Fortunately, it did possess vicious teeth and claws to make up for a lack of dexterity.

Breaking free had taken many years of patient planning. The creature was used to that, being able to quickly exit whatever body it was using at the time. Then revert into a form of suspended animation making it appear to be dead. During this period of suspension it was able to stop all signs of life. Nothing could be further from the truth.

The crash of its vehicle had been extremely violent, nearly causing death from being crushed inside the remains. When discovered, the human soldiers had no idea what it was other than being a thick, semi-liquid. Years slogged by just to regenerate and grow. Scientists finally concluded that it did, in fact, possess some aspect of life. Just not sure what. Nothing else was ever truly discovered because the humans on this planet had never seen anything like it before. There was really nothing to base their findings on.

Over many years it accumulated every single bit of data possible. It not only resulted from being totally alert since sleep was not an issue. It also possessed the unique ability to study its human captors, even lying completely dormant most of that long period of time. It discerned that the prison was an underground facility with eight foot thick walls descending eight floors down into the ground. Although it realized it could get free through the ventilation system, pursuing that path would be more difficult. When the time was right to escape, it steadily began to assimilate current information like guard schedules. Then get past the walls, doors, and fences that had been imprisoning it. Finding an adequate host body for conveyance would then become paramount.

Through mind control, the creature forced one of the scientists to open the enclosure it had been held in for over thirty years. Once free from the small enclosure inside the detention room it quickly killed the scientist, then entered the oral cavity. Alarms blared loudly. The alien got the scientist to open the outer door to the lab and immediately brought the guard outside to his knees. Blood immediately spurted from every bodily opening as the human dropped heavily to the floor. In less than a minute the alien left the body of the scientist and slithered inside the guard. Once the guard could stand it then moved out into the hallway, shooting anyone else responding to the alarm in the laboratory. Ten minutes later it was at the top floor forcing the guard there to open the thick outer door.

At last the entity was free from its long imprisonment. Standing outside in the dark there were no visible buildings, only two large tanks and a massive cement area on the ground. This was where the

THE REPTILIAN FACTOR

outer doors would've opened wide to allow firing of the missiles long ago. Two guards were on the outside near the front gate. Due to complete surprise and shock they were quickly shot to death by the guard the alien was using as a host. Alarms continued to blare throughout the facility. That mattered not since it was just moments away from total freedom. Nothing would stop it now after all these years.

It departed the body of the guard which then fell to the ground dead. Totally free now, it converted to liquid form so that it was able to slide easily through the chain link fence. It then crawled fairly rapidly away from the facility. Quickly, the entity began searching for a life form that much more resembled its own physical make up. A snake was the closest bodily type even though much too small on this planet. For now though it would have to do. The creature was extremely fast in natural state, but without a larger body it was only able to cover small distances at any one time before having to rest.

It selected a large rattlesnake which was much too slow, but shaking the rattle on the tip of its tail was fun. Utilizing the snake had other advantages as well. Those were concealment, camouflage, the speed of attack, sharp fangs, and deadly venom. The snake definitely held promise, but it would take too long to change the molecular structure enough to make it even stronger, faster, and much more vicious than its normal earthly form. Having no legs presented somewhat of a problem also. Since time was of the essence those alterations would take longer than it had at the moment.

About five miles away from its prison the creature came across a large, two and a half foot Gila monster skulking below a craggy outcrop. During the short period it utilized the rattle snake, an amazing structural alteration had made it faster and more deadly. It struck the Gila monster from behind, latching upon the neck and injecting a venom that was now not only fatal, but in smaller doses could cause immediate paralysis.

Once the victim was completely still the snake swelled and its mouth opened enough to release a twenty inch, dark reddish mass. It then entered the lizard by sliding through the mouth. As it did so the Gila monster began to shake violently. Rolling over several times it reached the lip of a small drop off where it tumbled about six feet into a gully. It quickly started to stretch longer than its previous length. Legs elongated and a much stronger spine began to stretch and bend. Eyes opened wide, bright red in color, as a loud hiss burst forth. Then a long stream of blood shot from the mouth.

After ten minutes of bodily conversion, what stood now upon four longer legs was something resembling a cross between the Gila monster and a small alligator. Length from tip of snout to end of tail was now over four feet. At full height it was give or take twelve inches off the ground. Though not finished with total conversion, for now this body would have to do. Even though it didn't need to feed as other life forms on this planet, the body it now possessed did. The creature then roamed at will, striking and killing whatever came within reach. Prey were animals of different varieties, thus leaving a long trail of blood and body parts throughout the desert. Heading for brighter lights brought it into contact with humans. This was a very different kind of meat.

After killing the nurse, the creature enjoyed receiving not only new genes and DNA to play with, but different intelligence was garnered from her brain. This allowed the creature to further blossom. With constant nourishment the body continued to develop. What raced across the highway earlier, nearly causing a multi-vehicle wreck, could easily run on four legs, at times able to walk on two. Length had now grown to almost five feet by then, still small for what it had been back on its home planet. At some point after several more transformations it would be able to begin forming wings.

The creature turned quickly and moved away. A lone coyote howled in the distance, the sun nearly setting. It yearned for more knowledge and DNA from other living beings, mostly human now. Soon it would be nearly unstoppable. Shortly after taking over the body of the Gila monster it discovered that the lizard was female. That was a stroke of luck even though reproducing didn't necessarily mean that it needed to originally possess the body of a female. Molecular structure could easily be altered to a point where reproduction could be accomplished in either sex. Now, however, eggs were beginning to form inside the animal's womb. It looked forward to producing hatchlings and becoming a maternal figure to a murderous, out of this world brood all its own.

Dr. Oliver Warring was very quiet, feeling an eruption might occur at just about any moment. Colonel McDowell paced back and forth like a caged tiger, hands behind his back, shoulders squared, shaking his head in obvious irritation. He was a large, imposing man and made everyone beneath him in rank nervous when he was in the same room. For that matter, he even made those of higher rank wary and on edge as well. It took years to build this type of reputation. He had done so in both Afghanistan and Iraq, along with other top secret deployments around the world. One thing could always be said about whatever command he was in charge of. They were most definitely the toughest, meanest, best trained, and most loyal units of any in the Air Force.

Stopping quickly, he spun around and glared at all five men in the room which were Dr. Warring with his two associates, Doctors Boyd and Fleming, Captain Pace and Lieutenant Spanner. Each of them felt they were in a world of shit. But at that moment they were needed by McDowell so the turds would fall on them eventually, not now.

"How could this disaster happen? Why the freaking hell hasn't the situation been contained, or eliminated? Jesus Christ, four civilians are now dead, plus nine guards and scientists. I don't have to tell you gentleman what turmoil is going to descend upon us if we don't locate this creature and soon. I mean like yesterday."

Clearing his throat, Dr. Warring stood and moved to the window which overlooked a large parking lot, along with rows of barracks on Davis-Monthan AFB. Even he still didn't know how the alien was able to break free. As a result, how was he supposed to tell the colonel what he wanted to know when he himself had no idea?

"Sir, I'm presently not certain I know all the answers to your questions. Possibly we had become lax in guarding this entity. Most definitely we underestimated what it was capable of doing. I will say that the escape occurred at night before shift change so part of the crew was asleep and the new team members had not yet arrived at the facility."

Warring paused and coughed slightly before proceeding. "For a long period this thing appeared dormant. By that I mean like over thirty years. We hardly ever got responses to anything we did, or tests ran. Yet we knew somehow that it lived, possibly in some animated state. Apparently during this time of suspended animation it was absorbing information, constant data buildup, whatever it needed to plan an escape. We have no idea how the life form obtained this information, but it did nonetheless. Possibly through some kind of mind invasion, we're just not sure. We have watched security film over and over, maybe a hundred times. We are able to see what happened. Just don't know how it was done. The dead servicemen and civilians are extremely difficult to grasp. But, we will capture, or destroy it. Trust me on that."

There was suddenly a thick, electric blanket of silence covering the men. All the colonel did was glare straight ahead, eyes unblinking, his large Adam's apple bobbing up and down, fingers entwined behind his back with fingertips beginning to turn white from clenching them so hard. He did this simply because if they were released then striking something, or someone, could easily occur. Definitely something would be broken.

"Jesus H. Christ, what a mess people. How do you propose finding this thing? It's been free now for almost a month and you have absolutely no idea where the heck it is, do you? Tell me the truth, Doctor Warring. I need to know exactly what we're dealing with here, plus what it will take to destroy it. If you think you're going to capture this abomination then you're more out of your mind than I've always thought you were."

Ignoring the crude remarks thrown at him by Colonel McDowell, he responded. "Sir, we have a way of tracking the creature because it definitely emits a peculiar type of electrical energy wave. During its captivity we developed specialized equipment geared toward frequencies that it emits. As far as what it looks like at the moment, we have no idea. What we do know is that it assimilates information very quickly and is not only able to convert bodily structure of something else entirely, it can also alter its own physical makeup as well. We never permitted it to stay in that state for any length of time. Along with the tracking equipment, we were also able to develop several weapons, one of which we hope will cause it to depart the host body. In all the tests we conducted over many years we honestly have not obtained that much information. Sometimes I think we're as much in the dark now as the very night we found it at the crash site."

The colonel shook his head, quite annoyed. "Just how long have we had this thing contained? You just stated in all that time you still know very little. Are we dumbass human beings so inadequate we can't discover what makes an alien worm tick?"

"I didn't mean that we haven't amassed lots of data. We have for sure. It's so new to us, different than what we're used to dealing with. How long have we had it? I came to this base back in 1994 and it was already here. When I first arrived my job was clearly defined. I worked on merely a small part of information acquisition. What I did find out though was that we discovered the crash site on March 14, 1983. Actually, let me digress. We didn't even really know at that point what we had. The debris found was obviously from some type of unidentified flying object, but nothing we had ever seen before. We transported all of that material here under extreme secrecy. It was while we were studying one particular part of the vehicle that the life form was discovered."

McDowell stared out the window. "Thirty-three years and you scientists were unable to figure out what this thing was, or where it came from. Now this damn creature has somehow escaped under your watch," the colonel accused, shaking his head. "We have no idea where it's at while people are dying. This is going to come back to bite us on the ass. Believe me, you will be in front of that line. Far ahead of me, I promise."

He moved to the desk and took a long drink of water. What he desperately desired was a tall scotch and soda, but that would have to wait. For now, he just really needed all his wits about him to somehow get through this disaster.

"Tell me what you're doing to find it. Don't bullshit me, either."

Doctor Warring looked over to Captain Pace and nodded.

The captain moved toward the front of the room and turned to face his superior officer, knowing full well that his career was probably on the line.

"Colonel, we have three teams of six operatives, each covering a particular area. All of them have the equipment we've developed to track it. Our goal is to capture the creature alive, but if that is not possible then we'll destroy it in order to save lives. One team is being led by Vince Flint. I believe you know him and how capable he is. If there is anybody who can locate and eliminate this damn thing it will be him."

There was a long pause, tension so thick that an explosion might occur at any moment. The colonel reached for the end of the desk, grabbed his hat and headed for the door. Over his shoulder he said forcefully, "I don't give a royal rat's ass who, or what, is looking for this monster. Find it, eradicate this creature, and then goddamn erase the freaking thing from my memory. If this abomination somehow multiplies then we are all in a world of shit. Not only all of us in this room, but Tucson as a whole. I don't even think God knows what might happen after that. Gentlemen, this is a classic military cluster fuck of the highest order! Keep me posted every half hour. AND I MEAN EVERY GODDAMN HALF HOUR," he yelled, slamming the door behind him.

Pictures on the wall shook. Windows rattled while nervous energy seemed to get even more strained. To say the least, he was one pissed off officer.

Chapter 3

We pulled into the congested Sabino High School parking lot a little after 6:30. It was already filled with a number of police and emergency vehicles, not to mention a growing crowd of curious and horrified onlookers. Feeling a slight bit of nausea already starting to coagulate in my stomach I realized that looking at the mangled remains of a young, innocent high school girl wasn't something I was looking forward to. Manny and I had stopped for a quick bite of dinner before heading out towards Benson Highway and the site of the bar killing. As a result, the cheeseburger, fries, and Diet Pepsi that I had shoveled down now swished dangerously in my stomach, appearing to seek release.

Winding our way through vehicles and human congestion, I glanced at Manuel.

"Tell me the truth, are you even up for this partner?"

He let out a heavy sigh. "Not in the least little bit, Amy. How in the hell can you ever get used to this? I'm not only really pissed off, but honestly scared at the same time. We have to find this damn monster and fast. How many more deaths before we do?"

"I agree, and we will," I replied, stopping beside Sergeant Dominick Salleria.

He glanced over and saw it was us. "Thanks for getting here so fast. You are not going to like this crime scene one little bit, trust me on that."

I dispelled a nervous laugh. "Yeah, we were just discussing that same subject. How does one ever get used to this? Where is the body, sergeant?"

He cleared his throat loudly. "Her name is Karen Culokis, seventeen, a senior here at the high school. Seems that she left drama class last night around seven o'clock, apparently on time. Called her mother and said she was going to walk over to the home of a friend, Sharon Taylor, and that she would give a ring when she was ready to come home. Come 9:30 that evening, and not getting the phone call for a ride, Karen's mother called her friend's house. Sharon told her that Karen had never come over and that she had not even been expecting her. It was obviously a ruse so that she could meet up with somebody else, possibly a boy. Apparently, young Karen did not have a boyfriend at this time. It may not be until tomorrow once the word gets spread around the school when we might actually find out who she was planning on meeting up with."

"Yeah, that figures," I replied, "Lots of kids don't tell their parents any more what's really happening in their lives. Makes parenting teenagers a little difficult. Then something like this happens and you hope that at least some kids realize how important it is to stay safe, not skulk around behind their parent's backs. Hell, I guess we all did it."

"Apparently Ms. Culokis learned that lesson the hard way," Sgt. Salleria replied. "Her body is over here behind the equipment shed. You should brace yourselves because this is not a pretty sight. In fact, it's one of the most distressing things I've ever seen."

Neither of us answered simply because we would never, ever be prepared for something like this. Not even over an entire career, or how many dead bodies we saw.

Shoving our way through a line of cops we saw the body covered up. Lots of blood saturated the ground as well as splashed all over the back wall of the shed. The odor wasn't all that wonderful, either. After tugging on a pair of plastic gloves I placed a mask over my mouth and nose. I had learned early on that trying to be macho at crime scenes when there was a mangled body like this was not something I did very well. I got ribbed about it early on, but then they all got used to it. In fact, I was surprised that a few of those very same *"macho"* detectives now did the same thing. Maybe doing it the female way wasn't all that bad and they could all learn a little *somethin'* from me.

Manny on the other hand did not place a mask over his face. Unlike my own weak stomach, my partner had maybe the keenest sense of smell I had ever known. So for him, however difficult it could be at times, he felt that inhibiting smell at a crime scene could possibly keep them from noticing very important information and clues.

"How was the body discovered? Who called it in?" Manny inquired. "This is a pretty discreet, out of the way, location."

"Apparently the neighbor two doors down reported a bad odor. He thought it was probably a dead animal so he called the cops feeling they could get animal control out here to dispose of the body. When a squad finally arrived at the scene they realized it was a young female and that it was most likely the missing girl."

"Damn, damn, damn," I said. "Let's not put off the inevitable partner."

I moved forward with distinct purpose and knelt beside the body, trying really hard not to get any blood on my shoes. Which, by the way, is why I had encased them in plastic booties. In fact, everybody within the crime scene area was wearing them so we didn't contaminate potentially valuable clues. Manny knelt on the other side as I reached for the edge of the cover over her body.

As I pulled it back I let out a moan and my fingers began to shake. Manny put his hand over mine. What a horrible sight, maybe the worst I've seen. I could also see the same distress in his eyes, especially since he had two young children, a son and daughter.

Her body was literally torn apart. Blood was everywhere! It saturated her blonde hair and face to the point of being unable to tell that she once had been such a beautiful young girl. I didn't have to move her head to see that the top of her skull had nearly been removed. What brain matter remained was most likely not where it should've been. I made a small squeaking sound when I realized that her eyes had been gouged out as well, sockets filled with drying blood. There was a vast assortment of insects crawling around, eager for a free meal. You never, ever forget seeing something like that.

Manny had now placed a white handkerchief over his mouth and asked in a muffled voice, "You okay partner?"

"Not so much, but I'll be alright. Good God, her eyes are gone. What did this?"

That was not all. Her neck had been savagely torn out, chest opened cleanly between her breasts, and the stomach was sliced apart like a watermelon. I stood quickly and stumbled backwards, turned and pushed up against the chain link fence. Tearing the mask off my face I threw up. So much for eating dinner earlier, and trying to be macho now. I didn't think having another meal anytime soon was going to happen, either.

I continued to dry heave even when there was nothing more to spew forth like some volcano. All at once a hand came into view holding a bottle of water. I looked up to see Manny there. I grabbed it and filled my mouth several times so I could spit out the vile taste of vomit. After the dizziness passed I stood and began wobbling away.

"I won't ask if you're okay," said Manny, "but what the hell, are you okay?"

Laughing weakly, I shot back, "Partner, you're such a big prick. I thought you weren't going to ask if I was okay."

"So shoot me, wouldn't be the first time," he chuckled in response.

"Damn it Manny, I'm really not okay. I can do my job, though. That's worse than degradation over there, it is downright slaughter. The violence in these killings is just getting worse. Like the damn thing is enjoying it."

"I agree completely. You ready to go back and take a closer look around? They've removed her body so we'll talk to the M.E. later when the body is cleaned off at the morgue. We can see the wounds then and hopefully he can provide something new."

I moved past him, determined to find something, anything that would help us. In fact, now that the body had been removed, most of the cops had left also. Guess the spectacle was over so only a few remained to guard the crime scene until we were done.

"Be careful partner," I said in a low voice. "CSI should be arriving any minute. We don't want to screw up this area for them."

A voice from behind stated firmly, "We are already here Detective Stephenson. And quite frankly, you are most likely contaminating my crime scene."

I didn't have to turn around to know it was Griff Mallory, head of CSI. The 'Griff' was short for Griffin, a first name he hated. So we called him that, and not 'Griff', if we really wanted to piss him off, which was often. All in jest though.

"Huh, so they brought out the big gun for this one I see," replied Manny.

"They had to it seems. Why in God's name are you two screwing up my crime scene? You should know better than this by now."

I shot back, "Come on Griffin, you know that we know what we're doing so stop busting our chops. Help a couple pitiful detectives out here. We really don't need any bullshit after seeing the body of that young girl. We're all on the same team, right? We have to find this monster before it slaughters more innocent victims."

"Whoa Detective Stephenson, back down lady and move aside. Watch where you're also stepping. That possibly looks interesting beside your left foot."

I stopped immediately and glanced down. A little to my left was a small piece of something that resembled skin off a baked chicken, all crispy-like. I knelt down and used the tip of my pen to move it a little. Griffin came up, knelt down and opened a plastic bag. With forceps he gently grabbed the edge and held it up to eye level.

"What the hell is that?" I asked in my most curious of voices.

"Looks like skin of some type. The lab will analyze it and I'm sure come up with something. Hey, look at all this stuff lying around. Appears to be scales like at the murder scene behind the bar. That was the first place we noticed lots of scales, right?"

"Yes, the nurse and teacher were killed, but not nearly as gruesome as the past two victims. There were some scales, just not nearly this many. For some reason this creature is becoming more ferocious. What the hell do these scales mean?" I asked him.

"Damn if I know unless there's some big hungry snake doing this slaughter."

I laughed rather nervously. "Yeah, right. Better *frickin'* not be a damn big snake. Absolutely hate those slithering bastards. Anything else with scales that could've left this stuff?"

"Yep, fish and lizards, plus some butterflies and moths," answered Mallory. "I think we can safely eliminate the fish, butterflies and moths, unless they are humongous with very large teeth and grew legs. Other than some transplanted Komodo dragon, the largest lizards we have around here are Gila monsters. No way could they do this."

"Maybe that talking gecko from the commercials grew up and is now highly pissed off about something," Manny responded, rejoining them. "It can walk."

"Hey partner, I thought you disappeared. Glad you decided to stick around," I shot back playfully. Something had to help alleviate the tension a little bit.

"While you two were horsing around over there looking at scales and skin, I found some clear prints that are extremely interesting. They don't appear to be human, either. Griff, do you think one of your guys can cast them?"

"Absolutely, where are they located?"

"Leading from the fence to the spot where the body was found. A good bit of the blood had hidden some of the tracks, but a few are still clearly visible," Manny replied as they moved over to the exact spot.

Mallory stared at the one print, dropped lower and took out a camera. After taking some pictures he motioned one of his associates, Teddy Franz, to come over and take the impressions.

"I don't think they're human, that's for sure. Something bothers me, though. Why does it appear that whatever made them was standing erect? Lizards have four legs and in some cases rear up on two, but they sure as hell don't walk, can they?" I asked.

"Well, you're partially right, Amy. The basilisk, or Jesus Christ Lizard, can walk on two legs and grows to about two and a half feet long. However, I'm betting that it's something else much more monstrous. Maybe the killer is somehow trying to make us assume we're dealing with an animal of some type," replied Griffin, moving towards the edge of the crime scene.

I stopped beside him and removed my gloves because I was done here for now. Apparently so was Manny who had started heading across the football field towards the parking lot. We tossed the gloves and plastic booties into a bag held by another CSI tech.

"Well Griffin, my gut feeling is that a human being could not have done that. No way! I don't care what anybody tells me to the contrary. Whatever is loose in this city is animal in nature, plus a man-killer as well. We'd better find out soon what the hell it is, or more people are going to come up dead. Necks may roll as well, ours to be exact."

He got angry because I called him Griffin as I began following my partner. I was actually in a daze, not really knowing what to think. This crime scene was the worst so far. Ghastly and disturbing beyond belief. In the back of my mind as I pulled open the car door was that damn thing which ran across Benson Highway right in front of us definitely looked like a very large lizard. Too coincidental for my way of thinking.

Chapter 4

The six man search team led by Vince Flint paused at the top of a small rise overlooking Catalina Highway. They had been on the trail of this creature for about five days now. Sleeping in the desert that entire time, they were tired, dirty, plus hungry for a thick steak and a cold beer. They were also dying to kill something, anything at that point. Vince was actually pissed off that they hadn't found their prey yet. He took great pride in being able to trail anything, and then kill or capture it with little or no problem. Actually, tracking was the tedious aspect of the game. Capturing or killing it the exciting and dangerous part. For sure he had been injured in the past, sometimes seriously, but he always survived. Too damn tough to die he was often told. He wondered if all the scars on his body wouldn't make Ripley's Believe It or Not someday. Nothing up to this point, human or beast, had survived unless he wanted it to. Or, the contract clearly stated so. He actually wasn't sure which one appealed to him more. Killing was final and it gave him total satisfaction. However, a successful capture could be much more exhilarating.

This particular challenge was very different, though. He knew from information provided to him at the outset that what they tracked was not of this world so the thrill was even higher. Now he was pissed off because for the first time in his life something was getting the better of him. That had never happened before. The trail changed often, other times disappearing completely like the thing just vanished. It took several of these changes, or disappearing acts, for Vince to realize he was dealing with an entity that could move and alter shape at will. Possibly assuming the bodily structure of whatever it chose. This was somewhat confirmed when they discovered the bodies of dead animals along the way. Dried skin as well, like it was shedding some outer layer as it grew larger.

"Hey Flint, what the hell is going on here? You know, I didn't sign on to track some damn ghost. Or, whatever the hell this thing is."

The leader stood and turned to face Clarence 'The Shadow' Hill, a wiry African American who was all muscle and had nearly zero body fat. They had been partners on a number of hunts and missions in numerous countries around the world. Vince knew he could count on Clarence no matter how deep the crap tended to get in any bad situation.

"What's wrong you big baby, ready to give up so easily? I thought you were tough. That's why I called you in. If you can't handle this shit then scurry on home."

The black guy stood and tossed a knife he was twirling in his hand between the feet of Flint. Vince didn't move, just stared straight ahead, a dark look in his eyes.

"You know how tough I am. No way am I quitting. I just like to know what I'm tracking. This has been a goddamn secret almost from the beginning. That's just not right man, and you know it's not. We need a lot more info and we're not getting it."

Vince bent over and pulled the knife from the ground. "Next time you throw a knife at me old friend you'd best make it stick in something other than dirt," flicking it back at Clarence who dodged just in time before it struck a large cactus behind him.

There was thick silence for about ten seconds and then both men laughed. Some of the tension had been released so it was suddenly a little better.

The other four team members stood, or sat around, watching the altercation between the old friends. They were Julius *'Kung Fu'* Prudot, master in a number of martial art forms; Jimmy *'TNT'* Baldwin, ex-ranger and explosive expert; Timothy *'Tiny Tim'* Rollins (obviously named because he was on the rather large size), who was an expert marksman with more actual weapons than anybody Vince ever knew; and lastly, Carrie *'Bad Ass'* Vaughn, the only female in the group. As her name implied, she was one badass bitch. Flint was pretty certain that she was the toughest of the four and would probably even give Flint a serious challenge in hand-to-hand combat.

"Okay guys, gather around because I'm not going to yell this out loud. Not that there's anybody out here in this god forsaken desert who could listen."

They all formed a tight circle. At least the sun had gone down so it was finally somewhat comfortable. Vince was dying for a damn cigarette, but he knew that was a no-no on the trail of whatever prey they were tracking.

"Okay, so here is everything I was told before we left. It seems that what we're searching for is not human. I think you all became somewhat aware of that fact a few days back. This thing is alien, pure and simple. From what galaxy, planet, or solar system I have no freaking idea. Just that it's damn sure nobody's pet dog or cat. It had been on ice for quite a while and don't ask me how long. I'm apparently not privy to that classified info at this time even as much as I feel it would help. This is one intelligent, mean, predatory bastard with no qualms about killing as you've seen. The only way we're going to catch this thing, and hopefully survive in the process, is to be extremely aware of what's around us at all times. Be prepared to kill with no questions asked. They would like us to capture this creature, but I don't feel we'll be able to successfully do that. Our lives depend on us being totally alert at all times. For that matter, all of Tucson and maybe the entire United States depends on us not failing. There are two other teams looking for this creature, but they are not as good as we are. This is our game to win or lose. Since I've never lost, I sure don't plan on starting now."

"Do you even have any idea what it looks like?" asked Carrie, ripping a bite off a stick of beef jerky.

"Apparently when not in a host body I understand from what I was told that it resembles a small blob, like a slug or worm, red in color, maybe a foot or two in length. I can't tell you that for a fact because I've never seen the little bastard. If you see what looks like a large, ugly, red earthworm with sharp teeth, then shoot the damn thing. Don't hesitate because it could sure as hell get inside any of us without even the slightest hesitation. That is some heartburn I don't look forward to experiencing."

They all laughed, trying to cut the nervousness a little. All of them were battle hardened survivors, killers, and experts at what they did. This crap was totally new. Something they had never, ever faced before. It was always difficult to kill something you never had the opportunity to scout previously, or had fought with at some point.

"So then let me understand something," said Prudot. "We have no idea what it looks like other than maybe some big fat polish sausage. We also have no idea where it is currently, or even what it might look like now, because it may have changed shape. For all we know it could be some damn rabbit, bird, wolf, snake, lizard, or who knows what else. That about the size of it?"

Vince smiled, his slightly crooked teeth showing brightly in the moonlight. "Fuckin' A, buddy. Pretty easy task if you ask me."

They stirred around a little, figuring Flint was crazier than a loon. Each of them thought they were all nuts anyway. Following something in this vast desert that could literally be trailing them, hiding behind the next cactus, ready to strike and kill in an instant. They also knew that they wouldn't want to follow anybody else other than Flint.

Carrie spoke up again. "So where do we go from here?"

Vince turned to stare down at the highway and then to the open ground beyond. The piece of equipment he carried took them on a trail that became both hot and cold. Each time the entity changed hosts the only thing left was either a dead carcass, or dried skin, like it had shed an outer coat. No telling what it looked like now.

"I believe it crossed the highway around here. Don't ask me how I know that, gut instinct I suppose. That dead snake we found not far from here probably meant it took over something else, probably larger and more vicious. No idea even to say how big it is now. I suppose we'll sure as hell discover that when we locate it. Or, the damn thing finds us. Check your weapons people and let's head out. The sun will be completely down in a few minutes and it's going to be really dark out there."

"Thankfully a lot cooler, too. Damn sun was beginning to bake my brain," shot back Tiny Tim.

"What brain?" asked Prudot over his shoulder, leaning down to check the three weapons he'd been toting for the last five days.

Tiny Tim spun around and with a size thirteen boot sent Julius forward where he fell and rolled twice. The fallen man jumped up, knife in hand, ready to lunge at the giant. Hell, he was ready for any action at that point.

"Whoa, whoa, no horsing around bullshit. Come on guys, save your energy for that creature we're following. You'll need it I have a feeling," said Flint, moving between them. "Hey Prudot, nice somersault. You should've been an acrobat."

The tension was at least broken for the moment while they all laughed. Five minutes later they crossed Catalina Highway when there was a break in traffic. Stopping about ten yards into the desert on the other side Flint knelt down when he noticed several distinct tracks. He then gazed forward before slowly standing.

"What's up boss?" inquired Hill, moving up to stand beside Vince.

"I don't know for sure. These tracks appear to be from a Gila monster, but much larger. Looks like it crossed the road right here. It's not a chicken, either. So boys and girls, it seems we are now looking for some damn big lizard. Since we know how vicious they can be then it's probably safe to assume it's five to ten times that size now. This isn't any boy scout expedition so be prepared every second and don't let your guard down."

"How in the hell can you eat after what we just saw?" I asked my partner.

Between bites of his juicy cheeseburger, slathered with hot peppers, Manny mumbled, "Hey, a guy has to eat, you know? I hated what we saw at the school too, but you know as well as I do we can't allow that to cloud our judgment, or keep us from going hungry. So you should eat up. We may never know when our next meal will be."

I finished off my diet coke and tossed the empty container into a trash can near where we sat. He was right, of course. I always tended to let this shit get to me and knew in the long run that it was wrong to do that. I was still relatively new to this detective game.

Somehow though I really didn't want to get so hardened to the victims that I couldn't let that emotion work for me. I could at times get really pissed off and felt like tearing something apart. Yet, it also worked in my favor because my mind never stopped working and assimilating details. I swirled with my French fries and ketchup.

"Yeah, well, sitting around here stuffing your face won't find this killer. You about ready to head out, lard ass?"

"Hey come on, you know my body is hard as a rock. You want this last bite?"

"Eat me Manuel, let's go," I shot back over my shoulder heading for his car.

A few minutes later we were on the street cruising towards the morgue. I didn't relish the idea of seeing young Karen's savaged body again so soon, but we had to get lucky and latch onto something that began leading us in a positive direction.

"Manny, something's really bugging me about all this."

He didn't answer and didn't have to. I knew he was waiting for me to continue.

"Each of these killings happened at night with only one of them being inside the city limits. That was the young nurse. The hospital is right on the edge of the city so I wonder if we can plot trails of the killings and follow them back to possibly where this thing may have come from. Plus, the first two kills had none of those scales on the ground. If there were any, then they were in such a small number that we didn't notice them. The last two, especially young Karen, had a lot of that creepy stuff lying around."

"Possibly, but the deaths could just imply the victim was in the wrong place at the wrong time. If we're dealing with an animal of some kind just roaming around, then these killings are most likely random. Unless you want to believe this creature is a very large snake, we still don't have much to go on," Manny replied.

"That's just it," I countered, "If this killer is an animal then most often they stay within a particular territory. My feeling is that maybe it's just strayed a little, but still remaining close to the area it knows best. Plus, if this is a damn big snake then you're on your own buddy. You know how I feel about those and this one would be so freaking big I'd most likely go into cardiac arrest."

He laughed and then took a long swallow from his large root beer. "Let's see what the M.E. has to tell us first before we start making snap judgments. Probably the wounds will give us some idea as to what kind of creature we're looking for. I still can't believe I'm talking about searching for some monstrous snake, or whatever the hell it is."

"Yep, makes me yearn for the safe confines of good old Philadelphia. Hell, all we have back there are werewolves, zombies, and vampires. Kind of tame compared to this stuff," I responded, wondering how he would react to that since he could be so gullible.

He took his eyes from the road and stared at me. "Really?"

I started laughing. "Partner, you're so innocent that you'd believe anything about now. Come on, let's see what awaits us in the morgue," as Manny pulled his SUV in front of the Pima County Medical Examiner's Office.

Ten minutes later we stood beside a long metal table staring down at the ravaged body of young Karen Culokis lying partially exposed. All I could think of over and over was what a terribly tragic ending for such a promising young life. That just such an innocent decision on her part to meet somebody else after school had placed her in harm's way. I kept telling myself to just try my best and keep it all together.

"So what's up, Doc?" Manny asked. "We're completely lost with these killings. We have absolutely no clues, other than some prints and scales. What are we dealing with? Can those ghastly wounds tell us anything?"

The Chief Medical Examiner of Pima County glanced up. "What you're dealing with detective? So you've pretty much decided that this killer is not human I take it."

"You tell us. Could a human being ever do this type damage?" I shot back.

"I can tell you stories that would raise hair on the back of your neck, but I won't so you don't get sick in my lab. In this case though, I think you're definitely looking for something other than human, although what that is as of yet I'm not completely certain."

"Then you're partially sure of something so let us in on it," Manny countered.

The M.E. pulled the cover down a little more to expose the sternum showing the large gash from neck to stomach that had split young Karen apart. "This was not done by a knife, I'm positive of that. It appears to have been made by a talon of some kind, a very large claw in other words. Probably more than one. This is all much too ragged to have been sliced with a knife blade, or scalpel. On the inside, her body looks like several organs were literally ripped out, mainly the liver and heart. Totally amazing!"

I felt bile begin to roar up my throat. I looked away and swallowed hard to keep it down. Certainly didn't need to vomit right here on the tile floor, especially after what young Karen had suffered through. I silently berated myself for being so weak.

"Can you possibly tell us what kind of animal might've done this?" I responded in a low voice, but at least not quivering like a scared little girl. "Or what could've done it?"

"Really hard for me to say right at the moment. We've sent off tissue and blood samples to be analyzed. That should hopefully return something positive. There actually was a small piece of what appeared to be a claw so I'm hoping that tells us something as well. I also feel fairly comfortable in saying that whatever killed this poor young lady was able to stand erect. Whether it has four legs or two, it was erect at some point."

"Then are you also saying that this could've been done by a human being?" Manny asked with surprise.

"No, no, I didn't say that, Detective Corroda. What I said was that the killer was erect at some point so it obviously stood on two hind legs. Many animals with four legs do have that ability, but how many are predators like that around here? I think until we get all the results back, your best bet would be to talk to some animal experts. Once we feel kind of sure of what type it is, then we could possibly know what you're looking for."

I cleared my throat. "Doctor, what about the brain? It looks like much of it is gone as well. Am I right about that? To be honest, I don't see many exposed brains."

"You are actually correct, Detective Stephenson. Apparently your parents did not raise a dummy, although that may be up for discussion."

"Thanks Doc, but I'm not sure my dearly departed folks would've agreed with you on that point. What can you tell us about the brain being destroyed like that?"

"A good part of the brain matter was removed I think to mainly expose the temporal lobe in the rear of the skull. That is the part of the brain which controls memory and perception. However, that's just my gut feeling. I can't be sure, especially since that part of the brain is missing. So, as you can see I'm very busy. Anything else you want?"

Both Manny and I moved away from the table. "No, I don't think so, not at this point anyway. When will you be completely finished, especially the lab results?"

"I'll be done with the body in about two hours or so. I would think we'll have the laboratory results back in the morning. I did place a rush on those and this case has everybody working overtime. I can let you know as soon as I have something positive."

"Thanks doctor, you have our cell phone numbers. Please call us as soon as you get anything that you think will help us find this monster."

Walking down the hallway towards the front door to the hospital I stopped at a water cooler for a drink because I was so dry. I also splashed it all over my face to kind of bring myself back down to planet Earth. Standing still for a few moments trying to compose myself I suddenly felt a hand touch my right shoulder. I screamed and spun around, grabbed the hand, twisted the arm, rolled to my right, and slammed whoever it was onto the floor. At the same time I pulled my service revolver and pointed it.

Manny stared up at me with eyes as wide as saucers. Instantly I felt totally foolish, but the damn guy should've given me some notice. Didn't he know that I was nearly strung as tight as a concert violin? He moaned slightly, mostly because I was still twisting his wrist. Also from the air slammed out of him when he hit the floor.

"Hold it right there," came a loud voice off to my left. "Put the gun down on the floor and step away. Do it now!"

I moved my eyes away from Manny's shocked glare and glanced up. A hospital guard, plus a Tucson cop, were in perfect shooting stances, guns aimed directly at me. Their eyes meant business as well.

The cop spoke again. "One last time. Put the gun down on the floor, release that man, and move back against the wall behind you. Do it now, no more warnings."

I let go of my partner's wrist, knelt down further, placed the gun on the floor, and shoved it towards the cop. Standing slowly I then turned back to the wall and took a deep breath which I realize I had been holding inside.

"I'm Detective Amelia Stephenson. That man on the floor is my partner, Detective Manuel Corroda. There's no problem here, I just lost it. Everything is fine."

While I talked, the two officers moved in closer. The hospital guard kicked my revolver further out of the way. The police officer then grabbed hold of Manny's right arm and pulled him quickly out of further harm's way. Hell, in harm's way? Yeah, I suppose so because at that split second I pretty much seemed like a crazed maniac.

The hospital guard moved over to check on Manny while the cop came forward, his gun still leveled directly at me. "Let me see some ID and do it very slowly. Any movement towards another weapon and I won't hesitate to shoot. You got that?"

"Got it," I replied, reaching slowly for my badge and identification in my back pocket. I rarely, if ever, carried a purse anymore. Too damn cumbersome. Sometimes I wore a fanny pack, but today when we left my house I just grabbed my ID wallet and some money. After all, that's all you need really unless you're driving and need keys.

Holding the identification out, the officer carefully took it from my quivering hand, checked it out, and then slowly holstered his gun. He made the sign for the hospital guard to do the same thing.

"What the hell happened here, Detective Stephenson? Did he do something where you needed to use so much violence? Do you want to report partner abuse?"

"Officer...," looking at his badge, "Gomez, things have not been going well. This case we're on, all these killings. We just looked at the latest body downstairs, stopped for a drink of water, and I totally zoned out. I suppose I was thinking so much of the killer that when my partner put his hand on my shoulder I reacted before I realized who it was. I'm sorry, truly sorry. In fact, I'll probably never be able to make it up to him."

"You can say that again. It's okay to straighten up and recover your firearm. I'm not going to report this incident, Detective Stephenson. I'll let your partner do that if he feels it's necessary. Abuse is abuse you know. Personally, if I were you I'd go home and get some rest, maybe take a few days off. If this would've been a civilian you could've done some serious damage and found yourself in a world of shit."

"Affirmative, I'll do just that," I replied, moving over to where Manny was just beginning to stand up with the help of the guard and a nurse who had been passing by.

"Are you okay, partner? I'm sorry, really sorry."

Holding his wrist and stretching his back, he replied, "Hey, remind me next time to alert you when I'm in the area at least ten yards away. Guess that proves you can kick my fat Mexican ass anytime you feel like it."

"Come on partner, I said I'm sorry. I'm really embarrassed so let me have your keys and I'll drive us back to my house."

"As long as you have liquor. If you don't, then I'm stopping at a bar along the way. I need something very strong right at the moment."

"I have a few bottles of something I'm sure from the holidays, and there's always beer. I don't drink much, but this is an exception. Come on, let me help you."

He moved back quickly and held up his hands. "I can walk without assistance just in case you get a flashback, or want to practice your karate moves again. You'll have to show me that one. Jesus, one second I was going to ask if you were doing okay and the next moment I was on the floor flat on my back. That was an awesome takedown."

"That comes from years of training and not much chance to use it lately. It's good to know that I can still react quickly when I have to," I replied, rather sheepishly.

"I'll vouch for that," he said, rubbing and moving his wrist around in a circle.

We were somewhat quiet on the way back to my house. I didn't know what to say, or even how to react. Had this case gotten to me so badly? It had to have been just seeing the mutilated body of the young teenage girl that caused something to snap inside me. What I really needed to do though was get my head out of my ass and harness those emotions into finding who, or what the hell, was killing people in our city.

We pulled into the driveway. Once inside, I quickly found an unopened bottle of Jack Daniels. We took it out on the patio and quietly sat down. After swallowing two double shots each I figured that my partner was just about shot as well. I still felt so bad about what I had done to him that I just kept apologizing. He kept accepting too which made me feel worse. Obviously, I would be apologizing and getting ribbed about this for quite some time, especially once it got spread in the squad room which I felt it would.

Since it appeared Manny was in no mood to drive home, I called his wife Anita who I had gotten very friendly with over the past year. I informed her that her husband just needed to rest a little bit, especially since he had at this point fallen asleep on my sofa. Thankfully she knew there was nothing to be concerned about sexually. After placing a light blanket over him to guard against the air conditioning I changed into shorts and an oversized tee shirt, crawled into bed, and was immediately sound asleep.

During the night my dreams evolved into nightmares of monstrous snakes and lizards chasing me around the desert. Somehow these damn little gray men crept in their too. Not sure why that happened other than they looked alien and I had seen them before.

Christ Almighty, what a night and the daylight wasn't getting much better. I began to wonder whether nightmares and reality would ever become separate. In fact, I prayed for that to happen and all of this to be over with soon.

Chapter 5

Michael Saylor had been driving his girlfriends out to a special lookout point, one that hardly anybody else ever used, for almost a year now. In fact, this magical spot was kept as secret as possible between Tommy, Greg, and himself. Sure, he'd go to the ones most of his friends utilized from time to time just to be part of the crowd, to have fun and drink, do some necking, a little feeling around so to speak, and whatever else teens took part in. When he was really feeling lucky though he brought his special dates here to overlook a vast open expanse of the Sonora Desert surrounding his home of Tucson, Arizona. It was close to Sabino Canyon where he also went swimming quite often.

He turned left off Catalina Highway onto a somewhat rough dirt road which led to a small rise where he then turned right. Another fifty yards further he came to a stop and parked. Thankfully, his father had given him a jeep for his last birthday knowing that his son loved going into the desert to explore and climb the surrounding Catalina Mountains.

Tonight at Kim's party he met Linda and was instantly captivated by her beauty and sense of humor. Plus, she was incredibly smart. To be truthful, it wasn't her humor, or keen intelligence he was interested in. Kim's parents were away for the weekend and had allowed her to have a few friends over. So then a few friends turned out to be near twenty-five. He was curious why parents ever trusted their children to just have a small party. Anyway, Kim would get punished when her folks returned home, but she thought the party was more than worth losing some internet, or cell phone privileges. Even getting grounded which didn't happen that often since she was normally a good girl.

"So, what do you think of this cool place?" he inquired softly.

She had only been living in Tucson for a little over five months, her father having been recently transferred to Davis-Monthan AFB. Never much of an open child, she found it difficult at times to make friends. Mostly because she was so smart. Her good looks and intelligence instantly gave her access to any school group she desired. But, there were some groups of girls who would not accept her because she was considered a *Brainiac*, and not the super villain in DC Comics, either. She hated having to put up a dumb façade just to be accepted, but sometimes it was needed just to crack the loneliness.

Her best friend Kim was different though, being pretty darn smart as well. Kim, however, would tell her that she just needed to ease up and try to act dumb. In other words, become more like a normal teen. Not that their friends weren't smart, just that intelligence and excelling in just about everything in life wasn't a major part of their own teenage lives. Being a potential nerd wasn't fun, either. Her friend would say there'd be plenty of time later in college and professional life to show just how smart she was.

So, at the party she really relaxed and let her hair down which was pretty stunning since her long blonde tresses nearly reached to her waist. It was an instant hit, drawing boys like bees to the sweetest honey. She just had to dumb it down so they wouldn't run in the opposite direction, afraid to be so close to this beautiful nerdy girl. As if, God forbid, her intelligence would rub off on them. Even though she rarely drank alcohol, after consuming a few beers the 'whooziness' hit her hard. She was now acting about as dumb as everybody else. Earlier in the evening she had removed her shorts and Grateful Dead T-shirt to show off her new, vividly pink, two piece swimsuit. The entire pool area became very silent. She always got a thrill out of how her body had that effect on others. After all, even really smart people sometimes could not contain their own vanity. Beauty and intelligence was a killer combination for any situation, or walk in life.

Leaping from the diving board she rose to the surface and looked around to find all eyes staring directly at her. A few seconds later Michael swam over and smiled.

"Wow Linda, I haven't seen a crowd like this become that silent ever."

The noise around the pool slowly returned to normal, the temporary trance broken. She treaded water and looked at Michael who was really cute with his curly brown hair and hazel eyes. There was a little acne on his face, but that was normal for teenagers. Linda, on the other hand, had nearly flawless skin. She worked hard at keeping it that way, too. Eating the right stuff and rejecting as much junk food as possible helped a great deal. She thought if Michael became an acquaintance, or more than just a close friend, then she would help him with his skin care. He was also the starting wide receiver on the football team so he was looking like a pretty good catch *(pardon the pun)*.

They stayed together most of the next two hours. He introduced her to lots of the kids, one advantage of being so popular. After having a burger and beer he asked if she would like to drive out to see a very special, beautiful spot in the desert. Immediately she was somewhat wary. However, at the same time curious. He assured her that nothing out of sorts would happen. She realized all guys used that worn out line. Ultimately, she knew he only had one thought on his mind and that would be getting into her pants.

Now, however, she stared out at the vast Sonoran Desert, lights from Tucson twinkling in the distance. The sky was so dark that stars appeared to be 3-D. Off to the east a nearly full moon glowed brightly. It was stunning and breathtaking to say the least.

"Wow, it's so magical here," was about all she could utter at that very moment.

Michael laughed. "Yeah, that's usually what I hear. In fact, I said the same thing when I first found this place. Heck, I still think that every time I come out here."

"Oh, you come here often?" she asked, curious if it was always on a pantie hunt.

"Pretty often since we go up to Sabino Canyon a lot to swim, drink some beer, and just hangout. Have you been to the canyon yet, especially Upper Sabino?"

"No, not yet, but I'd like to sometime. Sounds like it could be a lot of fun."

"The water is absolutely fabulous. It's so clear and cold because it flows in waterfalls down from higher up. Maybe we can go there some Saturday as long as you promise to wear that pink bathing suit you had on tonight," he said jokingly.

"Ah, you mean like the one I have on now?" she teased.

Pausing, he nodded. "Yeah, okay! Let's get out and walk around a little bit?"

They exited the jeep after he shut off the engine. She was quickly assaulted by the darkness once the headlights disappeared. It was a little unnerving to say the least.

"Wow Michael, it's really dark. Kind of frightening a little bit."

"You'll quickly get used to it. Not really as dark as it seems, just the effect of the lights going out on the jeep. Your eyes will adjust fast because of the moonlight."

She quickly realized he was right. Within a minute, light from the glowing stars and moon highlighted the desert, casting an array of strangely shaped shadows over everything. She thought it was maybe the eeriest place she had ever been, but stunning and mysterious at the same time.

He decided to take the plunge and reached for her hand.

"Do you mind, Linda? I don't want you to trip, or slip while we're walking."

She smiled, expecting something soon to break the ice and their nervousness. "Not at all, feels kind of comfy. Thank you for bringing me here, it's just breathtaking."

They walked a little up and down the crest of the hill staying clear of sagebrush and large rocks where rattlesnakes could be lurking. Eventually they returned to the jeep and crawled into the front seat. They leaned back and stared at the sky through the open roof. She took the moment to point out some stars and different formations since it was just so difficult for her to stay dumb for all that long.

She continued talking, mostly because she was so darn nervous. Suddenly, he reached over with his right hand and placed a finger on her lips. She stopped talking and turned her head with a questioning look in her lovely blue eyes.

"Ssssshhhh, let's allow the silence to work for us. May I kiss you?"

"I guess," leaning towards him, more anxious than she had been in a long time.

Michael was a damn good kisser too, as she found out right away. At first it was just lips on lips, but soon his tongue starting probing, anxious for things to possibly go further. She felt strong urgings between her legs and then suddenly jumped slightly as a hand gently cupped her right breast.

"Sorry, I didn't mean to scare you. Do you realize how beautiful you are?"

How does a girl really answer that question? To say yes, then you're showing how stuck on yourself you might be. To say no would basically be telling a lie.

"I've been told that before Michael, but coming from you it sounds different. Thank you. Hey, you're pretty darn good looking yourself, but then I'm sure you know that already. You really do have lots of girls at school staring at you in the halls."

He laughed, a throaty sound, excited to move this adventure forward and forget the small talk. "Oh, I'm nothing special. Just a tall, gangly guy with a skin problem that knows how to play football. If I weren't on the team I'd probably be insignificant."

She returned the laugh. "I highly doubt that. Hang on a minute though."

He stretched back into his seat while she leaned forward to slip the tee shirt over her head. Then she lifted her butt a little and pulled her shorts down so they dropped to the floor, kicking them off her ankles, along with the sandals. Now, she sat there in her bathing suit in the desert. Go figure! She felt brave and frightened at the same time.

"How do you like the view now?" she purred.

He was utterly speechless which didn't happen that often with this wide receiver. It took him a few seconds before realizing how freaking lucky he might end up getting. His buddies might actually kill for this exact opportunity and it was all his.

"Mmmmm, like is not even a word I would use, but yeah. In fact, I'm not sure if there is a word that I could even say at the moment," he replied, pulling off his own shirt.

"So what now Mr. Big Time Football Player? I'm getting a little cold."

He raised himself up and slid between the seats to the back, took her left hand and guided her through the opening. Immediately they locked lips and began running their hands over each other's bodies. Linda wasn't really sure if going all the way was very smart. In fact, she figured it was a pretty stupid thing to do. She also realized it was playing a dangerous game, yet she was ready. In fact, literally on fire. This would be her first time and she was really nervous. She was now prepared to relinquish her virginity to a first string wide receiver named Michael. She wondered if they would score.

Whispering in her ear, he asked, "Are you sure, Linda? I don't want to do this if you're going to be mad at me later. I also don't want you getting in trouble, either. We can wait if you want to. We can just let our hands and lips do all the work. I honestly don't want you to regret this moment."

"Michael, just please stop talking. Let's do this before I change my mind."

He took in a long breath and exhaled slowly. Sweet Jesus, he realized that he was possibly about to become the luckiest boy in Tucson, Arizona.

Suddenly, there was a sharp noise off to the left of the jeep. She glanced up quickly, pushing away from him. "What was that Michael? Did you hear it?"

"No, I didn't hear anything," he pleaded, wanting to hold her again.

The sound repeated, louder this time from just beyond the front of the jeep where the rise dropped down about ten feet. It was like a loud hissing noise. Then it sounded like rocks and gravel moving. This time Michael heard it as well so he sat up.

"You heard that, right?" she asked, her voice low and frightened. "I thought you said we were alone out here. That it was totally safe."

"We are, and it is normally," Michael replied, thinking maybe it was just his buddy Greg goofing around. Always the prankster in their group, he might've followed them here, parked further back, and then crept up to scare the hell out of them.

Not bothering to put his shirt on, he zippered and buttoned his pants before sliding out of the front seat. He then walked slowly towards the front of the jeep.

"Greg," he shouted loudly, "if that's you out there then just stop the bullshit right now. Linda is really scared and you're screwing up a very special moment in my life."

There was total silence other than his voice echoing slightly in the darkness. Then there was another movement, louder this time, just off to his right. Besides another loud hiss there was a sharp snap like possibly part of a cactus being broken off.

"That's it, enough crap," Michael shouted. "Hey Linda, turn the jeep lights on."

"Michael, just get in and let's get the heck out of here," she said, very frightened now. "I don't care who it is, I'm really scared. Please, let's get out of here."

"We will, just turn on the lights so I can look around for a minute."

Two seconds later headlights glared brightly, bouncing off Michael's back and shining all around him. His eyes opened wide in shock while she screamed. A long arm with sharp claws extended out of the darkness into the light, slicing across the boy's chest and neck, blood spraying over the hood and windshield. Linda continued screaming his name and reached out for the keys still in the ignition.

Michael was slammed back against the hood as a nightmarish vision appeared, swinging the other clawed arm. It struck the wide receiver's head, sending it flying out into the dark desert like a wobbly pass from an erratic quarterback. At this point Linda had totally lost her voice, mouth opening in a silent scream. The vehicle started up and she slammed the shift into gear. Stomping down on the gas as hard as she could the wheels spun crazily on the dirt.

That was all the time the monster needed. It leaped onto the hood and reach over the windshield through the opening in the roof, grabbing her beautiful face and long blonde hair, twisting to the right. A loud snapping of her slim neck shot into the night. Thinking that she had put the jeep into reverse she in fact had shoved it into drive. Falling forward into the dashboard her foot tromped hard on the gas pedal. The jeep shot forward, hurtling over the edge of the rise and plunged down to the ground below. The creature leaped free as the vehicle hit the dirt on the grill and then rolled over onto its top with Linda totally pinned underneath. Didn't matter though, she was dead anyway and so was Michael Saylor. A night of young teenage bliss had ended in terrible tragedy.

On the rise, highlighted in the moonlight and beneath the blinking stars, stood a large lizard-like beast. It was all that remained of the Gila monster, now transformed into a monstrous apparition never seen before. Covered with large armored scales, the head was more a cross between human and lizard, with teeth huge and protruding from a massive mouth, long forked red tongue flickering out to test the air. It was going to be a good meal the beast thought, plus more assimilation of intelligence. He would get plenty of that from Linda's brain. Michael would offer up only football plays and how to lure innocent girls out into the desert. But, he was much larger so would provide more meat.

Disgustingly slurping with great diligence and gusto this alien life form began gorging on a rather unexpected feast under the moonlight in the beautiful Sonoran Desert. No candlelight required.

Chapter 6

"**H**ey Flint, did you hear that noise?" whispered Carrie Vaughn.

"I sure did," he replied, equally as low. "Sounded maybe like a vehicle accident, at least some type of large crash. I think it came from our left over towards Sabino."

"Want to split up?" asked Clarence Hill. "You take three with you and check it out. The rest of us can continue moving forward searching for the creature."

"No, we all stay together," Flint replied. "Something tells me that what we're chasing may be the reason for that crash. If we split up then we weaken our force. We don't want to do that, especially if we locate this damn monstrosity. We'll spread out though. Just keep within sight and sound of each other. You all got that?"

Each of them sounded off and they changed direction heading east. Weapons at the ready, excitement stirring wildly inside their bodies. Just the thought of possibly finding this creature and engaging action was what they all had been waiting for ever since they had begun this quest. For soldiers like themselves, only the action meant anything at all. In this case, thoughts of the unknown drove them forward even more.

It took about thirty minutes for the team to cover the ground leading them to Michael Saylor's favorite lookout point. Vince held up his left hand to halt. Lowering his arm they knelt quietly waiting for what was to come next. He pointed to Clarence and then to the right, placing fingers to his lips. Motioning that he would go left, palm out meant that the others would stay behind, but on full alert.

Both of them crouched and then slid silently into the darkness avoiding cactus and sagebrush. Vince reached a small clearing at the top of the rise while Clarence came to a point where he could climb down the small hill. Flint allowed his senses to open up as wide as possible. He quickly detected the unmistakable scent of blood from someplace nearby. Moving to the right about ten yards his boot struck something so he stopped. Glancing down, it was a body. He switched on a small flashlight attached to his belt.

A quick intake of breathe signified that he was staring at what remained of Michael's ravaged body. Flint had seen numerous deaths and dismembered bodies throughout his career, but this sight was more than he was expecting. Stifling a gag, he turned off the light and moved forward towards the rise. He let out a soft whistle which was soon met with a returning signal. Glancing to his right Vince noticed the slow movement of his team member, Clarence. Sliding his gaze to the left he saw the large outline of the upside down jeep and motioned in the air for Hill to be careful. That there was something just ahead of them which they needed to carefully check out.

Being careful he stepped over the rise and half slid to the bottom. With his rifle pointing forward he waited a few seconds for Hill to join him.

"There's one dead body on the ground above," he whispered. "Chances are there will be at least one more down here. You go right, I'll go left. If you see anything move just be careful you don't shoot somebody who might've been thrown from the jeep. Be alert though in case it's that damn creature. Shout before you shoot."

They each carried comm. units attached to their collars, much like police have. That allowed each member of their team to listen in. When they reached the site of the crash, Vince spoke softly for the other four to come forward slowly, but to be careful.

Nearing the jeep Clarence knelt down and glanced underneath the smashed metal. There was lots of blood everywhere, but no body. He motioned to Flint who immediately thought the person had been pulled free, especially with that much blood spread around. Both men continued to move about the destroyed vehicle looking for signs.

Hill raised his hand and pointed to the ground where he was standing and then out towards the desert. Quickly, Flint maneuvered in that direction, weapon always at the ready. Even though he was an old hardened warrior, this shit never failed to give him a rush. Being careful, along with his super stealth abilities, had saved him numerous times.

A long, wide trail of blood led from the vehicle towards a large cactus and then beyond into total darkness. Flint felt movement behind and whirled only to see that the other team members had moved up into position. He waved Hill to follow him as they moved even a little further back.

"Okay, we know there was another body dragged away. This damn thing can't be invisible so spread out and look for signs, tracks, anything that's interesting. Stay alert and on your toes. I'm going to follow the left side of that blood trail. Clarence, you'll follow the right. The rest of you, spread out a little wider, but not too far. We're close to this thing and I want to nail it before we get slaughtered first."

They moved off, guns at the ready, all senses alert. At least the moon was full so there was enough light to maneuver rather easily. Although none of them would mind having the entire desert lit up like a damn football field at that moment. Then at least they could see if this creature was still one or two steps ahead of them.

About fifty yards further, Tiny Tim tripped over something sticking out from behind a large, fat saguaro cactus. Even though he was fairly agile for his size, once he started falling he couldn't stop. When he hit the ground his rifle went off and he cursed loudly. So much for being stealth, Vince thought. Even the best plans could go wrong.

Tim tried to get up and realized he was lying in something wet. As he reached out to push himself off the ground, his hand landed on what appeared to be a foot. Glancing beyond that he saw a leg up to the knee and nothing else. Letting go quickly, he rolled his big girth to the left and rose awkwardly to his knees. No use in whispering now, especially since the gun had exploded to give away their presence.

"Flint, over here, I think we found some of what we're searching for."

In less than a minute they all quickly congregated around what was left of Linda Evans. Even for a big, tough guy like Tiny Tim he finished throwing up before rejoining the team. Nobody said a word because they all felt like doing the same thing. There wasn't much left of the young girl, not to mention her boyfriend back on the rise. The problem with Linda was that only half of her was spread on the ground. The rest was anybody's guess. They all had witnessed death, but children were the worst.

"Okay, so look, we have to leave two of you behind. Call 911 and let them know where you are and that we've discovered two recently killed teenagers. Check the glove compartment for any identification of the driver. Tim and Carrie, you'll stay. The rest of us are shoving on because I think we're damn close."

Carrie stood. "No way Flint, I am not staying behind. Don't even begin saying it's because I'm a damn female. I can kick the ass of most anybody here, probably you too. Pick somebody else. I'm not staying behind and that's final."

Julius responded. "I'll stay, but as soon as the police arrive I'm coming after you guys so stay in touch. Vaughn, if you're set on going forward then you'd better sure as hell not screw up."

"Hey 'Pruddy', fuck off. You worry about your own ass and I'll do the same," she replied acidly, moving off into the desert just to get away from his macho bullshit.

Flint paused and then turned around to face Tim. "Call this in now. Try and get cleaned up a little bit, too. Maybe there's some water in the jeep. If you want to come with Prudot then fine, but we'll be moving fast. I'll leave that up to you. If it makes you feel better I would've probably thrown up also if I had landed in that mess."

"Just get the hell out of here and kill that damn thing," said Rollins. "I'm tired of running into mangled bodies and not being able to do anything about it."

Five minutes later Tim was pouring water across his hands, arms, and legs where he had fallen onto the bloody ground. The police were on their way and should be arriving at the crime scene shortly. Prudot scanned the area for other body parts, finding a hand, plus another foot. He sure as hell wouldn't admit it to the others, but he was damn scared. That was the main reason he volunteered to stay behind. No way was he rejoining the group, either. This was a screwed up mess. The way it was heading, they were all going to be slaughtered before the night was out. He was pulling out of this game while he had the chance. There was a time to be brave and another to be smart.

Flint and the other team members moved off like deadly shadows determined to find this creature, alien or whatever the hell it was, and then put an end to this bloody rampage. It had gotten to be a matter of pride at this point, especially since he had never failed to successfully complete a mission. He silently vowed to himself that this would be no exception. Not only these tragic young deaths, but all the others over the last month, would absolutely be avenged.

Several miles ahead, the entity stopped to rest behind a large mound. The life form itself did not need to halt, but the earthbound creature it had taken over as a host did. Especially due to the incredible energy expended in becoming much larger. In fact, what had been a below average heartbeat with the slow moving Gila monster had now become much faster. One clawed hand clutched the severed head of pretty Linda Evans. Using long talons it easily cracked the skull open from the back like you would a pistachio nut. Its long tongue snaked out and wormed inside the brain to the temporal lobe where it slurped greedily. It was preparing for another transformation so it needed as much energy as it could obtain, plus intelligence. It sensed this brain was a good one.

The creature was also completely aware that it was being followed by a small group of humans who were certainly persistent, if not inadequate. Also, with this next transformation it would begin to reproduce. Not in the sense that it would give birth to living, squirming young. It was far too soon for that as the first alteration with the Gila monster commenced internal re-workings. Now its own DNA could be implanted in embryos that were already forming. These eggs would be distributed in safe locations, primarily underneath the sand, until they hatched. Normally a Gila monster needed to mate in order to produce eggs, but the alien creature was able to supply what was needed without another male which came in pretty handy depending on the planet it landed on. Since the worm itself was sexless, the host body determined what physical sex it displayed.

Also, lizard eggs do not normally hatch for approximately ten months after being laid. Not so now, however, since one of the important aspects of this alien's life form was the time span in the process of going from embryo to egg to hatchling which only needed less than a month. This was based normally on the atmospheric conditions from the creature's home planet. Here on Earth, eggs would most likely hatch sooner because of the oxygen content in the air. Also, the spawn would grow incredibly fast inside the shell and need release. All that was required was heat and the exact reason it had originally chosen this area of Earth to begin with, the desert surroundings. There was no point in arriving on part of this planet which was encased in snow and ice.

Instead of a successful landing, careening through the planet's atmosphere had screwed up the anti-matter system on the alien's vehicle. As a result the ship was much closer to the ground than anticipated so when the propulsion system reversed thrust, there was suddenly too much speed to avoid a violent collision. The spacecraft was then virtually destroyed. The entity had nothing else to do but suspend all functions of normal life that it was accustomed to, appearing as nothing more than a thick, blob-like mass substance.

When U.S. Air Force personnel investigated the crash, this liquid mass was transported very carefully back to Davis-Monthan and placed in laboratory quarantine where it was analyzed in great depth. It was eventually determined that they had found some type of alien life form so it was very quickly and carefully moved into total confinement in a room with three foot thick walls in the middle of a larger room created for constant 24/7 monitoring. The alien entity could not stay in a suspended state indefinitely so eventually it briefly showed signs of life knowing full well that not much could be ascertained in such a short period. It was at that point where some of the top scientists in the field were brought on board to study and perform experiments. That was back in 1983.

Several years later it was transported under the very highest security out to only one of two actively remaining Titan II ICBM missile silos in the desert surrounding Tucson. Originally there were seventeen silo locations around the City of Tucson, but over the years only two remained. One was put into use as a museum with the missile itself being decommissioned. It had since become a highly successful tourist attraction. The other one was quickly altered into a full-time, live-in experimental lab used solely for the purpose of studying this particular alien life form. It was also one of the most well kept secrets in the military with only the highest security clearances permitted.

At times, scientists like Dr. Warring were excited about evident progress, but then feelings and emotions quickly got deflated when certain promising directions slammed heavily into stone walls. The alien was actually playing a game with its human jailers simply to see who was the most intelligent. Apparently now that it was free that answer was quite obvious – alien one, humans zero.

Aware that it was being closely followed, it now finished the succulent treat from Linda's skull. It began moving forward somewhat slowly at first, then at a more rapid pace. Unwinding its long, limber body was like a cobra uncurling and becoming more erect. In this case, however, the creature continued to stand on rear legs, somewhat bent because the spine was not completely altered in order to allow it to rise completely erect. Feeling that speed was more of a necessity it dropped down to get back on all four limbs to move forward quicker. Its left rear leg struck Linda's head sending it rolling forward and then down a small hill where it rested against a large cactus. It was sad that such a young, promising, and beautiful life had come to such a tragic ending, her body parts spread out across the Sonoran Desert like meaningless trash. To the alien it simply meant nothing at all.

The point of survival and overthrow was not to allow anything to stand in the way of domination. All that mattered now was to lay the eggs, help them hatch and find hosts, then move on to the next step. There was nothing on this planet to stop it.

Chapter 7

My cell phone, which had been resting quietly upon the nightstand suddenly, and rather rudely, woke me up. It was still dark in the room so the sun had not risen as of yet. Shaking my head to erase the cobwebs I reached out and angrily grabbed it.

Groggily I answered, "Stephenson here, what's up?"

"Detective, this is Chief Crosson. I've been trying to reach Detective Corroda as well. Would you happen to know where he is at the moment?

I hesitated, then answered slowly, "Yes sir, I do. Is there a problem?"

"We've had another attack and it's not good. Why the hell are you sleeping and not out chasing after this maniac? And where the hell is Corroda anyway?" At this point he was yelling so loud I held the phone away from my ear.

"Sir, Detective Corroda is here at my house sleeping on the couch in the living room. Where's the crime scene?"

"Two young kids were apparently torn apart out near Sabino Canyon. It's a goddamn mess detective and I need you two out there five minutes ago," he responded, still kind of yelling. "Why in the hell is Corroda sleeping at your house, Stephenson? Do I have to be concerned about something going on between you two?"

"Not at all, Chief Crosson. My partner dropped me off here at my house. We both needed a drink and one led to another. I thought it best that he crash on my couch. Don't worry, I called his wife so she knows. There's absolutely nothing to be concerned about."

"Okay, well, I don't need any more crap on my plate right now. So listen up Amelia. This was called in by a team member that's apparently been out searching for something in the desert. From the way I understand it they were dispatched from Davis-Monthan. Why I don't know, but you two are going to find out, correct?"

"Yes sir, absolutely. We're on it like flies on shit," I responded, realizing quickly that I should not have made that comment.

"Amy, just please don't let me down here. Heads are going to roll, trust me. In fact, as soon as you check out the murder scene, then find out what's going on with that search team. Has it been working on its own, or dispatched by the air force? Then get your two fat asses back here to the office. There was a task force started last night and both of you are on it. Now get your butts in high gear. I mean like five minutes ago. Or, quite frankly, you two are going to be the flies you mentioned directly on that shit."

I stared at the silent phone, slid to the edge of my bed and sat up.

"Who was that?" came an equally groggy voice from the hallway.

I jumped up yelling, "Manny, don't do that for Christ's sake."

"Sorry Amy, heard you talking and didn't want to interrupt. What the hell is going on now? Are we in trouble again?"

"Seems that we've got another killing, a double this time. Two kids out near Sabino Canyon. Chief Crosson says it's a real mess. So what else is new anymore? We've got to move and get out there. I need to hit the bathroom real fast. You can use the half bath to powder your nose. Oh, apparently there is also a rogue team looking for something out in the desert. The chief said it was dispatched from Davis so there is something very strange going on here," I said, slamming the bathroom door closed.

Five minutes later we were speeding out of town heading for Sabino Canyon. I called the precinct to get the location of where we were going since Chief Crosson so rudely hung up on me before I even had a chance to ask him. It took us about twenty-five minutes before we started seeing the distant flashing of police and emergency response vehicles. We had jumped into my car this time so I came to a grinding halt in the dirt about ten feet off the road.

Jumping out we both walked with purpose and intensity toward Sergeant Sanchez who seemed to be directing several officers to cordon off a large area.

"Sanchez, what the hell's going on?" Manny asked as we stopped on each side of him.

"Well, if it isn't Moe and Curley. Glad you could finally find the time to join us. Hey, when the hell are you going to do your job and catch this damn thing?"

"Cut the crap sergeant, just bring us up to date," I replied angrily. I was pissed off. Not so much at Sanchez, but at myself because two more had died on my watch.

"Okay," he answered with a heavy sigh. "It appears these two young kids, boy and a girl, pulled off the highway and drove out here. We can only assume for some extracurricular activity if you know what I mean. Obviously something greeted them. It seems to have attacked the boy first because his body was found up here on the ridge. Very mangled I might add. Somehow the jeep they were driving went over the edge and crashed below. The girl was inside the vehicle, but not for long. Whatever this thing is it apparently pulled her out of the wreckage and drug her body out into the desert. We have officers searching and have already received reports of finding different body parts spread throughout the area. I've never seen anything like this in my entire life."

"Do you have any names?" Manny inquired.

Sanchez flipped his notepad open. "The jeep is registered to a Michael Saylor so that obviously is the young man. We're in the process of contacting his parents right now. There was a purse in the wreckage that belonged to Linda Evans. Her family is also being contacted, but they may be out of town. Also, it appears that her father is stationed at Davis-Monthan. Jesus, I have a son and daughter almost the same age. This makes me sick to my stomach, I don't have to tell you."

"No more sick than we are," I murmured back. "Okay, so Chief Crosson told me that this was called in by somebody who was part of a search team from the air base. Who and where is that person, or persons?"

Sanchez turned and motioned towards one of the cars where a very, very large man stood talking to a police officer. It was also obvious from his clothing that he had been in quite a messy situation. Off to the left stood another man with his muscular arms crossed, staring off into the desert. He looked pissed and confused at the same time.

"Thank you Sergeant Sanchez," Manny said as we started walking away. "Say hi to your lovely wife for me."

"Will do and Detective Corroda, please catch this killer. Put an end to this shit."

Manny and I looked at each other and shook our heads in unison. As we walked up to the immense guy standing by the car it was quite obvious from his appearance he had been involved in some altercation. Either he had been in a scuffle of some kind, or fallen into something really messy. The other guy still hadn't turned around so I was really curious about him as well. I nudged Manny on the arm and motioned that he should go talk to that guy and I would question the stinky giant.

The officer turned around upon my approach. I recognized him as Troy Keeler.

We shook hands briefly and he smiled. "Detective Stephenson, this gentleman is Timothy Rollins, aka Tiny Tim. He's the one who called it in. The other guy over there is Julius Prudot, one of his partners. This little guy here is now thankfully all yours. I'll be over there if you need me."

"Thanks Officer Keeler," as I turned to face Mr. Rollins. I hadn't felt this small in a long, long time.

"Mr. Rollins, I'm Detective Amelia Stephenson and that tall, handsome looking Hispanic guy over there is my partner, Detective Manuel Corroda. What can you tell me about what happened here? Also, just how did you come across these two bodies?"

"Please, you can call me Tiny Tim if you want, everybody does. Or just Tiny is okay, too." He was obviously very nervous and worried big time about something.

I smiled. "Well, if you don't mind I'll just stick with Mr. Rollins, or Tim if that's okay."

He nodded and smiled back. "I'm part of a small team out doing nighttime maneuvers for the air force testing some new equipment to help find certain types of targets, especially at night. What else can I say? We got here, found the first kid over there, saw the wreckage of the jeep below and noticed all the blood which was pretty obvious. My team lead told us to stay behind and call this in. That's about it."

I tried to absorb what he had just said and pretty much realized he was lying through his broken yellow teeth. Not only did he have really bad breath, he also stank to high heaven. I actually couldn't wait to get away from him right about then

"Look Mr. Tiny Tim, don't think for one minute I believe that pile of crap you just spun me. You apparently informed somebody earlier that your team was searching for something and that you had been dispatched from Davis-Monthan. So hey big guy, what I need you to do right this very minute is tell me the damn truth. If you don't, then I'll have your big ass taken in for further questioning. Your call so you now have one minute," I stated as firmly as I could. I was really getting pretty pissed off at everybody.

Allowing the smelly giant to stew on that for sixty seconds I moved over to where Manny was talking in lower tones to Tiny Tim's partner in crime.

Manny glanced my way and gave me that million dollar smile of his. "Detective Stephenson, this gentleman is Mr. Julius Prudot. I suppose you would call him a modern day soldier of fortune. I don't think Mr. Prudot has been totally forthcoming with information yet. He has told me the group he's part of was searching for something that apparently is top secret so he's unable to say anything more. He would've just told me name, rank, and serial number, but I guess all he has is a name. That sound about right Mr. Prudot? If that is, in fact, your real name since apparently all this shit is a secret."

He looked at me and nodded ever so slightly. He was pretty damn good looking too in that cocky, dashing, pirate sort of way. Definitely dangerous, for sure. Even more so than his giant buddy standing over by the vehicle.

"The name is correct, at least the one I've been using lately," he said grinning. "I'm truly sorry, but I really can't tell you more than that. We were told not to talk to anybody about anything. Or if we had to, then reveal as little as possible."

I cleared my throat slightly and gave him my sweetest smile. "Look Mr. Prudot, we've got a really bad situation here. Not only were these two young people slaughtered tonight, but there have been at least five other deaths we know of. All apparently associated back to the same monster. We need answers now. Tonight, in fact. Your little pal over there already stated earlier that you were dispatched from the air base so we know where you're from. Now, we need to know the following."

Holding up my fist I raised my thumb. "Number one, who from the base sent you out here, how many are there in your team, where are the rest of them at this very moment, and what is this thing you have been tracking? That's four questions all rolled up into one big fist. I'll definitely have more questions, but for now we need those answers right this very minute. You may talk to us out here or find both of you under arrest for withholding information, as well as accomplices to this crime."

He laughed. "We didn't do this, surely you can see that."

I shrugged my shoulders and stared back, not smiling this time. "No, we actually don't know that. Your partner in crime over there seems to be covered in blood which is surely not his. I'm also pretty darn certain it will match at least one of the deceased so we have enough right there to haul both of your asses in. Not to mention that Mr. Big Timmy over there seems like he would possibly be able to tear a human body apart with his hands. Plus, I'm sure we could find a big knife on one of you. So, I'm going to give you about thirty seconds to respond. Otherwise, we will handcuff you both, haul you off to jail, and probably charge you with double homicide. Pretty easy really."

He stared back, glanced quickly at Manny and then back to me.

"My partner here is not going to help you. Believe me Mr. Prudot, this is not any 'good cop, bad cop' routine. We are at this point extremely on edge. I won't hesitate in the least to follow through with that threat, unless I get answers right now. We might even find out that one, or both of you, have criminal records that would make mighty interesting reading. Do you think that might be a possibility?"

I could feel a very large presence behind me and tensed, reaching for my gun.

"Tell them Julius, at least everything we know which is not a lot. Those two kids deserve that much," stated Tiny Tim Rollins in a very deep, but troubled voice.

Prudot's eyes flicked back and forth between me and his fellow soldier. "You tell them and I'll back you up. That way Flint won't rip me a new asshole first."

"Okay, that's fair enough," Tim said, then looked directly at me. "There are six members of our team led by a very dangerous and irritable man named Vince Flint. He and three others are out there in the desert right at this very moment searching for what killed these two kids. We were dispatched from Davis-Monthan four days ago, but I can't tell you by whom. Only Mr. Flint knows that information. We also do not know what it is that we have been tracking, other than the damn thing is some type of creature and extremely lethal. That's all we know, honest. We haven't seen what it looks like and this is the closest we've come to locating it."

He looked over at Julius Prudot for backing. "I concur totally. That's about it detectives. We really didn't know how deadly it was until we found this," waving his arm in a half circle. "All we know for sure, or at least what we've discussed, was that this thing is definitely not human and to be on full alert with weapons ready at all times."

A moment of silence stretched into a really long minute. I then took a step back and crossed my arms, staring back and forth at them both before I gave them my best warm and fuzzy detective's smile.

"Okay, I guess I believe you both to a certain extent. However, what I can't fully grasp hold of is that you people, experienced hunters and soldiers, would traipse off onto some dangerous mission without knowing what you were going up against. That just doesn't make any sense to me at all. So, you tell me why I find that hard to believe."

"Detective Stephenson," replied Prudot, "the money we were offered was extremely good and it was upfront. If we didn't come back from this mission we had made arrangements in advance as to where the money was to be sent. Flint told us we would become aware of things on a need to know basis. I'll be honest with you, I don't even think he was totally aware of what we were following until now. He probably still doesn't know for sure. You know the military I'll bet. They love to keep secrets."

Uncrossing my arms, I took a step towards Prudot. "Okay handsome, here's what we're going to do. You are going to take some of us out into that desert to link up with your buddies. Your stinky friend here is going to be transported back to the station where he can get cleaned up and then questioned further. Get ready to leave in five."

Manny looked at me. "Amy, you can't do that. We're not adequately prepared to tromp off into the desert. Plus, we need to get the chief's authorization to do that."

"You're not going with us, Manny. You need to take Tiny Tim into the station, then meet up with Chief Crosson and the task force. Let them know what's happening so they can send a team out to Davis and get some answers. Keep your cell phone handy, I'll stay in touch constantly as to where we're at. We can't let this opportunity pass us by. Besides, we have four dangerous people roaming around out there in the desert with some serious firepower. I'm going and that's all there is to it."

He shook his head, not in agreement with me at all. "I think you're one crazy, no nonsense woman. If you do find it Amy, please be careful. I'm just getting used to you after a year and I really don't feel like breaking in another partner."

"That's a big job for anybody, but thanks for the sentiment I guess."

Turning to Prudot, I told him, "Get ready to leave in five. Can you somehow communicate with them?"

"Yes ma'am, though it'll have to be through a code by tapping on the mic button. Any loud voice erupting in the darkness would probably give away their position."

"I don't care if you send up smoke signals. Just let them know we're coming. We don't need to be shot because your Mr. Flint thought we were monsters."

In the back of my car was a case that contained an assault rifle, plus a bullet proof vest. I wanted to be prepared for just about any circumstance. Checking the action and making sure it was loaded, I placed a few extra clips in my pocket. I had several pairs of pants with long, deep pockets for just this type of occurrence so I slipped a pair on over the slacks I was already wearing. I wasn't sure how much the vest would protect me, but I felt safer with it on anyway. Hell, if I got that close to this creature it would probably be more than my vest that would be torn apart. That I really didn't want to think about very much.

I gave Manny a hug and said we would stay in touch. Also, to let the task force know what was actually going on. At least as much as we knew anyway. I joined up with Julius Prudot just on the other side of the crashed jeep. Several swat team members had arrived as well. They were definitely pulled into the mix and were actually only too ready to head off into the desert to find who knows what. All macho, male testosterone bullshit really because truthfully, I was sort of quaking in my boots which I had changed into. I couldn't let anybody know it though because I freaking asked for this assignment.

"Which way, Mr. Prudot?" I inquired

"When they took off they were following the blood trail so I would say it's a safe bet to do the same thing, at least until the spot where we found part of the girl's body. After that I don't know because Rollins and I stayed behind."

"That's at least a starting point so let's shove off," I replied, wondering what dangers I was walking into and why I even decided to do something so insane.

Chapter 8

The creature had now moved a good five miles ahead of Vince Flint's small team. It then maneuvered so that it actually was coming up from behind them, slightly to the left. It also had altered shape for the third time. Still somewhat resembling the Gila monster that was closest to its original body type back on its home world, that's where the resemblance ended. It could stand more erect now with evident human physical traits as well. The head was no longer the long, narrow-snouted shape of a lizard, but a cross between that and a human skull. Its mouth and nose still jutted out in the form of a muzzle, just not as long. Teeth were extremely large and sharp. The entire body was covered in thick scales that now had an underlying layer that made it nearly bullet proof.

Inside was different as well. Eggs had definitely formed and would need to be laid very soon if they were to hatch in several weeks. In fact, it had already decided to go underground as well until the hatchlings could be tended to and instructed in the ways of killing. They would grow very quickly and be born with nearly an adult intelligence. This was required in that they would burst forth into a very hostile environment, needing to battle and survive almost from the beginning of life. For those that would survive they had to be small killing machines. World domination was at stake.

The entity had also decided that the group following closely on its trail needed to be eliminated also, or very nearly decimated to the point of giving up and crawling back home as failures. One of the additional traits it now cultivated was being able to blend in with the surroundings, very chameleon-like, but ever so much better. This would allow it to get extremely close before attacking. Appearing as near human as possible, but then strike like the creature it was. In other words, a virtually indestructible killing machine.

Sounds could be discerned ahead, not more than several hundred yards away. The creature could tell these human hunters were extremely alert and wary. It detected fear, but it was not because they were frightened. Rather they used that emotion to make themselves more alert and be prepared for attack. These particular humans would be a much greater adversary than those it had eliminated when escaping its prior prison. It actually looked forward to an altercation between enemies that would possibly put up a good fight. When the battle was over it would seek a place to hide, rest, and lay the eggs. A period of seclusion, probably several weeks, would allow the young to grow rapidly.

The closer the creature got the more sounds it detected, possibly some form of communication between members of the search team. Suddenly it stopped and turned around, gazing behind. For some reason it sensed a danger to the rear as well, but couldn't exactly be positive. Turning back around it hissed menacingly and then crouched so that all four legs hugged the ground. After this last alteration the body was over six and a half feet long. When it stood erect the upper part of the body leaned forward slightly which put the lethal claws lashing out in front. The tail was another three feet in length, whipping back and forth, a crushing weapon by itself for anyone getting too close. From snout to tail it was an awesomely large nine and a half feet.

There was a rather deep gully off to the right. It began moving undetected with great stealth considering body size until low voices appeared right above over the lip of the trench. The creature was anxious to feel the excitement of battle once again. Not necessarily slaying innocent humans, but facing someone or something that could fight back. However, the beast was still not in top fighting condition, only having just recently escaped its confinement and then passing through three transformations. This had taken a real toll physically even though it was much stronger now. The eggs within its womb vibrated. The creature definitely did not want to put them in any jeopardy. Yet, allowing these hunters to follow put everything at risk so they had to be eliminated, or stopped.

Crawling up the side of the gully it tensed, ready to spring. There were four humans, three males and one female, each with their own detectable odor. They did not appear to be lounging or lying around, but rather crouched with lethal weapons at the ready. Its teeth formed into a monstrous grimace as the body became taut, ready to pounce.

Without waiting another second it burst over the top of the trench emitting an extremely loud hiss which changed to a terribly menacing scream. Standing erect the creature swung to the left and struck Jimmy Baldwin across the right arm and chest. Dropping his rifle he yelled in pain and then was struck a debilitating blow by the tail. Baldwin was dead before he hit the ground.

The other three team members needed no more than two split seconds to fall into battle mode, something they were all used to. Vince aimed to his right and fired, bullets striking the target, but seemingly having no effect. Other than the hard pounding force of deadly bullets, the altered scales were nearly impregnable. To be sure, the extreme force of impact knocked the beast back and to the side, but not nearly enough to lose balance. That's why the altered size was needed so desperately.

With Jimmy Baldwin totally out of commission it leaped towards Clarence Hill. The black man had released one clip already and slammed another one home just as a vicious paw began its deadly arc. Hill saw it coming and dived to the left, never once taking his eyes off the monstrosity before him. At the same time he aimed his rifle with one hand and proceeded to fire in consecutive bursts. With his other hand he reached for his semi-automatic pistol and had it free before his body slammed hard onto the ground. Rolling over one time he ended up on one knee in a perfect shooting stance and held the pistol in both hands while dropping the rifle. Bang, bang, bang, bang...loud shots echoing in the desert, mixed in with all the other explosive fire power around him.

The creature was taking a devastating pounding, but shockingly to Flint it didn't seem to be phased. In the next instant the beast's tail made a long slashing swing and slammed into the left side of Clarence Hill sending him into the air and striking a large saguaro. He screamed as his head came away with needles sticking out of his cheek and eye socket. Falling to the ground with a hard thud he was stunned and broken. Not to let the moment pass the creature leaped and landed on Hill's body, the weight crushing a leg and shoulder. With extremely sharp claws it raked down the back of Clarence Hill's neck and left shoulder. Spinning around, it now faced the two remaining hunters, Vince Flint and Carrie Vaughn, who at this point had backed up against the edge of the gully.

"Flint, we're in really deep shit," yelled Carrie, her voice frantic.

On his third clip, Vince shouted back, "It's getting deeper, Babe. We die right now, or tear ass out of here to fight another day."

"Screw this Flint, I'm not dying out here tonight," stated Vaughn emphatically.

However, right at that moment when both hunters were about to turn and leap into the gully, a loud explosion rocked the ground around them. Both Flint and Vaughn were knocked off their feet as earth, rock and pieces of cactus flew in all directions. There was another explosion and then a blinding shaft of bright light. Human voices could be heard to their left and right. The creature at this point was hissing and screaming loudly, adding to the explosive echoes and total confusion around them.

"What the hell," Carrie screamed loudly, her voice barely heard above the din.

Vince slung his arm and upper body over hers in a protective embrace. Nobody could ever say that Vince Flint was not a gallant gentleman, even being the hard ass that he normally came across as.

"Thank God, reinforcements have arrived. Prudot and Tiny Tim must've gotten their point across," he yelled back, ears ringing from the explosions, another one to his right deafening and throwing debris into the air that now showered down on their backs and heads.

Suddenly, Flint felt rough hands grab his shirt and vest, pulling him over the edge of the gully along with Vaughn as well. They struck the ground below with a loud thud, both of them releasing 'whumping' sounds from their chests. Gun fire continued, volley after volley. Several screams were heard too, just emphasizing the fact that this damn creature was sure as hell not dead yet, and apparently pretty pissed off as well.

Loud shouts mingled with the sounds of battle until one finally became much clearer through the boom of explosives.

"Hold your fire," came a strong, authoritative female voice.

Then silence, the only sound being more debris showering down like a dirty rainstorm. The sounds of explosions and gun fire echoed throughout the desert. Flint's ears were ringing and his right arm hurt like hell where he had landed on it due to the fall, but at least he was still alive.

Rolling over and opening his eyes he gazed into the beautiful face of a woman he had never seen before. Wondering if he was truly alive or dead, he reached out to gently touch her cheek. Hell, it seemed to be real enough. He was suddenly in love.

"Are you an angel, sweetheart? Have I really died and gone to Heaven??"

I laughed just to ease my nerves. "Not likely Mr. Flint, but you sure as hell should be dead. And, I doubt you're going to Heaven at all. Can I help you stand up?"

He moved, wincing at the pain in his shoulder. "I think so. Just might need a little help if you can hold me tight. How's Carrie doing?"

"The woman over there? She's okay I think, stunned like all of us. Take my arm and let me help you up. Be careful."

Standing now on wobbly legs he held onto her arm, actually leaning in much tighter than he needed to. Even with all the dust and debris still falling from the sky, he realized that this woman smelled damn good. He breathed in her scent and immediately wanted more so his immediate instinct was to survive this mayhem.

"Thanks darling, I think you saved our lives," he shouted above the din.

"Well, you were in a world of hurt that's for sure. And get this straight big guy, I'm not your darling. We were following you, coming up closer when we heard the start of gun fire. Shit, I've never seen anything like that before. What the hell was it?"

He got a better look at her now. Not nearly as tall as he was, Vince could easily tell she was put together very well even under the armored vest and bulky pants. She had her hair tied back so he quickly saw how attractive she was. Definitely somebody he needed to get closer to when this was all over. That is if they both lived through it.

"Obviously some type of alien-type creature. Not what we were expecting by any means. How's the rest of my team?" he inquired, hoping to hear something good, but expecting the worst.

"My guys are checking on them. I think one is still barely breathing, but no idea how. He's pretty broken up. Sorry, but one of your men appears to be dead. So what were you expecting to find out here, Mr. Flint?"

"Which one is still breathing?" he asked, instead of answering her question.

"The black guy over there. He's bleeding profusely and really busted up. I don't know if he'll be able to get back to receive medical help fast enough. We've already radioed for back-up and helicopter assistance. Evacuation should hopefully happen soon.

We both moved aside to let the swat guys hustle past and then began scaling the side of the gully. Once at the top we lay back and breathed heavily.

"You need to talk, Mr. Flint. I mean right now. You have to tell me all you know about this thing and whether you're holding back on me, which you better not. Forget all this military top secret bullshit. If you lie, or are not totally forthcoming, then I'll slam your ass into a cell so fast you'll have metal burns on your cheeks. I don't mean your dirty, unshaven face either."

Covered in dirt, he grinned. "Yes ma'am, I do believe you. Can we move the hell out of here though? I'm choking on all this crap in the air. Need some water, too.

As they walked away he turned and looked for Vaughn. "Where is Carrie?"

"One of my guys helped her back down the path a ways so we'll head over there. I'll get you some water and then you're going to start spouting as much as you know about this. That a deal?"

"Deal, but let's just get out of here first. Who are you anyway?"

"I'm Detective Amelia Stephenson of the Tucson PD. I figure that you're Mr. Vince Flint. I don't know what the hell you are, but you're going to tell me. I have your comrade, Julius Prudot, over there. You can thank him for getting us here in time, or I'd be hauling your dead body out of here, probably in pieces. Now get moving."

They walked and stumbled for a few minutes before Flint sat down on a large rock with a thud, then drank nearly one entire bottle of water in one gulp. His face was covered with blood and grime. In fact, there was blood on his hands making him wonder how that had gotten there. Touching his face to wipe off some more of the dirt, his fingers came away blood covered as well. Obviously he had been hurt, but had been too damn numb to feel any pain.

"Dammit, seem like I'm bleeding quite a bit," he stated.

"Yep, you look like shit actually. There should be a medic here in a minute or so, but you'll live so don't act like such a big baby. How do you feel otherwise?"

He shook his head to help clear the ringing still in his ears. "I could use a nice vacation on some tropical island if you'll go with me. Other than that I'm okay, but I'm still really worried about Carrie and Clarence."

"She seems to be alright, about the same as you. Cuts on her face and arm, but she'll live. Your man Clarence, I'm not so sure about. He looks pretty bad. Now stop the bullshit and start telling me what the hell is going on Mr. Flint."

He hesitated, not sure what to say, but knowing he had to offer something. "We were dispatched from Davis-Monthan Air Force Base to look for some life form that had escaped confinement. Honestly Detective Stephenson, we didn't know what we were searching for. From what I understood, it was like some type of blob or worm, and that it possibly could've taken on another shape. We truly weren't sure in the beginning what we were looking for because quite frankly they didn't either. It appeared to them that it took over the body of the first human it killed, one of the guards. At least that's what they said. I mean, what the hell, we were just looking for some damn little worm. We weren't dispatched right away so we had to waste time just lurking in the background and looking for anything that could possibly lead us in the right direction. We found it at last, but sadly it took the death of those two young people to make that happen."

I hesitated. "You used the word 'alien'. Are you absolutely certain about that?"

He stared at me, his voice rising just a little. "Detective, you tell me what that was we just saw. Did that look to you like some normal little lizard running around in the Arizona desert? Not to me it didn't and I've been hunting large predators all my life."

Shaking my head, I had to agree. "No, it surely didn't. Never seen anything like that in my life and I hate lizards, as well as snakes. Do you think it was hurt at all?"

"I don't know." Flint responded. "Our bullets seemed to bounce right off those scales like it was some kind of thick body armor. Our military needs to develop that shit when we finally kill this creature. How did the explosions affect it?"

I had a coughing spell before answering. "Not really sure, I think somewhat okay," I replied loudly over the noise from a landing helicopter. "At least it left and there are some of those large scales scattered about the ground. We'll take those back and the lab can test them, see what they're made of. Oh yeah, another strange thing. One minute it seemed to be there in all its monstrous glory, hissing and screaming, and then the air seemed to ripple right before our eyes when it actually seemed to disappear."

"Disappear, like some magic trick?" he asked in disbelief.

"Can't really say for sure. Just '*poof*' and it was gone. Plus, while it was hissing and screaming, it was spitting out some type of liquid, like acid. It would start smoking and burning wherever it struck. I think it might've hit one of the swat guys on his vest. Thankfully he ripped it off in time. This creature seems to be indestructible and that's the frightening aspect of this real nightmare. How in the hell can we kill this thing?"

Flint stood and stared off into the night, the sound of at least two approaching helicopters overhead. "Nothing is indestructible detective, at least nothing that I know of. Mark my words, we'll find this monster and kill it. I have some buddies to avenge."

"They knew the dangers Mr. Flint when they signed on for your clandestine mission. This thing has killed seven other innocent civilians, three of them only high school age. We need to find and eliminate this abomination and soon. If you have any suggestions then I'm completely open and you'd better not hold back anything."

He shook his head. "Not at this time. We just need to keep tracking until we have it contained. I don't know how, but it very well could be injured in some way. I'm okay enough to do that on my own if I have to. In fact, going alone might be the best option. I can be much quieter and more alert if I only have to worry about myself."

"Let's get your wounds checked out and cleaned up first. Then we'll discuss that option. First though, I'll need you to talk to my task force and supervisors. They need to hear exactly what you've told me, as well as back me up on what we encountered here. After that, we'll go over it all closely and set a plan to end this once and for all."

Just at that moment an EMT tech came up and sat Flint down on top of a rock, immediately working on his face to clean off the blood and grime. I did, however, notice that he was pretty darn good looking in a very rugged way as his face became more noticeable. Maybe when this was over, well who knows what could happen. He had a number of small cuts and scratches on his face, several looking as if they might need stitches. I wondered if Mr. Flint would be macho enough to go without having them sewn up, or get stitches without crying like a baby.

Something told me he could do both. They'd be sore, of course, but at least he was still alive. I also knew that I was most likely going to need him desperately in order to locate and then finish off this devil beast. And I would bet my life that he would not be doing it without me right there at his side.

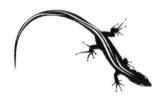

Chapter 9

The deep, extremely angry voice of Chief Crosson rattled the hallways and adjoining offices.

"She did what? She went where? Who the hell authorized that move? Does she think that she can just do any damn thing she wants? We'll see about that."

Manny was at least three inches taller than the chief, but he felt at least six inches shorter right at that very moment. He knew beforehand this chore wouldn't be easy so he was prepared for some type of volcanic eruption, just not quite this Vesuvius-like.

"Detective Stephenson continued tracking this creature into the desert along with Mr. Prudot and several swat members who were on site. Mr. Prudot seemed extremely capable and we had to make contact somehow with their other team members that had gone on looking for this thing. They were obviously in danger as well. "

Staring up at the ceiling, Chief Crosson shook his head back and forth. "Christ almighty, I can't believe any of this. For that matter, what the hell is actually happening here, Detective Corroda? There are innocent civilians dying left and right, while some monster is running amok in our wonderful city. I have detectives who can't find their asses in the dark, and now my newest detective, a woman no less, decides to be a loose cannon. That's not the way we work around here, is it Detective Corroda?"

"No sir, it sure isn't. However, this case is not what you would call normal and Detective Stephenson's being a woman shouldn't matter at all. You know that she's tough as nails, probably more than any of us."

There was thick silence while the chief tried to calm down before he literally blew a gasket and then very well might end up needing a casket. Picking up a stapler he slammed it down very hard on top of the desk anyway, lid flying open and staples soaring all over his desk and floor. That, at least, seemed to allow him to release some of his ire. For the moment anyway, even though there was now a mess to clean up.

He stood ramrod straight and sighed, trying to calm himself down. "Okay, okay, what do we really have people? Is everybody here at this meeting?"

"No sir, we're missing the M.E., but he should be here shortly," replied Sergeant Davis, "and two other detectives. I believe at the moment they're interviewing several possible witnesses to one of the killings. The newspaper deliveryman, I believe."

"Alright, we don't need them anyway right now. Manny, do we have anything at all? Are we even close to finding this creature, or whatever it is? Has anybody actually even seen what it looks like? I keep hearing that it can camouflage itself, so it seems to me we're hunting for a damn ghost."

"Well sir, we have gotten closer to finding it than at any time in the last two weeks. Honestly Chief Crosson, we haven't even known what we were looking for up until now other than it was one mean bastard and a total killing machine. If you would've been out there in the desert last night you'd for sure know what I mean."

Chief Peter Crossan lifted his arms, palms up and wriggled his fingers. "So then tell me what this thing looks like. How bad can it possibly be? Is it like some Stephen King novel? Some old X-files episode? Do we need that guy Fox something or other to help us get rid of it?"

Manny began to smile and then broke into a full blown laugh which lasted for nearly a minute. Wiping a hand across his eyes to clear away the tears he inhaled deeply before shaking his head. He thought that if it wasn't so serious, it would be comical.

"Obviously that's very funny detective so please let us all in on the big joke."

"No it's not funny in the least Chief Crosson and I'm sorry. I suppose it was just all this nervous energy exploding at once," Manny replied, trying to clear his throat.

Taking a deep breath he continued, "Okay, just imagine a large lizard, something like a Gila monster, which is normally around two feet long and that can stand erect on two hind legs. Now picture that lizard being nearly seven feet tall when standing upright, covered with virtually impregnable scales the size of bath tiles, possessing teeth and claws that could rip a man to shreds. Plus, it apparently has a three to four foot tail that lashes around like a battering ram, crushing anything it strikes. It also hisses like a damn steam locomotive, and releases some form of acidic liquid that can burn anything it strikes on contact. Oh, it also seems to be able to camouflage itself so that it appears nearly invisible. How's that sound?"

He hesitated slightly, thinking hard before adding. "That's about it sir."

There was a period of stunned silence inside the room. All that could be heard was the loud ticking of a wall clock and the window air conditioner humming merrily away. Manny wasn't sure if they were all going to bust out in laughter, or just get up and walk out of the room shaking their heads and muttering, *'Yep, he's done gone crazy'*.

"So then it seems to me we have one big alligator out there that can walk on two legs. Is that pretty much what you're telling us?" replied Chief Crosson, who had now slumped heavily back into his chair, all the time spinning a pencil between his fingers.

"Well, like I said," continued Corroda, "more like some gigantic lizard. And oh yeah I forgot, that tail I mentioned can knock a full grown man about ten feet in the air which it did on several occasions. It's like a freaking tank on four legs. Sorry sir, but that's it I suppose. At least for the moment anyway. It changes by the minute."

"That's it, you suppose. Who else has seen this creature besides your zany Amy partner?" asked Lieutenant Spencer who was standing off to the right while leaning against a book shelf.

"Nobody here at the moment." Manny replied. "We're relaying to you the exact description that Detective Stephenson gave to us over her cell phone. She's actually on her way into the office by the way. Should be here in about thirty minutes or less. I think that Mr. Flint will be with her as well."

Crosson stood and walked around the desk with hands clasped behind his back. Manny wasn't sure if he should run out of the office, or just stay to take his medicine like a man. Either way, he thought his career as a Tucson detective might be finished.

"Manuel, I barely have thirty minutes. In exactly one hour I have a meeting with the Mayor, his entire staff, and God only knows who else. Maybe even the governor of the state. I need answers and you're giving me descriptions of some comical monster from an animated movie passed on to you by somebody else who seems to be even crazier than you are."

"Yes, er, no sir. Shit, I mean Detective Stephenson, along with some of the swat guys she was with, plus members of this team looking for that monster, met and were engaged in battle with it. It's definitely not some animated dinosaur movie. Apparently only the leader of this search team, Mr. Vince Flint, plus a female member also, made it out in one piece although they are hurt. Oh, there is also some guy named Julius Prudot who led Amy out to connect with that search team. Also, from what I understand, there is one other member severely injured on his way to the hospital as we speak. The rest are apparently dead. Amy will back up everything she says because these two guys, Flint and Prudot, will be with her when they arrive, hopefully soon."

"Manny, you said early on that you had somebody with you, some guy brought in from the crime scene. Where is he stashed away at?"

"He should be here in a few minutes. He needed to get cleaned up really badly. Trust me, you wouldn't have wanted him inside your office. He was literally covered in blood and dirt. I also might add that he really smelled badly."

Just at that moment there was noise behind him so Manny turned around. Tiny Tim had finally arrived and was looking none too comfortable, but at least somewhat more presentable.

"Sweet Jesus," exclaimed Crosson. "You sure this isn't the monster? Maybe it followed you here."

Manny smiled, but was a little embarrassed. "No sir, that's not being very nice to Mr. Rollins who is a big man for sure, but I promise you he's not the creature we're looking for. He and Mr. Prudot were left behind at the crime scene so that they could call the killings into 911. They were planning on joining up with Mr. Flint when the police got there which Mr. Prudot actually did, along with Amy."

"You're absolutely right Manny, I must've left my manners in the men's room," replied Chief Crosson as he moved out from behind his desk and extended his hand to Tiny Tim. "Please accept my apologies Mr. Rollins. Trust me, I'm not normally this crass. It's just that this case has all of us on edge and saying things we really don't mean. That includes you, Detective Corroda."

Tim Rollins swallowed up the captain's hand in his massive fist and pumped robustly. "No problem sir, I'm used to those type of remarks due to my size. Quite frankly, I'm at a loss myself to explain any of what's been happening."

"So then it's my understanding that you needed to get cleaned up. Have a bad night out there in the desert, did you?"

Tiny Tim smiled, which surprisingly was actually nice for such a huge man. "You could say that. I slipped and fell when we were searching the area around the wreckage of the jeep. Damn if I didn't fall smack dab into a patch of wet ground that happened to be saturated with a lot of blood from the young female victim."

Chief Crosson stared for a moment and then looked quickly over at Manny. "Whose blood, Detective Corroda?"

"It was that of Linda Evans whose body was not discovered anywhere around the jeep. It had apparently either been thrown from the wreckage and then dragged away, or she was pulled from the wrecked vehicle and taken by this monster," answered Detective Corroda. "Uh, the jeep belonged to Michael Saylor and his body was discovered on the ridge right above the gully where the jeep had apparently crashed into."

"Have the parents been notified yet?"

"Yes sir, we started to notify them after the task force first was apprised of the situation. I'm not sure if they were contacted yet, though."

"What a damn mess Manny, right? You don't need to answer that! It was bad enough having to inform the parents of young Karen Culokis."

Chief Crosson paused and bowed his head as if he was saying a prayer. Nobody spoke in case he was doing just that. Then he pushed back from his desk, stood up and walked over to the window where he stared down at rush hour traffic on Stone Avenue which was steadily building for the morning commute.

Turning suddenly he crossed his arms. "Okay Lt. Spencer, make certain the families have been notified and see that it's done immediately. Have the bodies been already taken to the morgue?"

"I imagine they're already there, but we can check to make sure. I also need to advise you that the body of Miss Evans is not intact." Manny coughed to clear his throat.

"Not intact? You mean like the body is in pieces?" his boss asked quietly.

"Uh, yes sir. When I left the scene to come back the torso had been discovered, but was missing both an arm and a leg. Both limbs were found discarded about thirty yards away. And the head," Manny paused and then coughed loudly, not sure how to phrase it, "uh, her head had not yet been found when I left the crime scene to come in here. Hopefully it has by now, but I can't say for sure. Also, it is my understanding that her father is stationed at the air base."

"Oh my God," Chief Crosson whispered, shaking his head back and forth. "This is enough to push one's faith to the limit, isn't it?"

"Yes, but quite frankly God didn't have anything to do with this. Apparently it was a monstrous beast that has somehow escaped from the air base."

At the second mention of Davis-Monthan AFB, the Chief raised his head and glared straight at Manny, then over to Tiny Tim.

"How does that damn air base factor into this?" He hated the place because of all the airmen coming from there into the city, getting into trouble and the local police not being able to do much about it.

"Well sir, it appears," Manny hesitated, "and Mr. Rollins can hopefully explain it all a little better, that this creature apparently was being held in secret at either the air base, or at an unknown holding area out in the desert. It somehow escaped nearly a month ago. He doesn't know exactly what, how, or why, just that he was part of this search team headed by Mr. Flint that was hired to track it down. Apparently there were, or still are, other search teams out there as well. Possibly from the air base itself."

Chief Crosson turned to face Tiny Tim and smiled. "Okay, your turn Mr. Rollins and I would advise you to tell me the whole truth and nothing but."

"That's about the size of it. Our team leader, Vince Flint, probably knew more than we did, though honestly in my opinion he had no idea how this creature evolved over the last few weeks. In the beginning he was shown what happened, seemingly in what direction it escaped, possibly what the *friggin'* thing looked like at that time, and then was given instructions to locate it as quickly as possible. We were told to hopefully capture it, but once we were out in the desert for well over a week that eventuality became pretty much impossible after what we continued to see."

"So then did it escape from the air force base itself or not?"

"No sir, it's my understanding that it was being held at an old missile silo that had been converted into a laboratory and secure holding facility. Apparently, there were some guards killed when it got away. After we got geared up we went into the desert and have been following it now for close to a week. Tonight we got closer than at anytime."

"From an old missile silo which doesn't surprise me. They all should've been totally destroyed after the missiles were removed.

Figures the damn government would do something secretive. Did they say what this thing was and why it was being held?"

"No sir, but the six of us began thinking that it had to either be some military experiment gone bad, or it was some kind of alien," answered Tim, holding his arms up, as if to say, *'who the hell knows'.*

"Alien...a goddamn alien...that wouldn't surprise me in the least," Chief Crosson said, turning towards Manny. "So, you didn't see this creature then?"

"No sir, we had left by then," glancing at his watch. "But Detective Stephenson should be arriving any minute. She'll be able to confirm a description."

"Lieutenant Spencer, have Mrs. Potter contact Davis-Monthan AFB and tell them that we need to speak to somebody in authority right away and not just some damn lieutenant...sorry, didn't mean any disrespect Larry."

"None taken sir, I would've said the same thing. I'll get right on it, tell them we need to speak to the colonel and nobody else. That it needs to be right today. Do you want to come along, Chief Crosson?"

"I would love to, but don't know how I can," he said, glancing at his watch. "I need to be at the mayor's office in half an hour. So where in the hell is Detective Stephenson?"

"Right here, sir," I answered, somewhat apprehensively.

Everybody turned as I walked into what appeared to be an electrically charged atmosphere.

"It's about time detective. You have some 'splainin' to do and very quickly."

"Yes sir," I replied quickly. "Uh, this gentleman with me is Mr. Vince Flint. What would you like to know?"

"Lieutenant, you're dismissed so get on that right away. Don't forget to make sure the parents were contacted. Keep me informed constantly. In fact, I want reports every ten minutes."

"I'm on it" as Spencer walked quickly out of the office along with a sergeant that had been standing beside him.

Turning to me, he said, "Okay, I have twenty minutes for you to tell me what the hell is going on and what we're facing. Be quick, but concise. I need to let the Mayor know what is going on and it has to be the truth, no bullshit."

"Oh, it'll be the truth, trust me. We're facing an honest to goodness creature here. I told Manny what we fought out there and whatever he told you is the truth. Apparently, whatever escaped from that government facility is some huge monstrous lizard-like beast. At least it is at this point anyway. We threw so much firepower and explosives at it that the damn thing should've been destroyed. Yet, the creature still got away. In fact, it seemed to disappear as hard as that might be to understand."

"Disappear, like in a damn magic trick by the Great Houdini?" Crosson asked.

"Er, yes sir, like poof, but no fake smoke other than from the explosions that had gone off. Hard to say how many bullets struck the thing and several of the grenades went off very close. We found no body though. We had to have hurt it somehow, but we can't say for sure. It doesn't bleed like we do. And, the damn thing spits something like acid."

"So you didn't kill it then and it's still out there in the desert running free?"

"That's about right, sir. But, we're both prepared to leave as soon as we re-arm ourselves and get additional back up. It's gotten to be a real pain in the ass for me. A very personal issue and I need to kill this monstrosity."

Turning to Vince Flint, he asked, "How can you locate this thing, Mr. Flint?"

"Chief Crosson, everything can be tracked no matter how small the signs. I'll find it again, but I need to get back out there quickly before any of those signs are erased. And I really need to go alone because I'll move better that way."

"Not a fat chance in hell. Oh, you'll go out there again Mr. Flint, but not alone," the Chief responded, turning towards me and pointing, "and Amelia, you are absolutely not going. I need you here with the task force."

I got really angry and my voice rose. "Chief, please, I've seen this thing. I want to be there when it's destroyed. You can't do this, we're so close that I can feel it."

"No detective and that's final. Mr. Flint will go back out, but he'll go with my top two swat team members. I promise you that if and when they find it you'll be contacted and will have time to get in on the kill."

I turned to Flint who was slightly smiling. "Wipe that damn smirk off your face or I'll erase it myself. You better keep me informed constantly and do not let it get away. If you do then I'll track you down and tear you a new asshole. Got that Mr. Flint?"

He held up his hands. "Hey Detective Stephenson, I'm not the one keeping you from going. Honestly though, I'll move faster without you there."

"You rotten bastard! Why, because I'm a female? You had all your Special Forces buddies with you and they're mostly dead or severely injured so tell me why I'd be a hindrance?"

"Not in that respect, Detective Stephenson. I know you are one tough lady and can more than handle yourself. It's just that I need to be concerned about myself and nobody else. If I have to let these two swat guys tag along then believe me, whatever happens to them is not my issue. I've kind of gotten to like you in a very short period of time and can't be worried about your safety in a dangerous situation. I'll stay in touch constantly. I promise you that, or at least when I can talk and not be heard."

"I don't trust you for even one second Buster Brown, but it seems I have no choice," I shot back, turning to face Chief Crosson. "What then do you want me to do, Sir? Sit here with a thumb up my ass?"

"Watch your mouth detective. I'm in no mood for any of your smart ass bullshit. You're coming with me to the mayor's office along with Corroda and the gentle giant over there. In fact, we're leaving right now so get your butts in gear. We can't keep his Honor waiting. Let's get moving now."

I glared at Flint as I walked by. "Find it! Find it soon and let me know."

He nodded, smiled and winked at me as we walked out of the office. I wanted to just slap the guy and absolutely didn't trust him for one second. But he was a warrior and I felt positive he would locate the monster again. Whether this thing could be killed though was another matter entirely. However, all I could think of was that we were totally immersed in the biggest nightmare of our lives.

Chapter 9

Not far outside the beautiful city of Tucson quietly rests the majestic Catalina Mountains featuring absolutely beautiful and stunning vistas with stark changes in vegetation as you climb higher from the foothills to the highest peak, Mt. Lemon. It is known also as Sky Island and named for Sarah Plummer Lemon. The intriguing Catalina Highway wraps around like a festive birthday ribbon through the canyons up to the sometimes snowy peak. It's also very unique in that you can be running around in the city below wearing nothing but a tee shirt and shorts. Then jump in your car to drive along a winding Catalina Highway into snow during the winter months, approximately forty miles away. Unbelievable! Absolutely breathtaking scenery, dotted here and there with caves and mountain springs. It's a lovely ride that normally takes about an hour and a half. Unless, of course, one stops constantly on the drive up which happens quite often.

Part of the Catalina range is majestic Sabino Canyon, both upper and lower. A great tourist attraction where visitors can park their vehicles at the foot of the mountain and then hike all throughout the stunning ravines and cliffs. Then enjoy nature while lying at one of the cool mountain pools to relax and swim. Lower Sabino has clefts in the rock where water has been contained in narrow pools, great for swimming and diving as well. It's a wonderful place for local kids to congregate and have a great time.

It was now where the creature headed, feeling that it needed to find a safe haven in order to lay the eggs and let them hatch. It was also mountainous terrain and cooler, much more like its far off home world of Alkiron, a place that humans knew nothing about and most likely never would. Even though it had no fear, the battle during the early morning hours had done a little damage, mostly due to the exploding devices. It would heal quickly knowing that it still had one more transformation left and would then be virtually what it physically was before landing here on this godforsaken rock.

When the vehicle had crashed in the Sonoran Desert back in 1983, one way to survive was to dispense with its physical body and become semi-fluid. That extremely strange liquid became thick and viscous, nearly like oil, and then turned into a dense mass which resembled nothing more than a gelatinous blob. The contents of that small mass were the creature's blood that contained all its DNA, complete cell structure to reappear later on in a physical state. It also held vast intelligence, and never-ending memory. There was also an outer crust that protected all of the important organs and matter on the inside. It was a most unique life form able to adjust quickly within any type of atmosphere, but preferring it be oxygen laden. Here on Earth that atmosphere was more like it was used to back on its own world. That's the reason it could transform so many times within such a short period. There was also the matter of being detected before it was ready to do battle. It preferred being the hunter, not necessarily the prey.

Escaping the crash could've occurred at any time after being discovered and contained. But by using patience and fortitude it decided to at first go into a state of suspended animation. The humans could push, pull, prod, inject, and do all the different types of testing they wished. Very little, however, would arise with their inept investigations. Yet knowing survival was dependent upon existing, it now and then tossed the doctors and scientists a bone. Nothing would get them closer to full discovery.

During all those years it didn't need to eat actual food simply because it was a blob...no teeth, couldn't swallow, was unable to digest anything solid. But what it could do was pry into the minds of humans that toiled around it. So the entire time in which they thought they were doing testing, prodding, and digging, the alien life form was able to sustain life by stealing intelligence and memories from its captors. Obtaining this valuable information from some of the top minds in science and medicine, as well as other lab workers, provided a vast amount of nourishment to keep surviving. In fact, it flourished and continued to bide its time waiting and knowing when the exact moment would present itself. When it was time to strike it did so with a violence unknown to these pitiful humans who were relaxing in their rather inept guardianship.

Now as it moved through the desert it had traveled somewhere around ten miles, mostly in an undetectable state to reach the foothills of the Catalina's. It would stay clear of the main highway which began winding its way up through the mountains towards the top and majestic Mt. Lemon. Healing for the most part had taken place, but at some point it would have to physically reappear and acquire something to eat. The altered body of the original Gila monster had grown to such proportions that vast amounts of energy was being consumed just to keep it going forward. Even though it did not need to feed when it was in its own original state, the eggs now needed to survive on what it produced naturally from internal organs. Thus, this earthbound animal required to eat in order to keep the eggs alive. The creature was curious what the hatchlings would look like when the time came which would most likely be no more than two-three weeks. It had never been a mother before at any time so this was in effect breaking new ground in its lifetime.

Suddenly it stopped and listened closely, hissing quietly and beginning to feel the early morning heat. That was another reason it wished to be higher up in the mountains as soon as possible. The sounds were definitely human voices and coming from ahead, maybe fifty yards or so. Clinging close to the ground it moved with surprising stealth to the right, stopped behind a large outcropping of rock and detected three individual voices, two male and one female. The beauty of transformation was that it was able to use the original lizard's abilities like sight, hearing, and smell, but alas not speech. Without human vocal cords at this time talking was out of the question. So even though it was an expert at understanding human speech because of all the intelligence it had absorbed, as a large lizard it was unable to speak out loud. At least for now, anyway.

The creature could definitely tell that these three young humans were hiking and preparing at this point to scale a small cliff on the next rise. The huge lizard-like monstrosity slid to the right and began preparing for an attack, especially since all the hikers were facing forward and totally oblivious to the fact they were about to die. It realized early on that pretty much all humans possessed no real internal warning system to alert them that they were being stalked, which for the most part made them about the easiest prey the creature had ever hunted. Most times, if they finally heard something alarming or dangerous, by then it was simply too late.

Without waiting it struck with a violence never expected by these hikers who were just out having fun on a nice sunny day. Slashing left and right, crunching down with massive teeth, the two males were disposed of first and then the female last, just the beginnings of a scream erupting from her mouth. The entire attack lasted no more than thirty seconds. The creature crouched, rising higher on all four legs to crane its neck in order to see if anybody else was around. Satisfied that these three dead young people were completely alone it grabbed each one and carried them behind the outcrop from where it had launched the attack.

In the shade it fed and when it was done, not much remained but tattered clothing, blood-saturated ground, some scattered bone and three empty skulls. A little meat remained which it would take along for a snack later on. Not wanting this human waste to be detected it dug a shallow hole and disposed of the evidence with the exception of the bloody ground. However, before commencing the climb to higher elevations it kicked dirt over the stains. Much different than when it had left young Michael and Linda's remains behind to be discovered, which unfortunately had been a grave mistake. It ended up bringing dangerous hunters which developed into that nasty little skirmish. The creature vowed that would not happen again if there was any other way to avoid it. At least before the brood was born anyway. However, the possibility existed that there would be much bloodshed afterwards. Definitely something it looked forward to.

"Captain Pace, please let me introduce you to Captain Masters, Lieutenant Spencer, and Detective Manuel Corroda of the Tucson Police Department," stated Sergeant Miller in a very stodgy, military voice, cultivated over twenty years.

Pace stood and walked somewhat stiffly around his desk. He shook hands with all three visitors and cracked his official air force smile.

"Pleasure to meet you all. Please be seated gentleman. Can we get you anything in the way of refreshments? Coffee, tea, water?"

Captain Masters shook his head, a thin, tight grin displayed on his face. "No thank you Captain Pace, I'm afraid that this really isn't a pleasure visit."

"Okay, be seated then and tell me how we can help some of Tucson's finest."

Masters sat on the edge of the chair and looked the air force captain straight in the eye. He immediately couldn't stand this pompous asshole.

"Sir, I need to get right to the point because there is no time to spare. As I'm sure you are quite aware, there have been some very grizzly deaths piling up in and around Tucson. We now have information leading us to strongly believe that something, and let me emphasize something savage, escaped from your military quarantine. I'm not sure if it got away from here on the base, or some other secret location, but nonetheless it's loose in and around the city, killing people quite gruesomely. Captain Pace, we need to know exactly what this thing is. Plus, how the military is connected to it."

Pace looked at the police captain and displayed that pompous smile again. "I really would love to be of assistance Captain Masters, but I personally know nothing about something, or anyone, escaping from this military facility. I'm not quite sure where you obtained information that we might be involved, but it's in no way accurate. And quite frankly, I'm still not quite sure what you mean by the word 'thing'."

Masters rose quickly. "Listen to me and listen closely, Captain Pace. We have made physical contact with this creature which was in no way pleasant. In fact, it turned out to be quite deadly. Some of these individuals, at least those that survived, already stated that they were dispatched from Davis-Monthan so you can climb down off your high horse and start dealing on the up and up before somebody else dies."

"Please Captain Masters, there is no use getting so forceful, or accusatory. I've just told you that I personally have no information as to something like this occurring. I will be glad to check into it, however, and get back to you as quickly as I can."

"Oh, you'll find out something alright, but you'll damn well do it while we're here, sir! Detective Corroda has seen what this creature can do first hand and it's quite disturbing. Plus, from descriptions of this thing by my people, as well as yours who have fought this beast, you need to come up with answers now. We'll wait right here until you are forthcoming which I'm well aware the military does not do most of the time."

The Captain quickly stood, ramrod straight, tugged his jacket down and walked from behind the desk to stand three feet away from Masters.

"That absolutely will not be necessary. Now, I'm going to have to ask you to nicely leave and if you do not, then I'll have you politely escorted off the base."

Captain Masters did openly smile this time and replied, "Not on your life."

With that said he took out his cell phone and punched in the number for Chief Crosson. "You don't mind if I check in with my superiors, do you? After all, I was told to come here and get answers so if I go back without any then my ass is grass. And, if I get no answers then there will be more shit piled on your head than you can imagine."

Pace began to speak when Masters heard his boss say, "Hello?"

"Chief Crosson, this is Captain Masters. I wanted to check in and inform you that we're here at Davis-Monthan inside the office of Captain Pace. Sir, he has informed us in no uncertain terms that he has absolutely no idea, or information as to, what we've asked of him. He has basically told us that he would check on the situation and get back to us. He also would like us to leave the installation right this minute, or be led out."

There was a slight pause. "Yes, that's correct, and I might also add that he hasn't been very cordial about it either. In fact, he has just threatened to throw us off the base if we don't leave right this very minute. That is also correct, sir. Huh right, just a second Chief Crosson," Masters replied into his cell phone.

Looking straight at Captain Pace he smiled and extended the phone.

"Sir, if you have the time my superior would like to speak with you."

Not reaching for the phone, Pace shook his head. "I do not need to talk to your superior. This is a military installation and you have no jurisdiction here at all. I have informed you in as cordial a manner as possible that I would look into this matter and get back to you. What don't you understand about that?"

"Oh, I understand all too well what you're implying, Captain Pace. I understand that number one, you're blowing off my superior officer. Number two, you're definitely hiding something that is paramount to us finding and disposing of some monster that has already slain seven people that I'm aware of, probably more. And number three, I know only too well what you military people are capable of since I spent eight years in the army. Do I need go any further, or are you ready to speak to Chief Crosson? Because I guarantee you we're not leaving this base. And, if you as much as try to make us leave, then the local newspapers will eat it up. In fact, I'm almost positive they would love such a juicy story following up on all of these gruesome civilian deaths."

Captain Pace stared, anger turning his face beet red, clenching his fists together tightly. He reached for the cell phone and yanked it from Master's grasp. Taking a deep breath to calm himself down he finally spoke when somewhat more composed.

"This is Captain Pace, Military Adjutant to Colonel R. A. McDowell. What can I help you with, Chief Crosson?"

"Thank you for talking to me captain. I'm not sure if you understand the ramifications of this situation. Seven people have been killed in a most horrific way. Plus, at least two or three others have been torn apart while fighting it out in the desert. There is absolutely no reason for you to avoid the truth here and throw your cover up that military types like to do. We have four different people who have sworn to us that they were dispatched from Davis-Monthan Air Force Base in order to hunt down and either capture, or dispose of, something that escaped from a military facility around here.

"If you have to go talk to your superior, Colonel R. A. McDowell, some general out playing golf, or even the President of the United States, then you do so. But, I highly suggest that you do it fast. And, if my men are forcefully escorted off your installation there will be all out hell to pay. I guarantee there will be at least one air force captain who will be demoted. Now, have I made myself perfectly clear?"

Captain Pace swallowed hard and stared at Masters. "Yes, Chief Crosson, your requests and threats have been fully heard and understood. Your men can sit out in the hallway as long as they wish. I will contact Colonel McDowell and see what I can find out. This may take a while since I'm not sure if he's even on the base currently."

Crosson laughed. "Captain, I've played this game of tag before with the military for a very long time. After all, your base is in my backyard so to speak. You're his goddamn aide and I know full well that you know where he is at all times. I wouldn't be surprised in the least that he knows my men are there right now and is hiding in his office. Plus, I'm quite certain that he knows the reason they are there. He may even be cowering in the little boy's room. So listen very closely Captain Pace. You can tell my men to sit wherever you like, but they are not leaving there until they get answers and those answers better come quickly. Especially before another innocent person gets killed on my watch because some creature escaped from one of your puny little jail cells. That blood will then be on your hands."

Pace closed the phone without saying good-bye and handed it back to Masters.

"Please follow me gentlemen, there is a visitors lounge down the hall that has vending machines if you're hungry or thirsty. I will look into the matter and see if I can locate my superiors. If you'll please leave my office and turn right then the sergeant will escort you out."

"Don't be very long, Captain Pace. Innocent lives truly will depend upon your coming up with answers very quickly," stated Captain Masters as they left the room.

Taking a deep breath to try and get his anger under control he walked around the desk and paused. He had told the colonel when he was informed that the Tucson PD wanted to see him that they needed to cooperate fully. His superior, however, ordered him to stall as much as possible and get rid of them, but under no circumstances tell them anything. Pace knew different, because these deaths that had been occurring were directly as a result of the creature escaping and that the military was at fault.

Pressing a button on the phone a deep voice quickly answered. "Colonel McDowell's office, can I help you?"

"Yes Sergeant Frick, please inform the colonel that Captain Pace is on the line and it's extremely important. I'll hold, thank you!"

Thirty seconds later, the colonel answered. "Did you get rid of them, Pace?"

"No sir, they're in the visitor's room at the moment. Sir, can I speak candidly?"

A pause, "Go ahead captain, but I'm not changing my mind."

"Colonel, we really need to cooperate in this investigation. We possess information that they need and they absolutely know we're involved. Apparently that search team led by Vince Flint has engaged the alien in some type of firefight. They have also told the Tucson authorities of our involvement and that they were carrying out orders issued from here. Quite frankly sir, we have no choice. The shit is about to hit the fan one way or the other and I really don't want to be in the way of that avalanche."

"Captain, you'll follow my orders explicitly. What we're dealing with is top secret and I need permission from higher up to reveal information. I fully understand how much we're involved, but we just can't go off and be completely straight forward until we're in a position to do so. You just stall them a little longer. Tell them that you talked to me and I am contacting my superiors. We'll have something for them shortly."

"Thank you, sir." Pace hung up the phone, somewhat agitated.

What a mess he thought, what a damn grade-A cluster fuck. He was definitely caught between the proverbial rock and a hard place. He really wanted to tell Captain Master's everything, but if he did that then the colonel would have him cleaning out latrines. And, if he wasn't forthcoming then somehow he figured that shit landslide he mentioned on the phone would come right down on top of him as a scapegoat.

Walking around the desk he strode down the hallway to the lounge and walked in. Each of the men stood in unison.

"Gentleman, Captain Masters, I have been in contact with Colonel McDowell. What we apparently have here is a slight roadblock due to the delicateness of this situation, which I might add is top secret. The colonel will get back to me as quickly as possible so you're free to stay here if you'd like, or I promise I will get back you as soon as I know something much more clear and concrete."

Masters smiled. "Captain Pace, you can tell the families of the dead civilians how delicate the situation is. We're staying right here because if we leave then something tells me that we'll not be permitted access to this installation again. I've also contacted Chief Crosson once more. He has not only informed the Mayor of Tucson, but the Governor of Arizona is also being contacted at this very moment. If there is any more of a cover-up then I guarantee you it will climb up the ladder fast, probably to Washington. If I were you, being at the bottom of that ladder would not be a safe place at all."

Pace spun around and stalked out of the lounge without saying a word. His thoughts were totally upon salvaging his own career. He was totally pissed off that the colonel had put him in this very precarious position. What he needed to do was contact Dr. Warring and get him involved right away no matter what happened to him.

Chapter 10

I paced back and forth in the small lunchroom like a caged lioness. I had been walking around for almost twenty minutes holding a Styrofoam cup of really disgusting coffee, having barely sipped any of it. Without thinking I turned too quickly and it sloshed over the lip onto the floor, splattering my shoes.

"Damn it," I exploded, going quickly over to the sink and spilling the rest of the coffee into the basin.

Turning on the hot water I flushed the wasted coffee down the drain, turned the faucet to cold and cupped my hands underneath. Bending over I splashed it on my face. At this point I didn't give a rat's ass about my makeup. I was awake well beyond twenty-four hours now so it wasn't a stretch to say that I looked like hell anyway. With my emotions hedging on frustration and anger I took in a deep breath to try and calm myself down. It really didn't do much good. When I fell into this state of frustration, you just better watch out when you're around me.

"Everything okay?" appeared a deeply resonant voice from behind me. "Don't they have shower facilities in this joint? You have to take a bath in the sink?"

I stood and turned to face a grinning Vince Flint. At that point I wanted nothing more than to smack that smug look right off his terribly handsome face.

"So, you come here to gloat? I thought you'd be long gone by now, prancing around the desert all by your macho-self, maybe with your little puppies in tow."

"Hell no, it's too damn hot out there right now. I'm waiting for the sun to go down a little bit. So, how do you think the meeting with the Mayor went? Oh, by the way you have coffee on your shoes."

I ripped off a few paper towels, leaned down and wiped them off. Then I realized that my rear end was pointed in his direction so I wiggled it slightly before standing erect. Tossing the crumpled up paper towels into the trash can, I then moved toward the coffee machine which was the third time in less than an hour. Then I laughed out loud just thinking back to how the fiasco went in the mayor's office.

"Yeah right, meeting with the mayor my ass. It was like talking to a brick wall. Can you imagine he still had trouble believing these deaths were done by a creature running around out there? How in God's name could these have been done by anything human? Maybe we should take Mr. Mayor over to the morgue so he can look at the mangled remains himself, especially the three young kids. See if he can keep down his last meal like I was unable to. It was all I could do to keep my mouth shut."

Flint had also moved over to the coffee machine after I slumped down in a plastic chair that was cracked in the back. As he was pouring coffee into a small Styrofoam cup he said with his back to me, "Well, I do think in the long run he started to come our way. At least he perked up a little when he heard that the air base might be involved. There's certainly no love lost between city or state government and the air force. Oh, by the way, I really like the view from the back."

"You can say that again," I laughed before realizing what he had just said, regretting having answered so quickly.

He started to open his mouth and I held up my hand. "Please don't, no joking around right now. I'm clearly not in the mood for any bullshit from you."

"Hey, I was only going to say that when your Chief Crosson got the phone call from Captain Masters, and then relayed that information onto the Mayor's office, I think the seeds were planted for a deeper investigation. In fact, if you don't get answers from the air force then I'm sure the governor will be involved before the end of the day. He might very well be placing a call to D.C. right now."

I took a sip from my coffee and scrunched my mouth. "Damn that's not only hot, it sucks too. I don't know Flint, I feel totally useless right about now. I want to be out there looking for that monster and making sure it's dead. That it doesn't kill another innocent person. Plus, I'm really pissed off that you're sitting here drinking coffee when you should be out there right now tracking this freaking creature."

He sat back, crossed his arms and looked me squarely in the eyes. "Detective Stephenson, do you always do everything you're told to do? I highly doubt that."

"What the hell does that mean? Of course I don't, you know that already."

Smiling he shrugged those broad shoulders of his. "Well, I'm leaving in about an hour so if you really, truly, want to go after the big bad wolf with me then I'll make an exception this one time. I normally like to work alone. That way I only have myself to worry about. I didn't like this team idea one little bit, but it was forced upon me. So if you decide that you would like to just tag along then I'll be outside the front door in about," looking at his watch, "oh say, fifty minutes. If you just happen to open the door and jump in the vehicle then I won't throw you out. Please understand that I move fast and quiet. If you can't keep up with me, or you make too much damn noise, then I'm leaving you wherever you're at. You can worry about your own sweet little ass."

I stood and walked towards the hallway. "You worry about your own cute butt and stay the hell out of my way. See you in thirty minutes, unless you need the other twenty to powder your nose and apply lipstick."

Finishing his coffee in one large gulp, Flint stood and smiled to himself. He liked her grit a lot. This detective was one tough little fortune cookie and he thought that she could definitely be relied upon in a firefight. In fact when this was all over, if they survived, he definitely wanted to get to know her a lot better. Looking at his watch he realized that he wanted to be outside the front of the building before she got there. Kind of 'one-up-man-ship'. He thought this cute little detective was too sharp to pull tricks on.

The immense lizard-like creature had climbed about one thousand feet where it found a well hidden cave. Nobody would even know it was there unless they decided to crawl inside for some insane reason. With a spelunker though one never knew for sure. The mouth of the cave was a little narrow for the alien's size now, but it managed to squeeze through nonetheless. It had dined for quite a while on the three dead hikers so it was fully sated, both from the flesh and muscle to the delicious brain matter.

Safely surrounded by darkness it took a minute or so for the creature's eyesight to adjust. Once inside it noticed that the cave continued to be somewhat narrow and then opened into a larger chamber about ten by fifteen feet in length, plus high enough where if it stood on all fours its head didn't bang on the ceiling. Also, it had obvious evidence of prior habitation by animals unknown. So there was plenty of vegetation, sticks, etc., that had been dragged inside. After digging a hole about three feet deep with some pushing and pulling the creature got it somewhat organized into a type of bed or nest.

Walking around in a circle a few times, much as a dog will do before giving birth to a litter of pups, it released a heavy sigh and hiss, long tongue flicking out to sense any dangerous signs. There were none so it slowly plopped down and maneuvered into a relatively tight ball, kind of a fetal position. It would be time to release the eggs very soon, probably within the hour.

But for now it decided to just rest and recuperate from the battle out in the desert and that long climb up this rocky mountain. While resting somewhat comfortably it had time to reflect backwards, quite a long way in fact. Well beyond the time it crashed here on Earth in 1983. For the moment it had taken over the body of a Gila monster. This in effect was what it mostly resembled back on its own world. Altering body shape was something that just came natural because it had done this process hundreds of times before on other planets. It realized eventually that a human host would be required.

For now though, it had many different defense mechanisms, one of them being the ability to take over another host. It preferred the body to be lizard-like, but that was just primarily in the initial stages of transformation because it felt somewhat normal. Since the crash of the vehicle it had a number of earth years to gain as much knowledge as possible, to assimilate this data into different life forms on this planet from human to an array of creatures. Since it had escaped there was enough time to go through an adequate number of alterations to develop into exactly what it was at this precise point in time....a giant female Gila monster that had redeveloped traits and bodily structure. It certainly did not resemble the original lizard now other than a similar body type.

Another reason for selecting the Gila monster as a perfect host was that this unique creature *(heloderma suspectum)* was only one of two venomous lizards in North America. It also had very foul or toxic breath to go along with that fatal bite. This unique ability was a vital component of its original body type. Several transformations of the Gila allowed it to alter the venom to be even more lethal, that of possessing a much more acidic base to immediately burn upon contact. Thus, it did not have to actually bite prey now because the acidic venom could be expelled as a stream which ate into any exposed skin resulting in the same type of poisoning, but also quickly ate away the skin.

An additional defensive mechanism was the ability to become rather invisible for short periods of time, mainly because it took lots of energy to do so. Once done it could not be performed again until the host body built up additional energy. It wasn't that it became exactly invisible, more like blending in with the surroundings. Another ability it possessed was to sustain long stretches without food. However, it must to have eaten a vast amount before fasting so that it could be stored and then consumed rationally over a period of time.

It didn't need water when in its natural state either. That being its original life form. Here on Earth, however, water was required simply because the bodily structure and internal mechanisms relied upon this precious fluid to survive. In the process of feeding, it consumed as much food as possible which was good because part of that ingested material was fluid-based. However, on this planet water was a necessity other than that obtained from food once it had assumed an earthbound bodily structure.

In its natural state, that of a very viscous fluid-type mass, absolutely nothing was required. It could survive indefinitely and oftentimes placed itself in a unique type of suspended animation, completely different than what earthlings conceive it to be. As a result, the alien was sexless to start and had the ability to develop either trait depending on the situation it was in. In other words, uniquely transgendered. Reproduction could not occur in its original state. A host had to be present and then altered in some capacity, oftentimes being completed over several transformations. If the life form originally was male and the entity wished to produce babies then several alterations soon allowed it to create and lay eggs. If the host life form was a female and no reproduction was necessary at the time then it could alter the body to male in order to become stronger and much more aggressive. It was a win-win situation. Still, it was the host body that was transformed to be both sexes at the same time because its original form would always retain the worm, or slug-like, structure. Totally sexless.

Once the eggs within its body were laid then it could decide at that time whether to stay as it was, or enter another host body. However, due to the intense pounding the body took with each transformation it was limited to no more than four alterations with the same host body. After that, a new host would be required. Actual motherly duties were not necessarily needed after birth because it did not have to feed the young. Only blood provided by slain prey would be needed until the young found appropriate host bodies.

Either way, it was both difficult to catch and nearly impossible to kill. If the entity felt the body it had taken over was dying then it could eject itself through the mouth or any opening for that matter, then escape to hide until another host vehicle could be located.

However, now it was time to start the birthing process. The creature uncoiled and stretched, hissing due to a small amount of pain and aggravation. A hole had been dug deep enough to eject between twelve and twenty-four eggs. Now it moved back over top of the hole and maneuvered into a comfortable position. This particular alien life form had never before undertaken this birthing process so it was totally unaware of how painful it might be.

The creature hissed and growled low with each popping of an egg. The shell was extremely thick when first laid and only about eight inches in diameter. It would expand some as the embryo grew. Obviously the thickness was to prevent them from being broken upon ejection, or cracked apart by thieving predators. Another reason for this thickness was that on the inside of the shell was nearly an inch of protein lining that the embryo could then consume while developing. After ingesting this protein, when it was finally time to break free, then the cute little alien life form only had a thin, shallow shell left to poke through with several sharp teeth that would be ready to aid in its release.

However, the newborn had no basic form other than what it would normally be as an adult, a very thick fluidic mass that would eventually grow to double its original size, about two feet long when full grown, resembling a long worm. As a result of being extremely pliable it could stretch itself out like a long cigar or tube. That made it much easier to slide down the throat of most living things – animal, human, or whatever the living structure was on each planet. The creature also had the ability to curl up in a ball allowing it to roll quickly whenever it needed to escape something. In addition, it was not affected by extreme heat or cold, and could also survive underwater indefinitely.

There were drawbacks, of course. In this larval type stage, unless they were back on their own world where predators were kept to a minimum by *mukeli* guards, adult versions of lizards were lethal in the art of extermination. However, they were highly susceptible to actual fire since the skin had no outer protection. Certain alien-type gases found on numerous distant planets could also present problems. If crushed, however, they could break off in a number of smaller pieces and then spread out to then unite when it was safer. Water on some planets was not a problem because they would just move about like a jelly fish does in the earth's oceans.

The main point was that it was simply very difficult to eliminate these life forms when in fluid state. Within a host body it became open to the ways that any living being could be slain. This is why it attempts to look for creatures like the Gila monster, or any other form of large lizard as well as snakes, crocs, alligators, etc., because it could alter the already existing scales to make it nearly impregnable from firepower.

A painful groan escaped the giant lizard's mouth as the last egg squished out with a loud plop. At least it hoped that would be the last egg. Sometimes it was possible that all eggs could be ejected only to find one possibly still lodged inside. That was never fun because for the most part the creature had to use its internal organs to crush the shell and then eliminate it as waste. With the clutch of eggs finally released it was now time to recuperate and find food to replenish the energy expended in the birthing process.

Emitting a heavy sigh it used the hind legs to cover the hole with dirt and then curled its long, thick body overtop to supply heat. For the most part over the next two weeks it would perform this very important 'motherly' duty only to leave when food and water was required. Then it would quickly return to continue the incubation process. In the mountains there was a vast array of animal life so it decided to exist on that rather than actively looking for humans and thus attract undue attention. Unless, of course, there was a wayward camper or hiker that would be alone. Then there would be no chance of finding any remains. For these next two weeks it absolutely needed to assure that hatching would take place successfully. There would be plenty of time afterwards to enjoy killing and mayhem which it absolutely loved and looked forward to.

It also had covered over the opening to the cave with lots of brush and limbs. Now it simply closed its eyes and went into a deep, trouble-free sleep. In effect, for the next two weeks it would be on maternity leave. Just rest and regaining strength was all it needed. After the eggs were hatched the creature would then need to provide sustenance for them in the way of dead prey. That alone would quickly sap its strength. There would then need to be a period of regaining all the power it could possess before any more battles could be undertaken.

The alien hatchlings would not need to be taught how to kill, survive, or to transfer into a new host body. That all came naturally from the mother figure. In effect, upon birth they were individually as dangerous as the adult and just as deadly.

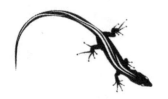

Chapter 11

Manny paced the visitor's lounge like an agitated puma, already sick of really bad coffee and feeling anxious to get the heck out in the field. He wondered what Amelia was doing so he told Captain Masters he needed to get some fresh air and a cigarette.

He had been trying to quit smoking and seemed to be doing a fairly good job, especially when he was on duty with Amy since she hated smoke in the car. He just really needed one right at that moment. Plus, he was also hungry. Those three cups of crappy coffee were churning in his stomach with nothing to eat since breakfast.

Looking out over the open expanse beyond the front door he noticed several other buildings, a large one appearing to be a hospital. Between there and the headquarters building where he now stood was what seemed to be the parade ground. Beyond that were several two story buildings that resembled barracks which he fondly remembered from his army days. Several platoons crisply marched by, either on their way to or from the mess hall. That made his stomach growl loudly even more. Tossing the half smoked cigarette into a sand filled container he reached for his cell phone. Pressing the pre-set number for his partner he let it ring while leaning casually against the handrail.

"Hey manny-man, what's up kiddo? Do you miss me that much?"

"Yes and I'm bored out of my mind. We're getting the run around here and I really need to get out. But, Crosson told us that we're staying until we get the news we want to hear. It's obvious that they're hiding something. Masters could stay here and I could leave. What are you up to, keeping a seat warm in the conference room?"

I paused before responding. "Right this moment I'm in the car with Vince Flint. We're heading out to where we battled that monster last night to try and pick up its trail."

"Dammit Amy, that's what I want to do," he replied, standing up and shading his eyes, staring at the mountain range in the distance. "You're obviously not doing what you were ordered to do so you most likely are probably in a world of shit about now."

"So what else is new? Tell Master's you have to leave and go home to handle a problem," I said, glancing over at Flint who looked at me with pursed lips.

"I'd love to actually. This waiting around crap is for somebody who has patience and I'm not that type of person as you well know."

I laughed because I did know. "Sure do partner. Hey look, we just left headquarters a little bit ago so lie to Captain Masters and then call me right back."

"Will do," Manny responded, slipping the phone back into his pocket.

Spinning around he opened the door and strode back into the visitor's lounge. He realized immediately that he could not state the real reason for wanting to leave.

Clearing his throat, he said, "Hey Cap, I just talked to my wife and one of the kids is sick. Since we're just sitting around here doing nothing and there are two of you, would you mind if I take off and get that taken care of? Then I'll report into the station."

Masters put down the magazine he had been leafing through and nodded. "Go ahead Manuel, nothing is happening here anyway, although I hope it does soon. You'd better be telling the truth and not throwing a load of crap at me just to leave."

"Sir, you know I would never do something like that," Manny lied.

"Yeah, well get the hell out of here. I'll talk to you later. Where's that partner of yours, getting into trouble again? She's a bad influence you know."

"I don't know where she's at right now. At headquarters I assume. Couldn't get her on the phone so I left a message. She's okay, just a wild banana sometimes."

"Yeah, well, there's always at least one rotten one in the bunch. Okay, buzz off. When you talk to her remind that partner of yours to keep her nose clean or she'll be heading back to Philly and walking a beat in Kensington."

"Will do. Thank you Captain Masters," and he quickly turned, walking briskly out the door. At least he had the intelligence to drive his own car explaining early on that he may be called away for some emergency.

Meantime, while Manny was pulling through the front gate of the base, Amy glanced over towards Flint. She had asked to be dropped off where her car was parked so she could grab her gear. So now they drove down Tucson streets in his vehicle.

"So, you're being very quiet. Are you pissed off at me?" I asked.

"Amy, I told you earlier that I prefer working alone on these missions, especially the bad ones. Allowing you to come was probably a big mistake on my part. Now it seems that you're inviting half the Tucson police force to join us."

"It's not half the damn police force you big jerk-off. It's only my partner who happens to be extremely proficient and will be an asset. Get off that damn macho high horse you're always riding. This isn't some child's game you can play alone. Three will be better than two, especially against that creature. Plus, you have a couple swat guys in the vehicle behind us and Crosson told them to come along, not me."

He looked at me and smiled. "It's not just that, Detective Stephenson. I was hoping to just have you all to myself for a while. I don't like sharing my women."

I stared straight ahead through the windshield at passing buildings for about ten very long seconds to digest his sick comment. Turning in the seat I flashed a half smile and then raised my eyebrows.

"You're completely impossible. At a time like this you can actually think about something other than this creature and the killings taking place? What about your own team members? Where's your damn loyalty?"

"Hey, I didn't really know them other than Clarence Hill and his condition does worry me. I know he's in good hands at the hospital though. He and I have been through many missions and battles together. Other than him, the rest are simply damages of war."

"You are such a big prick and hard ass. Why in the hell did I come out here with you? Is that what will happen if we face this creature again? You'll worry about your own safety and not mine, I suppose."

He laughed and I wanted right then to punch him in the mouth. Pissed me off too because I was actually beginning to like the jerk. See, my choice in men really sucks.

"Detective Stephenson, you are totally missing the point. In my line of work it's not good for one's longevity to form close attachments. It'll get you killed faster than anything. If you're worried about somebody else and then you let your guard down, well that means trouble every time. That being said however, I will not let anything happen to you. I can't say the same thing for your partner though. He'll be on his own."

"Trust me, Manny can take care of himself and I'll be looking after his back like he will mine even if you don't. You're a lone wolf and that can be dangerous."

We drove on in silence for the next ten minutes finally turning onto Catalina Highway. Just then my cell phone rang.

"Stephenson here."

"Hey Amy, I managed to get away. Lied my ass off so if Captain Master's does find out then I'll be in deep shit just like you are. Anyway, where are ya'?"

"We just turned onto Catalina," I replied, still fuming at Flint's attitude.

"You okay partner? You sound like you're pissed off at something."

Yeah, or somebody I thought. It's what I liked about having Manny as my partner. Not only did he have great perspective over any situation we found ourselves in the middle of, he was also extremely sensitive to my moods, which could be pretty manic at times. Plus, there was nobody I would rather have backing me up in crunch time.

I sighed. "I'm alright partner, just worried and a tad bit frightened. Just more anxious than anything to put an end to this creepy creature before anybody else gets badly hurt or killed."

"Same here. Are you going to park in the same place as the other day?"

"For sure. That way we can go out to the exact spot where we fought that thing and hopefully pick up signs we can follow."

"Don't worry Amelia, we'll nail this abomination," as the phone went dead.

I put it back in my jacket pocket and continued to just stare ahead.

Flint broke the silence first. "Detective, I'm sorry if we got off on the wrong foot. Please accept my apology. When we get there we'll get armed up and wait for your partner to join us. Our lives depend on watching out for each other, I see that now. You're used to working closely with the same partner, the same group of detectives and I'm clearly not. In fact, often I'm hired to track and dispose of a target on my own, a sniper's way of life. You were right calling me a lone wolf. That's what makes it difficult for me to get used to. So once again, please forgive me. Start over?"

I immediately felt myself melting like ice cream, damn him. He would have to show a human side right at this very moment. I released a heavy sigh as I gave in.

"Okay, truce. You're forgiven. I haven't been myself lately, either. These last few weeks have been wicked and I'm really on edge. I know this isn't my fault, but I feel responsible for some of those civilian deaths because we couldn't eliminate this thing."

I extended my left hand and he took it with his right, kind of a reverse handshake. He did hold my hand longer than I felt comfortable with so I pulled it free. I was surprised it didn't make a popping sound upon release.

"None of this is your fault. That apparently belongs to the USAF. So now that we're friends again may I call you Amy and do away with the detective part?"

"I suppose so if I can call you Vince. Or, do you prefer Flint? I'm actually tired of calling you asshole, prick, and jerk off all the time."

He laughed robustly which I liked. "Well, Flint is a tougher sounding name and most people call me that. Before this is over however you might be calling me worse names than asshole and jerk off. I'll try to be a good boy as tough as that may be."

We both hesitated and then laughed hard. At least for the moment the ice had been broken so it was nice to relax slightly. In fact, so much that I closed my eyes and took a quick catnap before we arrived at our destination. Lord only knew when I'd get a chance to rest again. I prayed that Flint was on our side because we needed his help.

"Excuse me, Captain Masters? Captain Pace has asked that I escort you back to his office so will you all please follow me," requested a different NCO.

They walked down to the end of the hallway and entered the captain's office without knocking. Five men were now in the room as the officer came around his desk. Not to shake hands again because he was still pissed off, but merely to meet them.

"Thank you for waiting. I'm very sorry for stalling you earlier. I think you'll realize after what I'm about to tell you that this situation is extremely sensitive and volatile at the same time. Not to mention quite embarrassing for us as well."

Masters nodded his head without replying. He was actually afraid that he would make a wise ass remark and didn't want to put a crimp in what they had been very impatiently waiting to hear. He just hoped to finally get some concrete answers for Chief Crosson and the task force. They needed a break and a big one.

"First, let me do some introductions. This tall gentleman standing to your left is Lt. Colonel Pike, Commander of Special Forces, based here at Davis-Monthan. Beside him is Master Sergeant Shoop who is also Special Forces. Sitting over there is Lt. Spanner, my aide and right arm, couldn't do anything without him. Last but not least the somewhat distinguished looking gentleman by the window is Dr. Oliver Warring who is our Chief Scientist in charge over a number of extremely sensitive experiments."

Masters introduced Lieutenant Spencer, explaining Detective Corroda had to leave. Then they all waited as patiently as possible for Captain Pace to continue. There was much to be said and Pace was unsure just how much to reveal.

"I conferred with Colonel McDowell who regrettably could not be here. I was finally told to be as forthcoming as possible considering that its highly sensitive material and to use my best judgment. Actually, that was like telling me that my ass is on the firing line. However, you need to know what's happened so I'll take the flack."

He paused then and sipped some water from a bottle on his desk. "Something did, in fact, escape from a highly sensitive and top secret testing laboratory at a different location than this installation. There really is no easy way to unveil this Captain Masters other than to say that what we have terrorizing the area is totally alien in nature."

The silence in the room could be sliced with a Bowie knife. Masters looked at Spencer, raising his eyebrows. Turning back to Captain Pace he broke into a slight smile.

"Alien, you mean like in extraterrestrial? Real, honest to goodness ET science fiction stuff?"

"You can certainly phrase it that way if you wish to. However, this entity is obviously quite more lethal than some little make believe alien from a movie. Dr. Warring is prepared to explain as much as he can in greater detail. Doctor, can you please take over?"

Clearing his throat, Dr. Warring shoved off the wall he had been leaning against and slowly walked forward. He pushed his glasses back up the bridge of his nose, a habit that others found quite annoying about him because he did it so often.

He coughed to clear his throat before starting out. "Captain Masters, back in 1983 an unidentified vehicle crashed out in the desert, about fifty or sixty miles from here, give or take a few. This unidentified vehicle was destroyed, but certainly came under the classification of the proverbial UFO. The wreckage was then brought to a large hangar here on this installation which was obviously sectioned off as a highly sensitive area and then manned by twenty-four hour guards, along with other surveillance systems.

"Within the crashed vehicle were several extremely interesting and valuable objects. One was the burned carcass of what possibly was a large creature which appears to possibly have been the pilot for this UFO. Apparently, it was quite difficult to tell exactly what it looked like because it was really destroyed in the fire. However, those remains were tested very diligently using x-rays and a full array of laboratory tests. It was finally determined from the skeleton, along with pieces of skin that were not totally destroyed, that it was some alien type creature, primarily reptilian based.

"In addition, a separate life force was discovered. It clearly appeared at first glance to be nothing more than a liquid-like blob, a thick and viscous mass. Possibly blood from the burned lizard-like carcass. The military at the time had no idea what it was, or even what to do with it. After being as cautious and gentle as possible it was carefully placed into a solid container and then transported here where it was kept under highly intensive quarantine. My predecessors ran intricate tests and an extensive battery of experiments. They apparently arrived at the conclusion that it was in fact alive in some unusual fashion, definitely alien in nature. Where it came from and why had it crashed on our planet? Obviously nobody knew those answers. So for the next thirty-two years it was kept under strict quarantine, monitored on a 24/7 basis. Over all that time tests were continually performed, without any real success."

"So, where was this thing being kept when it escaped?" Masters interjected in total amazement.

"One of the empty Titan II missile silos was converted at great expense into a laboratory that would only study one thing, this alien life form. It stayed in this liquid state for quite a number of years from what I understand. Then it began changing and this was all documented extremely close on a daily basis. The scientists and doctors at that time wrote some astonishing facts and papers about what this thing did during these times of change. Way before I got here it reverted back into some suspended animation phase. Nothing else happened for quite awhile. Just a short time ago it started moving again, showing possible signs of activity. To say the least we were ecstatic and detailed closely every single movement or change that we could document. However, it apparently was beginning the stages of an attack which we had no way of discerning. The entity escaped when our guard staff was at its lowest point in the day. As a result, a number of personnel were killed when it got free. We have been at a loss as to where it went and what it even looks like since it most likely has transformed shape."

"Transformed? You mean like shape shifting? Like in the movies? Werewolves, Lon Chaney, 'The Howling', crap like that?" asked Masters, utterly amazed.

"We truthfully don't know. It would appear that taking over a host body would be needed for it to move around easier. Somebody, or something, would have to be attacked and then that body utilized. We're not sure if the host would be animal or human, but it's out there and we haven't the faintest idea where. What escaped was a reddish mass about two feet long that resembled a thick worm, four to five inches in diameter. Even in that state it wreaked serious and deadly damage. From what was discovered concerning the burned carcass in the crashed vehicle we determined that the escaped entity must've looked for a reptilian-like body, possibly more like its own.

"Believe me, we are totally devastated at the loss of life so far. Not only the civilians here in Tucson, but our military and scientific personnel as well. We realize that it must be stopped. That is why we sent out three six-man teams to search for the entity and that is why the special force representation is here in this office as well."

"Okay," said a disgusted Masters, "so, what you're clearly telling me is that your efforts in finding and killing this creature has been inept at best. At least we now know what we're dealing with and that makes sense."

"In what way," inquired Lt. Colonel Pike?

"Our people did, in fact, make contact last night out in the desert near Sabino Canyon. Reports came in that they were fighting some type of large lizard-like creature like a giant Gila monster, believe it or not. Is that actually possible? Or, don't you have the slightest idea what this monster is capable of?" questioned Masters.

"It's highly possible I suppose since we have no idea what host body it will utilize. Obviously, it can alter size and shape into whatever it overwhelms. And please Captain Masters, we did not allow this creature to escape. When dealing with something alien like this we were totally in the dark for a very long time," replied Dr. Warring, annoyance spilling from his mouth.

"Right, anything you say. So the USAF feels that it hasn't any responsibility to the surrounding civilian public. You know, I've lived in Tucson now for twelve years and the State of Arizona nearly all my life. Never have I heard of an alien craft crashing into our state in my lifetime and being contained in captivity. So obviously, the air force along with our esteemed government, is very good at harboring dangerous threats to the public. Then this creature gets loose, you still show no responsibility to inform the local police so that civilians in and around Tucson can be warned that something dangerous is prowling their streets so that precautions could be taken. Oh I'm sorry, after at least seven innocent people died on our city streets. Then we have to come here and bust your chops to get answers."

"Enough Captain Masters," said Pace, standing erect from where he had been sitting back against the front of his desk. "This was top secret and our hands were tied. I think all we should be concerned about now is catching this thing before it kills again."

"Yeah right, fat chance that will be happening since it probably has already done so. We just don't know at this time where those bodies may be. Mark my words Captain Pace, and you can also pass this on to the powers that be above you, heads will roll for this when it's all over. You can also bet your ass that this thing will be killed and in no way captured. Not by the Tucson PD anyway."

"We will do what we can," replied Pace. "Now, I will allow you gentleman time to get back with your own people. We will then begin to coordinate activities with Lt. Colonel Pike. Hopefully, we will have this alien entity contained within a short period of time."

"Contained my ass. We'll blow it to smithereens. Call this damn life form, what you keep referring to as an alien entity, what it is. A goddamned monster, pure and simple. To my way of thinking, monsters are not captured and contained. They are destroyed," said Captain Masters, walking out of the office with Lt. Spencer in tow.

They stomped down to the visitor's lounge in order to report in to Chief Crosson and get instructions on what to do next.

Back in Captain Pace's office he shook hands with each man, telling Lt. Colonel Pike what he needed to do and that was to cooperate up to a certain point with the police. Dr. Warring was to stay out of the picture entirely unless he was asked to participate. As for himself, he was ready to take a damn vacation, especially since he had quite a chunk of leave piled up. Hell, for that matter, he might even be discharged after this disaster because the military always looked for scapegoats. He was on the front line when it came to that possibility.

Chapter 11

We pulled off the road and bumped down the rutted, dirt path to where the two kids had been butchered. Gazing through a very dirty windshield my heart felt heavy just thinking how sad it was that such young, promising lives were destroyed, not to mention the grief families would live with forever. And all they were doing was probably just a little teenage frolicking, maybe a tad more. Even then, it was no reason to be mangled to death by some monstrous creature. It was just that they were snubbed out so violently for no reason other than being in the wrong place at the wrong time. Two promising young lives never to be fulfilled. It was an absolute tragedy.

When Vince's vehicle ground to a rattling stop near the edge of the drop off to the gully a cloud of dust billowed across the vehicle from back to front. When it cleared away, the darkness was broken somewhat by glare from the headlights. We were now about ten feet higher than the ground below where poor Michael's jeep had plummeted. The wreckage had finally been cleared away and back at CSI for further investigation. All that remained was a large indentation dug deeply into the dirt. It seemed all I was doing anymore was sighing heavily. As if on cue I released another one.

"You okay, Amy? You don't have to do this you know. I'll be fine on my own and report back to you at definite intervals. You can stay here unless I need you."

"Not on your life buddy boy. I'm going out there, but you can stay back here if you're scared. I'm just breathing in deep to get some of this nervous energy dispelled. Let's go," I replied, jumping out of the truck.

He was really beginning to get on my nerves. I couldn't stand men who always felt that their way was the only way.

Flint raised the rear door on his vehicle and my mouth dropped open. Thankfully there were not any large flying insects flitting about to zip straight down my throat.

"Holy shit, are you serious? You have a small arsenal in here. I would imagine you have permits for all of these weapons, especially the semi-automatics and assault rifles? And all this ammunition. This is a small arsenal, Mr. Flint."

He smiled and then chuckled slyly. "Okay, so I guess that I'm talking now to Detective Stephenson, and yes I do, but not here at the moment. Would you like me to drive back into town and get the necessary paperwork you require?"

"Yeah, right, you're such a *fricking* liar. I'll assume that you're all legal, though highly developed police instincts tell me you're not even one little bit papered up."

"You know what they say about people who assume," he said over his shoulder while opening up one large case with two nasty looking rifles and a separate case of ammo.

"Smart ass," I shot back, reaching for a very large, incredibly mean looking weapon. "What does this do? Kill elephants and rhinos?"

"That my sweet little detective would put a hole through a dinosaur. So, if we see this creature and it stands still long enough, not to mention that it won't magically disappear, then that ammo will penetrate armor plating and I doubt lizard man can handle that. If it can then we'll have much deeper problems than you could ever imagine."

"For sure our bullets didn't make much impact last night."

"They were different types of weapons and ammo. This will do the trick believe me," he replied, turning around at the sound of another vehicle approaching.

It was Manny who pulled to the right of Flint's SUV and literally jumped out while the motor still chugged. I kept telling him he needed to do something about that pre-ignition issue as it eventually coughed, sputtered, and then died with a loud gasp.

"Hey partner, this is Vince Flint." I said, in the way of introduction.

"I'll only shake your hand if you call me Vince or Flint. My father who is long dead was the only Mr. Flint that I knew and at times even he hated to be called mister."

"Deal if you call me Manny and not Detective Corroda."

"Okay guys, now that the name game is out of the way let's gear up and get our butts after this thing. There's no telling where the hell it's at by now."

For the next ten minutes Flint handed out weapons along with vests for Manny and me to put on. He said there were only two of them and even though they were mainly used to stop bullets it should also serve as a cushion if anything like sharp claws or fangs came into contact with our upper torso. I told him that I wouldn't wear one if he wasn't going to, but that was totally my weak, very pitiful attempt at being macho. I would actually wear a suit of armor at this point after seeing that monstrosity last night.

"You both ready?" asked Flint. "You can still back out."

We didn't answer him, just nodded that we were all set and he should shut up.

Flint motioned for the swat cops to come over as well. They were armed to the teeth as you would imagine. Looking around I felt fairly comfortable that we certainly appeared to be prepared for most anything, maybe even a monstrous alien.

We half climbed, half slid down the bank to the ground below, then walked over to where Flint and his team had originally tracked the creature before it proceeded further into the surrounding desert. Without stopping we just moved forward and spread out a little bit from each other, no more than several arm lengths. Vince didn't think we needed to worry about being attacked this early. But then who the hell was he kidding?

Each of us wore something around our heads that resembled a miner's light, not as big though. Somehow this state-of-the-art bulb cast a pretty wide glow once total darkness descended. Even then I stumbled about every three or four steps, mumbling and swearing under my breath. All I got from Flint was 'ssssshhhh's' and dark stares. Screw him, I thought. Maybe he was used to this bullshit, but I definitely was not. Manny wasn't having as much trouble as me even though he still tripped a few times which made my heart swell. At least I wasn't the only clumsy oaf in the bunch. Hell, my hunting ground was the streets, not out in this sand and cactus crap.

After about twenty minutes we arrived at battle zone number one. We had been licking our wounds after last night's fiasco so now we spent a little time going over the scene, searching for anything that might give us some clue as to which way that badass monster had fled. I say 'fled' because it sounds better, like we scared it off. Flint had already stated to me while driving out here that if it wasn't for the fact Prudot and I showed up when we did, they would've been toast. He felt it was the explosives that ran it off, long tail between its ugly legs. Yeah right, believe that and I have a parcel of swamp land in the desert for you to purchase. Something clearly told me this creature was not frightened of anything, least of all some puny humans.

Each of us took a section of the area and started looking for anything that might help us. I was the first one to spy something interesting. Kneeling down I picked up what looked like a medium size bath tile from the shower stall. It was on the clear side though, a milky-white in color. Yet, under the light cast by my headlamp it had a sparkly tincture to it as well.

"Hey," I whispered as loud as I dared, "over here. I found something."

Both Flint and Manny were kneeling beside me in less than five seconds. Flint took the object and held it out before him, turning it different ways.

"Looks like some kind of very thick scale. I suppose that would fit since it was some type of gigantic lizard we fought with. From what I could see between shooting, ducking, and running, it looked like a Gila monster on steroids," as he tried to bend it, then struck it hard on the end of a rifle barrel.

"Damn thick and tough, too. No wonder our bullets bounced off it so easily, like we were shooting Superman with four legs. If it had an undercoat of these then it would virtually be just about impregnable. Thank God for those explosives. I wish we were carrying more with us right now."

Then he moved several feet to his right and bent over, looking closer at the ground. "Huh, look at this. Appears to be some type of fluid, like possibly blood or something," reaching down with the tip of the rifle.

He gave it a slight nudge and it moved. We jumped back!! The damn thing actually shifted, slithering a little and puffing up like it was some defense mechanism.

"What the hell is that?" I yelled, which actually came out sounding more like a jumble of meaningless words from somebody who was really freaked out.

Flint barely touched it again and the damn think scuttled a few inches to the right.

"What the fuck seems to be more appropriate," Vince replied, his voice low and concerned. "I think it certainly appears to be blood, or some type of fluid. It's somehow still alive, like the creature's blood even has a life of its own."

"Great, that's just goddamned great," I shot back. "We shoot the bastard, make it bleed, and the damn blood remains alive. How the blooming hell do we kill it then?"

Flint stood and we followed suit. He reached into his jacket pocket and took out three things...a box of matches, a silver metal tube about four inches long, and a pair of long tweezers that resembled forceps.

"What are you going to do now?" I asked, a little bit of disbelief in my voice. "Just destroy this abomination. Smash it into the ground."

"I'm going to do two things. First, I want to see if fire bothers it. Manny would you grab a long piece of sagebrush over there. We'll see how it reacts to direct heat. I will then attempt to pick it up and place it inside this vile. If it jumps on me then I might be in trouble."

"Uh, mmmm, I'm not sure about this Flint," I responded. "You're then going to carry it in your pocket until we get back to civilization? What if it eats right through that flimsy tube and then enters your body? Did you ever even think of that Einstein?"

"Come on Amy, we'll get back alive. What the hell, you're with me. Think positive, detective. This metal tube I'm holding is made from state-of-the-art steel. Once it's safely secured inside here then trust me it won't escape."

"First of all, I don't like people one bit who say 'trust' me," Manny responded quickly. "And second, the damn thing escaped from eight floors underground through eight foot thick walls. Don't tell me it can't escape from some tiny little tube no matter what it's made out of."

I smiled in total agreement. I always said that Manuel Corroda was damn smart.

Flint took the sagebrush and lit the end which quickly erupted into bright flame against the darkness. Extending his arm and the fire towards the small blob we were all somewhat apprehensive as to what might happen. Not surprisingly it started moving as the heat from the flame got near. Quickly pushing the burning sagebrush forward he touched the blood-like glob and it started to smoke, writhing in a small circle like it was really agitated. No wonder I thought. I would've jumped too if my butt was on fire.

Vince quickly knelt and grabbed the disgusting little blob, which was about an inch or so in length with the forceps, then quickly forced it down into the tub. Dropping the forceps he just as quickly slammed a thick rubber stopper into the tube opening, stood erect and then tightly screwed on a metal top for hopefully even more security. One had to wonder if anything was secure enough to contain this thing.

He held the tube out in front of him and grinned. The sick bastard.

"What's it doing?" I asked, actually in awe that he had the nerve to do what he had just done. I would've just slammed a large rock down and crushed it.

"I can actually feel it moving inside there, like it's angry at us," said Flint.

"Don't blame it, I suppose. Plus, it's mad at you, not us. So, what do you think it is?" I inquired, not really wanting to know the answer to my question.

"It appears to be blood or something. Definitely from the creature and absolutely alien in nature. Surprisingly, it appears to be alive which is amazing. Don't you think so?"

Manny and I looked at each other, shaking our heads. We realized right then that Vince Flint was most likely certifiably insane.

"Okay, so you got your little trophy and you'd better keep that thing inside the tube, well secured in your pocket. So where to now, Jungle Jim?"

He looked at me and smiled. "Amy, you're just too funny. Has anybody ever told you that? You're pretty damn cute, too!"

"Maybe a few times, but nobody as crazy as you. Which way do we go now?"

"If this is some of the creature's blood like I think it is then this is the spot where it was before disappearing. I would think we should find clues that show which direction it escaped so let's look around a little more. We'll see something, I'm sure."

He found something first naturally. That figured since he was the great tracker.

"It looks like it passed through here. See how the cactus was pushed over at the top like something large broke it down? That tells me that somehow it has the ability to camouflage itself like a chameleon. Yet it still retains a physical state, just nothing we can see. Plus, I somehow doubt it would be able to stay in that unseen state for very long. Let's push off in this direction and keep your eyes peeled for tracks. Also, scan for any place where the ground or vegetation is definitely disturbed."

Off we went, about five yards apart, looking for anything and everything. Part of me wanted to run in the opposite direction while the other part yearned for confrontation. Hell, maybe we were all as certifiably nuts as Flint because we actually followed him.

Chief Crosson was absolutely furious. If steam could really explode out of a person's ears then it was billowing from his. After pacing back and forth behind his desk he turned toward the few extremely nervous people in his office. Placing his hands on the desk he leaned forward and tried to smile, but it came out more like an evil grimace.

"Where the hell are they? Stephenson was supposed to stay around here and apparently Corroda lied to Captain Masters about going home for some trumped up emergency. And that damn soldier of fortune, whatever his name is, can't be located either. I have nothing else to do but assume that the three stooges are all together. Has anybody tried to reach out to them and find out what the crap they're doing?"

"Yes sir, but the phones for each detective will only take messages," replied Sergeant Avery, covering his mouth also as he coughed nervously. "I left one for each of them to call me right away."

"Great, just great," mumbled Crosson, looking at the desk surface and shaking his head like a cornered raccoon.

"Sir, if I may," inserted Captain Masters, "I would hazard a guess to say that they are both in situations that would not permit cell phones going off. Since Flint is gone too then I would imagine they are all together and probably out searching for this thing. I might also add that swat team members are most likely with them as well."

Chief Crosson stood up and tilted his head back and forth, neck actually cracking with tension. "Okay, okay so what do we have then? The air force has confirmed to some extent pretty much what our contact with this monster resulted in. That it's some type of alien creature, or whatever the thing is, and had been kept under lock and key for many years someplace off the base, apparently in one of the old missile silos. Also, that it got loose about a month ago and has since gone on a major killing spree. So, what the hell are they doing about this other than trying to wipe shit off their faces?"

Masters answered apprehensively. "Lt. Colonel Pike was supposed to dispatch as many choppers as they have available come daylight. I might also add that there are two aircraft flying up there now in a hundred mile radius that have heat tracking equipment aboard. The other two teams that were originally dispatched four or five days ago to other areas in the desert have all reported into the airbase. They will be going back out under the command of Special Forces, also to be deployed at daybreak. For now though, at least tonight, we have to rely on whatever Stephenson, Corroda, and Flint are finding."

"That is not enough, I guarantee you. They couldn't find their heads hung in a tree if you told them where to look. There will be some a-holes losing their stars and stripes over this," Crosson growled as he turned towards Avery. "Sergeant, set up an emergency meeting with the Mayor as quickly as possible even if you have to wake him up. Tell him also to prepare bringing the Governor in on this as well. We will need as much fire power that we can get, including the reserves. This fiasco has to end now. I will not have more deaths on my watch because of some military blunder."

He then glared over at Masters, "Get a few detectives and officers together. Send them out to where the kids were killed last night. Instruct them to call back here if they see any vehicles from Stephenson, Corroda, or that Flint character. I've had just about enough of this lone wolf bullshit. All they had to do was tell me where they were going rather than skulk off like a pack of scared rats. I'm understanding, right?"

"Yes sir," replied Lt. Masters, because he thought a response was needed. "Uh, but Chief Crosson please don't be too hard on them. You did instruct Flint to head out there anyway and he seems to be the likeliest choice seeing as he's some type of super-duper tracker and hunter. Plus, Stephenson and Corroda have been in on this since the beginning and it's become extremely personal. Just please go easy on them."

"Maybe," said Crosson, "we'll see. Right now I want you and the lieutenant to go along with me to see the mayor. That way there will be no third party screw ups on my part. We're already in the bull's eye on this. You convey exactly what that idiot fly boy Captain Pace told you, understand?"

"Yes sir. I'll be ready to go when you are."

"Be set to leave in ten minutes, no more than fifteen. This is top priority, nothing else matters. Get your butts in gear right now," muttered Crosson, shaking his head which he had been doing a lot over the last few weeks, especially the last several days.

At that exact moment Sergeant Avery reappeared. "Sir, I really do hate to tell you this, but we just received word that there are some missing hikers out near Mt. Lemon. A wife from one of the missing guys called in to say that he not only was supposed to have been back hours ago, he never called her either. It may be nothing and they could still be hiking on the mountain or maybe his cell phone battery went dead. I suppose we should look into it since they're out in that area."

"Christ Almighty, how can one damn little alien creature cause all this uproar on our planet and in my City no less? Captain Masters, get two groups together. One to go out to the scene of last night's killing and the other one out towards Mt. Lemon. Sergeant, how many are missing?"

"Three and nobody can be exactly sure that's where they went hiking either. Supposedly it was out in that area somewhere according to his wife, but they could've changed their minds at the last minute. She just hasn't heard from him and is very worried what with all the deaths recently."

After they all left his office Peter sat down rubbing his eyes, trying to massage away an exploding headache. Christ, what a mess he thought. Aliens of all things and in his beautiful Tucson to boot. Yes, he knew all about the stories concerning Area 51 and the UFO crash at Roswell in 1947. But this crash reportedly happened around Tucson, Arizona in 1983. He would've been twenty-two years old back then and nobody in his crowd heard about this although at that time he was just getting honorably discharged from the army. Now, aliens of all things were at his doorstep. On his watch no less.

Shit he muttered to an empty office as he reached for the Extra-Strength Excedrin bottle in his top desk drawer. He needed to call his wife Jenny and make arrangements to get them out of town before 'War of the Worlds' started up. Maybe good old H. G. Wells knew something even way back then when he wrote that book.

Chapter 12

A s the creature slept it regenerated the few body parts that had been slightly injured in the skirmish. Making sure the cave mouth was completely hidden it curled back over the eggs to settle in for what could amount to a two-week semi-hibernation. All it needed to do other than that was hunt for food. It had dragged what was left of the three bodies into the back of the cave where it was cooler and allowed the meat to stay fresher. In fact, there was a small pool with cold water at the furthest reaches which could also be used to keep the remains from rotting too soon. While covering the cave mouth it also caused a small avalanche to further block the opening to make any hunter/tracker/soldier not observe, or even wonder, that there was an opening there. It would be able to move the piled up dirt and rocks easily enough when it was time to move, but much harder for a weaker human to do so without the aid of equipment.

While it rested, slept, regenerated, supplied warmth for the eggs, it also dreamt. Yep, aliens dream, just not in movie format like humans do. This particular life form, however, was centuries old in human years and had traveled to many different worlds and galaxies. It thought back to a proud time from its birth society when it was an esteemed leader of the elite guard for the Royal class. Its name was *Quinotoa*. At that time it stayed primarily in its original host body that somewhat resembled the lizard-like humanoid it had recently transformed itself into here on Earth. Those original bodies were bred specifically for the newly born hatchlings. Their height back then was staggering, nearly eight feet with others definitely taller. They were vicious fighters, skilled in multiple forms of combat with exotic weapons and methods to kill. They were the leaders of armies, extremely skilled and very adept hunter/trackers which could follow and destroy, or capture any type of prey from any world. They lived well, deemed to be a higher stature between the lower workers and upper royalty.

Until the attempted coup. Back then the hateful ruler of their race was a tyrant who enjoyed killing indiscriminately, spreading a ruthless reign of terror and torture throughout its realm. The despised creature's name was *Xnniloi*. With the able assistance of others who were equally horrified at what was occurring they plotted an uprising in order to attempt a takeover and set things right. However, as uprisings will often go, there was a traitor amongst them and the Royals came down hard, killing many of *Quinotoa's* comrades. Along with several dozen other fighters they were able to allude capture, but not without surviving a bloodbath and sustaining serious injuries to very nearly each member that remained alive. At that point they became royal enemies.

In effect, they were banished from their home planet, never to return upon the threat of immediate death. So they wondered outer space for tens of thousands of years. They became a small army of mercenaries, landing on worlds that contained life, or were nearly uninhabitable. It was rare when some form of battle did not take place with whatever life forms populated each planet they landed upon. When they were able to they transformed into a liquid state and then took over the indigenous bodies as hosts. They also continued to incorporate strange new soldiers into their extremely unique and growing army as they spread their conquests. As a result, they multiplied and eventually grew to well over five hundred strong. They were badass warriors fearing nothing.

At a certain point it was determined that individual scouts needed to go out into the furthest reaches of space and search for possible planets they would be able to easily survive on. Possibly even make it their own. *Quinotoa's* orders were to head towards the planet Earth, a place where a large segment of its birth society had already landed somewhere after 6,000 BC earth time. The society back then was Sumerian, known as the oldest culture on Earth. It was the Sumerian's which profited from the knowledge and technology of what they referred to as the Anunnaki, depicted quite graphically in writings and hieroglyphics set on walls and in paintings. To them these beings were Gods, to be revered.

That brought *Quinotoa* near Earth back in 1983. Major problems occurred upon entry as it knifed through earth's atmosphere resulting in a terrible crash. Realizing it was about to get captured it transformed quickly into the thick liquid state the humans discovered. From that point on it just waited for the proper time to attack and escape.

Now it found itself lying in a state of semi-hibernation within this cold and damp cave overtop a clutch of nearly two dozen eggs. There was no way to tell how many young would live through the initial moments of birth. If only half survived cracking through the eggshells then that would be considered a successful birthing process.

With a heavy sound between a satisfied sigh and a worried growl that actually rattled the cave walls, it realized that possibly within a short period of time domination of this planet would commence. Only its direct mission was important, nothing else.

It was pretty apparent that I was growing tired, cold, and getting really filthy. After the sun goes down in the desert temperatures can fall dramatically. I had forgotten to bring along a heavier jacket so my long-sleeved shirt and bullet proof jacket would have to do. I was also getting damn fed up with tripping over rocks and stepping into shallow holes, my knees and ankles now displaying purple bruises to reflect that fact.

"Flint," I whispered, and then hissed somewhat louder. "We have to take a break if only a short one. I have to piss and really don't want to do it in my pants."

He stopped ahead of me and turned. Looking as tired and dirty as I was, he nodded. I dropped to the ground right where I was. Not only was I physically exhausted, but mentally drained as well which I didn't think was a good way to be at the moment. Especially not knowing whether some gigantic lizard might lunge for us at any time.

Moaning slightly I sat up, then stood, stretched and started walking towards a large cactus.

"Amy, where are you going?" Manny inquired.

"Honestly Manuel, I really don't relish the idea of walking around with wet pants so I have to take a piss. It seems that I forgot to bring a package of panty liners with me. Unless you or Vince have some in your pockets."

Flint got up and started walking toward me. "Where are you going?" I asked him.

"With you, of course. No idea where this damn thing may be lurking and waiting for us to screw up. Become too lax and we could end up being its next meal."

"So you're going to watch me pee? Will that excite you?"

He cracked a sneer and then laughed. "Amy, I don't have to watch women take a piss to do that. I'm sure you are quite aware that we he-men just need a centerfold. But, if you want me to watch then just say so and I'll be more than happy to oblige."

I turned and angrily stalked over to the saguaro, then quickly moved behind it. Thankfully it was extremely tall and had a very round trunk. Dropping my pants I squatted and let go. What a damn rush, a real weight off my mind so to speak. Reaching into my pocket I pulled out some tissues and wadded them up. My dear mother had always reminded me when growing up to be prepared for any situation, especially if you ended up in the emergency room. Like always make sure your underpants were clean.

After pulling my pants up I strolled nonchalantly out into the clearing.

"Was it as good for you as it was for me?" I asked, more jokingly than anything.

"Not really because I also took a piss. Couldn't you hear me?" he shot back while continuing to walk right past where I stood. I wanted to punch him.

"Detective Corroda, we just relieved ourselves so if you and the swat guys over yonder need to pee or poop, then you'd better do it now," Flint said. "I'm not sure when we'll be stopping again, or if we'll even have time. Oh, and don't forget to cover it up to hide any odor the creature might sense. Amy girl, did you do that?"

I replied hotly, "I'm not a complete imbecile even though you may think so. And, don't ever call me 'girl' again. I believe underneath this attire I'm all woman."

Flint laughed and just shook his head. "I totally agree with that comment."

After all potty breaks were taken care of we all knelt close to each other in a small circle and faced the ominous Catalina Mountains. The sun was beginning to creep over the horizon so we awaited Flint's directions in order to proceed.

"So where to now Mr. Elite Tracker?" I whispered, initiating a few snickers from the swat team guys. I liked them because they thought I was funny.

"Cut out the wisecracks detective. There will be plenty of time for that later when we get intimate," Flint responded, continuing to look towards the mountains ahead.

"Intimate my ass. Over your dead body. I'd rather sleep with the alien."

Chuckling, he now looked at me and winked. "We'll just see about that my darling detective. Okay, so the highway that curls up through the mountains is about a mile to the east. If we walk straight ahead it appears that we'll be going in the right direction. It also seems to be the shortest path. I've noticed a few tracks off and on, prints that were definitely not human and obviously quite large."

"Why didn't you say something to us back then?" inquired Manny.

"No need to since I couldn't really be sure the tracks even belonged to that thing."

"I highly doubt that Flint," I stated angrily. "You know what the hell you're looking for so get this straight buster. We don't keep anything from you and likewise, you don't hide anything from us as well. You got that mister?"

"Yes sir, or ma'am, extremely sorry. Let's go," as he started moving forward.

After about fifteen minutes of walking in the fading dark we began to hear noises. One definitely sounded like a siren unless somebody was playing around with something. Anymore the sound of sirens seemed to part of the Tucson landscape.

"Something's happening, I can feel it," I spoke up with deep concern.

"Seems that way. Sounds like it's coming from over there," as Flint pointed left.

By the time we neared the highway the sun was fully above the eastern horizon and I could feel the heat beginning to steadily rise already. Being from Philly I had to get used to the temperatures when I moved out here to the desert. At least back east it might be stinking humid and hot for a few months in the midst of summer, but the change of seasons was always such a welcome relief. Unless, of course, we got slammed with snow in the winter. When that happened, streets and highways around Philly could be a real nightmare. I had suffered through several over thirty inch snowfalls and it was not pleasant. Total gridlock on most of the surrounding highways and neighborhoods.

Philadelphia always seemed to be nestled in a pretty good location. Storms coming from the west and down from the north many times got broken up due to the proximity of the Appalachian Mountains running through the middle of the state, along with the Poconos to the north. Coming from the south, if there was a strong front blowing down from Canada, then unless it was a massive storm like a classic nor'easter it would often get pushed out to the Atlantic. Just the Jersey coast got hammered. The really big storms on record normally came from those classic nor'easters which could stall along the northeast corridor and then get blown back around in a circular formation. Then it would just dump, dump, and dump more snow. Those type storms were not that common, but when they struck it could literally cripple eastern cities along the northeast corridor for days. In fact, the last weather report that I heard was calling for just that occurrence since a large storm was moving east from the northwest part of the country.

However, this is good old Tucson, Arizona and the only snow I've been able to see here was up on the top of Mt. Lemon during the winter months when I would drive up to spend a nice weekend at the Ski Lodge and hopefully get in a little skiing. I had planned on going back home to Philly for the holidays, but now everything was on hold thanks to this damn pain in the ass alien

When we reached the highway there were a number of police and emergency response vehicles parked on each side of the road. That clearly was the reason for the sirens. To be honest though we looked like we had just been run over and dumped in the desert, we were so filthy and wild looking. A sergeant from headquarters strolled over and broke into a big wide grin, spreading his arms wide.

"Well, if it isn't the beautiful Detective Stephenson and her always trusty sidekick Tonto. Oh, I'm sorry, it's Detective Manuel Corroda if I live and breathe. Looks like you two, along with your mean looking friend over there, have been having a tough time of it. Just so you know, you'll both probably have new butt holes when Chief Crosson gets through with you," crowed Sergeant John McCorty.

"If you don't shut up John you'll have a new one yourself because I'm no mood for any crap," I shot back at him. "What's going on here? You can't all be looking for us, even though Crosson probably wants to string us up."

He turned and waved his arm. "Only half of this is for you it seems. The rest were dispatched because we got a concerned phone call from some guy's wife saying that her husband and two close friends came out here yesterday to do some hiking. They have not been heard from since, returned home, or called in to say that they were okay."

"None of them?" I asked with evident concern.

"Correct. So the chief sent us all out to look around, see if we could spot anything. It seems anymore you just never know why a person might come up missing, or even dead. Did you guys have any luck out there while frolicking in the desert?"

"Not so much it seems. There were some odd tracks that Mr. Flint felt belonged to the creature. They sort of were heading in this direction, but a little more towards the left. If it's up in those mountains right now all holed up, I don't see how we're going to locate the damn thing unless it decides to show up for some fun and games."

Just at that moment Lt. Spencer walked over. He started reaching out to shake hands and then had second thoughts, probably because we were such a mess and he was always known to be a neat freak. God forbid any dirt might rub off on him.

"Amy, Manny, Mr. Flint, why didn't you call in to let us know where you were? I left messages on both your cell phones which were turned off."

I reached for mine and realized that I had in fact turned the volume completely off. "Oh damn, Mr. Flint felt it best if we didn't get any undue calls that would cause ringing and alert the monstrosity we've been tracking."

"Your phone does have a vibrating feature I believe? You didn't think of that?"

"Yes sir, again I'm sorry. I just plain forgot. As for us leaving, I felt that if I asked permission then Chief Crosson might put me under lock and key. Plus, I didn't want Mr. Flint here roaming our great Sonoran Desert without somebody in authority alongside him. My apologies, it won't happen again."

He smiled and slapped my shoulder, a small dust cloud rising in the air. We both coughed. He suddenly wrinkled his nose and took out a handkerchief to quickly wipe the dirt off his fingers. Damn, I really needed a bath and a set of clean clothes. Spencer then turned towards Manny.

"I suppose your excuse is the same, Detective Corroda? You know, I think if you would've been a little more honest with Captain Masters he would've easily told you to leave the base. Now, he's just kind of pissed off that you lied to him. So, you'll have to deal with that as a separate issue when you get back and this is all over."

"I understand, sir. I also agree that it won't ever happen again."

The lieutenant smiled and shook his head. "Somehow with both of you I highly doubt that. But for now you're here and definitely in need of a bath and clean clothes. Anyway, bring me up to speed on what you possibly found out there."

For the next five minutes we reviewed how our night had gone. He also brought us up to date on the missing hikers although he didn't hold much hope in finding them anytime soon. None of us did, feeling that they were food for a hungry monster by now.

After Lt. Spencer shook our hands again and walked away I turned towards the bleak mountains. Where could it be I wondered? Did we in fact injure it seriously enough that it needed to mend? Or was it merely deciding to attack us again when we least expected it? Somehow, one way or the other, I knew we were still in for a rough trip before this was all over.

Chapter 13

What can I say other than I'm really angry, disturbed, annoyed, frustrated, and just plain old pissed off? I could probably think of a few more descriptive words. We hung around for most of the day at the foot of those foreboding mountains, even though we hadn't slept in a while. The growing crowd of searchers for the missing hikers turned up nothing, not even a missing shoe. I wondered if the damn thing was eating clothing as well. If so, then I hoped it was having one helluva' stomach ache.

As night fell with a heavy thud like the curtain falling on a horrifying play, the search was called off. Only a few officers stayed behind as a presence for the night. I didn't really want that duty.

Helicopters looped back and forth over the mountains and surrounding desert, but they came up short. The search was continued the next day as well with the same results. By this point a good portion of the mountain had been scoured until it was determined that the missing hikers were either having serious difficulties somewhere, or the big bad monster did in fact devour them, shoes and all. That still never answered the question as to why they didn't answer their cell phones, or even call or text their loved ones. Traces were sent out on each phone, but they came up dry. Could this damn thing be eating cell phones as well? Sadly I added what appeared to be three more lives to the climbing death toll in and around Tucson.

Flint, Manny, and I thankfully got a ride back to our vehicles. We were mostly sitting around with our thumbs up you nowhere. We rode mostly in silence. Flint dropped me off and said he'd be in touch, then drove away. Part of me wanted to ask him to come inside, but that was probably asking for more trouble. Definitely biting off way more than I could chew at the moment. In fact, I'd probably choke to death anyway.

I stood under a hot shower for twenty minutes letting the scalding water just burn away the pain and frustration. Then I filled up the tub nearly to the top and poured in several capfuls of my favorite bubble bath. I just wanted to relax my sore muscles, plus ease the growing tension. While the tub was filling up I padded naked and silent into the kitchen to fix myself a tall screw driver. I had really gotten to like Tequila sunrises, but they were too involved to make right then. Don't be alarmed, all the blinds were pulled down and curtains drawn. Once back in the bathroom I ever so slowly allowed my aching body to sink up to the neck. It freaking felt absolutely heavenly.

Since it was daylight, even though I had closed the curtains and turned the light out I still pulled night shades over my eyes which really blocked out most of the light. I fell asleep right there in the tub for who knows how long, but when I finally awoke the water was tepid at best. It was a miracle I hadn't sunk down under the water completely and drowned. That would've been a fitting end to a terribly stressful two weeks. Come to think of it, that's what they could've put on my tombstone – *'Here lies Detective Amelia Stephenson. An alien couldn't kill her, but drowning in a bathtub full of bubbles did the trick. At least she died clean.'*

I let the water out slowly. Then I turned on the shower and stepped in to wash off any last remaining vestiges of soapy film. Grabbing a thick, fluffy towel I dried off and then powdered my entire body so I could at least feel really fresh and feminine again, if

THE REPTILIAN FACTOR

only for a little while. Lord only knew how soon I would be tripping and falling through the freaking desert again, covered in sand and sweat. Maybe even blood, hopefully not my own.

Back in the bedroom I reached for a long, blue nightgown with thin spaghetti straps. It was really nice to feel girly again if only for an evening. Hell, even just a few precious hours would be heavenly until I received a call to go somewhere dangerous.

Old Man Hunger was also screaming out my name, insinuating that it needed food. Sadly, it was apparent that Mother Hubbard's cupboard was bare because a certain female detective had been virtually working 24/7 lately. Plus, traipsing around like a crazy woman out in the *frickin'* wilderness. Clearly though, this girl had to get grocery shopping soon, not to mention that I only had one roll of toilet paper left. I managed to grab a can of chili and still had half a sleeve of saltines that were getting somewhat stale. After a few minutes in the microwave I settled into my luxurious recliner and released a heavy sigh. To say that I was exhausted would be a humongous understatement.

Deciding not to turn on the TV just yet I wanted to enjoy the solitude and eat my chili with beans. Not the real stuff though. This was actually kind of mild, but the way my stomach was feeling I didn't think anything spicy would be too good. I like to crumble up a bunch of saltines in my soup, including chili, so at least it was filling. I remember asking Manny when he took me out for my first real, honest-to-goodness bowl of Mexican chili if there were any crackers around. He stared at me aghast. Almost hurt that I would ask such a thing. I didn't know I was breaking a cardinal rule of the Chili Eaters of America Society. After my first spoonful though of the *'real'* stuff, I wished to God I had a full box of saltines. It was about all I could do to get down the entire bowl. Manny was so proud of me when I finally finished. I couldn't say thank you because my freaking mouth was on fire. Later that night I was not a happy camper because as usual my butt was parked on the toilet seat. Remember what I mentioned earlier about the flames and ash? Yeah, you got it so I shan't be too descriptive. I'm still disgusting.

Putting the empty bowl on the coffee table I took a sip of cold beer and then reached for the remote. Maybe some stupid program would put me to sleep. I quietly drifted off into dreamland quite often reclining back in my chair, the one piece of furniture I had really decided to put some money into. Just as I was aiming the remote towards the TV there was a soft knock on the door.

What the hell!! I laid my head back and groaned.

Ah man, give a girl a break, I thought. I desperately needed this time to myself. It had to be Manny, but then he could've just knocked and walked right in since he has a key. The fact that there was a second knock pretty much told me it was not my partner so I got somewhat concerned. I really didn't think it could be a neighbor, but maybe it was.

Moaning loudly, I slowly stood and ran my right hand down the front of my nightgown to brush away some cracker crumbs. Sometimes I can be a slob when I eat. I also had the AC on, so because of it being nice and chilly I was wearing a warm plush robe, mainly because I liked to feel all snuggly sometimes. I pulled the robe closed in the front and shuffled slipper-less towards the front door.

Leaning forward I peered into the peep hole and then quickly stood back. I couldn't believe my eyes. I wondered if I should really open the door, or just pretend that I was sleeping. Another knock, louder this time, told me that my surprising visitor would not go away too soon, even if I pretended to be asleep. Breathing deeply I reached for the door knob, turned and opened it to find Mr. Vincent Flint standing upon my doorstep.

He smiled and held up a bag of food in the left hand along with a bottle of wine in the other. Well, chocolate would've had me in the palm of his hands like putty right about then. But hey, two out of three wasn't bad so this girl just smiled.

"Good evening Detective Amelia Stephenson. I hope I'm not disturbing you. Were you getting ready for bed? If so, then I can leave and eat by myself in the car."

I glanced down at my robe and nightgown. I was somewhat embarrassed as I looked back up at him. "Ah no, not really. I wear this all the time unless I'm walking around the house nude. Why would I ever decide to wear a nightgown to sleep in?"

"Ah see, you're just joking with me again. However, I must say you really look fantastic. So, I was hoping I might be able to spend a little time with you. As you can see, I have some delicious food here in the bag and a great bottle of chilled wine. All we need are two plates, some utensils, and a couple clean glasses. Or, we can drink out of the bottle. That is if you're up to it and maybe just a little hungry. I know that I am."

Hell, was I up to it? You betcha' sweet ass, my hungry stomach yelled out. He looked pretty damn good too, all cleaned up like he was going on a date. Plus, the chili did not cut the hunger pains at all. Not sure if I was going to regret this move, but I stepped aside and motioned him in anyway. Once he was over the threshold I glanced out at the street to see if there were any nosey neighbors ready to start some gossip.

Something told me that if I hadn't opened the door, then I would've heard him say, *"I'll huff and puff and blow your door in, Detective Stephenson."*

Quickly closing the door I turned with my back against it and observed him moving rather gracefully for a large man towards the dining room. Shaking my head I pushed off the door and shuffled towards the kitchen. This might be a mistake, I thought.

Ten minutes later I was actually moaning with pleasure at the warm feeling in my full tummy. The wine was actually delicious and went with the food quite well. He had thought about Chinese, but then thought better of it. So he stopped at a steak house not far from my house and ordered two huge steak dinners with all the trimmings. I was in Seventh Heaven and I'm not referring to the topless joint back home in Conshohocken. I had to admit that he knew the way to this girl's heart. Exactly through my stomach.

"Thank you, Mr. Flint. That was absolutely wonderful. My cupboard was so bare I had to resort to eating a crappy can of chili from a nearly empty closet and semi-stale saltines. So, this was sheer euphoria. Plus, the wine is really good, just as you said it would be. Oh well but alas, there is just that one special thing missing."

He raised his eyebrows and smiled, waiting for me to tell him what that could be.

"What else, but chocolate," I stated, presenting my most winning smile.

There was a moment of silence while he stared at me with that cute twinkle in his eye. Then, as if right on cue, he reached into a side pocket of his jacket and pulled out two Milky Way bars. I busted up and laughed solid for a full minute. The man had taste I had to give him that. He must've remembered when we were taking a break out in the desert while sitting on a large rock surrounded by cactus that I had mentioned all I truly wanted right then was a beer, a shower, and a Milky Way bar.

We cleaned and put away the dishes, grabbed the rest of the wine and moved out to the patio in the backyard with me clutching my precious Milky Way as if it was a solid gold bar. It was somewhat cool so being a real gentleman he took off his sport coat to drape over my shoulders even though I was still wearing the robe. I realized he was doing everything right and where this might be leading. I was certainly willing to see what direction that took us. Even though warning signals kept blaring away in my head.

"Have I thanked you yet?" moaning slightly, placing the last piece of candy bar into my mouth. At the same I reached for the glass of wine resting beside me.

"I think you have done that probably ten times. I'm really glad you enjoyed it though. I figured we both really needed something filling and I made a good choice apparently. Amy, you have a very charming house. Very homey and with a great view from out here. Even in the dark on this moonlit night you can see the ominous outline of the Catalina's against the sky. Very nice indeed. Kind of romantic, don't you think?"

"Yep, as soon as I first walked out the back door when looking at the house I was completely sold. I actually only moved in little over a month ago and sadly over the last two weeks I have not spent much time here. I desperately want to get a dog or cat, but with my crazy work schedule it just would not be too responsible on my part. So I'm just going to wait. Not for long though because I do get kind of lonely when I'm home. It'd be nice to have a wagging tail, or a loud meow, greeting me when I unlock the door."

Then he stood and turned around, wiggled his butt and meowed. I laughed, couldn't help myself. This side of him was totally new compared to the very macho 'me big hunter/tracker' mentality. I must admit that I sort of liked it.

"Well Amy, it's getting rather late so I should be going. I'm sure you also want to try and get some sleep, especially since we have no idea what's in store for us tomorrow."

Since he was already standing I pushed out of my chair as well.

"Yeah, I am tired. This was a nice surprise and I thank you. You're actually the first single male I've had in this house since I moved in. In fact, besides Manny and an electrician you're the only male who has gotten beyond that door. So feel privileged."

He bowed and took my hand, pulled it forward and planted a nice kiss over the knuckles. Oh crap, if he didn't get the heck out of my house fast I might not let him leave. And that would not be cool because we needed to keep everything professional for now. I didn't want him to think that I was some sex hungry, googly-eyed girl that was an easy target. Oh hell, you know what I mean…a slut, just like Manny always calls me.

He stood erect, but still held my hand and then gently pulled me towards him. With the other arm he slid it around my back and leaned over.

"I hope you don't mind Amy, but I've really been anxious to do this from the first moment I laid eyes on you. Even with all that blood and dirt, remember?"

Without another word he placed his lips on mine and I suddenly became totally weak in the knees. To say that I didn't respond would be a massive understatement. Geez Marie, I was completely lost at that point. I was ready to tell him that he could have his way, ravish my body, plunder me, use whips and chains (ah nah, not that, just a dirty thought). We remained lip-locked together for at least an hour…okay, it was just a full minute, but it seemed like an hour. I honestly didn't want it to end, but stop it did.

Our lips didn't pop when we parted, but he pulled away so slowly that I think our lips continued to stay together for a moment before they released. My head was actually spinning. I realized right then and there that it was the best kiss I was ever a part of. There wasn't one jerk back in Philly I had ever dated where I could honestly say knew how to kiss a woman. And, this coming from a man that I originally had pegged as a totally screwed-up, macho-centered asshole. Some of that description was probably still true, but I didn't want to lose my total focus on this one special moment in time.

"Wow! Whew! Do you end all your dates like that?" I murmured.

"Ah, was this a date? I thought I just came by, knocked on your door, and then totally imposed myself upon your quiet evening carrying gifts to lure you into my web."

I laughed. For sure the smart ass was a sweet talker.

"You're good, really good, Mr. Flint. The word date was just a metaphor for a *'get together between two friends'*. And yes, you actually did push yourself upon me. But it seems I've responded in a certain way as well so let's call that part of the ballgame all tied up. This was very nice tonight and we should pursue it further. But not now. Actually, this evening was so special that I'd like to treasure it for a bit knowing full well that I would like to have more nurturing in the future. How's that sound to you?"

He smiled and then hugged me very tightly. God, it felt like the air was about to explode from my lungs. Then he released me just as quickly. I turned and walked on shaky knees to the door, my hand still within his. At the door I turned and he kissed me again, albeit lightly on the cheek this time. I didn't think I could survive one on the lips.

"Goodnight Detective Amelia Stephenson. It was a most wonderful evening."

"Goodnight Mr. Vince Flint, I agree completely. Before you leave my threshold what are your plans for tomorrow?"

"Not sure yet. Probably see if anybody else is around. Try to make contact with Prudot and Tiny Tim. Then check on my people to see how they're doing medically. I suppose I should make an appearance out at Davis-Monthan as well since they are the ones who initially hired me. Plus, they still owe me some money. Hell, who knows when I'll collect that, or even live long enough to receive it."

"They paid you already? That's a shock coming from the military and U.S. Government. And hey, don't you even talk about not living long enough."

"We got half up front and the other half will be paid supposedly when the creature is bagged, tagged, and/or disposed of. I want to make sure that Hill and Vaughn get taken care of and the full amount now goes to Jimmy Baldwin's family. That was a prerequisite when we signed up for this insane mission. If we didn't make it all the way, whether this thing was located or not, the full portion would still be paid out with no questions asked. Tells you how desperate the military is to get this situation resolved."

"Are you going to continue working for them?" I asked.

He hesitated. "Well, I certainly don't like their secretive, underhanded ways, but they are paying me. Not sure if the Tucson PD would, but I can check. I actually want to work with you and the local police department. You're more honest and trustworthy."

I laughed. "Right, you're so full of crap, but I'll talk to Chief Crosson. I think he's done reaming me a new asshole, but there's always tomorrow. I'll let you know what he says. Actually, I'm pretty sure he'd like you on our side because I still don't trust the Air Force to seriously help us. I'm sure he doesn't either."

"We'll see I suppose. I'll contact you tomorrow," he said, opening the door. "Amy, I really did have a pleasant evening and want to make sure we see each other again when this is all over. You're actually a pretty amazing woman."

I placed my hand on his shoulder and grinned...my sweetest smile I think.

"Me too. Now get out of my house Mr. Flint, or I won't let you leave."

I watched him walk down the sidewalk to his SUV, jump in and pull away. We waved and all I could think of was, *'Amy, you're such a stupid, stupid woman'*.

Closing the door, I made sure everything was locked up tight. Then turned the A/C down a little, made sure the dishes were all cleaned and put away. Finally I headed for the bedroom because I was really tired. Placing the robe across the end of the bed I slipped in between the covers and enjoyed the feel of the nightgown against my body. Tugging the blanket and sheet up around my chin I couldn't help but smile. I had this glowing, toasty-warm feeling in the pit of my stomach that I had not felt in a long time, maybe never. At least I thought that warm and toasty feeling was coming from my stomach. Well, forget I even considered that it might be coming from another body part.

I fell asleep dreaming about how the evening had progressed. In my dream, however, I didn't actually do the stupid maneuver of pushing Mr. Hunky Chunky out the door. I smiled, moaned and fell asleep to my own special dreams. For the first time in two weeks I didn't have nightmares of dead bodies and a monstrous creature running around on the loose trying to eat us up. Instead, I was lying quite comfortably within the strong, warm embrace of one helluva' handsome man.

Chapter 14

L t. Colonel Pike stood in front of his men, twenty-four of the most highly trained and dedicated members of the 563rd Rescue Group. All but four of these particular men, including two women, belonged to the 55th Rescue Squadron. The remaining four were Special Ops brought in the night before. The 55th was paramount in deploying combat ready forces into harsh and dangerous situations, mostly under dire conditions. They all stood ramrod straight at rigid attention. They were not only crack young soldiers, but fine young people as well. He was exceedingly proud of each person.

He moved forward a little bit and smiled. "At ease gentlemen," he stated firmly. "Let's just relax a little bit. If you feel like sitting we can move over to the benches. Or what the hell, just plop right down where you're standing if you'd rather do that."

In unison they all shouted, "No sir, we're fine, sir."

Nodding his head he cleared his throat. "Most of you know that something major has been happening over the last two weeks. You four men from Special Ops will be brought up to speed shortly. In fact, you all will learn more about what has taken place over this time period and will most likely be quite surprised. I know that I was."

Clearing his throat, he continued, "What we have here people is a situation that needs to be resolved quickly. A number of deaths, both civilian and military, have occurred and the reason pretty much attributable to something that escaped our control. It is, quite frankly, like nothing you have ever faced before. Hell, nobody has."

He waited for a response, a murmur, a shuffling of feet, but none came so he continued, proud of each soldier who was standing before him.

"It seems an alien life form that had been under constant surveillance for over thirty years has escaped from what was supposed to be a highly secure facility. By our control, I mean the Air Force. This occurred about a month ago. We don't know how it happened other than the episode was very violent. Since then I believe seven or eight civilians in and around Tucson have been slaughtered as well. Three different teams of six contractors were sent out into the desert about five days ago. Nothing much happened during that time until the other night. One of those teams led by Vince Flint, who some of you may know already, came into contact with this creature. It wasn't a very pleasant confrontation, resulting in one death and another member of that team currently now in serious condition in the hospital. This creature got away to God only knows where. But for sure, it is out there in the desert someplace. I feel somewhat certain of that because it wouldn't have gone far and may have been seriously wounded."

He paused a few moments to wait for any response and then continued since there was none. "It's my understanding that when this thing was first discovered at a crash site out in the desert it was in some form of liquid state. Very carefully the people back then were able to encase it inside something solid and make sure that it was placed in a secret location. I'm not sure how it escaped, but it apparently has the ability to take over a host body, animal or human. It doesn't really matter, although so far it's been reptilian."

He stopped and let that sink in before continuing.

"So it seems that what we're preparing to do is start an intense search of our own, paralleling the efforts of the Tucson PD and those smaller search teams. This will be a combined air and ground operation. The four of you assigned to us from Special Ops will head four different teams of four members each, all on the ground covering different areas out in the desert. The other eight of you will fly shifts constantly from sunup to sundown covering a grid that we have created. Communication will be constant between air and ground forces, especially if those ground forces need assistance, both with firepower or rescue. This damn thing is someplace out there and my guess is that it has gotten up into the Catalina's somewhere. That alone will be extremely difficult because there are innumerable places to hide up there, especially if it got around to the other side of the lodge which is very rugged. From what I also understand, conventional ammo does not hurt it so we will be using more heavy duty firepower, armor piercing in fact."

Lt. Colonel Pike started pacing back and forth while they all stood at a relaxed parade rest trying to absorb everything he was telling them. They all for the most part had been involved in combat, some of which was extremely heavy and dangerous so they were battle hardened troops. It was apparent to each of them that they were about to search for, and no doubt face, an enemy that they had never in their wildest dreams thought about. Other than maybe watching crazy science fiction movies like *"Alien".*

He continued. "It also appears that three hikers went missing, at least reported by one of the wives. Police searched quite awhile before calling it off when they found no sign of any bodies. They most likely will resume the search come morning. We will, however, be heavily deployed before dawn and on the move before the sun rises. We also have equipment that each group will take along and hopefully be able to detect movement and danger. You will get some first hand knowledge of this a little later."

Pike clasped his hands behind his back and strutted back and forth, stopped quickly and then spun around. "So gentlemen, that's about it. Let me clearly warn you that this is going to be the strangest and probably the most dangerous mission you've ever been assigned. We hope that this thing can be located and captured without the loss of life. If we can't take it alive then it must be destroyed. I don't give a shit how you do it as long as the job is accomplished with nobody else dying. That's it! Any questions?"

There was some very obvious fidgeting, but mostly they were quiet. Perhaps lost in their own thoughts, maybe not even sure of what the hell to ask.

However, a sergeant over to the left spoke up first.

"Sir, quite frankly I don't think any of us care what we have to face. But, can you at least tell us what this thing is, or what it even looks like?"

Pike pursed his lips together, rocking slowly back and forth on his heels before responding. "Apparently from that violent altercation the other night, reports came back that it was some type of very large, lizard-like creature. A few statements were made that it looked like a giant Gila monster, but five times the size. That's about ten feet or so."

There was some low laughter now, more from nerves than anything. Then a continued shuffling of feet and low mumbles. This was definitely something new for them all and it came wrapped in some very obvious concern so it certainly didn't appear to be the nicest Christmas present. But in truth, they were soldiers and that was that. They followed orders and faced whatever enemy was placed in front of them.

"Excuse me Colonel Pike, but a while back you mentioned something about liquid. Was it in that state when it escaped from the facility, and if so, then how did it kill anybody from that type of bodily structure?" came a question from the back row.

Pike looked around at somebody who had just entered the hangar. Under his breath he muttered, *'it's about goddamn time'*.

"I'm going to turn this part of the questioning over to Dr. Oliver Warring who was in charge of this creature at a very heavily guarded facility off the main base."

The scientist stared angrily at the officer knowing that what he tried to do with that statement was place the onus of the alien escaping upon his shoulders entirely.

"Thank you Lt. Colonel Pike. But if I may say in my defense, I was in charge of experimentation, not security. That was your task if I can set the record straight. So even though this life form escaped, it did so because security was lax at that time."

"Okay, okay doctor, let's not point blame when we know that it belongs to everyone concerned. All I want you to do is answer questions from these soldiers who are about to go out and most probably do battle with your little lab experiment. Tell them something that will hopefully keep them alive. Did you hear that last question?"

Warring cracked a fake smile and turned to face the soldiers.

"Yes I did. While it was in captivity it stayed at least for the most part in a thick, liquid state. In fact, it remained pretty much that way from the time it was found in the wreckage of a UFO in 1983 out in the desert until its escape. At one point it displayed signs of life after being dormant for quite a while. There apparently were times when it changed shape assuming the qualities of different things, mostly strange animal-like shapes, but nothing we had ever seen before. Plus, it did not stay in those shapes for long before resuming back to something that resembled a small blob. All I have to go on are reports during that time. When I took over the operation it was in the inactive state. About four months ago it started showing continued, and at times, extreme movement. As well as some form of intelligence. I say intelligence because our instruments detected something resembling electrical impulses. We could not easily identify whether it was trying to communicate directly to us in some fashion, or it was instinctive on the alien's part."

He stopped for a moment and took a long sip from a bottle of water he had been carrying. Coughing slightly he then continued.

"On the night of the escape it apparently must have entered the mind of one of the doctors and had him unlock both the outer and inner doors. This obviously set off immediate alarms. By the time others got there, which was a very rapid response from what I understand, the entity had gotten loose. It still remained in this liquid state, but apparently moved with great speed. It was also easily lost due to its pliable structure. In addition, I think the ability to crawl into a person's mind and instruct them what to do was enormous. I cannot tell you how the three soldiers on that bottom floor died other than it must've killed them with some type of mind and body control. There were no physical wounds nor a lot of blood loss with the exception of blood pouring from noses and ears. In one case it came from the eyes as well. Several times it entered the body of a guard and forced that individual to fire upon other military and medical personnel."

Dr. Warring paused and took a much longer swig of water this time. He had been banging his head against the wall so much over the last few weeks that he nearly had a perpetual headache. Thus, he had consumed massive amounts of Ibuprofen. As a result, his stomach was screwed up also so he was then ingesting huge amounts of antacids. He wondered what was next, whether he simply should slit his wrists or take an overdose of something stronger. He had contemplated doing that, feeling so much so that these deaths of the guards, scientists, and an unknown number of innocent civilians were his fault because he had not noticed what might be happening with the creature before it was too late. Who the hell knew for sure? Maybe even that would not have been enough.

But, how could he have known anything that his internal voice kept repeating over and over? He was certainly not a mind reader, let alone one belonging to an alien. No human on this planet could've foreseen what happened, he kept telling himself.

He continued. "Once it had somehow gotten over the fence, or however it got free of the installation, we were at a loss as to know what might happen after that. Would it just skedaddle somewhere safe where every little alien worm went to and then contact friends? Might it take over someone, or something's body, and then control it? Would it become dormant, or cause mass mayhem? It was just a damn worm. We didn't know and it was nearly two weeks after it got loose that we heard of the first several deaths reported by the Tucson newspapers. Once that happened then we knew this was not, in fact, some friendly little alien out for a scenic tour of Tucson. Which we truly never believed anyway. That was the reason for so much caution over all these years."

He paused slightly and then continued. "We already had discovered that this creature, this alien life form, possessed and emitted some type of electrical waves completely different from that of a human. Actually, nothing known to this point on our planet. It was actually seven years ago when this became known so we brought in the best electrical technicians and scientists we could find. Over the next three or four years they continued working on a piece of equipment to record, analyze, and to try and duplicate these waves. It was very touch and go, hit or miss. Eventually, they arrived at patterns they could record and trace back to the actual life form itself.

"Obviously this data and information was invaluable for a number of reasons, one of them being the development of an echo-location device we could use on land. A few of these units have been developed. You all will be instructed in their use before you depart. I can't be certain that they will continue to be of any use now that it's free. Especially knowing that this creature has assumed the physical structure of something like a large lizard. So the question is, have the electrical waves been changed so much now after the transformation(s) that it no longer resembles what we had previously studied? We won't know that until we're out in the field. If you get attacked and nothing showed on the unit then do not smash it against a rock in frustration simply because it may leave the host's body and become a liquid state again. At which time you should be able to locate it. We're hoping the devices work no matter what physical body it's in."

Turning to Lt. Colonel Pike, he shrugged. "That's about it. We've developed some extremely strong serum that can hopefully be shot into the lizard's body and cause it to slow down, hopefully to the point it can be recaptured. This is again something else we won't know about until the opportunity arises. Plus, whether the needles which are as strong as we could get can enter the body through the scale-like armor it has now."

"Seems like that is what we're dealing with Dr. Warring, suppositions, guesses, hopes, and prayers. Thank you for your assistance."

Pike moved to stand in front of the team and re-addressed them. "Any more questions people?"

Lieutenant Spyker stepped forward. "Yes sir. Quite frankly, the lives of these soldiers depend on me and my judgment. I certainly want to keep casualties to a minimum, but that sounds like a pipe dream. If you order us to try and capture this thing we'll do so, but we won't wait around or hesitate even the least little bit in killing it if our lives depend on survival."

"I'm in total agreement. I've actually been on this base for quite awhile now and did not realize this thing was ever here, or in the surrounding area. That pisses me off to high heaven so I certainly have no love lost for anything, or for that matter anybody, in this situation other than people under my command. As far as I'm concerned you have my permission to eliminate this monster any way possible. Is that fully understood?"

"We fully understand. Thank you, sir."

Dr. Warring quickly stepped forward. "Excuse me Colonel Pike, but the value of this creature is invaluable and we should try everything possible to capture it first with total elimination the last resort."

The officer turned and put a death stare upon Dr. Warring that would've made a full blown rose wilt.

"Doctor, you had your chance for quite a few years. All you scientist geeks blew it. You go talk to the families of our military, plus those of the civilians, that have lost their lives because of this goddamned monstrosity your group allowed to escape. Unless you're willing to go out into the field with one of the teams and try to talk this thing into surrender then total elimination will be the course of action. That's what I'm instructing my people to take and that's final."

"I'll be more than happy to go out into the field, Lt. Colonel Pike. All I want is the first crack at slowing it down, hopefully to the point of recapture. If that doesn't work then your people may destroy it."

"Dr. Warring, you will have very little time to prove your point. In all honesty, if bullets and explosives couldn't stop it the other night how in heaven's name do you expect some stupid dart with sleeping medicine to work? Maybe you can plan on holding out a nice juicy bone in your hand and it'll just politely follow you right into a cage. The situation will play itself out. Totally understand that the lives of my men and women are paramount. There has been enough deaths attributed to this disastrous mistake of yours. We will definitely not make the same stupid errors."

Lt. Colonel Pike took the next ten minutes to divide the larger group into four smaller ones, each led by a Special Ops person which were all lieutenants. Over the next hour they were instructed in how to use the piece of equipment each team would carry. They were then dismissed to get back and prepare to be transported to their starting quadrant on the grid. Pike could only pray they would be successful in finding and eliminating this abomination. If they weren't then he shuddered to think of the body bags they may need. That is, if there were even enough bodies left to bury.

Chapter 15

I woke up the next morning actually smiling. During the night there had been several very pleasant dreams. A few that I very reluctantly had to leave on the pillow and beneath the sheets. After showering and gobbling down several pieces of cinnamon toast with coffee, I jumped into my Rav-4 and headed for the precinct. Manny and I had already been in touch and were looking forward to getting together with the task force to make things happen. I put a call out to Flint, but had to leave a message. Maybe he was still sleeping, or even sitting on a toilet. Somehow though I presumed he was already out in the field, most likely alone, or with Julius and Tiny Tim.

"Chief Crosson, how are you?" I inquired, grabbing a large powdered donut and coffee, then dropped into a chair.

"Fine Detective Stephenson. Did you get a good night's sleep? It might be the last one you get for a while."

"Yes sir. I'm totally rested and ready to locate this damn thing so we can kill it and hopefully put an end to this nightmare."

"Agreed. You ready to be a team player again?"

I smiled. "Sir, you know I'm a team player and always have been. What Manny and I did the other day needed to be done. Somebody had to get out there and search around. It won't happen again. At least I promise to let you know where I am if it does. Please understand that my cell might be turned off because even the vibrator could be noticed by the creature. No telling what type of sounds, even low ones, can be detected by this thing. But I'm totally on board, you know that."

He slapped me hard on the shoulder as I choked on some donut. "I know Amelia. Okay, let's get this ballgame started so we know what we're going to do."

Just then my partner walked in and handed me a cup of coffee, plus a glazed donut, even though I already had both of those in front of me.

"Glad you could join us Corroda. How's your family and the sick child?" a back-handed remark due to Manny using that excuse to get away from the air base.

"They're fine sir, thanks for asking."

Chief Crosson walked to the front of the large squad room and turned around. All talking stopped and eyes stayed riveted on their esteemed leader.

"I've been informed by Lt. Colonel Pike from the base that they are sending out four teams this morning, troops trained for this type of mission. In fact, they're probably out there already knowing how early they get up. In addition, they will be using helicopters with thermal devices to scour the area as well. As a result, our search will primarily be within the city and outer suburbs. All calls and leads, no matter how trivial or silly, will be followed up on. Every squad car will be equipped with two full assault rifles. Each detective will carry one also, so you will be sent out in teams of two and thus have two extra powerful weapons at your disposal. That's in addition to the weapons you will be toting. Also, each of you will wear vests and that's an order. If I hear any of you are not wearing it then your ass will be hauled in here and be slammed in a chair behind a desk. We've battled this creature once, hit it with enough firepower to kill most living things. Yet it still got away. I don't want any of you taking unnecessary chances, but at the same time we need to find and kill the bastard.

"We feel strongly it scurried back up into the mountains, but that does not mean the thing is still there. It's very possible now that it has had a taste of human flesh and blood it will be tempted to once again venture into populated areas. If that happens then we need to be prepared. It's very possible all hell will break loose at any given time."

He stopped talking so we weren't sure if he was opening up to questions, or just thinking about what to say next. So we all remained silent. Either way, we knew enough to wait until it was obvious what he was doing, or going to say next. Chief Crosson was a great guy, but he could also be one hard S.O.B as we all knew.

He coughed and then continued. "Okay, you're already partnered up and will continue to stay that way at least for the time being. We have sectioned off the city and there will be many patrol cars out there as well. Do nothing on your own without radioing into dispatch and having adequate back-up. I absolutely mean that boys and girls, trust me on that. Nobody goes rogue and strays away on your own," as his dark eyes fell on me and my partner.

"Also, be prepared for long hours and let your families know so they don't hog up the phones calling in here. I would also suggest that if you haven't already, then instruct them to stay home unless going out is absolutely necessary. I wish it were the weekend, but at least its Friday so we just need to get all the kids to and from school safely. Once they're home make sure they stay there. Now get your butts on the move and be careful out there. This is something we have never faced before."

That's exactly what we did. Within half an hour Manny and I, along with dozens of teams, hit the pavements. My partner and I were assigned the area around the Univ. of Arizona. Up to this point, other than newspapers blaring out their headlines concerning a series of grizzly deaths, no curfew had been put into place, at least not yet. However, I thought Chief Crosson was probably only one more civilian death away from suggesting to the mayor that a declaration may be needed.

As we patrolled the streets, the life of a cop did not stop. Crime continued to happen all the time. The radio never ceased screaming out calls. We had to stop by a Hispanic convenience store where a fight had broken out between two rival gangs. Three bangers were shot, one seriously wounded and two dead. Three blocks away a gun battle broke out between several guys, possibly the same gang members, and several patrolmen. One guy was brought down with a bullet to the right shoulder, another tossed his gun onto the pavement and stood with hands raised, while several others apparently got away. The chase continued, but Manny and I stayed clear of it. Seemed like it was just now a matter of capturing those gang bangers and hauling them into the precinct. Then prepare for the next altercation which would come soon enough. It was the way of the City.

I called Flint and had to leave messages. Obviously he was gallivanting around out in the desert and his phone was turned off. Last night still lingered upon my mind and the kiss continued to lie softly upon my lips. Really made me want more. I definitely wanted to say, 'Hi honey,' which was on the tip of my tongue, but I realized it was not quite professional enough. Hopefully, we would live through this manic extra-terrestrial turmoil and be able to explore some form of relationship.

All in all though the day was pretty boring. Really hot, too. We were used to working nights so this dayshift crap was for the buzzards. A little before two o'clock we stopped at a snack truck to have a late lunch. It was too damn hot to sit outside so we plunked ourselves back in the car with the A/C running.

"This is going nowhere," I exclaimed, between bites of my beef taco.

"Yep, I think we need to be out there with Flint because that's still where this damn creature is," Manny replied. "Apparently just waiting, resting, and preparing for whatever will happen next. I don't know Amy, I just have a really bad feeling about this. Who the hell knows what that monster is doing? It could be transforming again into something else entirely, or if it has the ability, maybe creating little baby monsters which would be a real nightmare."

"Hey partner, just get those thoughts out of your head. We'll get through this like we always do. But, I do kind of agree as to where this thing is. Nothing we can do about it though. We used up our 'get out of jail free' cards the other night with good old Chief Crosson. He would bust us down to patrol in a heartbeat if we screw up again. Hell, he'd probably throw us in a cell just so we wouldn't be in his way anymore."

"You got that right," as he wiped hot sauce from the corner of his mouth and then grabbed his mega-size soda.

I took a long drink from my iced tea and stared out the window. "What if it's not around here anymore? I mean, what if it already went over the mountains and is in the basin beyond? Hell, what if a space ship picked it up? This whole situation is wickedly fluid and the information shouldn't be contained to just the surrounding Tucson area."

"That's not our call, Amy. We have enough to be concerned about. The powers that be need to work on that aspect."

Six hours later after already putting in nearly eleven hours we were relieved without any serious incidents occurring. Manny dropped me off at home and I told him that I would pick him up the next afternoon. I also wanted to ask Crosson if we could work nights again, but was afraid to ask any favors at this time. I was just feeling somewhat fortunate that I still had my shield after leaving the precinct without informing the chief.

After opening the door to no puppy wagging its tail, or kitty meowing and brushing up against my leg, I grabbed a cold 'brewsky', a bag of chips and headed for where else, my recliner. I was still way too keyed up from the night to try and actually fall asleep in a bed. Realizing I should've grabbed two beers, I flipped on the TV, grabbed another one from the fridge, and then dropped my exhausted butt into the chair.

I surfed through channels which I always did anyway even though it always got on my nerves when somebody else did the same thing. But it was my TV so I could do whatever I wanted to. Jumping from sitcoms (I wasn't in a laughing mood), to all the various 'CSI's' and 'Law and Orders' (I had enough of my own real stuff to deal with), to freaking reality shows (there was enough crap in my own life which could be a hit show), to movies I had seen or didn't interest me at all. So I finally just let it stay put on CNN where I knew the news would be constantly repeating itself.

I also leafed through the mail which ended up being a few bills, a postcard from my sister Irene who was on vacation, plus tons of advertisement crap, and two fitness magazines. Tossing it all on the coffee table I grabbed the handle and pulled back, leg rest springing up. By that time I had finished both beers and a large bag of chips. Closing my eyes I sighed and allowed the day's events to replay in my mind.

It was troubling in the end that we actually had no idea what we were doing. With a human 'perp', we had a history of doing specific things, searching for clues, patterns to follow, etc. At least it was somewhat disorganized organization. Dealing with this freaking creature, we were more lost than a newborn trying to reach for a musical mobile hanging from the ceiling with tiny little bears swirling around. We had no idea when it would strike again. Who would die next or possibly already had and we didn't know as of yet because a body hadn't been discovered. Even what the damn thing looked like now. Had it shed the lizard skin and would it now be walking or crawling around as something totally different than what we were searching for?

We just had no *frickin'* idea. However, what I did know for sure was that the doorbell had just rung. I moaned for a few seconds, but then I perked up a little thinking just maybe it could be someone special. Hey, a girl can always dream for Mr, Right.

Looking through the peep hole I was correct which caused me to smile. Dreams do come true sometimes. Opening the door there stood Vince covered in dirt from his daily romp in the desert, looking extremely tired and frustrated. Yeah, he was cute.

"I'm afraid you really look like shit, Mr. Flint."

"I feel like shit, too. Any chance I could maybe take a shower, clean up a little bit and relax? Maybe even get something to eat if you have anything?"

I quickly stood aside and let him come on in, glancing back out to the sidewalk. Thankfully there were no neighbors walking by. Don't know why I was really concerned about that anyway. It was my life and they didn't know me at all as it was.

He had a small gym bag with him. "You moving in?"

"Not unless you ask me to. This is just some clean clothes and a pair of sneakers. Sure you don't mind me doing this? I could leave and head for the motel, but it's all the way on the other side of town."

"Now how in the world can I resist such a romantic request from a handsome man to take a shower in my house? That surely doesn't happen very often. Besides, since you look rather homeless and relatively harmless it'll be my good deed for the day," I replied, a wide smile spread across my face. "I actually haven't even had time to change clothes myself so you do what you need to do and I'll see what I have around here to eat. I still have not gotten to the grocery store yet, but I'll figure something out."

I realized that I was actually acting kind of giddy, like a young school girl as I heard the shower start up knowing Vince Flint was now actually naked in my house. Shivering at the thought I pulled on a pair of white shorts and my red Phillies World Series T-shirt. I decided to be wicked and left the bra off. I slipped into my slippers and then padded out to the kitchen. Rummaging around I was able to find four eggs, six slices of bread which hadn't started turning green yet, and one opened package of Canadian bacon that didn't smell too dicey. I also started a large pot of coffee.

As I was frying up the bacon I suddenly felt a strong arm encircle my waist, pulling me back into his firm body and I do mean firm in all the right places.

I leaned back and said, "Don't you know that you should never silently creep up behind a woman standing at a stove with a hot frying pan in front of her?"

"Well, if I knew that beautiful woman didn't want me to be here, but I sure hope she does. So then, I shouldn't have to be worried too much about being struck on the head with that frying pan, right?"

Spinning around slowly I pushed away from the stove since I didn't want grease splattered on my back. Placing my left hand on his chest, I let the other touch his cheek.

"I must admit, you do smell a lot better. Feeling somewhat more human now?"

"For awhile there I wasn't sure, but yes it feels a lot better actually. In fact, holding you this close kind of makes me feel really good in all the right places."

Yeah, I could feel exactly what he meant by that. Shit, this was all certainly happening faster than I ever expected it to. But, I was not about to avoid a good thing when it was staring me straight in the eye.

"Would you like to eat?" is about all I managed to mutter, especially since he was pulling me even closer. Any tighter and I might suffocate, but then what a way to go.

"You know, I am really, really hungry, but right this very moment not for bacon, eggs, and toast although it smells delicious. What I'm actually hungry for is you, Detective Amelia Stephenson. Are you on the menu? Any price is fine with me."

Oh baby I thought. What a line that was, but they were the only words I could think of right at that very moment. I pushed away from his warm body to squirm free. I reached behind me and turned the stove off. The bacon would just have to wait.

Holding onto his hand very tightly so that he couldn't get away I slowly led him down the hallway to my bedroom. We didn't turn on the light. No need to because if I was truly dreaming then I didn't want it to end. I was used to exploring strange desert terrain in the dark anyway. Without a doubt he was also experienced in that area. In fact, since he was a well-known tracker my own terrain was entirely open to be searched.

He spun me around and looked into my eyes, his gaze burning with a lustful intensity that I hadn't seen in many years. That is if I actually ever had seen it at all. Philly guys were more interested in their next mug of beer and/or hoagie to possess this type of sexual fire. Taking my head in his large, rugged hands he tilted my face upwards and kissed me...hard, with more passion than any man had ever shown me. Oh yeah, you can be hard, but you better have that thing called passion. Works every damn time.

To say the least I responded, giving back as much as he gave me. Can I say that I had been one horny little girl now for a very long time? Okay, if not then I obviously have been. There was one guy back in Philly by the name of Keith who I had a big crush on. But alas, he was married. Not happily, but married with three kids. No way was I going to get involved in that hornet's nest. I'm not too proud to admit we did have one night in the sack which was quite extraordinary. But, I couldn't travel to those blissful pastures again though. No way was I going to get locked into a no win situation.

The few guys I had been involved with here in sunny old Tucson were for the most part just okay. But frankly, they were cops. I had decided long ago that I would not get too overly involved with anybody in law enforcement simply because of the work we each did. However, at the same time becoming extremely close to a civilian was not great either due to the hazardous conditions of my job.

So this ruggedly handsome man, holding me so tight that I couldn't breathe, kissed me hungrily. To say that it was exactly what I needed right then would be an understatement of major proportions. I reached down and fumbled for the clasp to unhook my shorts. Why didn't I wear something with just an elastic waistband that I could easily slip out of? Vince reached down, pushed my hand away and pulled hard. The hook broke, as did the zipper. Shit, these were my favorite white shorts. Then that thought passed quickly as they slid down my legs to lie at my feet in what looked like a white cloud in the darkness of the bedroom. Sounds pretty romantic, right?

"Mr. Flint, don't you dare rip this tee shirt," I mumbled into his broad chest, "it's from the 1980 Phillies World Series victory and is priceless to me."

He laughed through our locked lips as I raised my arms. He gently pulled up and our lips popped free. Slipping the shirt off completely he let it drop reverently to the floor. My braless breasts were now on display. He then pushed me as gently as possible back onto the mattress. I don't even know when or how he did it, but his sweat pants had already been discarded. Damn guy was a freaking magician or he had lots and lots of practice with women all over the world. I didn't even want to know that information.

I leaned back onto my elbows and watched as he pulled his shirt off. A little gasp was all I could muster because quite frankly he was built like a brick shit house, abs standing out in perfect symmetry. Coming forward his knee spread my legs apart as he leaned forward with his hands planted on each side of my body, his face just above mine. Holy crap, this was actually going to happen and I couldn't wait another bloody second.

"You're a goddamn tease Mr. Flint. Just get the hell down here big guy."

He didn't need a second invitation. Both his tongue and other lengthy appendage entered me, searching and hungry, moving slow and methodical. Oh Lordy, Lordy, look who's going on forty. My birthday was a year and a half away, but it sure as hell was close enough to accept this wonderful gift. I grabbed him, nails probably scratching away at his arms and back. If they were he didn't seem to mind. Scratches could always heal and it would be difficult to tell those marks with all the other ones he received from traipsing through cactus in the desert. Not to mention the numerous scars on his body.

I won't even begin to say that we first made love in a tender and passionate way. Quite simply, it was totally apparent we were both extremely horny and hungrier than hell. Not for any bacon and eggs, either. He also didn't appear to me to be the type of guy who would be sex deprived, but I hoped he was and this unplanned lovemaking would be as wonderful for him as it was for me. I certainly didn't need to ask him if he was excited because it was pretty damn apparent to me that he was.

So the first time took less than ten minutes. That was due mainly to wild passion and being as horny as I was. The second time was performed in a much more tender fashion, bringing me to a climax that I truly had never experienced in my lifetime. It was absolute heaven and quite frankly, I forgot all about aliens, snakes, and lizards.

Now we lay totally spent beside each other on the rumpled bed sheets, panting and breathing heavy, glistening with perspiration even though the A/C had been blowing away. I sure as hell didn't know about him, but my whole body was humming a happy tune which wasn't from some animated Disney movie either. He had actually brought me to a climax twice and that my friends had never happened before on one lovemaking session. I can honestly say that it would be very cool to happen again.

"Wow," was all I could barely whisper.

"Double wow," he returned, a little deeper, but still low and throaty.

"Mr. Flint, that was absolutely incredible. It doesn't mean we're engaged or anything, right?"

He laughed. "No, at least not yet. However, give me another try and maybe we can start planning a wedding. And, would you please stop calling me Mr. Flint? Sounds like you're screwing my father."

"You want to do it again right now?" I asked, more than a little breathlessly.

"My God girl, not right this minute. I think you've drained me for a little while anyway. I'm going to the bathroom first and I can still smell that bacon lying in the pan if you're still interested in frying it up. I could eat something other than you right now. Maybe the third course can happen after our stomachs are somewhat fuller."

"Man, you just say the most romantic things," I murmured into his shoulder. "Then you go and do what little boys do after sex. I'm just going to lie here for a while inhaling the aroma because I don't want to lose this glow. That doesn't mean the bacon, either. I honestly don't want this moment to disappear anytime soon."

He leaned over and kissed me much more tenderly this time. It was nice and I was hooked like a damn trout at the end of a fishing rod. Lying there with my eyes closed I just allowed myself to bask in the afterglow until I smelled bacon and eggs frying. However, it was the aroma of freshly perking coffee that really got me moving.

After jumping into a lukewarm shower I pulled on a pair of gray sweatpants with Eagles spelled in green going down each leg and an old throw-back Eagles jersey, sleeves cut off, with Montgomery across the back. I then started moving towards the kitchen. Look, I might be living in Tucson, Arizona, but I will always be a Philly sports girl, especially the Phillies and Eagles no matter how bad they might be.

We mostly ate in silence with the only sounds coming from forks hitting plates and spoons stirring coffee. Well, my spoon because I liked mine with plenty of cream and sugar. His was black so he didn't need a spoon. I finally pushed away from the table after putting the last piece of toast in my mouth and smiled.

"That was delicious, although the bacon was a little burned and hard. But, I don't believe that I've ever had my fill of both food and sex in such a short period of time. So where do we go from here Mr. Flint, er sorry, I mean Vince?"

"How 'bout out to the patio? There's still some coffee left."

I grinned thinking yeah, he's really good at this romance stuff.

Sipping away at another delicious cup of hazelnut coffee, I glanced his way and actually saw him smiling.

"I do believe you're quite relaxed," I purred to him, trying to be sexy.

"You could say that. I think we both needed to release all that built up energy."

"Oh, so is that all that was to you? Just a need to get your rocks off? Like scratching at some irritating itch between your legs?" I asked him, somewhat pouty.

"Hell no Amy and don't even think about getting all prissy on me. You know damn well what I meant. That was the most incredible love making I've had in quite a while, maybe ever. If you think it was simply a quick lay in the hay you've got nothing between those cute little ears of yours."

I laughed. "Okay, okay don't get all hot and bothered. I'm glad to hear you say that because it sure as hell was awesome for me, too. Incredible, in fact."

We let a few quiet minutes slip by while staring at the outline of the mountains in the distance. I truly didn't even want to think about any damn alien creatures and dead bodies. But sadly, that was reality and it was my job to do so.

"How was your hike in the desert last night?" I asked, actually a little interested.

"Not so earth shattering I have to say. It was an awful lot of walking and nothing to show for it other than sore feet to be quite frank. There was definitely a military presence for sure, helicopters flying overhead and making enough noise to cause every living creature in the area to run and hide in fear. The ground troops were good though. I only detected them once. Not sure they noticed us, but they never made contact."

"Us? I thought you were going out there alone."

"I had thought about it, but then Prudot contacted me. So he and Tiny Tim tagged along which wasn't really a bad move. We were able to spread out to cover more area. Wherever this thing is hiding it's well hidden and seems to be concealed for some reason. Maybe we injured it more than we thought, I just don't know. Or possibly it moved on entirely and we're wasting our time out there."

"That's what I said to Manny earlier. If it has moved to another location then I was just wondering if the neighboring communities should be alerted. But like he said, that isn't our call."

He turned and looked at me, still with that afterglow in his eyes which was nice to see. "I still think it's around here Amy, possibly underground. There are a number of caves in that mountain range though why it would be hiding out we can't be sure. All we can do is continue searching, be prepared, and not let our guard down even the slightest."

"Sounds like a plan I guess, as good as any. My night was boring as hell, thanks for asking," I said, smiling and squeezing his hand. "Did you contact the brass on the air base? Do they still want you doing your thing for them?"

"Yep, they weren't happy with me because we spilled the beans to the police, but then I explained that I was better on my own and would report anything I found so that seemed to appease them somewhat. I sure as hell don't trust them and quite frankly they probably shouldn't trust me either. There is no love lost between me and the military."

"So you obviously have a strong military history?" I asked him.

"For sure and truthfully I can't tell you much other than I was trained to do just about anything the military or government wanted me for. To do the jobs they couldn't give to anybody else. There was also a number of sniper missions that maybe I'll tell you about someday. After the military, I worked under rather clandestine situations with several agencies that you probably are not aware of and don't want to know either. There were also assignments with civilian contractors that I can't talk about at all. I still do jobs and missions for the government from time to time. It's why they called me in on this situation. They should've called ghost busters because we're all just pissing in the wind."

"As long as it's down wind then we're okay," I responded.

Standing I walked around his chair, still holding his hand and smiled. "I'm going to lie down for a while. Would you like to come along?"

"Is that an invitation, my dear Amelia? If so, how could I ever refuse a romantic request from such a lovely lady?"

"Ha, it's an invitation to lie down only. I'm tired and really need some sleep. You do too, Mr. Soldier of Fortune."

Thirty minutes later we were both sound asleep locked securely in each other's embrace. Yes, we had round three as soon as our butts hit the mattress. But for now, it was just nice to dream about pleasant things and not have alien monsters running around in the night killing innocent people. In fact, I was really one happy detective for a few short hours anyway. I figured that reality would hit soon enough.

Chapter 16

The next week and a half inched along very slowly. In fact, it seemed to crawl by considering how chaotic the weeks before had been. After the first three or four days I think we all began thinking that just maybe the creature was either dead or had moved on to ravage another location. However, there were no reports coming from neighboring communities so there wasn't much more we could do but continue to wait for the next reported deaths. The military had not stopped their searching apparently, but had scaled back a little. Vince and his buddies still continued to go out on their little desert jaunts and had come up with nothing other than some really good exercise and suntans.

Things in the city got somewhat back to normal. Manny and I actually did what detectives normally do, try and lock up hardened criminals. The three hikers were never found although it was still an open case. We figured they were alien fodder, but with no traces or body parts we couldn't be certain. I think in general we all were waiting, albeit somewhat cautiously, for the next shoe to fall and hoping that it wasn't a size 13 boot.

Vince and I continued to explore this relationship we had going for want of a better description. The sex was incredible and we actually liked each other's company quite a lot which was even more amazing considering our strong personalities. I think it was simply that our attitude about most things was very compatible. Plus, we decided right away that there would be no ties beyond what was happening at this current place in time. His profession could at any time yank him to the deepest jungles and face the most dangerous of circumstances. Still, it was nice from a girl's perspective to dream just a little bit. I did have to continue reminding myself that I did not need to have a broken heart if he did walk away and was never seen again. I really could not make plans for a white picket fence anytime soon, though still hoping for a cute little cat or dog sometime down the road. At least I could cuddle with them, if and when Vince departed my life which was always a distinct possibility. I did not even want to think about that.

I pulled up in front of Manny's and waved to his wife who knelt alongside their house watering flowers, doing her best to help the plants survive in the ever present Tucson heat. She got my *'Best Gardner Award'* for that massive effort. My partner closed the front door and waved to me. He then walked casually over to his wife, gave her a big hug and kiss, then stooped over to ruffle the hair of his youngest child, little Contrella, named after Manny's loveable grandmother who was still hanging in there at 89 years young.

"Hey partner here you go," he said, handing me a cup of steaming hot coffee which I accepted graciously.

We were really a good tag team, always knowing what the other was most likely thinking. Also, having consideration for what the other desired which quite frankly was coffee most of the time. Being able to make each other laugh was important too.

"So where we heading? Hear anything about creature feature?" he asked.

I shook my head. "Nope, not a peep or squeak from anybody lately. I'm assuming that the military is still searching in some capacity, but even if they find something I don't expect them to divulge anything. They can't let that thing continue to stay free so they still need to send out search parties. Flint thinks that they've started using some kind of infrared technology to see if it's hiding underground in some cave, or maybe somewhere lying dead. I'd just like to get this all over with and get back to normal everyday crime solving stuff. You remember, like the good old days. I always liked reading science fiction novels and loved watching the 'X-Files', but this has been too damn real for my taste. Actually, Fox and Dana can have it all back."

"I agree." Manny murmured. "So partner, are we heading into the office?"

"Yeah, I have some paperwork that needs to be completed and then submitted. After that we'll see where we're supposed to patrol tonight."

Oh by the way, I forgot to mention that we had been put back onto night duty again, thankfully. At first I really had a hard time getting used to it after arriving here. Now that's the only shift I really wanted to work. All the best radio stations in Tucson played country music, what else. So we listened in silence, lost in our own scrambled thoughts. It's really funny how I had gotten to enjoy the shit kicking stuff since moving here, just like hot and steamy Mexican food. Deep down inside though I was still a Philly gal hungering for a good old cheesesteak from Pat's or Gino's, maybe a huge Italian hoagie on a long, fresh Amoroso roll. Even a really warm soft pretzel smothered with plenty of yellow mustard. I'd be floating on cloud nine if that were to happen.

Like I always say, you can take the gal out of Philly, but not Philly out of the girl.

Meanwhile, deep inside the cave where the alien had been maternally taking care of the nest, it came awake after feeling some movement beneath. It was a little surprising that the young were getting restless, but it had been two weeks almost to the day so they were ready to hatch into a new and very dangerous world. Since they would be coming forth in a liquid state, not physically structured with arms or legs, then it took much less time than the normal hatching of turtle or lizard eggs. It was even fast for alien eggs.

Slowly raising its large bulk the huge creature walked a few steps away from the hole in the ground containing the large clutch of eggs. It stretched and felt a sharp inner pang of hunger scratch strongly at the lining of its stomach. It had been awhile since finishing up the remains of the three hikers several days ago. Now that the eggs would be hatching shortly it could search for food. Then it would be interesting to see what happened after that. It was going to be a whole new ballgame shortly.

Staring curiously at the clutch of eggs, the mommy alien *(or queen)* noticed that one egg shell suddenly started to crack, rocking back and forth. Something inside wanted desperately to pop out and join this new brave world. Several others started performing the same ritual until soon nearly the entire mass was moving around. The first egg to start the process split open further and then a red mass started pushing forth. Cracking the shell completely the two sides fell away and a small red blob about the size of a vibrant soft ball slid forth towards the closest wall of the hole where it began to stretch out. It was followed by more eggs splitting open, some at the same time as more of the extremely strange brood started rolling and wiggling around inside the hole.

Shortly, most all the eggs had broken open. Several had not moved or even shook slightly. So mommy lizard felt they would apparently not do so well, deciding they would be instant nourishment after all the other little life forms got completely free of the eggshells. Within half an hour the birthing pit was vibrantly alive with little red, squirming blobs, each definitely showing some form of early intelligence just in how they moved around. It had been important for the creature to originally take over the snake, absorb important DNA that it needed, and then move into the Gila monster's body to provide some of the alien's original physical structure.

However, absorbing the DNA obtained from the human prey, along with memory and intelligence as well, provided the young with all they needed upon birth. They would grow rapidly within the next twenty-four hours to a length of about two feet. Their early intelligence would soon become even more acute. After that twenty-four hour period then it would be time to exit the cave and go hunting for food, sustenance needed for what appeared to be twenty ravenous baby aliens.

For the moment, however, the brood would need to remain within the hole. To make sure they did exactly that the creature pulled over a large, broken slab of wood that originally had been a sign signaling that this was once a working, thriving ore mine. The young didn't need to breathe or have light at this point so the hole was covered entirely. That way none of the more precocious babies would sneak away until the proper time.

Waiting until nightfall the creature carefully removed some of the rubble that blocked the cave mouth and narrowed its body to where it could somewhat easily slide through. Ripping out a large bush it was placed over the narrow aperture just created by leaving the cave. With huge head erect it sniffed the air for any imminent danger. Lately during daylight hours the sky had been filled with whirling sounds and voices could be heard around the cave. The alien figured it was some type of search team and it stayed completely still and silent, not concerned in the least that it would be detected. But if that had been the case then it would've easily disposed of any human coming near to protect the precious brood.

A full moon brightly lit the foothills below as well as the side of the mountain the cave was on. Even still, much of the terrain was dark and gave plenty of protection as the creature moved with easy grace across the rocks and large boulders. The highway that wound around the sharp ravines and steep cliffs up to the peak was several hundred yards away. The creature slowed down and climbed into a shallow gully just off the pavement.

There was no traffic at the moment so it waited. Patience was something the creature had plenty of. After all, it had waited over thirty years to make its escape at just the right time. It now reveled in the freedom.

However, it did not have long to hide as the approaching glow of headlights careened around a sharp curve to the left. Straight sections upon this winding highway up the mountain were few and far between, at least until you got near the bottom and approached the desert floor. As the bright glare of headlights came closer the creature tensed, preparing to pounce.

Many drivers didn't even apply brakes, especially when there were no other vehicles in sight because one of the fun aspects of this crazy drive was careening around the sharp curves, hearing both the engine revving and the squeal of tires on the pavement. This was no exception. When the vehicle, an older white, two door 1980 BMW 320i got to within about twenty yards the creature lunged from the gully into the center of the lane.

"Watch out," screamed a voice on the passenger side through the open window.

The driver was at that moment too terrified to scream or yell. There was only but a few seconds of life remaining anyway. The driver slammed the brakes hard and yanked the steering wheel to the right. Not enough time, or enough road surface remained as the car knifed across the lane, bounced roughly over the gravel and then flew through the air. It came down hard in front of a large rock before slamming into it head on. The sound was deafening, but there were no other humans nearby to hear the noise.

The driver who had been wearing a seatbelt slammed up against the windshield with a violent jolt. The passenger who was not wearing a seatbelt flew through the window. Glass sprayed everywhere, mingled with screams of pain and terror. The flying body slammed hard against a large cactus and then fell roughly to the ground where it lay totally still. The engine coughed and sputtered until it gasped to a final stop. The one headlight that remained unbroken glared accusingly across the desert floor while the horn, now jammed, blared angrily into the night.

This all took no more than fifteen seconds at the most. The creature had already moved off the road and crawled quickly to the wrecked vehicle. Inserting a claw into the open window it jerked outwards and the door fell away. It then bit down on the steering wheel and yanked it free with a loud grinding sound. The horn stopped and complete silence enveloped the area. The headlight still glared out into the darkness, while a cloud of steam poured from the mangled engine.

Totally dazed with copious amounts of blood streaming down his face the driver stared straight ahead until the muzzle of the great lizard moved directly in front of the car. The mouth opened wide and swallowed the man's head, crunching down easily to sever it from the neck. Blood spurted everywhere as the creature backed up and placed the amputated head gently on the ground to be kept as a tasty morsel for later.

Moving to the front of the vehicle its tail slammed into the one lit headlight and now there was total darkness with the exception of moonlight from above. It followed the sounds of painful moaning until it came to the fractured and torn body of a young woman lying at a crazy angle against the base of the giant saguaro. She was practically dead, barely breathing. The creature finished her off easily enough.

Bending down, the mammoth lizard turned the body over with a large paw and then slit her down the middle. The heart was what it needed right at the moment while it possibly still struck a few remaining beats. Inserting its long muzzle into the open body cavity it grabbed the organ between sharp teeth and yanked. As the head came back up blood dripped freely. Lifting a terrifying muzzle towards the sky it open its mouth wider and the heart slid down its throat as the creature swallowed greedily, but not before the teeth tore the organ in two. At the same time a loud growl echoed across the desert.

What followed was a quick feast to replenish the energy it had used while lying on the nest and going several days without food. The wrecked vehicle was far enough off the road that it couldn't be seen by passing motorists, but the creature wanted to make sure so it easily pushed the car behind a high mound. Only one body could be carried so it chose the lighter female, mainly since it was already out of the vehicle and quite frankly her blood was extremely sweet. Much more so than the older male.

It took but thirty minutes to crawl carefully back to the cave. Dropping the dead female to the ground the alien cleared the debris and found that it had to widen the opening in order to squeeze through. Once inside the dark interior it dropped the woman and covered the cave mouth again. Nosing the food roughly to the edge of the hole, it slid the piece of wood away so the hungry brood could crawl out and partake of their first real meal. The creature opened the skull so that the brain was exposed. It then widened the long slit down the middle of the carcass providing much easier access to those vibrant internal organs.

As the small red blobs crawled up and out over the rim of the hole they sensed food and eagerly began searching for ways to get inside the pile of fresh meat lying there. Soon the dead female was covered in a wriggling sea of red worms, slithering in and out of any orifice they could locate. The mother had moved back and watched with pride as the hatchlings did exactly as they were bred to do. Within a matter of minutes the body was vibrating with a life all its own. Soon the carcass would be nothing but skin and bone. Even much of that would be gone as well. Not a great way for a human life to end, but like all deaths in nature, everything became useful to some other living creature.

Communication was beginning to develop as well between the huge lizard and it's young. Not human language, but more electrical impulses detected telepathically, an alien-type code. The eggs that did not hatch completely were broken open so that the creature could suck out the insides. It already had its fill of human flesh and blood anyway. This protein was more like a late night snack. Nothing ever went to waste.

Standing inside the dark cave the alien turned and went through the process of opening the cave mouth completely. This hole in the ground was no longer a safe haven and thus did not need to be kept hidden any longer. Five minutes later the doorway gaped wider and the creature moved out into the open space. The moon was still full so enough light was splashed across the mountainous terrain.

What needed to be done now was another vital step in domination. Hosts needed to be found quickly so the hatchlings could begin their own transformations. The mother had needed to find the closest physical entity to its own and that was the lizard. For the newborns, however, the hosts would have to be human and then alterations could take place, but not until then. Each step of the process was simply part of the overall plan.

It was actually a very weird sight under a clear nighttime sky cut sharply with stars and a glowing moon. The large hybrid-transformed-Gila monster moved slowly over the rough desert terrain with twenty or so little red, liquid worms slithering and squirming behind it. Kind of like the Pied Piper of Aliens, although there was no flute music or ugly little rats following closely behind. The creature detected sounds from far off which possibly meant a large enough gathering of more humans to hopefully supply hosts galore. That was now the direction it began homing in on.

Chapter 17

We weren't back in the office more than thirty minutes when Chief Crosson informed us that there had been a serious car accident out on Catalina Highway at the base of the mountain. His voice was strained as he informed us about the condition of the bodies, or lack there of. He didn't think it was just your normal car crash either so he told us to check it out and take Carl Most along as well.

Great, just *frickin'* great I thought. Exactly what I didn't need at this point in the investigation, or rather search for some damn demonic beast. Take along the only monster-like detective in the entire unit. I glanced over at Manny and shook my head in disgust. He would have to inform Most that he was coming along with us since I didn't really want to even talk to the guy.

We didn't verbalize much on the drive out to the accident scene, either. Carl Most was a miserable S.O.B. anyway and we were not the best of friends. However, I had to admit begrudgingly that he did his job well and was a good detective. Hell, he should've been since he'd been at it for so damn long. There were rumors that he would be retiring at the beginning of next year. I, for one, would be toasting his departure with great glee. In fact, I definitely planned on getting drunk as a skunk.

Finding an open spot close enough to the crash site was somewhat difficult due to all the police and emergency vehicles on each side of the road. I steered my Rav-4 onto the gravel shoulder and hopped out. It was hot which enhanced the smell of gasoline, oil, and blood, quite a mix. I held up my hand to slow down one lane of traffic getting by so we could get to the other side. A tow truck with huge tires had backed onto the desert floor about as far as it could maneuver without getting stuck. From that point a long metal line had been snaked out towards the wrecked vehicle. A greasy covered driver with a large belly was hooking it to the rear bumper, at least what was left of it anyway.

Walking very carefully over the ground we said hello to a few guys that we knew. There was a crowd around the vehicle so we had to push some of the hot, sweaty bodies aside. Quite frankly I was immediately stunned by the sight of the wreck and all the blood around. What was left of the body in the driver's seat didn't leave much to the imagination. Especially since it had been gutted and torn apart, not to mention being decapitated. It was anybody's guess where the head was at.

I turned away and glared up at the mountain range, mainly to get my eyes refocused, but also to take a very deep breathe and then let it out slowly.

"You okay partner?" inquired Manuel who moved up against my shoulder.

"Yeah, just not prepared for this," I responded. "I don't know why considering what we've seen over the last month. You'd think by now we would be somewhat hardened to this. I noticed that the windshield was broken out so there must've been a passenger inside. Was anybody else found?" I asked, wanting to walk into the desert and find a nice shady, secluded spot. As far from this nightmare as possible.

Manny shook his head. "Corporal Rivera said there were signs that the body had been thrown straight ahead about thirty feet or so, landing against a large cactus. Again, lots of blood, but no one else was discovered. Not even a body part. So that person was obviously carried off to be used for something we don't even want to think about. I highly doubt the body will ever be found just like so many out here that have gone missing."

Detective Carl Most responded in his normal gravelly voice, "It appears to have been a trap most likely. This killer must've been waiting and scared the driver off the road. Gives a new meaning to 'road kill'."

"Very funny Carl," I replied acidly, "but then again, not really. Kind of sick, but you're not well known for your consideration of others, victims especially."

He made a loud snorting sound through his nose which always disgusted me and then shook his balding head. "I didn't mean it to be a funny remark, Stephenson. As always you took it the wrong way. You need to grow up. You women are all alike."

I hated the fact he never put detective in front of my name. "Yeah, well," I replied, "consider the miserable source it came from, Most."

"Okay guys cut out the bickering, or just shut the hell up," Manny said. "I agree with Carl though, the creature must've been waiting for something it could attack. The first vehicle coming down the highway would've been fine and dandy. It apparently wanted food, or just simply desired to kill something. Being at night it was probably easy to scare the driver off the road, definitely serving its monstrous purpose."

"Smart sum'bitch," Most murmured, thankfully walking over to a group of three cops, probably just to get away from me.

Mumbling under my breath, 'screw him', I walked over to the car and bent down to glance inside. What a way to die, I thought. Just coming down the mountain, happy after having had a nice time during the day doing whatever they wanted. Probably had consumed a good meal at the ski lodge, maybe a pleasant hike along the trails. Then they end up with such a horrible ending. No different than any of the other deaths I supposed, just very sad and disturbing. I was becoming so damn angry I couldn't stand it.

I stood up, wincing a little at some pain in my lower back, something that had been bothering me now for a few weeks.

"Hey partner, think this damn thing is still around here," I asked, "or is it coming back later for an after dinner snack?" I then realized that remark was as bad as what Most would probably say.

Manny moved up beside me and placed a hand on my shoulder. "You're a weird broad, Amelia. You don't need to answer that because you know it's true. To answer your question I kind of doubt it. There are just too many human guinea pigs running about and it might get hurt again if it came around here with all this firepower. For some reason though I get the odd feeling it isn't far away. Probably maybe even observing us as we speak. It's like when you feel eyes on you from somewhere. How about you?"

"I agree. And don't forget that you're a male chauvinist pig. Do you feel like taking a slow ride up the mountain with this weird broad?"

He chuckled. "We can't do anything here. Plus, there are just too many people standing around doing absolutely nothing. We can pretty much figure out what happened here. Since there's nobody to interview we might as well look around someplace else."

We made it known to the sergeant in charge, Harold 'No-Action' Jackson as we called him, that we were going to take a short ride and that we'd be stopping back. Avoiding Carl Most like the plague because I really didn't need him in the vehicle with us, we jumped into my car and pulled slowly out onto the road. After moving about twenty yards from all the turmoil I put my headlights on high beam and started driving about thirty miles an hour. Manny looked out the right side of the car while I scanned the left, both of us definitely continuing to keep the road surface visible as well. If this damn creature jumped out in front of us then I sure as hell wanted my free hand resting on the butt of my gun for quick release.

It was really dark out now, especially since there were no lights along this stretch of the highway. I had a spotlight on the floor in the backseat which Manny grabbed and plugged into the cigarette lighter. It covered a nice broad area and since I couldn't see anything on the left side of the road I had to leave it up to my partner to notice anything unusual. We drove a few miles, about the point where the highway began its gradual rise up the mountain side. Suddenly, Manny held up his left hand.

"Hold it, slow down," he said, almost in a whisper.

Since I wasn't driving too fast at that point anyway I came to almost a complete stop in seconds. Nervously, I glanced to my left, afraid at any moment this creature's claw was going to rip the door off and yank me out onto the pavement.

"Well damn it, what did you see or hear?" I asked, trying to sound calm and brave, but I know it didn't come out that way.

"I don't know," he replied, still in a hushed voice. "I thought it was a large shadow moving in the direction we're coming from, but I couldn't be sure. I didn't see an actual body, just a large shadow across the light."

"Think we should turn around and go back where it might be safer?"

"Well, unless you want to start up the mountain I suppose so. Can you turn this buggy around right here?"

"Hey, this is a Toyota Rav-4. I can do just about anything. Plus, I didn't just get my driver's license yesterday. You just watch me perform miracles."

Revving the engine a little I swung the wheel as the vehicle spun left, but I quickly had to stop. Since I was unsure how wide the gravel was I braked hard, backed up and spun left again. I didn't want to get stuck in a gully. Guiding the vehicle back onto the lane I gunned it a little faster and we headed to the accident/crime scene.

Manny laughed nervously. "Well, since you just gave me whiplash I'll be going out on disability tomorrow so you can catch this damn thing yourself."

I turned my head slightly and smiled. "No great loss partner, you're really just unnecessary weight around my neck anyway. Like a damn yoke. Besides, I can probably get more accomplished with Vince."

"Oh, so you two are casual enough now that he's on a first name basis. That's nice, really swell. Anything I should know about him and my horny partner?"

"Just keep your sick Mexican mind out of my personal life."

We both laughed as the car moved back down the highway.

Chapter 18

The creature paused about thirty yards from all the loud activity occurring at the crash site. It sensed a number of humans which was a good thing because there would be plenty of unwilling hosts for her anxious and thriving brood. The slow and very ill equipped humans going over the accident scene actually served two purposes. Much needed food to replenish its own strength and a nice supply of additional host bodies for her hatchlings. While remaining in a prone position and scouring the area, the small red blobs squirmed and slid up their mother's legs and body. It would be easier to get them all into the action at one time so it just ignored how anxious they were.

Rising slowly, it crossed the highway just beyond where the glow from the accident scene reached. Nobody noticed the large, shadowy form that went from one side to the other. It decided to move inland about thirty yards and then veered left until it came to a stop behind a high sand mound with several large cactus. Moving its head slowly back and forth it surveyed the area, making sure it knew where each human was.

Without any hesitation it launched the attack, moving in quickly, silently and deadly. It immediately severed the heads of two cops leaning against the tow truck.

The creature moved rapidly. As it did so it was suddenly noticed by other police officers standing about. Guns were raised and shots began ringing out, striking the well armored body of the creature. The bullets were of no consequence, bouncing harmlessly aside. The area itself was no more than a sixty foot radius so the giant lizard stood on hind legs towering over each terrified human. In their most horrifying nightmares they never witnessed such a frightening apparition, especially one that was actually real. This slight moment of fear gave the lizard all the time it needed to kill indiscriminately.

Slashing to the left and right with massive claws that had grown with each transformation it was like an erect lawn mower, savage blades swirling death. Some bodies were cut in half, others cleanly decapitated, while a few lost arms that continued to pull triggers from their useless firearms. Others were stunned by a widely sweeping tail that knocked them unconscious. In all, there were twenty-seven emergency personnel, both police and medical. For the most part they were no threat to the alien.

As human bodies collapsed right and left, the red blobs dropped off the mother's rear part of her torso and quickly squirmed to the closest available host that was not severely damaged. If there was a large enough gash from their mother's claws then they could enter that way, but it was best through the mouth. That was open most of the time as each individual writhed on the ground in pain, screaming from agony, as well as terror. It was also best to gain access to the host when it was still alive. Not totally necessary, but better because if the body stopped breathing then to properly start the heart it had to be accomplished by an electrical charge issued by the entity from inside the body and quickly before the life was too far gone.

In these cases, however, none of that was required as each human host was still breathing. The hatchling would quickly expand once inside the mouth and squirm down the throat into the lungs. The absolute rush of now having a host body was exhilarating to the tiny alien life form so it would quickly take over the heart, central nervous system, and brain. After gagging and retching terribly for about thirty seconds the human host lay totally still. Even though the body remained alive, the actual person was not. If the entity had to switch hosts later then the original body would still be dead and quickly deteriorate.

The entire rampage took no more than three minutes. In all, some sixty bullets had been fired at the horrifying creature, none of which made any serious impact. One of them did, however, strike the alien in the eye causing some initial pain. It quickly began to heal the injured organ and realized that it was a vulnerable spot. So during the next, and possibly last transformation, it would need to repair and enhance that function.

Once the sound of rapid gunfire and screams began to fade away the creature turned and surveyed the battle ground. Twenty of the humans were now moving slowly, new hosts for her eager brood. Six or so other bodies would suffice as food because it needed to feed and quickly. The creature leaned over and grabbed one large body which smelled of grease and grime, obviously the tow truck driver. His name had been Rich when alive. Einstein was the moniker attached to him by his boss and was scribbled in script across the left pocket. The ample gut provided a nice array of juicy organs as the beast split it down the middle. It gorged quickly on the succulent innards and then threw the body aside as nothing more than scrap. Not enough time to nibble on the bones.

At that same moment it heard the squeal of brakes as a vehicle slid to a stop and two doors slammed shut. The immediate concern was whether to face these two new antagonists, or leave while the getting was good. The creature looked around to survey the area. The entire brood had obtained hosts with most of them actively stirring. They would all be fine on their own, learning enough in this short period of life to survive.

None of them would be dispersed to survive alone because they had an inbred connection with the maternal host and would follow her orders as they transformed. For now, it was more important to get away safely, not that it was worried about two more pitiful humans. Rather than leave completely it moved to the edge of the killing ground, blending in completely with the surroundings to appear nearly invisible. That way it could still attack if it felt the brood was in any imminent danger.

Since they had captured humans to be their new host bodies it all looked like each person had survived a nasty battle, nothing more. At least until the first transformation took place, most likely in a few days. Once that happened, the next phase of the plan would begin.

Before we got there, Manny heard the gunshots first. I tromped down hard on the gas pedal as we sped down the road until lights from the emergency vehicles came into view. Sliding to a screeching stop in the gravel we opened our doors and jumped out at the same time. We had our guns out and pointed forward, completely on the alert.

"What the hell is going on?" I questioned in shocked amazement.

"Looks like we might've found the creature, or worse, it found us."

Moving slowly to a small gully we jumped to the other side and knelt. The gunfire had stopped the moment I slammed my foot down on the brakes. Now it was unnervingly quiet. I motioned for Manny to take the right side and I would take the left. As we moved I could see bodies sprawled on the ground, lots of bodies. Some of them stirred, attempting to stand up, while others either moaned, or remained motionless.

Manny saw the body of the tow truck driver lying in a mangled, bloody heap near the front left tire. It was easy to interpret that the creature had made a sudden and deadly appearance. I came upon one dead body, a police officer completely eviscerated. I didn't know his name, but had seen him on several occasions and if memory served he had three young children. The next body was moaning in pain but alive, trying desperately to stand up. He stumbled several times going down to one knee and then stood again, albeit very unsteadily. His name tag said Perkins.

"Hey, are you okay?" I questioned with concern, putting my left hand on the back of the injured cop.

The officer jumped and spun around, his eyes wide and terrified. It was the frightened look of somebody who had absolutely no idea what just happened.

He tried to speak, but it was like something was choking him inside. Coughing and sputtering he suddenly bent over and spit out a torrent of blood. I quickly jumped back, hoping to avoid getting my shoes violated with slop. When the officer was done retching I helped him rise. He now seemed more in control, but definitely still terrified.

"Officer, what the hell happened here?"

His voice came out in a hoarse whisper. "Not sure...detective... this damn monst..." he coughed some more, "monster came...out of no...where. I was hit hard...by something, a tail maybe...at least I think so. Felt like....a two by four."

"Okay, okay, just sit down here and relax. Let me see if anybody else is alive," as I helped him down to the ground.

On the other side of the battle ground Manny had assisted several officers, one male and one female, who were sitting with their heads bowed. I had knelt beside one cop who was slit across the chest and then helped a female ambulance tech. The front of her white shirt was covered in blood, but she didn't look terribly injured. I figured she had thrown up like the first one I assisted. In fact, come to think of it as I looked around all the cops standing or sitting had vomited, or were in the midst of doing so. It was kind of sickening actually, especially since I had a weak spot when that happened. Funny how I could look at blood and gore at a crime scene, but throw up around me and I would just about lose it. I used to hate when my cats threw up those damn hairballs.

Moving forward slowly, I kept my eyes quickly switching from the ground and then straight ahead. Looking downward I came to a sudden stop. I just stared and wasn't sure how I actually felt right then. It definitely appeared that Detective Carl Most would not be reaching retirement. His body was literally torn in half above the waist. An actual gap of about a foot separated the top from the bottom, only shreds of flesh connecting both halves. As much as I had disliked him, those feelings mostly resulted because he constantly displayed such a low esteem for women cops, something I could never fully understand. However that being said, it was no way for anybody to die. I knew that he had four grown children and a wonderful wife, Cynthia, who I had met during the past Christmas party. All at once I actually despised myself for not liking him that much and made it a point to not have feelings like that for anybody else. Life is too damn short.

Moving forward I had to wipe away a tear which suddenly began trickling down my cheek. Damn it, quit being an emotional female detective, I thought to myself.

Suddenly I stopped and turned. There had been a discernible movement, like a rippling of air to my right. I motioned for Manny to stop and pointed toward a high mound with several large cactus. Holding my gun in both hands I crouched and started moving forward slowly. Then the air rippled again so I took direct aim and fired point blank. The sound of the gunshot exploded in the night air, startling in that only the occasional moan or retching noise from more and more police officers could be heard.

Manny saw where I had shot and fired as well even though there was not a visible target. A loud hissing sound erupted and the rippling air became more solidified, but still not a physical body. One of the cactus was pushed over while dirt erupted from the mound, as if something large seemed to be moving away from us even though we couldn't clearly see it. I ran toward the commotion and fired several more times.

There was a loud growling sound and before I knew it I was hurtling through the air after being struck on the right side by something hard, but invisible. Landing with a severe jolt on the open ground I rolled several times gasping for air. Surprisingly, I still held onto my gun. Completely dazed I didn't know if the form rippling in my vision was simply my imagination, or the damn alien. Trying to rise I winced in serious pain, as if my left shoulder was caught in a vice. Shit, this was all I needed. To get injured and not be able to continue looking for this creature. I would be really pissed off then.

Strong hands held me down as I gazed up into the wavering face of my partner.

"Stay down Amy, you might've broken something. I'll get one of the EMT techs to take a look at you."

I pushed his hands away. "Not on your life buddy. I got stunned by something, not sure what or where it came from. Did you happen to see what it was?"

"Nope, one minute you were firing and moving forward, the next you were flying through the air. Ever think of trying out for the circus?"

"Yeah, very funny partner. You make a better cop than a comedian. It had to have been that damn creature. All I saw was the air rippling in front of me. Did you see it?" my voice rising hysterically.

"Settle down. Yes, I saw the air shimmering and I do think it was that creature, but not sure how it pulled off that trick. It's like a damn chameleon. Not only is the body armored to protect it from our bullets, now we can't even see the bastard either when we need to. How the hell can we fight this freaking thing?"

I was now barely on my feet. With my left shoulder aching like hell I was somewhat grateful that at least I could move it so I didn't think it was broken. However, I would be willing to bet that in the morning it would hurt like the dickens and be stiff as a board. Looking around I saw at least twenty of the emergency personnel, cops and EMT, those that weren't torn apart moving around albeit very slowly. It was like they were totally in a daze, almost zombie-like. Maybe we had the walking dead right here.

"We'd better call this attack into Chief Crosson," I said. "Maybe get Flint and his team out here. I also think these police and emergency technicians need to be relieved. They look okay physically, but something's not right, like they're totally in shock."

"Come on, I'll help you to the car so you can sit and relax," Manny told me, holding on my right arm tightly so I wouldn't fall. "Sure as hell we definitely need help out here."

On a small hill about fifty yards away the creature lowered itself to the ground and rested. It observed the man and woman who had fired their weapons as they headed for their vehicle. Even though it didn't totally understand the human language as of yet, it somehow determined that the names sounded like Man'e for the male, and Ami' for the female who limped heavily from being struck by its tail. She would be a good adversary the creature pondered. It definitely looked forward to further confrontations which would be fairly one-sided, or so it thought. There was also something interesting about her.

The twenty host bodies were all up and moving around. Already there were electrical impulses being transmitted back to the mother. It would stay close for a little while longer, but it really didn't need to know where each one went individually after they left this site. For the next forty-eight hours they would need to transform their human hosts and prepare them for the upcoming battle when called to action.

Chapter 19

I slept for nearly ten hours after being admitted to the hospital and having my injuries tended to. The left shoulder was apparently dislocated and I had one really nasty, ugly looking purplish/black bruise on my right thigh. I wouldn't be wearing a bikini anytime soon. However, at least I was hurting on both sides of my body to make it all equal. I was now just one big pain in the ass like Manny always told me that I was.

Moving slightly on the bed I moaned loudly, sharp pain waking me completely. I started rummaging around for the remote gizmo that controlled the TV and bed because I wanted to sit up a little. When I glanced over to my left I broke into a big smile. The sweetest, most caring and thoughtful partner in the whole wide world had been asleep in a very uncomfortable chair beside the bed. He stirred and then stood up, stretching and moaning like it was the worst nap he had ever taken. Maybe it was, but he cared!

"Hey Amy girl, how're you feeling?" he inquired, continuing to stretch the kinks out of his handsome, angular body. "Man these hospital chairs really suck."

"The beds are not much better, believe me. Did you happen to catch the crazy truck driver that hit me? It had to have been a huge semi."

He laughed, rubbing sleep from his eyes. "Well, apparently that crazy, rotten semi-extraterrestrial didn't want to stay around long enough to be questioned. I guess it can be charged with *'alien leaving the scene of an accident'* if we ever catch it. That lizard's tail whacked you so hard you must've flew nearly twenty feet in the air. Thought I lost you right about then partner."

"Huh, it'll take more than being slammed by the tail of giant lizard to stop this girl. Any water around this joint? I'm really dying of thirst. My lips are so dry."

"No, I think they're still monitoring you for a possible concussion. I'll check to see if you can sip something though. Maybe swab your mouth and lips with water."

"Doesn't really matter anyway because I'm not staying in this place. Where are my clothes so I can get outta' here?"

"Whoa, you're not leaving until the doctor releases you. Just get that idea out of your stubborn little head. Don't be a pain in the ass patient. You were hurt pretty good."

"Screw that Manny, I can walk and I sure as heck don't have any concussion," I shot back, throwing off the blanket and trying to swing my feet over the side of the bed.

"Ouch, goddamn it. Man that hurts," I groaned loudly, but not giving up until I sat precariously on the edge of the mattress. I let my feet dangle above the floor.

"Amelia Stephenson, have you been like this since you were a little girl?"

"Yes, my mother always told me I'd pester the crap out of some man one day and right now that's you, partner. So just be a good little boy and get my clothes. Or, do I have to find them myself? Can you please help out a weak little girl here?"

He stood with both hands on his hips, angrily glowering at me. "As I've stated many times, you are one big pain in the ass. You know that, right?"

"Yeah, yeah, of course I know it. You can say that as much as you want," trying to move my frozen shoulder. "Look partner, we don't have any time to fart around. If I couldn't walk at all then I'd have no problem lying here, even though it would upset me. I know for a fact you wouldn't be staying here either, so if it's good enough for you then it's the same for me. I owe that monster an ass whipping when we finally catch it."

He was chuckling as the doctor came through the doorway.

"Hey Detective Stephenson, what in the world do you think you're doing? That shoulder is not in good shape and we still don't know how badly you hurt your head since we had to put a few stitches across the front. You need to rest and recover completely."

"What?" I asked in shocked surprise, moving my hand up to touch my forehead.

Sliding my fingers higher I felt stitches sticking out going across my scalp just about where the hairline should've been. I stress 'should've been' because apparently they also shaved some of my hair off as well. It had felt numb, but I just didn't think anything about it. Now I find out that I'd been all stitched up.

"What in the hell did you do to me Doc, scalp me?" I shouted loudly in shock. "I must look like the bride of Frankenstein. Manny, help me over to a mirror so I can see."

I started to stand and sat down right away, suddenly more than a little bit woozy.

The doctor moved to the other side and between them they supported me enough to stand so I could get my sea legs underneath me. I grimaced in pain as Manny pulled a tad too high underneath my left arm.

"Sorry partner, I didn't mean to hurt you like that," he murmured.

"Yeah sure, you're probably having the time of your life. Quit being a mother hen and let me see how ugly I look now after some doctor disfigured me."

To say the least I was totally stunned. The emergency room butchers (*well, doctors really*) had shaved my hair in an arc, like half a salad bowl shape. Straight across my skull was this ugly looking strip of stitches and dried blood. I groaned loudly because for sure no man would ever want me now I thought, least of all Flint.

"Oh man, this just gets worse by the minute. Let me sit down before I faint," as they guided me back to the bed where I appropriately fell back onto the mattress.

A nurse, hopefully not named Ratchet, had just entered the room since apparently Doctor Gonzalez pressed the help button. Once lying prone on the bed, my head now spinning as it rested back against the pillow, the nurse pulled the sheet and blanket up to my chin. I actually let loose a few tears which was then accompanied by a loud moan.

"So tell me the truth, Doc. When can I get out of here and I mean the bare minimum?" I asked.

"Three or four days at the least Detective Stephenson and that would be barring any surgery you might need on that shoulder."

I shook my head and then stopped immediately as the room started spinning which actually made me a little nauseous. "Nope, no way Jose. I'm leaving here tomorrow. So give me pain pills, wrap the shoulder, whatever you need to do Doctor Gonzalez, but I'm outta' here after tonight even if I have to dress myself and stagger through the doors. Your call, but it would be easier with your help. If I need surgery then it can wait until we catch the monster we're looking for."

He smiled. "That's funny detective since Jose is my middle name. Obviously from a medical standpoint you need to rest that shoulder and I would highly recommend a stint on disability even if we don't need to operate. But seeing as how you're going to be a difficult patient I don't see why you can't leave tomorrow. It will definitely be against my better judgment and I'll write that on the discharge orders. We'll put the shoulder and arm in a sling, but something tells me that you won't leave it there very long, or even be careful with it."

I smiled back. "I promise I'll be a good girl and do everything you tell me to do."

Laughing, he started walking out the door, stopped and turned. "Eat a good meal tonight and get lots of sleep. In fact, I think we may just aid you in doing exactly that. Tomorrow you'll be discharged, but don't start bugging me too early since I have lots of sick patients in this fine hospital who actually want to get better and need my help. Got that, Detective Stephenson?"

Saluting with my good arm, I smiled. "You're the boss, Doc. I'll be up early."

"Women and detectives, not a good combination," he mumbled, shaking his head as he left the room.

Manny looked at me as I grinned back. "See? A little female persuasion goes along way, don't you think? You should try it sometime."

"You're a really messed up person, Amelia Stephenson," as he looked at his watch. "I'm going home to take a long hot shower, eat a decent meal, sleep with my beautiful wife, and hopefully not have nightmares about this damn creature we're after. Follow orders tonight for once in your life. I'll check with you in the morning and be here when you get freed. And do not sneak out of here without me, got that partner?"

He bent down and kissed me on the cheek. Sometimes he would give me a peck on the forehead, but not today since I definitely felt un-kissable. As he walked out the nurse changed the bag of goodies connected to my IV and also made me swallow a few pills. She asked me to open my mouth to make sure they went down. Damn medical personnel just wouldn't believe that I could be a good girl. This somewhat tall, but attractive nurse, was like the secret hospital police making absolutely certain that I followed orders. She didn't know that I rarely followed them. Hell, aren't they meant to be bent just a little bit anyway?

Dinner came shortly thereafter. It wasn't too bad for hospital chow, but not all that great either. It was something resembling meatloaf, but I wasn't totally sure. The mashed potatoes were barely warm and the green beans definitely cold. I toyed with all three and suddenly found that I had created what somewhat resembled a lizard in the mashed potatoes. I cracked a thin grin thinking of when Richard Dreyfus had a *'close encounters moment'* at the dinner table. Smashing it all angrily with my fork I felt right at that moment they had better shoot me up pretty good if I was going to sleep nightmare free. Damn, you know how much I hate lizards and snakes, but the monstrous ones are even more frightening. I would try to dream of Vince, if he still wanted me that is.

Police officer Robert Perkins had been glad to get home in one piece. He truly had no idea why he was still alive, especially since at least six were killed at the accident scene. He had some bruising on his back and right hip, along with a few cuts that seemed to be healing pretty quickly. After hugging his wife tightly he took a long, hot shower, pulled on a Cardinals tee shirt and jeans, then reached for a can of beer sitting on the closed toilet seat. His wife Jeannie had fixed his favorite dinner of chicken quesadilla with black beans and rice. It was funny because he felt like he had an appetite, but when he tried to eat after a few bites he felt very nauseous. Not wanting to upset his wife he ate more than half and then begged off, telling her that he was just extremely tired and needed to lie down. Instead he headed straight to the bathroom and vomited up the vilest, thickest black crap he had ever seen. A violent spasm threw him to his knees as well.

That was nearly seven hours ago. Now the clock by the bed harshly glared two forty-five a.m. in large, gaudy white numbers. He had turned the air conditioner off after going into the bedroom because he felt chilled as well. Locating another blanket from the closet he finally fell asleep curled up in nearly a fetal position on the floor.

Now that he was wide awake he was extremely cold even though the chill felt more from inside than out, like his body temperature was changing drastically. He glanced over at his beautiful wife Jeannie and saw that she was sound asleep. Not wanting to wake her up he slid out of bed as soundlessly as he could.

Trying ineptly to put his slippers on, he moved quickly to the bathroom and eased the door shut before turning on the light. The sudden brightness was harsh and hurt his eyes. He didn't know why, but he was about to throw up once again which is exactly what he did. He was bent over the toilet for close to fifteen minutes, most of the time with his eyes shut. Completely exhausted he found it hard to believe that the noise from his retching did not wake his wife or kids. But no knock came on the other side of the door which he was thankful for.

Opening his eyes wider he was quite startled to see the water in the toilet completely red with globs of gelatinous crap floating upon the top. Some of it was chicken quesadilla and beans. But, he truly had no idea what the additional stuff was other than it erupted from inside him. He moaned and needed something to drink, preferably water since his mouth tasted like a waste dump.

Rising slowly he staggered a few steps to the sink, turned on the cold water, splashed some on his hot face, and then cupped his hands. He sipped for several minutes until his thirst was somewhat quenched.

Backing up he flushed the toilet, lowered the seat and sat down pulling the trash can over in front of him just in case round two commenced. He felt really dizzy, but thought it was more from over sensory activation. The water dripping in the sink sounded like a single bongo drum pounding away. He saw a thousand-legger crawling up the wall beside him and suddenly got hungry. He could literally see every tiny little hair and leg sprouting from the insect's body. Quickly he reached out and stuck it between his teeth, biting down as he felt the soft squish of flesh and some vile-tasting fluid. He shuddered over what he had just done, but it also felt somehow natural. He had tried chocolate covered ants one time. It just wasn't the same thing now.

Not only could he still smell the lingering blood odor from the toilet, he also detected the sweet, intoxicating aroma of his wife from the other room. Shaking his head back and forth as if to clear cobwebs, he held up his hand and was completely startled. The skin upon the back of his hand and forearm was now covered with square scales about an inch across, overlapping each other. His fingers appeared to be elongated and narrow, bent like claws with nails much longer than they had ever been. The scaling went up each arm so he held the tee shirt away from his chest. Not surprisingly, the scales were on his chest as well. Totally shocked he realized that something was terribly wrong. He thought maybe this was all just a bad dream and prayed he was still asleep.

Rising, he dropped his jeans and almost fainted. The scaling went from his feet up both legs to his crotch area. He quickly sat back on the toilet seat and started shaking violently. Thinking he was about to throw up he stood, spun around and lifted the seat. He hovered for several minutes and realized that there was probably nothing more in his stomach to come out. Inside, his body felt totally different. Like he had been eaten away and renovated, restructured, transformed. It was crazy he thought, but he felt completely different, totally alien to how his life normally was as a human being.

He had no idea that this very same scenario was happening in nineteen other households throughout Tucson. Fellow cops and emergency personnel who had been out at the crime scene were all feeling the same effects that he was. All of them had been sick in the bathroom, or wherever they ended up being violently ill. Each one was experiencing the same terrifying thoughts and reactions. They didn't know it right then, but they were united in a horrifying plot, a nightmarish jigsaw puzzle that was about to come together very soon in a monstrous crescendo.

One other thing they all now had in common was a ravenous hunger and not for items in the fridge or pantry, either. Perkins stood, feeling extremely strong and walked over to the mirror above the sink even though he was now somewhat bent forward at the waist. Walking wasn't really the word to use, it was more like shuffling. He glanced down and saw that one slipper was barely hanging onto the right foot while the left had come free. Both feet were now elongated, resembling that of a wild animal.

When he glanced in the mirror he saw that his eyes were nearly green. Opening his mouth unveiled somewhat human teeth, but now much longer and sharper. He was then startled by something flickering out between his gums and realized it was his tongue, also long but jet black. Staggering backwards his back found the other wall as his chest heaved in and out. He felt like weeping, but whatever had happened to him would not allow such a weak, human emotion. In fact, very few human traits remained.

The driving hunger continued so he shoved himself away from the wall and moved to the bathroom door which he opened, not even thinking to shut off the light. Moving into the bedroom he pointed himself toward the bed. The bright light from the bathroom fell across the blanket and Jeannie's beautiful face. The glare caused her to open her eyes, squinting while lifting her left arm to block out the harsh light.

"Honey, what's wrong? You're just standing there looking at me so strangely. Do you feel okay sweetheart? Did you turn the air conditioner off? It's warm in here."

There was no answer from him other than just a heavy, animalistic breathing, accompanied by a soft hiss that came from deep inside his throat.

"Robert, you're beginning to scare me. Why don't you turn off the bathroom light and come back to bed. You've had quite a day sweetheart," she said, patting his side of the mattress. "Come on honey just let me hold you tight. I think you really need to rest. You didn't eat much for dinner tonight so you're probably hungry."

In a growl that even startled himself he responded menacingly, "Yeah, I'm really hungry. You have no idea how bad a day I've had. But my dear loving wife you're about to find out."

At least that's what his mind heard. Rather it came out as a low, throaty growl that was an ominous threat uttered, not sounding like human speech in any shape or form. He then lunged onto the bed and covered his wife's body. By this time his claws and teeth had emerged to even longer and more deadly lengths. Jeannie was so stunned she had been unable to scream, but that was a moot point since her neck was cleanly slit open. All that remained now was the terror bulging from her eyes amid a silent scream, especially now knowing the man she had loved was gone forever. She had no idea who the monster was that now desecrated her body other than it no longer resembled her loving and adorable husband, Robert. It looked like a cross between a man and lizard.

His hunger was ravenous. He fed greedily, having no idea why he was devouring the woman who had loved him terribly for over twelve years. Simply put, Officer Robert Perkins was no longer the person he had previously been. Nor would he ever know that feeling again. When he was done gorging on his wife then the children were sleeping soundly right down the hall. He would continue his meal because he was damn hungry. There was only one thing it needed to do now. Feed and become stronger for when he received the message from the mother.

Throughout nineteen other households within the City of Tucson his fellow officers and EMT responders were no longer what they had been less than forty-eight hours prior. With unexplained gusto they fed as well on whatever, or whoever, was unlucky enough to be available. Obviously loved ones were the easiest and closest meals. This feeding frenzy was simply vital for their next transformation. Robert Perkins and all the others really could not be held accountable for these horrifying actions because in reality they were all virtually dead. Their bodies were no longer their own, even though some lingering thought patterns remained. In effect, they were simply horrifying puppets now. What resided within their bodies was monstrous and alien, bent only now on destructive domination.

Chapter 20

I was anxiously wide awake long before breakfast was delivered, nothing more than runny eggs, burnt bacon, cold toast, tepid water for tea, and some type of gruel-like cereal that I wouldn't feed to my dog if I had one. I was completely dressed thanks to clean clothes Manny had brought back for me right before visiting hours were over. So I just waited, very impatiently I might add, until Manny finally strolled nonchalantly into the room. Like he didn't have a care in the world.

"Where have you been?" I exclaimed harshly. "This place is driving me crazy. Nobody tells you the truth around here. Doctor says the nurse will be in to sign me out. Then all the nurses say is that the quack still has to write up the release orders. Well, they didn't really say that. I'm just upset that I'm still stuck here."

I rose from my very uncomfortable bed much too quickly and got slightly dizzy, putting my hand on the mattress for support. Manny moved quickly to help steady me.

"Amy, this is absolutely insane. You won't be much help to me in the condition you're in. I'll be so worried about you that this creature will probably devour me, you, and anybody else stupid enough to be with us."

I grinned and pushed him away. "Don't worry partner, you're way too tough and stringy. It would most likely spit you out. Besides, it might not like Mexican food. Let's just get out of here," I shot back, grabbing my purse and slinging it over my good shoulder. "We have some monstrous, lizard-like, alien something or other creature out there that I don't think some normal mouse trap is going to be helpful in catching it."

"Well, I might be tough and stringy," Manny shot back at me, "but you're actually so spoiled rotten it would undoubtedly spit you out, or it might die from contacting food poisoning."

I couldn't stop laughing as I shuffled somewhat slowly down the hall, right hand hugging the railing on the right wall for support. Behind me a nurse called out for me to stop. Hah, no way I was doing that. She had her chance earlier.

"Miss Stephenson, you need to wait for transport so they can wheel you down to the front entrance. You can't just leave on your own like this. I have your release forms here to sign anyway. Plus a few prescriptions from Doctor Gonzalez."

Shaking my head I just kept walking as I mumbled *"watch me"*. I was not about to waste another half hour in this place for somebody to do something I could do myself. However, just then the good doctor appeared ahead of me from around the corner of the next hallway. He grabbed an empty wheelchair and used it to block my path.

"Sit down Detective Stephenson, its hospital rules. You're not about to fall and then sue us for negligence. If this stubborn streak of yours won't allow you to wait for a hospital employee to provide transport then your partner here can push you out. But detective, you will sit on this wheelchair, or I'll happily tear up those discharge papers in the nurse's hand. Then you'll very quickly find yourself back in a hospital bed, held down by restraints I might add."

In a huff I growled, turned around and dropped roughly into the wheelchair. Shaking my head angrily I held my arms out towards Manny, basically saying, *'Well, what are you waiting for?'*

The doctor glanced at my partner and shook his head, an angry and concerned look on his face. "Is she always this stubborn?"

"You have no idea, Doctor Gonzalez. The only reason she's partnered with me is nobody else will work with her because she's such a royal pain in the ass."

"Hah, that's a laugh," I exclaimed. "Our captain at the time teamed me up with you because he knew you couldn't figure your way out of a paper bag, or even a taco shell."

As Manny started turning me around the doctor remained standing directly in my path. "The nurse also told me that you would not take the medicine I ordered for you upon release. You will take that before leaving this facility, or as previously stated I will tear up the discharge forms and you will stay right here as our guest."

"What the heck is this? I'm not in prison you know so I can do anything I want," I responded angrily.

"Not really. Let's just say that I'm your warden and you're being released into the capable hands of Detective Corroda for the next twenty-four hours. The one prescription is for pain and the other will make you sleep. You are being released only to go home and rest until tomorrow. After that you can do just about anything you want. Hopefully you won't be returning to this hospital and if you do then not as my patient. I would rather spend my time healing those people who actually want to get better."

"No way doctor, I am not taking anything to make me sleep. Don't you realize we have a killer out there on the streets of Tucson? I can't do that if I'm flat on my back sawing logs. I'm not even really in that much pain. It just hurts when I move."

Doctor Gonzalez crossed his arms and stared down at me, shaking his head.

THE REPTILIAN FACTOR

"Right at this moment detective you're not capable of helping anybody, let alone yourself and Detective Corroda. That shoulder is not in good shape at all and you suffered what could easily be termed a slight concussion. All you will do is put your partner in danger, along with anybody else nearby. Now quit whining like a darn little baby and take those pills, or believe me you're heading back to the room you just exited. So do it now! It's your call. You're a big girl so make up your mind."

I let loose a sound that was a cross between a growl and a scream. Yanking the glass of water from the nurse's hand I reached for the pills, popped them both in my mouth and swallowed. Of course, I was now also soaked since water from the glass spilled all over my top and slacks in anger.

He leaned down. "Open up wide, let me take a look."

"What, you don't believe I swallowed them? I'm not some baby you know."

"That's highly debatable," he replied. "Now open up or you don't leave this hospital."

If looks could kill the doctor would've dropped to the tiled floor right then. I opened my mouth and stuck out my tongue directly at him. He smiled after opening my mouth with his gloved fingers and then moved aside.

"Nice to have you visit us here at this wonderful hospital, Detective Stephenson. Stay safe so we don't see you back here. Yet, somehow I think we should just keep your bed warm."

I decided the best action was to just keep my mouth shut in case I said anything that would further harm my chances of release. As Manny pushed me down the hall towards the elevator it was like going through a gauntlet of stares, both patient and hospital personnel gawking at me. I have to admit that I was a little embarrassed in how much I was acting like a child, but I just wanted freaking out of the place.

A lot good it did me though because by the time Manny got me to my house I was so darn drowsy that he literally had to carry me inside and straight back to the bedroom. Deciding not to have me get undressed and put on pajamas, he simply turned down the bed, slid my shoes off and then eased me onto the mattress. After covering me he kissed me lightly on my cheek. I wasn't totally asleep yet so I patted the mattress beside me.

"Mmmmm, that was nice," I mumbled, "Come on partner, keep me company. I would love to feel the presence of such a big, strong, hunky man like you with his arms around my lonely and tortured body in a protective embrace. Pretty please? Your wife won't mind, I'm sure. She knows that I'm harmless."

He laughed. "Oh Amy, there's absolutely nothing wrong with your slutty mind. A concussion couldn't even bother you. It's still as filthy dirty as ever. Just sleep tight and we'll hit the streets tomorrow. I'm going to stay until Flint gets here. I don't trust you being alone."

However, I barely heard half of what he said. I was already searching for some diabolical monster out in the desert, albeit in my nightmarish dreams. Either way, reality or dream state, I vowed that it would die in the end. If not, then we were all in for a world of shit.

Chapter 21

When I woke up it was very dark. The thought crossed my mind, *'maybe I'm really dead'*. I laid there for a few minutes to see what might happen next. The deathly silence was soon broken by what sounded like a low growling noise so I figured that I was, in fact, either lost in the dark depths of Hell, or there was possibly a large animal prowling around my house. Maybe searching for a sweet detective as its next meal.

I slowly reached out towards where the nightstand should've been until I touched the clock. My shoulder hurt, but was somewhat bearable because I was tough. Turning it slowly I saw the big green numbers displaying 3:58 a.m. So unless the afterlife had alarm clocks I figured that I was still somewhat alive, albeit very groggy and hurting like hell. Still, that low rumbling growl persisted from somewhere outside the bedroom.

Rolling over onto my left side the pain shot through my shoulder and upper arm. Trying my best not to scream loudly and alert whatever predator seemed to be roaming the house I put my face in the pillow and moaned. Then I tried sitting up slower and held my left arm as securely as possible with the right. I suddenly remembered what the pain was from and the thought hit me, *'you are not going to be worth a shit out on the street'*.

Still, I was a cop and the rumbling growl continued. I stood and balanced myself until I felt somewhat oriented which wasn't saying too much. Quietly as possible I slid open the top drawer in the nightstand and reached for my Glock 41 Gen 4. After quickly checking to make sure it contained a full clip I turned slowly and began taking baby steps towards the bedroom door. Well, I was really shuffling more than actually walking.

I felt like it took me an hour to reach the doorway, but in reality it was only about a minute. Apparently I was a fast shuffler. I think the pain in my left shoulder and the dizziness inside my head didn't help with the disorientation. Sliding through the open doorway the rumbling growl started to get somewhat louder. I remembered Manny dropping me off at the house after leaving the hospital so all I could think of was maybe he had left the back door open and a wayward coyote wondered inside thinking it would make a nice cozy den. Wait a minute though, could it possibly be that damn alien?

Reaching the end of the hallway the living room was dark other than a little light from what the early morning moon was still casting onto the street and coming through the front window. The rumbling was much louder now so I figured whatever animal it might be, it was definitely large. I continued to shuffle against the wall until I bumped up against the table where I threw my mail and car keys upon arriving home each day. The room's light switch was on the wall just above the table. To my left, what else.

Holding the gun out with my right arm as firmly as possible I reached towards the switch with my left even though it really, really hurt. Suddenly flicking the switch up I moved my left arm forward to grab my right hand. The pain shot through my shoulder like a steel blade, but I was a tough cop so I did what needed to be done.

The room suddenly became very bright. That was then accompanied by a loud shout of surprise.

"What the hell?" Vince Flint yelled out loudly as he fell off the couch onto the floor with a thud.

"Just stay right there and don't move," I hollered back.

Vince rolled over and glared up at me. "What the hell are you doing, Amy?"

"What the hell are you doing in my house sounding like a goddamn animal?" I yelled back, totally confused as to why I was screaming in the middle of the night.

He put his head down on his folded arms while groaning loudly and then started to slowly crawl back up until he sat back on the couch.

"Amy, please put that damn gun away in case it goes off accidentally. I took over nursing duties from Manny so somebody would be here while you slept. I didn't think it was going to be that dangerous of a mission. What time is it anyway?"

Lowering the gun and placing it on the table I leaned back against the wall.

"Must be a little after 4:00 a.m. You could've told me you were here you know."

"Amy, the point was you were supposed to sleep so why would I wake you? It got late and I basically got sleepy. Since I didn't think that I was in much danger, especially of being shot as an intruder, I decided to get a few hours of rest."

I slowly pushed away from the wall and began slowly shuffling my feet towards the kitchen. Damn men I thought, they're always screwing with my life.

"Well, I'm sorry I scared you, but I woke up and didn't understand what the noise was. Sounded like a damn wild animal and here it was only just you snoring like one."

"I don't snore, Amy," was his annoyed rebuttal.

"Hah, I'll record it next time. Maybe you can use it on one of your missions to scare the enemy. Anyway, I really need some coffee and maybe a pain pill or two."

I started stumbling to my left before two strong arms grabbed hold of me. Then Vince guided me towards the same couch that he had just fallen from.

"Please sit here or lie back. I'll make a pot of coffee. Where's your medicine?" he asked over his shoulder with a frustrated voice.

I eased back into the couch to clear my head which was at this point seeming to spin out of control. "The pills are on the kitchen counter I believe. The big ones are for pain even though I shouldn't take one. Damn, I really need it though."

"You should've stayed in the hospital like the doctor wanted you too. But since you're so stubborn that was never going to happen."

"Do me a favor, Mr. Flint. Shut up and start the coffee brewing, or just get the hell out of my house. I'm getting tired of people telling me what I can and cannot do."

Five minutes later he came back and I was half dozing. Vince held out my hand and plopped a pain pill in my palm. I took the glass of water and washed it down.

"Coffee should be done in a few minutes. Do you think you can eat anything?"

I started shaking my head just a little too fast and moaned slightly.

"Not yet. Hopefully the caffeine will pick me up a little bit. Maybe then I can eat something light. Vince, I'm sorry for scaring you and thanks for being here."

He knelt down in front of me and took my right hand which he brought to his mouth and kissed it just like a true gentleman, albeit a very rugged and handsome one.

"No problem, I wasn't doing anything anyway. Things have been somewhat quiet the last few days."

I looked at him with more than a questioning glance. "A few days? How long have I been out of it?"

"Well let's see, you got hurt Tuesday night, admitted to the hospital and then released Thursday morning around ten. Manny stayed until I got here around three in the afternoon. You were asleep when I arrived and it's now Friday morning about 4:20 a.m. So I guess you slept for around eighteen hours, but you really needed it."

"Wow, so almost three full days have gone by since we fought that damn creature. Have you been out there looking for it at all?"

He stood up and then sat beside me, all the time holding my hand. "We went out on Wednesday for about twelve hours. I was also advised that the air force dispatched four new teams on the ground, commando-types, plus a few more helicopters. I haven't heard anything as of yet. I had been planning on going back out to a different location Thursday afternoon. However, Manny called and I changed my plans to come here. Prudot and Tiny Tim went out, but I haven't heard from them yet either."

I squeezed his hand. "I'm sorry for being such a big bother and grade one pain in the ass. I would've been okay on my own, but thanks for being here. It means a lot."

He leaned over and kissed me. "Well, if I wasn't here then you most likely would be lying on the floor after getting dizzy when you woke up. But hey, you would've done the same for me, right?"

I hesitated slightly to see what reaction I would get. None came so I laughed.

"Yes, I would've been there for you. Hey, think that *cawfe'* is done?"

Rising he held my hands and helped me while I moaned.

"Sorry, where does it hurt?" Vince asked.

"Everywhere at this point, but mostly the left shoulder. Apparently, it was dislocated pretty badly when I was knocked for a loop by that lizard tail. My head is pretty messed up, too," as I reached up to my forehead. "Oh no, I forgot. I must look like a creature myself with these damn stitches. You probably think I'm so ugly now."

"Not at all. I admit it's a different look, but I wouldn't worry. I'm sure the hair will grow back. Actually it is kind of sexy in that Elsa Lanchester sort of way."

I punched his arm with my good hand. "You're impossible and I know that I'm anything but sexy at this point. I need to wear a hat when we go out later today."

Vince pulled out a kitchen chair and helped me to slowly sit down. Not saying a word he just walked over to the coffee pot, grabbed a few mugs from the cabinet, and then returned to the table. Still without saying anything he got the milk from the fridge and the sugar bowl from the counter. For the next few minutes it was fairly silent with the only noise being the spoon stirring my coffee.

I broke the silence. "What are you thinking inside that handsome head of yours?"

He coughed loudly, took a long sip of his coffee, and then sighed.

"That's good coffee if I do say so myself. Listen Amy, I know you really want to go out and help us search for this creature, but honestly babe you are absolutely in no shape to go anywhere. In fact, you should be back in the hospital. I'm not going to argue that point with you though. For now you're here and this is where you need to stay, at least for another day or so. You have to see that you'll be no help out there in this condition. We are going to worry more about you than about our own asses. If you need help getting from the couch to the kitchen then what the heck are you going to do out in the desert? We can't take a walker with us for you to use."

I kept my head lowered, watching the steam rise from my mug.

"You're absolutely right, I know that. I'm just being really stubborn as usual. But, if this were you then you'd probably be out there right now. It's just because I'm a woman that you're all being cautious."

He laughed and shook his head. "My God, you are one screwed up chick. Quite frankly Amy, if I was hurt as badly as you seem to be then I'd probably still be lying in a hospital bed being tended to by all the cute nurses. Hey, have I been on missions when I was hurt badly? You bet your sweet little ass and we can compare scars sometime. But, I was in the field and needed to get free and clear of danger before I could get medical attention. I once was in a hospital healing for two weeks even though the mission I had been on was not totally completed. I knew that while I healed I also had very good and capable people still pursuing our objective. That's what you have to begin seeing clearly, Amy. I know that you're not going to go back to the hospital, but you need to rest that shoulder and get your head straight before you go out with us again. In this condition you're not only a danger to yourself, you'll put everybody at risk."

I remained quiet through his entire speech and clearly knew he was absolutely correct. I raised the mug to my mouth and finished it off, then wiped my lips.

"I'm really hungry. Are there any eggs left in the fridge that aren't rotten?" I asked in a somewhat meek voice, especially for me.

Vince stared for a few second before standing and taking a few steps to the refrigerator. Looking inside he grabbed a carton of eggs missing only four, and saw an open package of bacon which he took out as well. Inside the cold cuts drawer he took out some cheese and then grabbed the tub of butter.

"I make a mean bacon and cheese omelet. Want more coffee?"

I smiled rather sheepishly. "Yes please. And Vince, I know you're right so I'm not going to give you all anymore problems, at least for the moment anyway. It was all I could do just to hold the gun out in front of me and I just wanted to collapse the entire time. So let me just have more coffee, eat a good breakfast, and then head back to bed."

"Manny said you were smart. Rest up, take the meds, and we'll keep you informed. When you're ready I know you'll be right out in front of the line. Now let me get this omelet started. Do you want toast if the bread isn't moldy?"

Smiling I nodded. "Yes please. Will you stay with me until I fall asleep?"

"Amelia, I'll stay with you just as long as you need me to. Now shut up, drink your coffee, and get ready to eat the most fabulous omelet of your life."

Chapter 22

The all black van stopped in front of the Headquarters Building for the 355th Fighter Wing, assigned to the Twelfth Air Force, part of Air Combat Command (ACC) at Davis-Monthan Air Force Base. The sprawling base lies five miles south-southeast of downtown Tucson, and is one of the two largest employers in the city with the other one being the University of Arizona. It was originally activated in 1924 as Davis-Monthan Landing Field where Charles Lindbergh actually conducted the official base opening ceremonies. The airfield was named after two local aviators who died in separate accidents, 1st Lt. Samuel Davis, and 2nd Lt. Oscar Monthan. The 355th is comprised of six different squadrons. The base is also known as the famous '*aircraft boneyard*', the largest in the world, containing older retired aircraft going back to World War II.

The driver's side door opened. A tall and trim, but obviously well-built, good looking young man climbed out. He wore a well-tailored black suit, white shirt, relatively thin black tie, and sported a very black pair of sunglasses. Oh, and he also did not wear a hat which obviously did not make him a chauffeur. His hair was cut very short, almost in a crew cut style. Sort of military, but not completely. He left the door open and reached for the door handle on the left passenger side.

Once the door was open he kind of stood at attention, stiffly erect nonetheless. The most notable aspect of his persona was that it was quite obvious he was prepared for anything at any time. To say that he was quite lethal would be a gross understatement.

A few seconds later an older gentlemen with a white, well-cropped beard and somewhat longish white hair that stopped just below his shirt collar, slowly exited the van. At first he stood somewhat stooped over, mainly due to suffering from a severe case of spinal stenosis and arthritis. He also wore a black suit, but not as well tailored as the drivers. Plus, it was a little more on the wrinkled side. He slowly began to stretch his cramped muscles and older bones since it had been a somewhat rather long drive to get here from his home in New Mexico. After straightening out all the kinks he bent over, reached inside the backseat and pulled out a large black briefcase.

Smiling to the driver he leaned closer, whispered a few words and then began walking around the back of the vehicle. During this ritual another imposing gentleman exited the front passenger side, standing in more of a rigid, military-style pose. He was, not surprisingly in the least, dressed all in black with the same type of crisp white shirt and black tie just like his twin brother. They were aptly known as double trouble.

"Phillip, what say we go inside and get out of this brutal heat?"

Phillip nodded slightly and started up the small flight of steps ahead of the older gentleman. He opened the door and they both entered the building while the black van pulled away to find a nearby visitor's parking space. The driver would stay with the vehicle until it became obvious that his boss would be longer than anticipated, at which time he would then securely lock the van and go inside to the waiting room.

Once inside the building the older gentleman walked up to the front desk where a well-trimmed, attractive female staff sergeant sat erect with perfect military posture. She glanced up and displayed a smile with gleaming white teeth.

"Good afternoon, sir, I'm Staff Sgt. Reynolds. How can I help you?"

He smiled back while the much taller man dressed in black stood about four feet behind and slightly to the left. Behind the dark glasses his eyes never stopped moving even though they were in a headquarters building on a large military installation. His job was simple. Stay on high alert every second and be prepared to react, sometimes quite violently, in a split second if danger presented itself.

"Hello Sgt. Reynolds, my last name is Smith, first name Howard. I'm here to meet with a Colonel James McDowell. I believe you'll find that he's expecting me."

Once again displaying her perfect smile, she replied, "Yes sir. If you and the other gentleman would have a seat over there I'll buzz into Colonel McDowell's office."

They moved over to a small waiting area with about six chairs and two tables. Nothing swanky, just military-style serviceable. The older man sat down while the younger one stood a few feet to the left facing the desk and the front door. When on duty neither he, nor his twin brother, rarely sat down. Always alert and prepared for action.

Sgt. Reynolds quietly hung up the phone and stood, her blue uniform perfect with not a crease showing. She walked quickly over to Howard and Phillip.

"Sir, Captain Pace will be coming out in a few minutes to take you back to the Colonel's office. There's a water cooler there in the corner if you're thirsty."

The older gentleman smiled and thanked her. True to her word in less than two minutes a door opened at the other end of the main entrance where Captain Pace stiffly strolled through. Walking by Sgt. Reynolds desk he tilted his head and smiled at her. It was obvious to any trained observer that there was more than just a working relationship between the two individuals even though Captain Pace displayed a wedding band.

"Mr. Smith, I'm Captain Gerald Pace. Welcome to Davis-Monthan Air Force Base. I trust that you had a nice trip?"

Standing up the older gentleman reached forward to shake hands with the officer. "It was fine, though at my advanced age sitting in a vehicle for any length of time can cause the old bones to get somewhat stiff. This tall young man behind me is Phillip."

Captain Pace turned and extended his hand. Hesitating slightly, the much taller Phillip returned the handshake firmly. Not a crack of recognition showed on his face.

"Now if you will please accompany me then we'll head back to Colonel McDowell's office. Phillip, there is a snack room right down the hall on the left side beside a larger and more comfortable waiting area. You'll find it's quite nice."

Mr. Smith smiled. "Phillip goes everywhere with me Captain Pace so he'll be coming along if you don't mind."

Pace smiled in acknowledgement and spun around, starting to walk toward the door he had just entered from. They quickly found themselves in a fairly long hallway with a large, open office area immediately to the right which contained four desks, each separated in cubicle fashion. Walking down the hallway they passed six offices on each side until they reached the last office on the right. Captain Pace knocked on the door and upon hearing a somewhat muffled 'come in' he opened the door and stood off to the side.

"Gentleman, if you please. This is Colonel McDowell's office."

Mr. Smith entered quickly while Phillip paused until he motioned Captain Pace to enter the room which he did, somewhat reluctantly. Phillip never, ever allowed anyone to follow him into any enclosed area. He then immediately closed the door with his back firmly flattened against it. Nobody would get in unless he let them.

Colonel McDowell quickly walked around his rather massive desk with hand outstretched in a welcoming gesture, a broad smile spread across his weathered face.

"General Smith, really good to see you again. It's always such a pleasure."

Howard Smith was a retired Air Force General with thirty years of proud service behind him that covered part of Vietnam thru Bosnia. Having spent many tours of duty all around the world, numerous times without family, his career progressed steadily as he scaled the ladder of promotions. Highly decorated, plus wounded while fighting in Vietnam that left him with a noticeable limp, he finally called it a career in May of 1996.

The first year of his retirement was an absolute joy. After thirty years of service to his country, many of those spent away from his family, he welcomed this time with great anticipation. Finally he and his wife could travel, spend quality time with his four grandchildren, and even more importantly get to know his son Peter and daughter Carol, who sadly had been deprived of those formative years with a devoted father. He had been far from filling that duty primarily due to his career that kept him away for long stretches at a time. It was quite apparent over the years the animosity that grew between he and his son. The first six months when he was no longer in the military were spent mending broken fences and sewing the torn sections of familial structure back together. The last six months of that first year was spent in building a stronger family base, just totally enjoying his fantastic son who was also an awesome father and loving husband.

In the second year of retirement his wife June suddenly became quite ill with pancreatic cancer. When it was finally detected it had just progressed too far. Nothing could be done other than make her last days as peaceful and pain free as possible. He was completely devastated as the building blocks he had been establishing began to unravel. He reeled deeply into a black hole filled with alcohol and pure anger at life. What he had worked so hard to reconstruct in that first year all came tumbling down.

After spending two months in a rehab facility at the request of his children he began reaching out to old contacts in the Air Force. Maybe there was something he could do, anything that might keep him busy as a civilian, but somehow militarily related. He needed to become deeply involved in something where he could feel self-worth again.

In February, 2001 he got reacquainted with several officers of equal rank who had also retired. They had gotten together several times for dinner at which time he was then introduced to a larger, rather secretive group of influential individuals. He was told that not only was his experience as a leader of men needed in this secretive society, but his past strange alien-like encounters that he rarely discussed were also of valuable interest.

Now he stood in front of the colonel and smiled back.

"Please Colonel McDowell, I've been retired for quite some time now so the rank of general is certainly not required anymore. I would just rather you call me Howard, as one old friend to another. I do, however, wish our meeting was under better circumstances."

The colonel grinned back and slightly slapped Mr. Smith on the back. "Totally Howard, not a problem at all. If I call you Howard, please call me Jim. Is that a deal?"

They both laughed as Colonel McDowell walked behind his desk and sat down, while Howard also sank back into his chair. Phillip and Colonel Pace remained standing.

"So Howard, you called me the other day with some evident urgency and here you are. You now have the floor. How can we be of assistance?"

At the same time he glanced up to Pace and Phillip. "Are you two going to stand the entire time? Why don't you either grab a chair, or sit on the couch and hold hands."

Captain Pace glanced at Phillip who in turn did not change his facial appearance, or even move a fraction of an inch.

"I think we're both fine standing, Sir. Isn't that right Phillip?"

There was a very slight turn of the head and the barest of nods. So they both continued to stand even though Captain Pace did actually want to sit.

McDowell laughed and shook his head. "Unbelievable. You two just have your little pissing contest then. Anyway Howard, please proceed. I actually have a staff meeting scheduled in thirty minutes. What's so important to bring you here?"

"Well colonel, I think it would be a good idea for you to cancel that meeting. I'm here due to the extremely serious nature of the situation you've been having for the last month. You truly do need my assistance. The wonderful City of Tucson, this facility, as well as all civilians and military personnel in this area are in grave danger."

Colonel McDowell stared ahead and hesitated briefly before responding.

"How could you know anything about what has been happening around here? We've been keeping everything as low key as possible while at the same time deploying ground and air teams to bring it to a conclusion. Plus, trying to work with local law enforcement. We feel strongly that the situation should be controlled shortly."

Howard Smith leaned forward in his chair and gazed powerfully at McDowell.

"Jim, it's very important that you listen to me very closely. Don't miss a word of what I'm about to say. I'm part of a large group of people who not only have been aware from the very moment when this nightmare began, but have also been following it step by step going back to 1983. We don't believe that you truly have any idea what has been unleashed upon the city. This is not like any enemy you have ever encountered. And hopefully never will again in your lifetime. That is, if we survive at all."

Smith coughed and then rose slowly from his seat. "I'm not sure what you had planned on discussing in your staff meeting, but I would cancel that immediately. Then you need to quickly gather together all the appropriate players in this deadly ballgame, including Dr. Warring and his associates. We have very little time to act and God help us all if we've run out of time. Now, Phillip and I are going to get some coffee. Captain Pace can come to get us when the new meeting is set."

Turning he began walking towards the door which Phillip now had open. He then stopped and turned to look directly at Colonel McDowell. "Jim, when we walk out this door your hand should definitely be on that phone. We'll be waiting in the lounge."

Chapter 23

Manny slipped the cell phone back into his jacket pocket. He had just received a very strange call from the night desk sergeant relaying the message that a 911 call had apparently been made from a hiker out in the desert claiming that he and his buddy had entered a cave for some fun exploration only to find what appeared to be the remains of at least one body, maybe more. Plus, there was some other very odd stuff lying around at the bottom of a big hole obviously dug out by a large animal. When Chief Crosson was informed he said to immediately contact Manny so he could check it out.

He was just finishing a breakfast of toast with strawberry jam, a bowl of Shredded Wheat which he loved, and two cups of coffee. Since the call was received at 7:30 a.m. on Saturday morning he just told his wife to stay in bed and go back to sleep. The kids, well, it was Saturday morning and they would not wake up until close to noon anyway. He could never remember doing that because his father was always an early riser. As a result, he would wake Manny every morning around 5:00 a.m. during summer vacation from school. Since his father ran an old Atlantic gasoline station where he also did mechanical work, he decided to use a little family child labor by making his son wake up before the roosters so he could pump gas and learn to do minor jobs on cars like oil and tire changes. He paid his son two dollars an hour and Manny was fine with that.

His father, Jose Miquel Corroda, had sadly passed away two years ago at the ripe old age of 87. Manny had not really taken the loss well being extremely close to his dad and losing his biggest supporter. Jose was so very proud of his only son's service in the Army since he had served heroically during the war in Afghanistan. He was honorably discharged with the rank of First Lieutenant in 2004. A year later he joined the Tucson PD. Manny remembered how his father had smiled all throughout the day he retired, and never stopped boasting about his son whenever he met up with all his old cronies at the barbershop, the bowling alley, or neighborhood bars. When Manny told him that he was going to join the Tucson PD and be a detective, the pride blossomed even more.

He glanced at the picture on the wall as he opened the front door. Touching the image with his fingertips he whispered, "Love you Dad."

Once inside the car he removed his phone and touched the number for his partner. After three rings a male voice answered.

"Yeah.........ah, morning. Who's this?" came a very groggy male voice.

"Who the hell is this?" asked Manny, as if he didn't already know.

There was a muffled cough before Flint answered. "You know who the hell it is because you're the prick who left me here on this nursing assignment."

"Is she awake yet? How's she doing anyway?"

There was a slight pause and then a muffled, "Who's calling so damn early?"

An equally muffled voice responded, sounding as if a hand was covering the phone, "Its Manny. Here, you talk to him. I'm not going to be a go between."

Another pause before I answered after slowly grabbing the phone from Vince. "Morning partner. What the hell are you doing up so early on a Saturday morning?"

"Amy, where are you?"

"What the heck does that mean? I'm in my bed you idiot, you just woke me up."

"So where the hell is Mr. Flint?"

"Oh, well he's in bed, too. But hey partner, don't get any sick ideas in your head. That couch is too uncomfortable to sleep on and I needed to be held last night. After all, you weren't here to do the job," I responded, now sounding somewhat more alert.

Manny realized he was having a jealous moment. It was more protective rather than pure jealousy. After all, he didn't really know Vince Flint that well and positively did not want his partner hurt any more than the physical pain she was already suffering at the moment. He felt somebody in her life had to be protective.

"Okay, better not be any more than that going on. I care about you Amy and don't want anyone taking advantage of you. Especially in the condition you're in."

I laughed. "Wow, I haven't had that happen since my mother gave me a good talking to when I was dating this creep back in my senior year of high school. I'm okay buddy, honest. Your concern is heartwarming though. So what's up partner?"

"How are you feeling physically? Are you up to taking a small road trip to check out something very strange?"

I quickly sat up in bed, moaning louder than I actually wanted to. "Strange is my middle name, you know that. I'm okay, I guess. Stiff and sore, but that's the way it's going to be for a while I'm afraid. Not every day that you get knocked nearly twenty feet by the tail of some huge monstrous lizard. Christ partner, I can't sit or lie on my big ass around here, you know that. Let me just get up and walk around a little bit to work out the kinks. I was up in the middle of the night to pee and moved better than I had during the day. Besides, you know I'm right handed so I can shoot the arm off any cactus if I need to. I'm not totally incapacitated partner, just a little slow at the moment."

Manny laughed. "Well, there may be some walking involved if you definitely think you're up to it. I'm just leaving the house and it'll take me about thirty minutes to get over to your place. There is a chopper waiting to fly us out to the location of a cave discovered yesterday by a few hikers. Apparently they found the recent remains of at least two bodies inside, maybe more. I understand that it was a pretty gruesome sight for those two young men. Could be where the creature has been hiding out all this time. They will try to get us relatively close, but we will still have to walk and climb some of that rough terrain. Amy, if you don't feel you're up to it then tell me now."

I was already sliding out of bed. At least there wasn't any obvious dizziness from the head injury like there had been over the last few days. If there had been a slight concussion then it must've just been a teeny weeny one. Can't hurt this hard head.

"I'm getting ready as we speak partner. We'll be ready when you get here."

"We? You mean Vince is coming along?"

"Of course he's going with us partner. Don't forget, he was out in that desert looking for this damn thing before we were so he has just as much at stake in this."

"Amy, this is official police business we're checking out."

"Oh, just shut up Manny. When did anything like that ever bother you before? Just get here when you can and we'll be ready. Bye honey bunny!"

I had already started moving towards the bathroom so I could freshen up as much as possible, grabbing my jeans and a tee shirt along the way. I was in no mood at this point to dress for success, especially since we were heading out into the desert. I also had to remember to grab my Phillies cap so I could hide my partially bald, stitched up head.

"What's up Amy?" asked a still sleepy Vince Flint.

I laughed because I truly had forgotten he was still in my bedroom. "Come on, get yourself all prettied up. Apparently some hikers found a cave with at least one dead body, maybe more. It could very well be the hidden lair of our little creature. Manny should be here in about twenty minutes so we need to dress quickly and have a little breakfast if possible. No telling when we'll eat again. There is a helicopter waiting to fly us out there."

"Amy, are you truly up for this? It could get really rough out there."

I grabbed the door frame and spun around. "Damn it, will everybody quit asking if I'm okay? I'm not some weak little female who needs to be coddled and taken care of by some big macho-spouting male assholes. Now get off your damn band wagon and get ready if you're going with us. That is unless you feel it's going to be too much for you."

With that I slammed the door shut and headed straight for the toilet because I really had to take a wicked piss.

In the bedroom Flint smiled and shook his head thinking that Amelia Stephenson definitely was not weak and fragile in any way, shape or form. In fact, he had been around some very strong, tough women in his life and was pretty confident that he had not met any like her. Definitely none crazier than this girl who he was beginning to become very fond of. And that really surprised him because he rarely let that happen.

The alien, previously known as Quinotoa on another world very far away, paused for a short time on a high rise near where the last skirmish had previously taken place. It had a very firm grasp now of the day/night cycles on this planet and realized that three full cycles had passed. Other than physical destruction to the terrain from the battle, all bodies and wreckage had been cleared away. That also meant that its young brood was spread out in the surrounding area now firmly in control of the human bodies each one had taken over as vehicles. It also realized that they had transformed and fed over the last few days, thus becoming much stronger. Now they were simply hiding low and waiting to receive orders from their birth parent.

It anxiously sniffed the air which constantly held hundreds of different scents. Now it mainly searched for only one in particular. That didn't take long. The human it hungered to meet again was the female who had struck the creature's body with almost every single shot she had fired. When its tail violently struck her body, the creature also extended one of its rear legs. A long, sharp claw gouged across the top of her head before she went sailing through the air. The beast then quickly bent backwards and licked the blood coating the claw before it got impaired and contaminated in any way.

Once her tasty blood was ingested then every single cell and molecule making up her human DNA was at once part of the creature's memory bank. That's all it needed to track down any living thing, especially here on this unique planet. There were definitely some entities on other worlds in different galaxies that contained very little in the way of tracking material and those times had been rather rough even though it had prevailed in every instance.

However, this planet called Earth was quite easy. It now stood erect and stared far off into the distance across the relatively flat desert landscape. Since going through the different transformations over the past several weeks, this lizard's body had also acquired eyesight that was now incredible. It could detect not only actual objects from many miles away, but notice ethereal waves in the air that were just as easy to follow. All creatures on this planet, whether it be human, animal, or insect left an ethereal trail every single time it moved from place to place. If it lingered too long in any particular location then the ethereal cloud was deeper in color and more noticeable. These waves lingered for a while until the body moved. But the longer it stayed in one place then the easier it was to find. None of these ethereal waves could be detected by normal eyesight.

There were thousands of these ethereal-like wave patterns floating or hanging in the air, but having ingested her DNA sequence made it all relatively easy to follow her. This trail led east towards the glow on the horizon that apparently meant a large gathering of humans. That most likely was the colony where she lived.

The lizard started moving in that direction, sometimes quick and at other times rather ponderously. Whenever necessary it utilized the unique ability to blend in with the surroundings, very chameleon-like. If more stealth was necessary then it appeared to just ripple the air and nothing could be seen at all in substance or bodily form. Now it yearned to only find the human female and hopefully transform one last time.

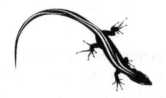

Chapter 24

Howard Smith sat on the couch, head slumped forward, his eyes closed. Half his coffee was left in a white plastic cup and had long grown cold. It was difficult to tell if he was actually asleep since he was well known for appearing to doze off in meetings and waiting rooms. Actually, he was wide awake most of the time. He amusingly told everybody that he was just resting his eyes. On the contrary, he was normally more alert than people who were wide awake.

Phillip stood to the right of the couch a few feet off to the side of the window. He had a perfect view of the entire room including the hallway outside the entrance to the waiting room. In addition, he could see anyone who might enter through the front of the building from outside. Jeffery, his twin brother, had come into the building when he found out they would be longer than originally intended. He now stood off to the right of the door, but not in view of anyone entering. Together they made up a formidable security team that guarded General Smith pretty much 24/7. Definitely anytime he traveled. Attempts had been made on the General's life before so they never let their guard down.

Suddenly footsteps were detected in the hallway followed up by Captain Pace walking stiffly through the door. Upon entering he was quickly startled when he noticed Jeffery. Quickly composing himself he looked at Howard Smith and smiled.

THE REPTILIAN FACTOR

"General Smith, we are now ready in the conference room so if you would be so kind, please follow me."

Opening his eyes Howard smiled and started to rise. Phillip quickly moved forward and grabbed hold of the older man's elbow to help steady him.

"Thank you, Phillip. I'm not sure what I would do without you and Jeffery."

He walked forward and nodded slightly. "Captain Pace, if you would please take the lead then we will follow."

The officer hesitated, at the same time glancing nervously at the two brothers.

"Sir, this will be a highly sensitive and top secret meeting. I'm afraid your two companions will need to wait outside in the hallway, or in this waiting room."

"Captain Pace," Howard responded in a soft, but authoritative voice. "Phillip and Jeffery have taken part in more top secret meetings than you will ever attend in a lifetime. In fact, they have been in meetings that you absolutely would not be able to attend at all. So if you would please proceed, once again we will follow you."

In somewhat of a huff, Captain Pace turned sharply and started walking towards the main reception area. They all walked with purpose and then passed through the door that Pace originally came out of. Once inside they immediately turned right and stopped at a large double door to the left. He knocked once, opened the door and stepped aside. Howard Smith walked through followed immediately by Phillip. Jeffery stood stiffly and stared through his dark glasses until Pace walked into the room. Jeffery followed and closed the door behind him.

Colonel McDowell quickly stood erect upon their entering the room and forced a somewhat fake smile. The put down from

Howard Smith earlier in his office was still sticking in his craw and he wasn't happy about it one little bit.

He held out his left hand, palm up towards a chair opposite him at the table. "General Smith, please have a seat and I will introduce you to the other people in attendance."

Smith smiled, but remained standing for the moment. "Colonel McDowell, I apologize for my curtness earlier and possibly ruffling your feathers. Please don't take it personally because that was not my intent. I honestly believe you will shortly understand my insistence and being rather abrupt earlier. Also, please remember that you may call me Howard."

The colonel returned the smile. "Not a problem, sir. However, if you don't mind, since we're in this official venue, I would rather refer to you as General Smith."

Howard smiled slightly and nodded, then sat in the chair. Phillip and Jeffery stood stiffly at the door. Nobody was getting in or out, that was pretty obvious.

Colonel McDowell took in a long, deep breath and then released a heavy sigh before continuing.

"General, to my immediate left is Lt. Colonel Pike and beside him is Major Andrews. Captain Pace, who you have already met, is sitting at that end of the table. To my right is Dr. Oliver Warring, and to his right in order are Drs. Peter Neville and Sandra Crawford. Dr. Warring is head of our research facilities and will take the lead in most of this meeting."

There was a slight pause before Colonel McDowell sat down. The room was already chilly from the air conditioner, but the overly tense atmosphere was downright icy. A very long minute passed while several in attendance poured water. Coffee was on the table against the far wall so Howard sat back, tilted his head in the direction of Jeffery, and mouthed the word *'coffee'*.

Another long minute went by while the younger man filled a plastic cup, added cream and two sugars, then placed it in front of his boss. Quickly returning to his guard position, and after the General took a sip, all was finally ready. Colonel McDowell had been drumming his fingertips on the table the entire time.

"Okay gentleman and lady, my deepest apologies for taking you all away from any important duties that you were possibly involved with. Spending thirty years in this Air Force I know only full well how busy you all can get. My sudden visit to your wonderful facility this morning, however, is one of grave importance. Everything to be said and discussed within this meeting is of the utmost secrecy, and strictly – I repeat very firmly – strictly, on a need to know basis. I represent a group of very strong and influential people from around the world, the majority of whom you have no idea who they are. That in and of itself is not important. However, what is of vital importance is that the situation you have going on here is life threatening to every living person not only on this facility, but to the populace of Tucson and surrounding areas as well. This fact should not be anything new to you as a result of the deaths, both military and civilian, that have been occurring over the last few weeks."

He paused slightly to take a few sips of his coffee and clean his glasses. Those in attendance waited for him to continue, all with their own thoughts, questions, and fears. Colonel McDowell had been drumming his fingertips on the table since he sat down.

General Smith glanced over at Warring. "Doctor, we have known all along about what occurred in your desert back in 1983 concerning the crash of that alien vehicle. In addition, we have also been aware, and following very closely, any research performed. As well as care and security provided for the alien entity that was discovered. Our government, and the military in general, are extremely adept at keeping secrets as you well know when it comes to anything unexplained which, of course, this definitely falls firmly within that category. There isn't a person in this room not aware of Area 51 and other secret facilities throughout this vast country. So that being said, I am here this morning at the behest passed down to me from the highest authority of this country. I don't believe that I need to be more explanatory about that comment."

There was a pause while Howard Smith opened the briefcase beside him on the table. Taking out a sheet of paper he passed it across the table to Colonel McDowell.

"This rather short, but very explicit memo, backs up what I just said so that you all know the seriousness of this situation. After you read this memo please pass it around. Then give it to Phillip so it can be destroyed. Now, the escape of this alien organism that you all have been taking care of for so long can be disastrous if not handled properly and expeditiously. When this escape first occurred, far too much time was lost because of embarrassment before you started to take action on a higher level. When it first got loose there should've been contact made within the first few hours. None of that was done I believe until early last week and that was no doubt because of all the civilian deaths piling up. After all, military deaths can be covered over somewhat as you well know. But civilian deaths cannot, especially if it falls back onto the military."

Colonel McDowell started to say something in response and was immediately hushed by a raised hand by Smith. Cold silence suddenly pervaded the room.

"I'm sorry colonel, but the time for bitching, yelling, and complaining has passed. The time to act is now. Believe me when I tell you, there may not be much time left. What you have running around in your desert is an alien creature that is near impossible to kill. It apparently has the ability to take over a body as a host, doesn't matter if it's animal or human. I think you can certainly attest to that fact since there is some huge lizard running amok. This thing also has the unique ability to produce offspring and very quickly. It can also exit a dead body and then take over another one extremely fast. So, even though you may think you're killing it you're actually not. That being said, I believe this eventuality has probably already taken place. This transforming, and then regeneration process, is something we know little about. The question is, has this birthing already occurred? If it has, then how many, or what bodies they have now taken over, is not even known yet. It is our absolute opinion that you will shortly have more of these creatures running around and that's a nightmare."

General Smith paused and gazed around the room waiting for responses. He could see the stunned look on each of their faces.

Finally Dr. Warring spoke. "Sir, can I ask how you know all of this?"

Smith chuckled. "How we know is not important, at least for now. What knowledge we do have though is hopefully going to help us put an end to this critical situation."

He glanced down at his watch before proceeding. "It is now ten-fifteen a.m. At precisely noon there will be several large transport planes landing here at the base so I would immediately advise your air traffic control as soon as possible. These aircraft will be carrying sophisticated equipment, as well as an attachment of special commandos highly trained and ready for battle. Colonel Pike, I believe that you are in charge of the 563rd Reserve Group. I would suggest that you call them all to service immediately and be prepared to deploy when orders are received. Captain Pace, I would also request that you make immediate contact with local law enforcement. Have a delegation here on the base at exactly twelve noon because at some point there is going to be a world of shit come down on this wonderful City of Tucson. We had better be prepared."

Standing up he slowly looked around the room. "Please trust me when I tell you that we do not have any time to spare. I will also greatly emphasize the most critical nature of this situation. Get over any embarrassment and hurt feelings you may be feeling. You are military and there is no time for such frivolous emotions when battle is imminent. Pull those quivering tails from between your legs and get moving. Phillip, Jeffery, and myself will be out at the airfield awaiting the arrival of those aircraft."

Picking up his briefcase he pushed the chair back and proceeded to the door. He then turned around. "I don't see anybody moving yet. Go, go now!"

As he exited the room everyone did just that.

They climbed out of the helicopter which had landed on a relatively safe and level piece of ground. Bending over from the wind, the three of them scurried away from the whoosh of the beating rotors and swirling sand. Thirty yards away they met with a small group comprising two Arizona Highway Patrol officers, one Arizona Park Ranger, two Tucson police officers, and the two civilian hikers.

"Detective Stephenson," I yelled, extending my hand. "This is Detective Corroda and Vince Flint. We understand some human remains were found near here."

The patrolman with the name tag of Krebs spoke first. "These two men were out hiking early this morning and found a cave about 800-1,000 yards up there," turning and pointing in the exact direction. He also turned to one of the civilians.

"Mr. Anthony, would you please explain to these detectives what you saw."

A young and well built, very good looking guy around twenty-five years of age stepped forward. It was very evident he was really shook up.

"Ah, wow, what can I say? Well, like Patrolman Krebs was saying, me and my friend here, Jimmy Salvino, was following somewhat of a narrow trail up the side of the mountain right over there. So about 800 yards up the hill he noticed a dark hole that was partially hidden by lots of brush. We went over, pulled the stuff away and saw that it was the mouth of a cave. I'm very experienced at spelunking so I went in first. It was pretty dark inside so we switched on our flashlights and walked slowly further into the cave itself. I would say about fifty feet in we reached a relatively deep hole that I almost fell into. Thankfully I did not because at the bottom was what appeared to be bones and tattered clothing. Hard to tell if it was just one person or more, but let me say that it was really distressing. Something I'll never, ever forget the rest of my life."

He stopped talking and bent over looking like he was going to throw up.

"Mr. Anthony, are you okay? Please take your time," I said, resting my hand on his shoulder.

Then he slowly straightened and smiled. "I don't think I'll ever be okay after seeing that nightmare. However, there was something else down in that hole as well."

"What was that, Mr. Anthony?" asked Manny.

"I couldn't tell exactly, but honestly it looked like some type of large, thick egg shells that were broken apart, pieces spread all around. It was a really strange mess so we just backed out and immediately called 911."

"Thank you gentleman, you did the right thing. Are you okay to drive home? Where is your vehicle?" I asked as gently as possible, yet trying at the same time to contain my obvious interest.

"Yes, thank you, I think we're okay for now. I won't be sure until I finally try to fall asleep tonight. Plus, I may never go searching in caves anymore either," he replied, laughing rather shakily. "I don't ever want to discover something like that again."

"You'll get through this experience, Mr. Anthony. I'm sure in time you'll be spelunking once again and enjoying it. But at least you certainly will have a good *'fish story'* to tell," I replied, both of us laughing while they walked away.

I turned at the same time Manny and Vince did. Each of us stared with concern up towards the side of the mountain, lost in our own nightmarish thoughts.

"Well, are you ready to take a little stroll partner?" asked Manny. "It's going to be a really tough hike up that trail they pointed out. It's not going to be easy even if you were in good shape. Nobody is forcing you to go up there."

"Just lead on *'McDuff'*. Quit trying to baby me. If I fall down then just pick me up, dust me off, and keep on climbing. If you have to drag me then just go ahead."

Manny laughed. "You're one tough lady, Detective Stephenson."

"Yeah, I'll tell you how tough I am once we get up there if I'm not in tears by then. Now go on, both of you. Quit treating me like I'm some weakling."

It took us nearly an hour to get up to the cave. To say that I barely made it would be an understatement. Vince actually put his arm through mine and helped me the last fifty or so feet. My left shoulder was screaming in pain and the right thigh was aching like hell. At least I wasn't dizzy. I guess two out of three wasn't bad. Thankfully I was also wearing my stylish Phillies cap. The sun was starting to get hot and I certainly didn't need a sunburn on my already ugly looking bald head displaying a ghastly line of stitches across the front. Vince had helped me clean some of the dried blood away so it looked and felt a little better. Still damn ugly though because I felt like Igor.

Now standing in front of the cave mouth, somewhat rather apprehensively I might add, Vince spoke up first.

"Let me take the lead. I'm used to this kind of thing. Even though I think it's going to be pretty safe in there since nothing happened to those hikers, you just never know what might still be hiding someplace."

"That's so gallant of you Mr. Flint, allowing yourself to get attacked before us," I replied, trying to break the tension somewhat.

Vince didn't answer. He just had a scowl on his face. Both Manny and I motioned for him to enter and we followed. The darkness hit us pretty quickly so we switched on our flashlights. Just like Mr. Anthony had said earlier, in a few minutes we reached the hole which I would say was about three feet deep and seven to ten feet long. Shining our flashlights into the dark abyss we were somewhat stunned to say the least. It was totally the way the young hiker had explained it as. At the far end of the hole was a partially devoured human body that appeared to be that of a male just from what was left of the clothing. Further in towards the middle of the pit lay more remains of what appeared to possibly be that of a female. I assumed that because there appeared to be a shredded pink and white vest lying amid the blood and bones.

"Jesus Amy, what is this?" asked Manny in a nervous voice.

"Your guess is as good as mine. I would have to say that this was where the creature was holed up for the last few weeks. Apparently starting a family of its own."

Flint spoke then. "Detectives, from what I'm seeing here it appears that this creature laid eggs. They hatched and the dead bodies were used as food. At least I hope they were dead at the time. I think a closer search may detect more bodies as well."

"So you're saying that now we have multiple little baby lizards running around out there?" asked Manny. Then he added, "I don't think I'll ever eat eggs again."

"Detective Corroda, we can't really tell how many until we get the bodily remains out of that hole and look closer at those shells. We don't really know they were lizards at time of birth. God only knows what was hatched here," Vince responded, walking around the right side of the hole before suddenly stopping.

"What's wrong Vince?" I whispered loudly, even though it echoed in the cave.

"Ah, I don't think we should go any further. There definitely appears to be more remains on the far side of this pit. No idea if it's animal or human. You need to get a forensic team out here quickly and go through this cave with a fine tooth comb."

Once we were finally back down on level ground I stood alongside Flint looking out into the vast Sonoran Desert. Manny was making a call to get a crime scene unit out to the location as quickly as possible.

"Vince, we're in for a world of shit aren't we?" I asked.

"That's probably not even the half of it. We are obviously dealing with something completely alien, excuse the pun. We have limited information on this creature other than it's huge, deadly, can seem to disappear, regular bullets don't seem to harm it because of this armor plating it has, and now the damn thing appears to be able to lay eggs and have freaking babies. Not sure about you, but it's not something I've ever encountered before. So Detective Stephenson, you tell me what we should do."

I started to respond when my cell phone rang, braking the tension.

"Stephenson here, what's up?"

THE REPTILIAN FACTOR

"Amy, this is Crosson. Obviously you are still not listening to anybody including your doctors. I'm honestly not sure if I should be furious at you, or happy with your dedication. Either one doesn't matter at the moment. You're there with Manny I'm assuming and not sure who else. I need you both to get over to the airbase right away. There apparently is a very important meeting being held at noon so myself and Lt. Spencer will meet you there. Now, tell me what you found inside that cave."

I spent the next five minutes detailing what we saw, what it possibly meant, and that Manny was arranging to get a crime scene unit out to the site as soon as possible.

"So then it just keeps getting worse," he replied. "If I live through this then I'm going to give retirement some serious consideration."

"Ah Chief Crosson, you can't do that. Who else would bust my chops on a daily basis?" I asked in jest.

He chuckled before responding. "Well, I can still bust'em now since I haven't retired so get over to the base right away. We'll see you there."

Flint tilted his head in my direction with a questioning look as I ended the call.

Shaking my head I told him, "Something big is happening at the base, some top secret meeting I guess. We need to get over there post haste. Crosson and Spencer will meet us. I'm sure all the military big wigs will be in attendance, too. Although I highly doubt that they are aware of what we just saw, so that will add to the situation."

We turned to get Manny and jumped inside the chopper. It was a short ride to the base so the entire time I sat there securely strapped in with my eyes closed just letting everything run through my mind like some horrifying science fiction movie. By the time we landed I was still unable to figure out what the ending was going to be.

I just prayed that nobody else was going to die. But, with all my experience in dealing with serious situations, we at least had a plan of action. Here we were all just flying by the seat of our pants, literally. It was as if every hour something was happening beyond our control and we were acting after the fact.

In any event, I was really getting pissed off because I was feeling so inadequate. I also had no idea why we were needed at the air base. Something about this just didn't sit right in my stomach. But for some reason I strangely felt that my life was about to change.

Chapter 25

Robert Perkins sat quietly on the couch appearing to be somewhat normal, at least physically. What lay upstairs in the bedrooms, however, was something else entirely. After feeding on his succulent wife he went to each of the children's bedrooms to continue with his tasty meal. Thankfully, he had no idea what he was actually doing from the human perspective because Robert was officially dead. In nineteen other households throughout the glorious City of Tucson, Arizona the same scene was being horribly unfolded. Human hosts who were nothing more now than deadly puppets.

Feeding time over, the thing transformed back into a more human appearance. Skin became less scaly, nails and teeth receded somewhat even though they still remained sharper and much longer than normal. Covered in blood, a shower was definitely needed. Afterwards, he got dressed in cleaner clothes, but nothing matched at all. The blood saturated clothes remained on the floor. After all, cleanliness was not an issue anymore.

Even though Robert was dead internally, his mind was still fully intact which allowed the creature to obtain as much information as needed to perform quasi-human functions. Since there had only been one transformation up to this point, Robert's physical body was still pretty much the same. That would eventually change. He had never been a large man at only 5' 8", 165 pounds. In fact, he and his wife Jeannie were pretty much the same dimensions although she was about twenty pounds lighter and an inch or so shorter. Of course, he was built more solidly which came from working out on a daily basis and running ten miles every other day. Jeannie was, of course, a lot curvier.

Even though the creature had total use of Robert's memory it really was unable to use it in the way of common sense. The human's memories really meant nothing. It had no previous experience to pull from other than what was initially provided by the parent when reproducing. As a result, it sat quietly on the couch dressed in a red Cardinal's tee shirt and long floral skirt of Jeannie's. It selected the skirt because it was much easier to put on and quite frankly felt much more comfortable. For some strange reason it detected hidden thoughts in Robert's mind of previously wearing female clothing in secret. It had attempted to pull on a pair of jeans, but after ripping them it selected the skirt instead from the wife's closet. On its feet was a pair of Robert's black Nike sneakers. None of Jeannie's shoes would fit since her feet were much smaller, especially the heels which were impossible to walk in anyway. The outfit now being worn could definitely be classified as trans-unisex-punk.

About twenty five miles on the other side of town its parent was hidden in an empty building close to where the female's strongest scent lingered. It had tracked Amy's ethereal trail to this area though there came a point where different trails merged. Making it somewhat more difficult to decide where she was currently, the creature elected to follow this particular path leading to this present location. The trail wasn't extremely strong so rather than going on a total wild goose chase to find her it just made a decision to remain here and wait until she showed up.

Arriving at this location had been somewhat of a challenge because this large cement colony had thousands of humans walking around, as well as numerous odd looking vehicles maneuvering all over the place, some of them small and others large. Attempting to camouflage its body resulted into more of a wavy, rippling effect in the air. Crossing several streets caused minor vehicular accidents because the drivers thought they saw something in the middle of the street, but nothing of substance. Just as quickly it disappeared. However, those vehicles in front ended up having fender benders.

It decided to just lie low until the female appeared nearby. It would be quickly alerted when her scent grew stronger. Then it would quickly travel to the best meeting place. The location it now found itself appeared to be some type of residence where a human family unit would reside. The building was definitely too small for the creature's massive bulk so it merely broke through a double glass door in the back where a porch and patio was situated. There was plenty of open space on both sides from other structures so any undue noise didn't seem to present any issue. The rooms were all empty other than a few pieces of furniture. Yet it was quiet and relatively safe. As it moved through the house a few doorways had to be renovated which it did easily enough.

The thing had also decided to contact each brood member by sending out thoughts and directions telepathically. The main instruction was to just stay where each of them were and rest, grow strong, and try to utilize the human mind it now possessed within safe enclosures until they received orders on what to do next. Even though it was hungry and there was plenty of food nearby, the parent also needed to rest after a somewhat arduous journey through the desert to this large human nest. There would be plenty of time to feed later.

Now it curled up and dropped to the floor, allowing its long tail to wrap around the body. Resting its head on part of the tail and front feet it fell asleep. However, always remaining completely on alert to the barest of sounds which might be threats. Even though it was not really concerned at all when it came to any outside dangers.

Chapter 26

The chopper pilot radioed ahead to the airbase for permission to land in front of an older hangar on the outer edge of the base. It was used now primarily for just storage. When we finally touched ground it was quickly apparent that the building was now a beehive of activity. The hangar doors gaped wide open like the wide mouth of a carnival clown. Lights glowed brightly with vehicles driving in and out of the building, people moving around resembling an overactive anthill on Prozac.

It was pretty obvious that whatever meeting was scheduled it would be held right at this location. I looked over at Manny who just shrugged his shoulders since he was as confused as I appeared to be. Glancing at Vince, it was obvious he was now once again totally in his element. However, I also noticed a concerned expression on his face.

"Mr. Flint, you suddenly look really intense. What's up?" I yelled, trying to be heard over the rotor noise, also trying to hold down my Phillies cap. The very last thing I wanted to happen was attend a meeting and look like I had been recently scalped with a long slash of stitches ghastly displayed. Hell, I'd rather battle a fiery-eating, disappearing, scaly-covered, lizard-like dragon. On second thought, maybe not!

He turned and smiled. "This is my life, Amy. It has been for well over twenty years. Something big is about to come down and

I think we're going to be right smack dab in the middle of it. I'm really excited and can feel lots of adrenalin building up. Come on, let's get the hell out of this windstorm and head over to the hangar."

The three of us bent down and jogged towards the open building trying to avoid any careening vehicles at the same time. I could see Chief Crosson off to the side so I tapped both Manny and Vince on their arms, pointing in that direction.

Crosson looked over his shoulder and noticed us at the same time. He broke free of his group and started walking over to meet us.

"Glad you got here so fast," he yelled, trying to be somewhat heard over all the din. "There is going to be a meeting very shortly inside the hangar. So far I have no idea what's happening, but it's pretty obvious that the military is finally going to get off their asses and start some type of military campaign against this creature. Probably because the shit is hitting the fan so they need to wipe their 'you know what's'. So come on and follow me. There are a few people I need to introduce you to."

A few minutes later we stood around as part of a larger gathering, some wearing uniforms and others in civilian attire. I noticed an older, very distinguished looking gentleman towards the center of the hangar talking to two taller and mysterious, but very athletic looking guys. They were both dressed exactly the same wearing very dark shades inside the hangar. I shook my head and motioned for Manny to look that way.

"What do you think partner, men in black?" I asked him.

Laughing, he responded, "Nothing would surprise me in the least right about now. That older guy appears to be somebody very official and ex-military. He's definitely governmental, probably some top secret hush-hush type."

I turned to where Vince had been standing, but then noticed he had moved off and was now sequestered with both Prudot and Tiny Tim, along with a very attractive and more than capable looking woman. It appeared to be the injured Carrie Vaughn from his original search team. Her right arm was heavily bandaged from above the elbow down to the wrist, but she looked better now. Even though she also sported some large sutured wounds and bright red abrasions on her chin and forehead. Apparently she was like me, not going to be tied down on an uncomfortable bed in some stupid hospital. I liked her right away. Especially because another female was displaying stitches besides myself.

Manny and I followed Crosson over to where Colonel McDowell and Captain Pace were standing with a first lieutenant and a master sergeant. At the same we were joined by the older gentleman and his two sunglass wearing security guys.

"Gentlemen, allow me to introduce you to Detectives Amelia Stephenson and Manuel Corroda," said Chief Crosson. "They have been involved in this right from the beginning due to all the civilian casualties. I've brought them into this meeting because they will continue to spearhead our efforts in the city. As a result, they absolutely need to know everything there is concerning this creature we are searching for. Also, some new critical information has come to light which I doubt you are aware of yet."

Colonel McDowell then introduced us to each member of his group. At the same time, Vince Flint and his three team members also strolled over so they were now added to the name giving and handshaking. The older gentleman in a black suit was introduced as Retired Air Force General Howard Smith. He turned towards me and displayed a smile that was actually somewhat engaging. Something else quickly nibbled at the back of my mind saying this nicely dressed older gentleman was nobody to screw around with.

"Detectives, I don't know whether to extend my condolences since you need to be part of this meeting, or provide my sincere gratification for what you've already done up to this point. So," he said, continuing to smile warmly, "I will give you both if that's okay."

We all laughed and just kept quiet, assuming he was going to continue.

Just then, however, we heard the sound of two huge aircraft flying low overhead. As if it was some kind of a signal we started walking to the open front hangar doors. Standing in a straight line we could see two large transport planes make a smooth turn and then begin coming in for a landing. I would find out later that these were both C-5M Super Galaxy transport aircraft which happened to be the largest in the Air Force. Also, that they were manufactured by Lockheed Martin. I was somewhat in awe because I honestly had never seen such a huge plane in my entire life.

They landed not only gracefully, but rather majestically as well. Once reaching the end of the runway they turned slowly to start heading back in our direction. This all took close to fifteen minutes before both planes taxied side by side up to the tarmac in front of our hangar. The noise was actually deafening so there wasn't any talking at all amongst our group. Finally when the engines were shut down and it got somewhat quieter, General Smith took several steps forward and then turned to face us.

"The reason I wanted to wait before talking to you all was the arrival of these two magnificent transport planes. Being carried aboard each of them is not only highly sophisticated equipment, but two platoons of very skilled, specially trained commandos. They also need to hear what we are going to be facing as well. So, I would suggest that we allow them all time to disembark and get organized. That shouldn't take long as they are very efficient. In the meantime, however, I think that we can return to the hangar and possibly have some coffee or something cold to drink. Would that be agreeable to everyone?"

We all just nodded and started walking back towards the hangar which appeared to be a very old structure. Other than recently being used for storage, it had been put into emergency use strictly for us. I came to a sudden stop and stared at the structure.

"Hey, what's up?" asked Manny.

"Oh, nothing really. I just seem to remember this building. I think it was the second month after my arrival in Tucson when I took a tour of the base. You know, just getting familiar with my surroundings so to speak. Plus, I've always been somewhat interested in the Air Force and older aircraft. Anyway, if memory serves, this is a very old hangar from around 1932, one of the first ones built here back when it was known as Municipal Field. It became Davis-Monthan Airfield around 1926 and the following year changed to Davis-Monthan Air Force Base. Hell, Lindbergh and all those famous pilots in history landed and took off here. If you stand and listen real close you can almost hear the whispers from thousands of pilots who walked through this very hangar."

He looked at me and smiled. "Wow, so nostalgic and poetic. I never knew you were such a history buff. I just continue to learn more and more about you every day."

I laughed and punched him in the arm, then turned around to start walking back towards the transport planes.

"Hey, where are you going now?" he asked, voice still loud due to all the bedlam surrounding us.

"I'm not really thirsty right at the moment and honestly I wouldn't mind seeing what comes out of those two planes," I responded, beginning to retrace my steps.

Suddenly I felt not only Manny, but also Vince and his three team members, beside me. That was somewhat gratifying. They were actually following yours truly.

We watched closely as the two large rear doors swung down to the ground. Within five minutes some movement was finally noticed and from each plane, walking in unison but not really marching, were two groups of twenty highly armed soldiers. One group of twenty exited each aircraft. They wore large backpacks, had serious looking pistols belted around their waists and large powerful rifles which appeared to me to be something resembling machine guns slung over their shoulders. It also looked like a first lieutenant led each group. Once the two platoons had completely disembarked, they turned and orders were then barked out whereby the soldiers began to march in unison towards the front of their respective planes. They completely ignored us as they passed by. It was easy to figure out that these commandos, as General Smith referred to them earlier, were some very highly trained and dangerous SOB's.

Following the soldiers disembarking from each plane came two M1128 Stryker Mobile Gun System (MGS) vehicles. Each of them carried a 105mm cannon which was the same type cannon that the original M-1 Abrams Tank displayed. I learned all of this later so don't get the impression that I was up on my commando/army badass firepower. Once the parade of soldiers and cool equipment had ended, then it was just supplies being unloaded so we all turned and walked back towards the hangar. It was actually good timing because the meeting was just about to start.

The commandos, dressed in camouflaged fatigues, stood off to the right. Until they were instructed otherwise they all seemed to be standing at parade rest. Colonel McDowell and his officers took up the center, while Captain Crosson and we civilian law enforcement figures banded together on the left. Howard Smith walked to the front of the group and turned slowly to face us. His two 'men in black' henchman stood behind him about five feet, to the right and left. I never once saw them break their intense stare which was actually kind of freaky. If I needed any guards, I wanted those two guys.

"Gentlemen and ladies, thank you all for being so precise in attending this meeting. I will not waste any of your time and spout a lot of nonsense simply because we don't have precious time to spare. To bring some of you up to date though, I will need to provide some background. Back in 1983 an unidentified flying object crashed in the desert outside of Tucson. I believe if you had the time to research this occurrence you would definitely find articles in the local papers back around that time concerning numerous sightings. The Air Force responded very quickly and made the area off limits. After securing the site, the wreckage was loaded onto transport vehicles and originally brought here to this base. If I'm not mistaken it actually came to this very hangar. But that's beside the point. This is no time for a history lesson by some doddering old fool.

"In addition to the unidentified vehicle itself, some form of alien-type entity was discovered within the wreckage. It was at first thought to be liquid in nature, but did have some unexplainable gelatinous-type structure. The extreme violence of the crash apparently caused this strange material to be totally immobile. It was very carefully recovered and placed within a thick, glass enclosed unit, then moved to a very secure location under strict twenty-four guard. It was kept here on this facility for a short period of time until it was subsequently moved to a very highly secured location outside of Tucson, which was actually a decommissioned Titan II missile silo site. This action was taken after a good deal of renovation was performed to not only create a highly secretive environment, but able to provide much higher security around the clock. Any of you who have toured one of those locations would immediately see why that was done."

Smith paused and took a few sips from a bottle of water he held in his left hand. Coughing once, he then continued. "Other than not being too successful in discovering much at all about this entity over its thirty years of imprisonment, it apparently learned a great deal about us. As a result, it was able to escape using some type of mind control. It first appeared to take over a scientist's body as a host. The videos that I've seen show it entering the doctor through the mouth while he lay on the floor twitching and bleeding through the eyes and nose. It then vacated that host and took over a soldier, thus having control of a firearm where it then commenced shooting other guards. That body was discovered topside where at some point it must've reverted to its original state and passed through the gate. Outside cameras showed nothing.

"So then after thirty years what did we really learn about this thing? Number one, it appears to be extremely intelligent. Number two, that it can take over a host body and then apparently transform it into something larger and more terrifying. Number three, it is difficult to kill because of thick body armor in the way of scales. And number four, it also apparently has the unique ability to camouflage itself extremely well, almost to the point of seeming to disappear right in front of your eyes."

Smith paused, more for effect apparently, and then smiled.

"Any questions so far, or anything more to add? Dr. Warring, Colonel McDowell, Chief Crosson?"

After a long moment of additional silence I stepped forward.

"Yes General Smith, there is something of vital importance I believe that needs to be made known. Something that we just discovered this morning, in fact."

Smith smiled and moved back, using his left hand to request I come forward which I did. Never liking the prospect of addressing any group, no matter how large or small, I realized that I quickly needed to get over my nervousness. Turning around I faced the group which was extremely silent, all eyes pointed directly towards me.

"Okay, so some of you are aware there was a confrontation with this creature several weeks ago that was pretty rough to say the least. There were some deaths and injuries. Then nothing happened for a period of time. In fact, the situation became strangely silent. We began to wonder whether it had been mortally wounded, or whether it had just fled to a completely different location to heal. However, earlier this week there was another violent confrontation. It was total chaos, believe me. The worst fighting that I personally have ever been involved in. Yet, as strange as it seemed at the time, bodies were going down left and right with what appeared to be serious injuries only to slowly rise again about five or ten minutes after falling unconscious to the ground. It was like they were in some kind of hypnotic state, very groggy and talking slow, mumbling total nonsense. Almost like they were trying to learn everything anew."

I hesitated at that point, not for added effect. Just thinking how to continue.

"So, we received a 911 call early this morning from a few hikers who came across a cave up in the Catalina's. They ventured inside only to discover at least one body, possibly more. I was accompanied by Detective Corroda and Vince Flint to investigate the crime scene. Believe me, it was as gruesome as you could ever imagine. We saw what appeared to possibly be three bodies in various forms of decay and dismemberment. I'm explaining it that way because two of the bodies seemed to be somewhat intact, but......", suddenly pausing so I could compose myself.

I quickly felt a hand on my shoulder. Glancing around I noticed that it was General Smith who smiled at me.

"Please take your time detective. I'm sure you're doing better than most of us would be after seeing all of that. Are you okay to continue?"

I smiled back. "Yes, thank you. Okay, let me just say that there were human remains scattered all about. At least two of the bodies seemed to be somewhat intact, but really torn apart badly. I mean like ripped down the middle. Outside the pit and further into the cave we viewed quite a few dismembered limbs and other body parts just lying around in a haphazard fashion. I can't say more than that other than we did not want to search any further in case we screwed something up. However, even more distressing, especially mysterious, we noticed at the bottom of this deep pit broken material that resembled cracked egg shells. I'm no biologist or mathematician, but if broken stuff resembled egg shells then that sort of meant to us that something hatched in that cave."

I turned around. "That's about it, General Smith. The cave itself was empty in regards to anything alive besides maggots and other thriving insects. At least what we could see. The pit and scattered remains was about fifty-sixty feet inside. But as I stated earlier, we did not venture any deeper."

"Thank you detective. It certainly sounds like an extremely upsetting scene and I feel completely certain that I probably would not have handled it as well as you did."

I wasn't sure if he was just patronizing me, but it was nice to hear anyway. There was about a minute where people shuffled around nervously and talked aloud amongst themselves. That is until Howard Smith moved forward and held up his hand for total silence.

"So Detective Stephenson, what you've revealed to us is that we have a fifth, and rather disturbing, ability that this creature possesses. Apparently it can now lay eggs and thus reproduce."

"Yes General Smith, that's the way it appeared to each of us. The bottom of the hole was a mess with the two bodies and lots of blood strewn around. Also, there was all of that cracked egg shell material and other disgusting white and yellow fluid caste about. Apparently, that must've come from inside the eggs after the evil lizards, or worms, hatched. How many were there before they broke open? Hard to say until a CSI team attempts to put the pieces back together like Humpty-Dumpty, or a mad jigsaw puzzle. I'm going to somewhat go out on a limb and say that it may be at least fifteen or more."

The general shook my hand and patted me on the back like I was a little girl although I didn't think that truly was his intention. Maybe I was just being a little too sensitive, but I thought I deserved to be after everything I had been through. Turning towards the crowd he remained quiet until all the murmuring died down.

"So now you have some idea of what we're up against. Conventional weapons don't seem to bother it that much because of this armor plating it has covering the body. By conventional, I'm referring to bullets from regular firearms, i.e. standard pistols and rifles. We may, in fact, need to use armor piercing ammunition. I believe it was also made known from the first altercation out in the desert that some type of blood substance was found so possibly it was temporarily injured as a result of explosions from hand grenades. That at least tells me it can be seriously hurt, or killed, as all living creatures can. But please remember people, what you are physically doing battle with here is just a body, human or animal, that can bleed and will die. This alien entity uses these bodies to get around just like any vehicle, but it also appears to enhance them beyond their natural capabilities. Possibly through some form of transformation. The key to possibly being able to destroy it will be when the thing leaves its host because destroying the body it has possessed will only destroy the host. And, now it appears we not only have the original one to deal with, but who knows how many more."

He definitely paused for drama this time, adding just that more tension to the situation. Then he looked intensely out at everybody.

"Any questions? Now's the time to ask them before we start preparing for what happens next."

One of the commando officers stepped forward. "Sir, Lieutenant Frawley here. Can you give us a description of what this thing might look like? And, do we have any idea where it might've gone?"

"Let me have one of the people who faced it out in the field address that. Mr. Flint, would you please be so kind?"

Vince strolled forward. I was thankful that Smith didn't ask me to address the crowd again since public speaking was apparently not my niche. My stomach was still roiling after my last dissertation.

Flint coughed before starting to talk. "This thing, whatever the heck it is, or wherever the hell it came from, apparently took over the body of a Gila monster once free from its prison. Possibly through several transformations it has grown to monstrous proportions. Think Gila monster times five or more, but with thick scales like armor plating. It also has a huge tail like a battering ram. We found some of the scaly material lying on the ground and have samples if anyone would like to look at them. Experiments are being done right at the moment to see what they might be. This creature not only has the ability to camouflage itself with its surroundings, but can also nearly disappear utilizing some damn form of rippling effect in the air. Meaning, if you see the air in front of you wavering like water then it may be a good idea to shoot first, or it might be too late."

A voice spoke up from the commando group, "You mean like in 'Predator'?"

Laughter rippled through the crowd. "Well, that does sound kind of comical doesn't it?" Flint responded, but he wasn't laughing. "However, when I tell you that several of us witnessed something very similar to that, then maybe we should put out a call to Arnold. He's free at the moment I believe and making movies again."

Laughter broke out, but it was more tension filled this time.

The same wiseass voice spoke up again. "So then it appears we are looking for a blob-like creature who can appear and disappear like the predator, but also looks like a creature from the black lagoon. That really sounds peachy. Do we have any idea where this thing is?"

Lieutenant Frawley spoke up. "Quit being a smartass, Sergeant. Gray. We obviously know we are dealing with something alien oriented and this is no goddamn science fiction or horror movie. This is real time shit that is happening. What we need to know is how to locate and then kill it. Plus, if there are little baby worms or lizards, then they need to be disposed of as well."

There was silence again which was quickly broken by General Smith.

"Well people, what we need to do right this minute is get prepared. Lieutenants Frawley and Spinner, get your teams ready to respond at a moment's notice. I have been informed by Colonel McDowell that currently there are four teams of five soldiers out in the field, and have been for several days. In addition, helicopters have been flying over that area non-stop. I know you all have armor piercing ammunition so get it ready. Be prepared to move as soon as we have an idea where it is, or might be heading.

"Chief Crosson, I would suggest that your officers prepare as well. There is no telling where this thing may be at the present time other than it left the cave site and has at least fifteen or more offspring of some kind. Until the situation is taken care of then it would not be a bad idea to end all leaves and vacations. Get your force ready to respond to any serious altercation within the city. I will for the time being remain here on base with Colonel McDowell. We will monitor everything between the four teams in the field and the two platoons of commandos. We will stay in constant touch with everybody."

With all the talking taking place I thought of something that might be important.

"Excuse me General Smith, I was just thinking of something additional that may or may not be important. In the battle we had with this thing back on Tuesday night when I got injured we witnessed a number of officers appearing to be hurt seriously. Yet, they all seemed to recover within five or ten minutes. Do you think it's possible that each of these individuals could've been taken over by the offspring?"

General Smith stared at me for a few seconds and started nodding his head. Then, he looked over at Crosson.

"Sir, do you think you can contact each of those individuals that were hurt in the altercation to see how they're coming along? Did any of them end up being admitted to the hospital for further examination and treatment?"

Chief Crosson responded, "Other than three that were outright killed, to my knowledge only three or four with serious injuries were admitted to hospitals. The rest were examined by medical personnel at the site, or from the ER, and then released to go home and recuperate. Some of them had injuries, but nothing life threatening or of a serious nature. When I get back to headquarters we can find out who those individuals were and contact each of them either by phone, or directly with responding officers."

"Okay, sounds good. Please report back to us here at the base with your findings," replied Smith.

After a few moments to let all of that sink in, General Smith looked at everybody once more. "So, without further ado we need to start the ball rolling and get prepared so that you can respond at a moment's notice. Each officer in charge of their respective group will report back to Colonel McDowell's office which will in effect be home base. Let's get going everyone. But please remember, be alert and stay safe at all times."

We had been inside the hangar for well over an hour before walking outside only to find the weather had changed quickly. That was how it could be in Arizona, especially Tucson. The morning could be sunny and bright, plus very hot. Within hours a storm could cross over the mountains and a quick deluge could fall down upon the city and surrounding desert area. Depending on the severity of the storm, streets and highways could also quickly flood since the drainage system left something to be desired. In fact, there literally wasn't any drainage system 'per se' in and around the city. So when there was a deluge it normally flooded, simple as that. The good part was after the rain stopped within a few hours it could very well be sunny and blistering hot again, thus helping to get rid of all the water.

Since we had flown onto the base in a helicopter we had no vehicle present. So Captain Masters, who had driven over to the hangar since he was already on the air base, reluctantly agreed to drive us out to the main airport where we had left Manny's car. The going was slow because of all the rain and subsequent flooding. We got there none the worse for wear. Captain Masters said that he was going to stop by his house and get a change of clothing, plus a good meal, before heading into police headquarters. He suggested that we do the same.

Manny dropped me and Flint off at my house, also reluctantly. What the hell, Vince's SUV was parked in my driveway so where else was he supposed to go. I kissed my partner on the cheek and told him not to be an old mother hen. I would be fine.

Which was true. Vince and I went inside, had a small lunch of tomato soup and grilled cheese sandwiches. Oh yeah, I finally had a chance to make a quick stop at a grocery store. We talked for a while and soon fell asleep in each other's arms because quite frankly we were exhausted having gotten up early. And that's all that happened, honestly. Cross my heart and hope to........., well I'm not going there.

Chapter 26

A low rumbling noise disturbed the creature from its partial slumber. Glancing quickly out the window it noticed that the day was somewhat dark and dreary, raindrops heavily coating the glass. However, it wasn't the storm making the noise that had really alerted it. The creature noticed that some type of large, extremely loud vehicle had pulled into the driveway. It was actually a 2006 Dodge Ram truck whose engine was quite noisy. When the motor finally shut off the driver door flew open and a thin, but attractive, middle-aged blonde female jumped onto the wet pavement. She quickly raised a large umbrella over her head to at least try to keep her white short sleeved blouse and black skirt dry. Sadly, she knew her shoes were about to get soaked. As she slammed the door shut, the passenger door opened. Sliding out of the seat from that side was a young man in his mid-twenties who did not have an umbrella. So he pulled his jacket up over his head. She had decided to pick up Ricky Fallon from her office on the way to this house, figuring she didn't want to come out here alone.

Sheila Moore was the realtor and had received a telephone call from a neighbor saying that he had heard some noise last night that may have come from the rear of this particular property. After making sure their own house and property was secure, he and his wife went back to bed. Since they waited and listened closely for about half an hour, hearing no other worrisome noises, they just didn't think anything more about it. Then over breakfast in the morning they had second thoughts and decided to call the phone number on the 'For Sale' sign in the front yard.

She thanked them and decided to stop and check out this property since an earlier appointment to show a different house had canceled because of the weather. It actually started pouring rain on her way over so she started to somewhat regret her decision thinking it was going to just be a wild goose chase anyway. Now she was here and since the neighbor had stated he and his wife had heard a noise possibly from the rear of the property she decided to walk around the left side. She instructed Ricky to go around the other way. If anybody had broken into the house then the last thing she wanted to do was just barge in through the front door and get accosted, or even something much worse.

Tucson and other beautiful cities in the southwest have wonderful perks like nice weather most of the time. No frigid temperatures, exquisitely sharp night skies, as well as definitely little snow to shovel. However, having really nice lawns that grew naturally was not one of them. Many residents just gave up and filled in their properties with colored stones which was great because you didn't have to buy a lawn mower and you could paint them any color you wanted. Other property owners, especially those from northern and eastern states, liked the beauty of green yards so sod was installed quite often. You could grow grass of course, primarily Bermuda, but it took lots of work.

For this property it was a combination of both. The front of the house was more a blend of dirt, stone, cement, and plants, even two cactus. The rear of the house had sod installed around the porch, back deck, and pool area. So she simply stayed on the sidewalk which went around the left side of the structure to the backyard. When she finally approached the rear of the house she was stunned to see the double sliding glass doors completely shattered and the frames bent in towards the kitchen like little twigs.

Ricky had finally come up beside her. They both stood staring at the destroyed door. To say they were completely stunned would've been an understatement.

"This does not look good at all," Sheila whispered nervously. "What the hell could've done that? We need to call the police right away."

"Yeah, I agree. Want me to take a look inside?" he asked, rather tentatively.

"Let me first make a call to report this. Then we'll both go in together," getting out her phone and dialing 911.

After letting the emergency operator know who she was, where they were, and tried to describe what seemed to have happened, she was told to just wait and not to venture inside the property. She was to go around front and stand near her vehicle. A squad car would be responding shortly. Also, to call back if the situation worsened.

"Well, the operator told me to wait. But, I have to see what's happened in there. Let's at least go slowly up to the door and peek in," Sheila whispered.

"Why are you whispering?" Ricky whispered back.

"Shut up, don't make so much noise. You never know if something is in there like an animal, or maybe some homeless person. We'll just stop on the outside and look in, see if we can hear anything. Come on," she said, grabbing his hand and tugging.

"Damn big animal Sheila if it could break through those doors like that," he responded in just a little higher voice than a whisper this time.

Sheila squeezed his hand tighter to be quiet. They very tentatively moved forward on the stone patio and then climbed onto the porch. Another few steps brought them to shattered glass that had fallen onto the deck. The only illumination inside the house came from what small amount of light fell across the doorstep from the dreariness outside. They could easily see more shattered glass strewn all over the white and green tile on the kitchen floor. She shuddered at the damage they would have to repair.

"Sheila, we're not going in there," whispered Ricky. "They told you not to."

"Yes Ricky, we are going inside. At least just into the kitchen. The police should be here any minute. I just need to see what's happened in there."

Still holding his right hand very tightly she heard him mutter, 'this is not right'. She tugged him harder behind her. With glass crunching beneath their shoes they stepped over the damaged threshold into the dark kitchen. Sheila wished that she had had the forethought to bring along a flashlight. Unfortunately, that was stashed away inside the glove compartment out in the truck. Great place for it, she thought.

Sheila listened closely and heard nothing so that seemed to give her a little bit of courage. "Ricky, you go through the doorway on the left into the hallway and I'll go through this one on the right into the dining room. We'll meet in the living room. Just please be careful. Yell out if something doesn't look right."

"You don't have to tell me twice to do that. I don't really want to go anyplace so you better believe I'm going to run like hell if I hear or see anything. Do you want the light turned on?" he replied, in a loud whisper.

"No, if something or somebody is in here sleeping it might alert them," she said, leaning her closed umbrella up against the refrigerator.

They each took a few steps before she stopped suddenly, hearing Ricky hiss loudly. Turning, Sheila saw him pointing to the shattered doorway like something very large had forced its way through. Her heart dropped even more because not only would they have to install a brand new double sliding glass door in the kitchen, that entire doorway would have to be rebuilt, also. She immediately saw profits dwindling away.

She motioned him to go forward anyway as she turned to cross into the dining area. Then she heard a loud hiss like a snake and a thud behind her. Quickly spinning around, she didn't see Ricky at all so she assumed he must've bumped into something in the darkness, knocking it over. He had always been a clumsy kid anyway.

Moving forward she noticed that the dining room looked somewhat to be in good shape, but it was fairly dark so she couldn't really tell for certain. Placing her right hand on the table using it as a crutch, Sheila took a few more steps and then stopped suddenly. There was definitely a strange noise now, like something sliding along the floor. Then a very low rumble from the darker part of the living room. Her instincts screamed to just turn and run as fast as she could. But this was her property dammit. She wasn't going to let anything, or anybody, scare her away. As stupid as that sounded in her head.

Another two shuffle-like steps brought her to the arched doorway leading to the living room. As she started tilting her head to the left something large came out of the darkness towards her. Alarmed, she screamed loudly before it struck and propelled her spinning backwards against the heavy oak table. Hitting her head hard, she slid down and was totally unconscious before hitting the floor.

The creature quickly turned and moved back to Ricky's battered body His throat had been sliced wide open, nearly decapitated, a dark stream of blood now running across the floor. Quickly the beast dropped down and began to feed by tearing large chunks out of the young man's chest and stomach, nearly swallowing them whole. It gagged out whatever clothing it ingested. Within five minutes his body was literally torn apart and the beast's hunger was somewhat sated. At least for the moment anyway.

Suddenly the monster heard a loud, shrill sound and then saw flashing lights outside the structure. It remembered a large open field not far away so it moved quickly, grabbed the body of the female in its mouth, and scuttled very quickly out the shattered back door. There was a five foot high wooden fence in the rear of the yard that it smashed through easily enough and then quickly disappeared. It had more important plans for the female. At least it had also pretty much stopped raining which was good.

In front of the house, two Tucson cops, Matt Kent and John Swanson, had gotten out of their vehicle and glanced in the truck. Not seeing anybody inside the vehicle, or even outside for that matter around the house, they moved towards the front door. Kent knocked and got no response. He then tried the door handle which was locked.

Swanson motioned that he would take the right side and for Kent to go around the left. They met at the deck, looked at the shattered back door and pulled their service revolvers. Kent hit his mic and radioed in that the person making the 911 call was not outside, and that the house had considerable damage in the rear. They were going in and requested additional backup.

Once inside the kitchen they continued to see damage, shattered glass all over the floor and the small dinner table pushed to one side with several broken chairs. There was also a pink umbrella lying on the floor. Kent went left and his partner moved right.

In less than a minute Officer Kent responded in a low voice, "John, we have a body over here on the floor. It's bad, really bad. All torn up! My God, what a mess."

"There's some blood over here on the floor, but no body. The table is shoved out of the way and there appears to be a blood trail like something was slid or carried."

They checked the three bedrooms and bathroom which revealed nothing more. They both unlocked the front door and went outside. Kent called in again to report what they had found. They would remain outside so as not to contaminate the crime scene any more than they may have already. Back in their car they waited for back-up.

"What the hell is going on in this city?" questioned a somewhat nervous John Swanson. "I mean, that poor kid was literally torn open from waist to neck. Nobody should die like that. I don't even see how another human being could've done it."

"Yeah, that just might be the most gruesome thing I've ever seen," his partner responded. "I don't know what's running loose around this city, but to me it's like a serial monster terrorizing Tucson and I don't like that even one little bit."

At that moment they heard sirens from several cars approaching. Neither one truly wanted to go back into that house with such a really gruesome crime scene.

Chapter 27

Chief Crosson slammed his fist down on the desk. "What the hell is going on here? How can it get from a damn cave in the desert to an empty house in the suburbs without being seen? Is this creature some type of diabolical magician as well?"

Sergeant John McCorty wasn't sure how to answer those questions, but figured he had to say something, or else look like a pure dumbass.

"Sir, whatever this thing is, it's definitely nothing like we've ever seen before."

Crosson glanced up and glared in McCorty's direction. "What are you, a dumbass? Sorry, forget that remark. Please John, tell me something I don't already know. In fact, that's probably the only damn thing I do know because we don't know a damn thing. Is there any capable people in the squad room you can send out there?"

"Yes, we have Sanchez, Phillips, Mills, and Smith."

"Where is Stephenson and Corroda? Does anybody even know?"

"I believe they're still at home, but it's still pretty early. Maybe they went to church since its Sunday morning," McCorty answered with just the hint of a smile.

"I don't give a holy crap what day it is. Besides, I don't even think Detective Stephenson ever saw the inside of a church. She'd be in confession 24/7. Get hold of them now and if you have to leave a message tell them they're going to be arrested if they don't get their lazy asses in here within the hour."

"Who do you want sent over to that house? It's actually close by, about three or four blocks away," the sergeant asked.

"Do your job McCorty. Pick somebody and get their worthless butts over there. Also, make a phone call to those dickheads on the air base so they know what we've found in that house. Maybe they want to send somebody out there."

McCorty walked out of the office, closed the door, and took a deep breath. He figured that his hair was going to turn gray pretty quickly if this creature wasn't found and soon, especially having to deal with Peter Crosson all day long.

He strolled down the short hallway into the larger squad room. Normally on a Sunday morning there would only be a few lonesome souls hanging around, primarily the detectives who had no family, no life other than tracking down criminals, and/or still hung over from a night of drinking away their miseries and personal problems.

"Sanchez and Smith, pull yourselves together and get over to this property," as he handed them a sheet of paper. "It's not that far from here. From what I understand there is one deceased male that was torn up pretty badly. Plus, one older female that seems to be missing. Check it out and then get back to me as soon as you can because Chief Crosson wants answers and results, like yesterday."

They both started moving, but not nearly fast enough.

"Come on guys, hit the bricks now," McCorty yelled, "I'm not going to get my ass chewed out anymore because you two are still hung over. I need to contact the air base to give them information on this attack so I'm going to give you half an hour to look around out there before they show up in all their military glory. Move it guys."

He turned and headed for his desk, took a long gulp of cold coffee, and reached for the phone. On the second ring Manny answered, actually sounding pretty alert surprisingly. He was told to report to headquarters as quickly as possible and hung up before the detective had a chance to bitch about anything.

On his second call, the phone rang five times before a groggy-voiced Amelia Stephenson answered.

"Yeah, this is Amy. What's goin' on?"

"Detective, this is Sgt. McCorty. Get up, take a cold shower and get your skinny butt in here within the hour. Direct orders from Chief Crosson. I've already gotten hold of Manny so he's probably getting in his car as we speak. Don't worry about trying to look beautiful, that's a lost cause. Chop, chop Amy. You know the way Crosson gets and he's constantly pissed off at you as it is. Please make him happy this one time."

He hung up and I just looked at the phone, then dropped it on the nightstand. Throwing the bedspread off me I started turning over to crawl out of bed. The pain shot through my left shoulder like somebody stuck a freaking bowie knife right into the rotator cuff which I had to have repaired four years ago. As a result, I groaned and moaned quite loudly. That elicited some movement on the other side of the bed.

"What's up Amelia? Who was on the phone?"

"It was McCorty. Appears we've been summoned by Chief Crosson to attend a meeting in the office. I need to take a quick shower, throw on anything I can find that's clean, and then head into the shop. Manny's on his way supposedly. I kind of get the impression something else happened by how agitated the sergeant was on the phone."

I tried standing up straight and additional pain shot through my right thigh where the deep bone bruise was.

"Ah man, that really freaking hurts," I groaned again as I stood slowly.

Flint had also thrown off the bedspread and stood up, naked as a jaybird. I glanced over at him and was amazed at the body he possessed. I know the saying, *'built like a brick shithouse'* is mainly intended to describe a hot chick, but in this regard it definitely fit one Mr. Vince Flint, soldier of fortune.

"Hey buddy boy, don't even think for one minute that your special endowments will entice me into jumping back onto this bed. As much as I'd love to do just that, I'd rather keep my job for at least a little while longer."

He laughed while reaching down on the floor for his jeans. Coming around the end of the bed he put his arm around me, I think simply trying to help support my somewhat crippled body. However, his right hand cupped my right breast and I kind of moaned. Trust me though, not in pain. I reached up and lightly slapped his hand even though I didn't want to.

"Cut that out you big pervert. I need to get ready to go," I responded.

Then I turned and faced him. "Vince, what the heck are we actually doing here? I mean, I really do like you a lot. You're a terrific guy, a real gentleman when you want to be, you have a magnificent body, and the sex is out of this world. But honestly, I'm not sure where this is heading, and if it's even the time for this type of a relationship."

"Amy, I'm not holding you down to anything. I really like you too, a lot in fact. But right now we're helping each other get through this. Whatever happens afterwards we'll just have to see if it goes anywhere. Right at this very moment I'm spending time with a beautiful woman that is hotter than hell and funnier than shit. Let's just enjoy this time together and if we live through it then we'll see what transpires later. Deal?"

"Yeah, it's a deal I suppose. Want to scrub my back anyway?"

He smiled. "Oh yeah, and a few other body parts as well if you don't mind."

Twenty-five minutes later we were racing to headquarters at 270 S. Stone Avenue, both in our own cars. No telling what was going to happen, or where we would have to go. At least if we were split up then we'd have our own vehicles available.

The creature moved as quickly as possible and sought out a rather secluded section of the area originally known as Military Park Plaza. More recently it was referred to as Armory Park Plaza. There were buildings dotting the grounds with enough hidden space to remain somewhat secluded. There were some trees, lots of grass, and a knoll that provided some protection for what it needed to do next. However, what was convenient on this particular day was that the earlier rain had clearly deterred the normal amount of people spending time in the park so it was relatively empty.

Even though it utilized camouflage techniques to hide its own massive bulk, the body of the female was another story. It had noticed this relatively large open area when it had been searching for somewhere to hide. Several streets had to be crossed so great care needed to be taken because the female's body could still be noticed. If it saw an oncoming vehicle on one of the streets then it placed the body on its other side trying to somewhat hide it. If anybody noticed, they didn't yell out simply because they were unsure what they were actually seeing.

What needed to be done next would not take long to accomplish. It realized during the night while resting that it had to be rid of this huge, monstrous body. The need to pass openly within this human colony was now much more critical. Out in the desert the transformations that the lizard's body went through had been important. Successfully surviving the few battles with humans, then being able to give birth to the hatchlings was just the next steps in taking over the entire area. Now it needed to transform again, but in a different way. It had to blend in and become more human in appearance. Like the entire brood was now. That way it could move around in the open much easier.

The creature dropped the unconscious body of the female onto the wet grass and stood over top of her before glancing around to see if the area was somewhat clear. Without wasting time, mainly because it sensed that humans would soon be searching with great intensity after crashing free of the structure it had been hiding in, it forced opened the lizard's mouth as wide as possible and then began regurgitating. It wasn't trying to throw up the food it had just ingested from Ricky's dead body. Rather free itself from the animal's framework.

After gagging and retching for about thirty seconds, its natural form started to ooze out. It had to release control of all the internal organs. Finally, it plopped right onto the stomach of the female. The creature's actual form was between one and two feet long, bright red, and looked like a long, thick tube of gum, well chewed and lumpy. It immediately began crawling towards the woman's mouth which it opened easily enough with its pointed snout-like head. Once her mouth was agape it started invading her body.

Sheila was not dead yet, only unconscious. Her eyes burst open as her body began violently jerking up and down on the ground like she was having an epileptic seizure, gagging the entire time. Fear and shock clearly registered in her face, but at this point she had lost control of her own body. In less than a minute the creature had completely disappeared inside her. Sheila Moore, loving wife and mother of three, excellent realtor with a vivacious and bubbly personality, was now a living puppet.

The lizard's body just fell to the ground where it stood. It would not revert to its smaller original size because of the physical transformations. Someone would come across it and receive the biggest scare of their lives when seeing that monstrous form.

Sheila was virtually very still now other than a few tics in her face and fingers. The creature reached out with tentacles from its own body, slithering up the spinal column and brain stem, boring into the vital organs like the heart, lungs, kidneys, etc. Some of the vital organs were really not required anymore. Up to this point Sheila was still barely alive although she had absolutely no control over anything. She would not officially die until it exited her body and was now simply a vehicle for this alien creature. It would continue to work on her inside structure because the reptile DNA was now the master component. Being able to alter shape was still paramount. Several bodily conversions would be needed to allow scales to cover her skin, much larger teeth and claws to extend outward, and a stronger body type to be created. Then she would no longer appear human in any way when in battle mode.

After allowing the body to rest for about ten minutes it began to test motor functions. Sheila's legs and arms began to pump while still lying down on the ground. She moved her head back and forth while fingers and toes curled and straightened out. Finally, she sat up easily enough and then rose on her legs, a little wobbly at first, but not too clumsily. Now the vocal chords needed to be tested.

It yelled out, "Hello! Please! Thank you! My name is Sheila!"

The creature was pleased now that the body would move human-like and be able to speak when required, though it would attempt to keep that to a minimum. Now it needed to see if the claws and teeth would work. Sadly, nerves were still active in her body so as the fingernails extended out at least two inches into claws and her teeth began sprouting to more animalistic size and sharpness, she moaned aloud in pain. The creature felt nothing so it didn't matter that Sheila's body did. The final step was to allow scales to appear on her arms and face. Once again the pain was enormous. Within a minute, large and extremely thick, one inch square scales covered her arms from hands to shoulders. Her cheeks and chin also changed, becoming more pointed in appearance.

It moved Sheila around by walking back and forth, much like a diabolical puppet master. Now it was secure in knowing that it was prepared to move. The very last action it needed to do before exiting the park was send forth a signal to each brood member, advising them to get on the move and away from the locations where they had recently transformed and fed. They would hide in more secure locations until a stronger signal would be sent out so they could follow it to where they would reunite with the parent.

Now the creature started Sheila moving out of the park area towards the spot where it had followed the ethereal trail from the female out in the desert, that being 270 S. Stone Avenue, Tucson Police Headquarters. If she didn't show up then it would be able to find somebody there that had been with her recently. One way or the other the creature was going to locate its prey.

Chapter 28

Officers Geraldo Ruiz and Janet Lacey knocked on the front door of Robert Perkin's house. After rapping hard two more times they backed away and looked at each other.

"What do you think?" asked Ruiz. "He should be at home resting from what I understand since he was injured during that battle. Is the car in the garage?"

"Yes, I glanced in one of the windows as we walked past the door," answered Lacey. "Let me take a walk around back and check it out."

"Okay, give a shout if you find anything. Just be careful, no telling what's happening here. I'll keep knocking in front. Maybe take a peek in the windows."

Lacey walked around to the backyard and once there immediately saw that the backdoor was standing wide open. She noticed what possibly appeared to be their dog, a light brown cocker spaniel, which was lying down at the end of the patio.

"Hey buddy, come here. Come on, I won't hurt you," she coaxed, patting the ground as she knelt down on one knee trying not to scare it away.

At first the dog wouldn't move, just kept staring at the open door. After some more prompting by Lacey it got up and slowly moved cautiously in her direction. As it got closer the officer began to take notice that there was something on the dog's paws, stomach, and rear end. When it got to within a few feet Janet realized what it was. Reaching out she gently pulled the dog towards her and noticed how badly it was shaking. Plus, it definitely appeared to be blood on the dog's fur and feet.

Once she had the animal secure she yelled out, "Hey partner, get back here. Hurry up, too. I think we have a serious issue on our hands."

Ruiz quickly came around the side of the house and walked over to where she was kneeling in the yard with the dog.

"What's up? Hey, is that blood on the dog?"

"Yeah, sure as hell looks like it. The backdoor is wide open, too. You want to call for backup because we may have a crime scene here. We should also take a look inside because something doesn't appear right at all."

A few minutes later they were both approaching the backdoor. The dog remained outside on the patio seeming to be too frightened to enter the house. Ruiz cautiously took a few steps into the kitchen first, Lacey following right behind. Everything seemed to be in order. Nothing appeared to be broken or out of place. They continued through the kitchen into both the dining and living room areas which also appeared to be okay. There was just some books and magazines lying around on the floor near the couch and coffee table. However, it was eerily quiet in the house, especially since somebody should've been home with two cars still parked inside the garage.

Ruiz tapped Lacy on the shoulder and held up his hand, then pointed towards the staircase. He silently mouthed the word, 'slow'.

"This is the Tucson police, anybody in the house?" he yelled loudly. "If anyone is upstairs please holler down to let us know you're okay, or whether you need any help."

No response came from his request. They then moved towards the bottom of the staircase. At this point their firearms were out and ready. They began slowly climbing the steps with their backs sliding against the wall. At the top they stepped quietly onto the hallway where Ruiz reissued his request. It was received again with no response. Immediately to the right was a bedroom. Straight ahead was the bathroom, then three more bedrooms were positioned down the hallway on the right side, as well as a large window at the end of the corridor. Ruiz noticed what he thought could possibly be a smeared bloody handprint on one of the glass panes.

"Check out the bathroom, I'll cover you," Lacey whispered, her service revolver held tightly with both hands and pointed forward.

Ruiz carefully pushed in an already slightly open door and glanced quickly inside. Immediately he noticed a good deal of blood splashed all over the sink and carpet. He turned back to Lacey and shook his head, whispering 'blood'. He then pointed to the larger room where the door was closed, obviously the master bedroom. They both carefully moved to where they stood on each side of the door. It was shut so Lacey knocked once, placed her hand on the knob and turned, then gave the door a gentle push.

"Anybody in the room? If you are, let us know before we come in. This is the Tucson police!" she yelled out.

No verbal response of any kind came from inside, but a very strong odor assaulted them right away. They both had started smelling something out of place when they first entered the kitchen. Now here in the bedroom it was extremely strong. They both spun into the room, Lacey high and Ruiz low.

"Oh my God," Lacey whispered immediately. "Geraldo, do you see that?"

"Yeah, I see it. Sweet Jesus," he responded, holding his gun out in front with his left hand and at the same time making a cross on his chest with the right.

"I can't tell who or what that is on the bed other than it's a body. I'm going to guess its female because of what appears to be a torn nightgown. I can't see how she could still be alive. My God, all that blood," said Lacey, trying to hold her stomach together. "Should we go in any further?"

"I don't think so. She definitely appears to be dead. With all the blood on the floor we don't want to screw up the crime scene," answered Ruiz, in a voice that definitely quivered.

"Yeah, but we need to make sure she's gone," replied Lacey. "I'll be careful where I walk. Just keep your eyes open in case anything is hiding in the closet. I don't feel like being lunch for some damn monster."

Lacey kept her eyes focused on the floor trying her best not to step in any blood spots or prints on the floor. When she got to the side of the bed she just about vomited right there. In fact, she did turn towards the window and made a nauseous sound in her throat. The woman's neck was nearly completely torn out and her stomach was sliced opened from bottom of the ribcage down to below the waist.

Letting some dizziness pass she quickly stumbled back around the bed to stand shakily beside her partner. "She's definitely dead. Oh my God, I've never seen anything like that before in my entire life and hope never to again."

They backed out slowly into the hallway. "We need to check out the other rooms. You ready?" asked Ruiz.

"Hell no, but we have to do our job. You first, but watch where you step because there are bloody footprints all over the floor," responded Lacey.

""Yeah, I will. Thanks Janet, you're really good to me."

"Don't think anything about it partner. You'd do the same for me."

Ten minutes later they were standing outside in the front yard. Lacey had already thrown up into some bushes and Ruiz was just about to do the same. They had radioed in the crime scene and were now just waiting for backup to arrive. They had found the torn up bodies of Jeannie Perkins and their two children, Mark and Sherry. There was no sign of Officer Robert Perkins. At this point it was unknown whether he did the killing. Or, something else did and forced him to leave the house. Either way, there were three more dismembered people inside the house, one adult female and two children. The body count just seemed to go even higher.

However, completely unknown to both Ruiz and Lacey, this same scenario was being carried out in at least nineteen other households throughout the City of Tucson.

I walked into the conference room with Vince tagging along right behind me. Manny was already there, along with Chief Crosson, Captain Masters, Lieutenants Spencer and Tolliver, Sergeants McCorty and Flanders, and Dr. Frederick Morgan who was the Chief Medical Examiner, along with several civilians who I did not know.

Nodding to Manny, I went to the side table and poured a cup of coffee, adding cream and sugar. Then grabbing a powdered donut, which I seemed to be hooked on lately, I turned and went to sit in an empty chair beside Flint. I guess he didn't want any pastry to hurt his girlish figure.

I got the sense that something had happened and those of us who did not know what it was were about to find out. I hoped my female intuition was wrong in this case because no news anymore was good news. Taking a few sips of hot coffee, I bit down into the powdered donut just as Chief Crosson stood up from the table.

He removed his glasses and rubbed the bridge of his nose which he normally did when he was really pissed off, or confused about something. I think it was his own tailor made form of anger management. Then taking a deeper breath he looked up.

"Thank you all for coming as quickly as you did. Detective Stephenson, why is Mr. Flint at this meeting? He's obviously a civilian. And you have powdered sugar all over your lips and chin. Quit being such a big slob."

Wiping my mouth with a napkin I then glanced at Vince before responding. "Since we got home pretty late last night and his car was parked out front of my house, he just crashed on the couch. When I got the call this morning from Sgt. McCorty it just felt right that he should be here. He needs to know whatever we know. Plus, he can also get onto the base easier than us and get important information there that could help out. Besides, you have a few other civilians here I believe that were not introduced yet."

When I mentioned that he had slept on my couch there were a few snickers and Crosson just shook his head.

"I'm not even going to pursue that dark avenue any further other than to say you have a lot of men sleeping over at your house lately. Welcome to the party Mr. Flint. Maybe you can actually add something sensible to this mess. Since you asked, sitting at the end of the table are Larry McDonald and Selania Manos from the mayor's office. They are here to listen, observe, and then report back to him with their findings.

"So here's what we've got. None of the phone calls made to any of the twenty responders were answered. Since they all suffered various physical injuries, none requiring admittance to a hospital I might add, they all should've been at home recuperating. A car was dispatched to each location. What they all found to say the least was a complete nightmare. An absolute slaughter was discovered at each household including the children. When I say slaughter, apparently from what could be determined by each responding officer the bodies were not only torn apart, but fed upon as well by something animalistic. The words monster and creature were used quite a lot."

He paused allowing that to sink in. However, it did nothing but crash like lead balloons in all our stomachs.

"What about each of the people that originally got hurt out at the battle site?" Manny inquired. "Were they dead also?"

"None of them were anywhere to be found. Not in the house, not outside, not in the neighborhood. Neighbors are being questioned at this time to see if they saw or heard anything. At this point we don't know where those individuals are, or even what may have happened to them. Maybe they were taken away by whatever monster committed these crimes. Hell, it might be even worse if they did the killing themselves."

At those words a loud murmur broke out around the table.

"Chief Crosson, if you're phrasing it that way then you must be implying that each of these people was taken over by whatever came out of those eggs in that cave." I stated in a very concerned and somewhat fearful voice.

"Amelia, what else do we have to go on? Some of the officers responding to those locations are tough, seasoned veterans and they were puking their guts out in the yard. Hell, some of them even did it in the houses. Sergeant McCorty has put out an APB on all twenty of these individuals so if they're out there roaming the city streets we'll locate them, unless they're hiding out somewhere. I just don't know what we're going to find when we do. I'm as much in the dark as everybody at this point."

Dr. Peter Morgan stood up from the table. "Chief Crosson, you'll have to excuse me from this meeting. I have the feeling things are going to become somewhat chaotic when these bodies start arriving. Besides, there's not much I can add to your locating these individuals, or killing this creature. I will keep you informed as much as possible. Obviously the earlier bodies brought in over the last few weeks could definitely be classified as some type of animal related death. I won't know causes or times of death until we can examine the bodies closely. It's pretty obvious from what little information I've received so far, they were torn apart quite badly."

"You're excused Dr. Morgan and thank you for coming. Somebody will be over to your area at some point for information and be a liaison. I'm quite certain you don't relish what's on your plate, or examination table I would suppose."

"I'm not sure if that was intended to be amusing, or just to relieve some of the tension, but you're right. I'm not looking forward to any of this even one little bit. I'll stay in touch," as he picked up his PC and quickly exited the room.

After about a minute of strained silence, Chief Crosson addressed us all again.

"Okay, so we need to brainstorm here. Throw out onto the table any questions or ideas, thoughts or fears, no matter how crazy they sound. It seemed that at first we were just looking for one creature and now it appears we may have a number of them on the loose."

"Has Davis-Monthan been notified, Chief Crosson?" asked Flint.

"Yes, Captain Masters called them right before this meeting. Oh shit, I nearly forgot. There was another phone call received from a different crime scene a few hours ago. Apparently a realtor by the name of Sheila Moore visited one of her properties near Armory Park Plaza because a neighbor called their realty office to report hearing some noise in the rear of the house. She and a young man from their office by the name of Ricky Fallon got there to check it out. Apparently they took notice that the back door had been smashed in. Ms. Moore called 911 and was told to wait out front near her vehicle. Apparently she didn't listen and they went inside. Officers Kent and Swanson got the call and responded quickly. When they arrived and entered the house they found the body of a young man all ripped apart. However, they did not see Ms. Moore. There was also quite a bit of physical damage to the house."

"What are your thoughts, Chief?" I asked, finishing the last piece of donut.

"Detective Stephenson, how should I know what's happening? I really have no idea. I want you and Mr. Flint to get over there as soon as this meeting is over. It's not far from here. Sgt. McCorty will give you the address. Colonel McDowell is sending out some of his commando guys that came in on those transport planes, probably as we speak. They may already be there for all I know. I can only ascertain that this creature took her out through the back of the house before the police arrived because the rear of the structure going out to the deck was literally destroyed, as was the fence in the back part of the yard. You two get going right now. Check it out and report directly back to this office. There may also be a couple detectives there when you arrive."

"What about me?" asked Manny, feeling somewhat pissed off that he was being split from his partner, especially since it was for this damn Flint, a civilian no less.

"Sorry Detective Corroda, you're staying right here with us for the moment. Something else is going to happen soon, I'm sure of it. So I want you to be prepared to respond quickly. Don't get your pink panties in an uproar. You're not being split apart from your better half. So Amy, go now, go, go, go! Listen to your superiors for once."

Chapter 29

Sheila walked rather stiffly, quite zombie-like, in fact. The rain had started to ease up somewhat to just a mere drizzle. She obviously had no umbrella because that was back at the original property she was attacked at so her hair and clothing were soaked and plastered to her skin. There had been some blood on the face where the creature had struck her as well as on the back of her head when she whacked the table in the fall. The heavier part of the rain had washed most of that away even though she displayed quite a gash over her left eye that still seeped blood. Not a pretty sight if a passing driver or pedestrian took notice of this wild looking woman on the street. Nobody dared stop.

She struggled along a wide sidewalk out of the park to the corner of S. 6th. Avenue and E. 13th. Street. From there she turned right and walked a block past the Children's Museum on her right to S. Scott Avenue. She crossed that to where E. 13th turned into E. McCormick. From there she walked another block to S. Stone Avenue.

Crossing the street she moved slowly through the open parking area at Tucson Police Headquarters. It was this exact location where the creature detected the female's scent to be the strongest. The problem was that the building was quite large and the creature detected numerous humans inside. Plus, a few that moved around outside. It strained somewhat to pick her scent out of so many. Suddenly it was right there, very close by.

Sheila stopped quickly and began slowly turning. This female the creature had been seeking was walking outside at the far end of the building, then got into a vehicle with a large male. It began moving its host body as quickly as human legs would carry it, albeit running. The damn shoes still attached to her feet made it rather difficult to run while staying erect on three inch heels. Several people got out of the way quickly after seeing this startling apparition of a woman running, soaked to the bone, with blood now starting again to flow freely from the gash on her face.

The creature was too late. The vehicle that the female crawled into had pulled out of the space and was now turning right onto the street, then speeding up. When Sheila got to the empty space the car was gone from sight. She raised her head and screamed. Then bending each leg tore off the shoes and threw them onto the pavement.

"Excuse me miss, are you okay?" came a very concerned male voice behind her on the sidewalk.

Sheila turned and looked wild-eyed at a man dressed in a police uniform who stood in front of some bushes with a shocked expression on his face. She immediately walked over to him and smiled which ended up looking like a tortured grimace now that the blood had reached her mouth and chin. Not taking the time to stop she reached out with both hands and pushed the startled cop off the sidewalk and back into the bushes where he landed on the ground with a hard thud.

Lying flat on the ground she squeezed his neck tightly with both hands to open the mouth wider. At the same the creature forced open Sheila's mouth and it quickly slid worm-like out of her mouth straight into his. Within thirty seconds the transfer was completed. Sheila's discarded body fell to the side, dead of course. At least she had been somewhat useful. The creature was thankful, however, because those damn shoes and tighter fitting clothes had been a real pain in the ass for easy movement.

Nobody else had seen the altercation because it happened so quickly. The officer raised his head, glanced around and slowly rose on unsteady legs, brushed off the dirt and small leaves, then stepped quickly onto the sidewalk. Moving his head in both directions, cracking the neck loudly as it did so, the creature forced it to turn and walk towards what appeared to be the main entrance. When he got there several police officers were exiting. One of them with a nametag of Miller held the door open.

"What's going on Kramer? Hey man, you really look like shit."

The creature just nodded and murmured something that sounded like hello. Then continued through the front door. Once inside it moved to the right and stood still to observe what was going on. It could strongly tell that several people in this building had just been with the female it longed so much for, and who it almost nearly possessed. The scent was on the bottom floor because she apparently had just come through here to go outside. Other humans who had been with her recently appeared to be on the higher level.

Relying on the policeman's mind it quickly accessed the information needed to get further into the building. Then moved over to a door marked 'STAIRS'. Suddenly it was inside the stairwell and started ascending. While it moved up the steps the creature also began transforming the host body by allowing scales to form on the outside of the skin. This was no time to be careful or take chances. Enough damn time had been wasted as it was and the thing was getting tired of following its prey. Taking over the body of the one human she seemed closest to was paramount. It would not fail this time.

We took my car and left Flint's vehicle parked there at headquarters. Since I pretty much knew where the location was that we had to respond to we got there in a shade over ten minutes. That was just because we were unlucky enough to hit most of the damn red lights. I thought about switching the emergency lights on, but figured we would be there quick enough anyway. I hated displays unless necessary.

"I thought you were going to go right through that one red light," Vince joked.

"Apparently the victim is dead with no monsters present at the scene. So there's no need to rush. I might've done that if the address was further away. Why Mr. Flint, you scared of my driving? Would you rather have a thrill ride with the siren blaring?"

He laughed. "I'll hold the thrill part until later when we're alone."

I responded back with my own light banter. "Let's live through all this crap first before we start planning our next sexual encounter. That is if I think I know what you're dirty mind is considering," as I pulled up in front of the crime scene directly behind an ambulance. But not too close in case I had to get out quick.

There was a large brown military vehicle parked there as well, pretty much taking up half the street. We got out of the car quickly and walked towards the officer stationed at the front entrance to the property.

"What's up Swanson?" I asked.

His face had a somewhat ashy, sickly look. It was quite obvious he had puked out his guts. Not too many individuals would've been strong enough to hold it in anyway.

"Detective Stephenson, if I never see anything like that again in my entire lifetime it won't be too soon. One would expect to maybe find that mess out in the desert where vicious predators live, but not here within the city. Anyway, they're all inside, maybe outback in the yard. That includes the army guys as well. Good luck because I'm going to stay right here. Unless you need me, of course," he added, with a cute, crooked smile.

I patted him on the shoulder. "It's okay, I totally understand. I've felt quite nauseous since this whole killing spree started. I think most of us have upchucked as well over the last few weeks when we've seen these bodies so don't feel too bad."

He smiled in acknowledgement as we entered the building. Once inside we saw the body bag being spread out onto the floor. To say the least there was a lot of blood. One of the crime scene techs I knew as Carlson looked up, tried to smile, but found it kind of impossible. So it resulted in more of a lopsided grimace.

"Hello detective, do you want to look at the body?" he asked.

I glanced down and shook my head. "No, it's pretty apparent what the COD is. You just finish your rather difficult job which quite frankly I do not relish in the least."

He chuckled. "Well, the good part is that we just need to convey this body back to the medical examiner's office. You on the other hand need to find a monster. Oh by the way, there were two other detectives here earlier. Sorry, I forget their names. They stayed for about ten minutes and left rather quickly. I think they got another call."

I just smiled and muttered 'thanks'. Vince and I walked as carefully as we could through the living room and noticed even more blood on the floor in front of the dining room table, as well as on the surface itself. Looking up I saw several commandos in the kitchen and then others standing around out in the backyard.

"Come on, Vince. Let's see what the hell's going on."

We walked slowly into the kitchen as Lieutenant Frawley looked around.

"Detectives, thanks for coming. We're just about ready to track this damn thing."

He pointed out the huge hole in the wall where the large sliding glass doors once had been. "You can see that the fence in the back of the yard is also wrecked so we have to assume that it escaped through there. The female, name of Sheila Moore, is not at this crime scene so the thing must've took her body for some unknown reason. We have no idea where it went without being noticed by anybody. Apparently though it did just that. There seems to be a blood trail in the yard and beyond the fence."

I allowed him to talk before saying anything. You know, the military way so to speak. "Hello to you also Lieutenant Frawley. Obviously this is what you guys do so I'll hang back. You can take the lead on this operation. However, I want to be involved in everything since this is definitely police business. By the way, this is Mr. Vince Flint. He's a civilian contractor being used by the Air Force and is extremely qualified when it comes to tracking just about anything. I would imagine his skills might be valuable."

The two men shook hands as we walked outside. The rain had finally receded to just a little sprinkle now and then. Hell, the sun was actually beginning to show through the storm clouds which I had become pretty used to ever since moving to Tucson. Back in Philly it was drab and dreary for hours after a storm ended.

Five soldiers had accompanied Lt. Frawley. It was apparent they were loaded for bear. Or, something much larger and way more vicious. Sgt. Gary Gray (I would come to know him as GG which all his buddies called him), walked over to where we stood.

He smiled in acknowledgment because he talked to me briefly after the meeting.

"Sir, we're ready to go," he stated firmly in a very no-nonsense voice.

"Thank you, Sergeant Gray. This is Detective Stephenson and Vince Flint. He apparently is very experienced at tracking so let him kind of take the lead here."

"Are you sure, sir? He's a civilian," Gray responded, which I immediately felt was absolutely the wrong thing to say. I waited for Flint's response.

Vince spoke right upanyway."Don't worry Sgt. Gray, I was tracking everything from wild animals, to criminals, to enemies of all kinds before you were even born. Promise I won't lead you guys into an ambush if that's what you're worried about."

Sgt. Gray let his gaze scour Vince from head to toe. "Yes sir, I'm sure you have. If you want to take a quick look around the yard before we go then please follow me."

He and Flint walked off towards the shattered back fence.

"Sorry about that. My men are very sensitive to outsiders," said Lt. Frawley.

I smiled and followed that up with a light chuckle. "No need to apologize. I thought the same thing when we first met. However, Mr. Flint is more than capable. Probably what you and your men would call 'one bad motherfucker'. Please excuse my French."

He just laughed and nodded. "I think we're going to need all the help we can get. And, your French is pretty good. Come on, they're about to start the search."

Vince took the lead with Lieutenant Frawley and GG about four feet behind him. We all moved cautiously through the broken fence which led into a narrow area of about six feet that bordered another house directly behind it. This narrow lane appeared to go the length of the block, thus dividing the homes in somewhat of an alley-like effect, but not for vehicle use.

They put me at the rear of the line with Corporal Winston Jarvis, a rather tall, very good looking, dark-skinned African-American. At first, I was somewhat pissed off about that positioning, feeling it was because I was a female. You know, put the girl in the back of the line kind of thing. But I quickly reconsidered because I could tell that the corporal was a really no-nonsense kind of guy. So if we ended up being attacked by this creature then the thought occurred to me that being further away was better than being first in line like Mr. Flint was. Plus, since Corporal Jarvis was a really big guy, and apparently very athletic, it was a pretty good place to be. I also noticed that when Jarvis did occasionally smile in my direction I could see that his teeth were extremely large and brilliantly white. A million dollar smile for sure, but probably the reason why he didn't smile all that much when they were on a mission. It would've been like turning on a bright light and saying, 'Here I am, go ahead and shoot'.

Each of the commandos carried identical firepower which Jarvis explained to me in a low, whispering voice were M16 A-1 rifles with light weight plastic NATO STANAG 30-round magazines. Underneath each barrel was attached M203 40mm grenade launchers. To say the least these guys were loaded with lots and lots of testosterone. Each man carried extra clips and grenades along with hand guns. Depending on the taste of each soldier they either toted a Beretta M9, or a Sig Sauer 226, both holding fifteen rounds in clips. I noticed that Corporal Jarvis carried a Sig.

From what I could see, Lt. Frawley held an M4 Carbine and was not loaded down with as much ammunition as his men. Guess that's an officer for you. I did not notice what firearm was holstered around his waist. What was I carrying? I always preferred the Glock models and was totally aware that there was a new model available which I believe was the G43. I just liked the Glock 41 Gen 4 model because it simply felt more comfortable in my hands with good weight distribution and balance. Plus, it carried a thirteen round clip and I always figured that more firepower was always better. I could just keep shooting until the bad guy went down on the ground.

At any rate, whatever each soldier carried I felt this was a pretty badass outfit.

Vince knelt and saw that apparently the blood trail went right so he started moving in that direction. I guess he felt that nothing was going to attack them in the small alleyway. Quickly, we found ourselves on the sidewalk of a major street which I knew to be E. 13th. I moved forward towards Flint and knelt down beside him.

"What's up? How could it come this way and not be seen by people out on the street?" I asked, more curious than anything.

"Amy, come on. You know as well as I do because we saw it happen out in the desert. This damn thing has the ability to camouflage itself very easily so once it got out here in the open I'm pretty sure that's exactly what it did. The heavy rain also may have kept anyone from really noticing it too clearly."

"Yeah, but the heavy rain had pretty much stopped probably. It's obviously carrying the woman's body whether she's alive or not. So how in the world could it do that and not be seen?

"Detective, if I really knew all the answers then maybe we would've caught this freaking thing already," he responded, more in frustration than trying to be a smartass. "Maybe it concealed her body somehow. I haven't the faintest idea."

He looked over at Lt. Frawley. "Sir, the blood trail goes to our right so we need to walk in that direction and we'll be out in the open for everyone to see."

The officer had been listening closely so he nodded. He then turned and gave a low voiced command for each soldier to sling their rifles, but also to remove their pistols and hold them down against their legs. No use causing any undo alarm to the populace, at least that's why I figured he was doing that. However, they also would be prepared.

We walked slowly up the sidewalk in single file formation at this point. We then crossed the intersections at S. Herbert, as well as the one at 6th where we soon found ourselves at a large, sprawling building. This was the Armory Senior Citizen Center. Beyond that was Military Park Plaza. We continued moving forward until we stood on the grass. Glancing down I saw that the blood trail left the cement at this spot and then moved onto the grass.

With the buildup in traffic, both vehicular and pedestrian, we were beginning to draw much more unwanted attention than we desired. After all, it could be kind of scary seeing six heavily armed soldiers and what appeared to be two police officers entering the park. The good thing, because of all the rain earlier there were fewer people around. A few joggers and people walked dogs. Other than that it was pretty empty.

"Where to now, Mr. Flint?" inquired Frawley.

"The trail leads that way and obviously the blood is from the female. We should probably spread out in a tight line and move in that direction. Motion any civilians to get out of the way. This creature could very well be hiding someplace so be prepared for anything. Remember that it can camouflage its body so be on the lookout for any place where the air may seem to be rippling, or shimmering. It might be better to shoot and ask questions later even though I don't recommend that in normal situations."

We spread out in a tight line as Vince suggested with no more than three feet between us. At least I wasn't on the end. I had Jarvis taking care of that position which actually made me feel rather safe. The soldiers all unslung their rifles and held them in the ready position as we slowly moved forward. I can only imagine what went through the minds of civilians staring in awe at this very strange action taking place in their beautiful park.

A few minutes later Vince held up his right hand signaling for us to stop. We were now about ten yards from an area that had a small gully and was surrounded by trees. We all knelt down and moved together in a tighter knot.

Vince whispered, "If I was this creature and going to hide it would be in there. Looking around this park, it's pretty open with the exception of this area. Let me go first and see what's in there. We don't need any surprises at this point and I'll need backup."

Lieutenant Frawley responded very officer-like. "You won't go alone Mr. Flint. Sergeant Gray and myself will move forward right behind you. Let's go."

I could tell Vince was offended somewhat because he was used to giving the orders. But stealth is stealth so the three of them started creeping forward, legs somewhat bent, weapons held in front and at the ready. They got to the tree line when Vince slowed and pointed down at the ground, obviously where more blood sign was. At that point they spread out with about four feet in between and entered the treed area.

For about three minutes they were lost from sight. To say the least, tension around us was so thick you needed a knife to slice through it. Yes, these were highly trained soldiers, but that didn't mean they couldn't display edginess. The difference though was my taut nerves could be termed possible fear. For them, it resulted in being much more alert and prepared for any type of potential altercation. To say the least I felt safe. But hell, I was no hero by any means. I was just really glad to be in their company.

We saw Lt. Frawley come out first, a very strange look etched across his face. He was followed by GG. Apparently, Flint was still poking around in the secluded area, but since there was no shooting I had to assume the creature was gone. Maybe they found Ms. Moore's body.

I moved towards the Lieutenant where he stood scratching the side of his head.

"What did you find in there?" I asked, extremely curious.

He laughed slightly and then looked at me. "No human body was detected, but there is one helluva' large, dead lizard lying on the ground. Looks like a damn Gila monster on steroids. The woman is not in there so I'm even more confused than ever. Something is not being conveyed to us and it pisses me off to no end. I'm going to explode at somebody back at the base. We need to know everything there is about this creature, or my men will be in more jeopardy."

"Well, it was mentioned back at the hangar in our meeting that this thing has gone through multiple transformations and also has the ability to take over a new host body. Apparently, the babies do also. If the female is not in there then it's highly possible that the creature left the host lizard and moved into the new human host which would be her. God only knows where she is now, but we need to find out quickly." I replied.

Just then Vince came out of the trees and walked over to us.

"The lizard is dead as you would imagine," he said, shaking his head. "Just totally amazes me how it could enter the body of a Gila monster which is so much smaller and transform it literally into the body of that monster lying in there. Anyway, the woman's body is not there so apparently it is now using her body as a host."

"We need to get a photo of her quickly and put out an APB so she can be located. Can you track it at all anymore?" I asked him.

He pointed to the ground. "Looks like smaller footprints walking out of the trees. By the looks of the prints it is some type of heeled shoe."

Vince moved away from us and followed the trail to the sidewalk where there were some muddy and broken footprints. They only went so far before disappearing because of the rain. There was no more blood so either the wound had closed up or she was dead, only being used by the creature. Possibly the heart was not pumping anymore. None of us had ever been through an alien hunt before so we knew virtually nothing yet.

"There is one thing though. At least we can see where the trail ended. It looks like it went back out onto 13th street and then turned right. I guess we move off in that direction, but let your men know we're not looking for some damn big lizard any longer. I would advise them to definitely be on the alert for a very soaked and muddy looking female, probably bloody with a wild look on her face."

GG spoke up, "That sounds like most of the women I've been with over the last few years. Some of them, I definitely would not take home to mama."

His buddies laughed, but I didn't think it was that funny. Just another macho, tough guy remark. Well, maybe it was just a little funny since I had no love lost for the jerks I've dated in my lifetime.

Chapter 30

O fficer Eric Kramer opened the door and stepped out into the hallway. He raised his head towards the ceiling as if he was smelling for something. In actuality, the creature inside his body was most definitely searching for the female's ethereal trail. Although its actual prey was not in the building any longer there was definitely a human male on this floor that had very strong ties to her. It needed to locate this individual soon because its brood was waiting for a signal as to when to move and where to come.

There was quite a bit of noise arising from different rooms off the hallway, along with a number of humans walking back and forth, some fast and hectic, while others were slow and nonchalant. The creature forced Eric's head to move back and forth. Feeling the trail was stronger behind, it turned and began walking in that direction, feeling that it was in a room on the left..

Suddenly a loud voice boomed out, "Hey Eric, what the hell you doing up here?"

He stopped and turned slowly, trying to locate which human had called his name. Suddenly, a large male in a uniform stopped almost directly in front of him and then went to put a hand on his shoulder. The creature did not realize what was happening so it quickly reached out feeling it was some form of attack and grabbed the other human's hand, squeezing and turning hard at the same time.

"Whoa Officer Kramer, what the hell are you doing?" declared a shocked Sergeant McCorty, startled at the rather offensive move made against him.

The creature allowed the human's brain to quickly format what was happening and then released the other person's hand just as fast.

"Sorry Sergeant McCorty, I've been a little jumpy lately," Kramer responded in a rather monotone voice. "Hope I didn't hurt you too much."

McCorty was rubbing his wrist and stood back a couple steps. "Well, you'd better get a grip on whatever's bugging you. There's too much crap flying around here at the moment. Why are you up on this floor? Looking for somebody in particular?"

"Yes, I have some information for somebody."

"Who're you here to see?" McCorty asked, moving aside to let somebody rush past.

Eric hesitated because he actually did not know the male's name. The creature realized it had heard what sounded like names being yelled after one of those skirmishes in the desert so it attempted to transfer that information into Eric's mind.

"Well, who the hell is it?" the sergeant asked again, waiting rather impatiently for over a minute.

"Ah, mmmm, somebody by the name of Man," he replied in a low, confused voice.

"Who the hell is that? You want to see a man? We have lots of those assholes running around here like chickens with their heads cut off. Officer Kramer, give me a name and I'll point you in the right direction."

Kramer hesitated and his mouth formed into half a crooked smile. "No, not 'man'. It sounded more like *Mane'*, or *Mani'*, something like that. I know what he looks like, but I only heard part of the name and there was lots of noise around me."

"Detective Corroda? Manny Corroda? Is that who you're here to see?"

"Yes, I believe that's who it is. Sounds right," Kramer responded.

McCorty looked at the officer with some concern. "Okay, he's two rooms down on the left. He's about the only detective that I have on the floor right now. They're all out at crime scenes. The whole goddamn City of Tucson is blowing up. You know what he looks like, right?"

"Yes, I believe he's possibly Mexican, dark skin, dark hair, rather tall."

"Hells bells, that describes close to half of our police force. Okay Kramer, go do what you have to do and then I would suggest you head on home and rest up. You're so damn tense you look like you're about to explode. Plus, I don't like the sound of your voice. Get too rundown and you'll be no help to anybody."

"Thank you sir, I'll do just that."

"Don't sir me. Now go get it done and then get the hell out of here."

Kramer turned and walked down the hall to the second office on the left. The door was half open so he pushed it wider and slipped in as quietly as possible. He then closed it behind him and silently as possible reached back to lock it. At the end of the room to the right sitting at his desk was the man the creature remembered seeing before out in the desert. Finally, he was another step closer to locating the female it desired.

Manny looked up and saw Kramer. "Can I help you?"

The creature didn't respond right away because it was partially forming the human host's hands into claws.

"Let me repeat that very simple question. Can I help you officer?"

Kramer started shuffling forward. "I have some information for you," as he got closer to the desk.

"About one of the crime scenes? One of these killings? Something about this thing we're looking for?" Manny asked, in a frustrated voice. He was still pissed off that he had to remain behind at headquarters while Amy went out to have all the fun.

"Yes," Kramer simply replied.

"Okay, so now you're really beginning to piss me off. Yes, what? Can't you see I'm busy here? Spit it out dammit."

At this point the creature had slowly shuffled forward to within a foot of where the detective was sitting. He then quickly reached out and grabbed Corroda by the neck. Startled, Manny tried getting out of his seat and began choking at the same time. The grip on his neck was extremely powerful as he also began feeling something like claws digging into his flesh. Then he felt himself being lifted out of the chair like he was a rag doll until he was being held upright directly in front of Officer Eric Kramer. He was suddenly filled with total fear, realizing what might be happening and that he was about to die.

The creature continued to squeeze extremely hard, Manny's eyes beginning to bulge out. Corroda was swinging out wildly with his fists, but the blows seemed to have little effect. Using the other hand it opened Manny's mouth as wide as possible, to the point of cracking the skin and causing blood to start trickling down his chin. At the same time Kramer's mouth opened very wide, being split apart by the creature's worm-like body which started sliding out. Their faces came to within an inch of each other. The transfer itself from old host to new host took less than a minute. Once it was complete the dead body of Officer Eric Kramer fell hard to the floor, discarded like day old trash.

Manny coughed and gagged, nearly falling onto the floor. In the last seconds of his life he thought quickly of his family and wondered where the hell Amy was. He placed his hands on the desk and then sat back heavily in the chair. His body started to convulse violently and after close to a minute it stopped. Manny sat completely in his chair looking straight ahead. He still continued to cough and gag every now and then.

Suddenly, he bent over in the chair, grabbed hold of Kramer's uniform and pulled the body past the desk and against the wall so it was wedged between there and his chair. At least for now the body was hidden. He sat still stiff as a board, breathing heavily. The phone rang loudly and he jumped. It rang four more times, but he didn't answer it. Then it stopped and the office grew very quiet. At this point the creature was finishing initial alterations in order to have complete control over the new host body.

A loud rapping on the door made it more alert and Manny turned his gaze in that direction.

"Corroda, you in there? Manny, why the hell is this damn door locked?"

The detective stood and walked slowly forward. Seeing that it was locked he clicked the switch and pulled the door open. Sergeant McCorty stood in the hallway and was just about to rap hard on the door again.

"What's going on here? Why was the door locked when I told you not to?"

"Ah, I don't know Sergeant. Maybe when that officer left he locked it by mistake," Manny answered in a monotone voice.

"So officer Kramer left already? What did he want?" inquired McCorty.

"Nothing much. We saw him out in the desert one day and he remembered something. I wrote it down, but it didn't seem to be overly important."

McCorty looked at him oddly. "Are you okay, Manuel? Christ, you almost look like Kramer did. You all better not be coming down with the same blue flu."

"I'm fine, just tired. Here anything from my partner?" Manny asked.

"Not yet, but she may have her phone off if they're tracking that damn creature. As soon as I hear something I'll let you know. If she calls you then inform me as well. You got that?"

"Yes, got it," Manny responded in a very monotone voice.

"And keep this damn door open so it doesn't accidentally get locked again," McCorty said, as he stalked away.

The creature moved back to the desk after closing the door and sat down. The time was getting closer to sending out the signal for its offspring to move and let them know where to come. It would at the appropriate time send out its own ethereal signal, but from its own natural body and not specifically the host. At this point though it needed to hold on and wait for the female to hopefully reappear soon. Once that transformation was completed then it would be ready to start the takeover in earnest.

General Smith stood on the tarmac draped by his two matching shadows, Phillip and Jeffery. They watched intently as the sleek private plane landed and then taxied in their direction. Off to the right sat a large black limo with the motor running. Behind that was the general's long black van, windows very darkly tinted. It was obvious they were waiting for somebody aboard the plane that was just pulling up.

Late the previous evening he had spoken to his own superiors. He advised them on what had been happening and that they wanted to get Smith's own thoughts and concerns. They, in turn, had him contact one individual in particular which he would do.

"General, what is going on out there in the great Sonoran Desert and the beautiful City of Tucson, Arizona? What steps need to be placed into motion in order to put an end to this apparently serious situation?" the deep voice on the other end of the phone asked. "I would say before it gets out of hand, but it sounds like it already has."

"Jason, we are facing a very dire problem. The alien entity that broke free of its confinement has apparently transformed and altered shape numerous times, becoming stronger, deadlier, and more adept at stealth upon each occurrence. Plus, it was able to hide for a period of over two weeks inside a cave out in the desert where it laid eggs that hatched. From what we have been able to ascertain there were about twenty of them. In a serious confrontation with the creature in the beginning of this week a number of the responding individuals, law enforcement and medical, became hosts to the creature's young. In turn, these new hosts then went on to slaughter their own families and also avoided capture. At this time we have no idea where they are at."

There was silence on the other end of the line that seemed to go on forever. In reality it was less than a minute.

"Howard, what's being done currently?" asked Jason, sounding very concerned.

"Forty more commandos from Florida arrived the other night, plus plenty of serious equipment and firepower. Six of them which included Lt. Frawley responded to a crime scene not too long ago where possibly the entity itself was hidden, but who had killed and partially devoured one young male. Seems that it was able to escape with a female. I can only imagine at this point that the damn thing is no longer in lizard shape, but rather that of the female's body. That is if it has not passed into a different body by now. To my knowledge there are at least five or six military groups out in the desert searching different sectors. We also have thirty-four commandos from the first group led by Lt. Spinner here on base, at alert and ready to respond at a moment's notice."

Smith paused and after thirty seconds continued.

"Jason, we need additional help here right away. Dealing with one of these things is bad enough, but at least twenty others may be nearly impossible even though we have a large force available, including air power here on the base. I think that it's time we contacted you know who. If this goes any further and more eggs are produced it could result in a complete disaster for Tucson and the state. Hell, the entire country."

"I completely understand. It sounds like a real mess. Let me take over on this end to get everything in motion. Is there anything else that I need to know before we end this call?"

General Smith was quiet for just a moment before answering.

"There is a female here, a Tucson police detective. She's a very lovely young woman by the name of Amelia Stephenson. Jason, she is the same young lady that we've been monitoring for so long now. From when she was a child, in fact. She may be aware of being previously abducted and has just suppressed it, or intentionally hidden it away so that she could lead her life as normally as possible. She came here from the Philadelphia area and possibly either moved here to get away from there completely, or as strange as this may sound, been summoned somehow by something, or someone.

I have not addressed this directly with her since I felt that it was not my position to do so. I think that we need to let her know what the situation is regarding her life. It appears to be the moment when we need to proceed further with her enlightenment. Do you agree?"

Jason made a low groaning sound on the other end. "That's a very interesting scenario, Howard. Let me quickly address the Organization and I will get back to you promptly."

Howard was contacted several hours later and was told what would be happening, as well as instructed to meet the private plane now coming to a complete stop in front of the hangar. He took a few steps closer as the jet's two powerful engines shut down. In about five minutes the exit door near the cockpit opened and steps lowered. Six men dressed all in black, just like Phillip and Jeffery, filed out and climbed down to the ground. They stood ramrod straight, alert and on guard for any possible altercation. The pilot and copilot followed.

Several minutes later a very tall individual, well over seven feet, bent low and exited the door to stand on the upper platform. This person, however, was not wearing a black suit, but rather a lighter gray one that seemed to hang on his gaunt frame. Even though this extremely tall individual was very thin, it exuded a power that belied his obvious look of frailty. The face was long and angular, eyes narrow and appearing to have a yellow cast to them. The nose was very thin and flat with two large black nostrils clearly visible. The mouth was a wide slit and the head was totally bald. The entire shape of the head itself was long and narrow, kind of oval in appearance. Howard noted that he was extremely reptilian looking and pretty damn scary.

General Smith had seen several of these individuals once before, back in 2006. They were rather disturbing then and it was the same feeling he had now. After glancing around for at least one full minute the male turned, bent down, and appeared to be talking to somebody still inside the plane. Smith turned to his right and motioned for the limo to pull up slowly.

When he glanced back at the plane he was stunned to see a young Nordic-looking female exit and stand beside the giant. She herself was obviously shorter, but still nearly six feet. What was amazing about her was that she had an almost albino-like appearance. Her hair was cut short and barely rested on somewhat muscular shoulders, primarily white though with hints of blonde. She wore an off-white dress with what appeared to be muscular and longer than normal arms, especially for a female. Her head was also very oval looking with somewhat pointed ears and eyes that were lower than a normal humans would be placed. On each side of her head right above both ears were somewhat deep grooves, much like when you might take off tight fitting glasses after wearing them for a while and then removing them, or from constant wear. The bridge of her nose was very wide and flat, almost blunt at the end with very little nostril flesh. Her lips were narrow and red in color, but she wore no makeup at all. The eyes, to say the least, were quite startling in that they had a distinct reddish glow to them and seemed to sparkle when sunlight hit them a certain way. To say the least, her entire appearance was both enthralling and disturbing, quite mysterious at the same time.

She glanced up at the tall male, obviously her protector. He nodded and she turned to start descending. General Smith, along with his own shadows, Phillip and Jeffery, moved towards the bottom of the steps to greet her. The limo driver had also gotten out of the vehicle and quickly moved around the car to open the wide rear door.

The young woman moved with a fluidity and grace not normally found in any human female, even runway models. It was almost as if she floated down the steps even though her legs moved in an obvious descending motion. At the bottom of the steps General Smith greeted her by bowing and then extending his hands which she took by reaching forward.

"Welcome Aimee and thank you so much for coming so quickly. Sadly, we don't have time to show you around so if you would, please follow me so that we can proceed in accomplishing your mission and then get you back home safely."

She smiled, displaying just a brief hint of sharpened teeth, and then followed General Smith into the limo. Phillip and Jeffery also got in, along with the young ladies giant guardian. He definitely had to bend rather low in order to get inside, but the ceiling on this limo was somewhat high so he had no problems once sitting down. At least there was plenty of leg room. The other six men entered the van that had pulled up right behind the limo.

The two vehicles then immediately sped off towards the entrance to the air base while General Smith explained to the young lady why she had been summoned.

Chapter 31

When I reached the corner of S. Stone Avenue, along with my little group of soldier boys, we abruptly stopped. A rather nice surprise was seeing the remnants of Flint's op-team standing on the corner, that being Julius Prudot, Tiny Tim Rollins, and Carrie Vaughn. I noticed that she had removed most of the bandages on her arm. I wasn't really sure how they had known to meet us at this very location, but I made it a point to ask Vince about it later. I had to assume that Manny, my highly pissed off partner, was still being held against his will by Chief Crosson at police headquarters, which was just cattycorner to where we now stood.

"Okay Mr. Flint, where to now? I don't see any blood on the sidewalk anymore so it feels like we're just aimlessly moving around," inquired Lt. Frawley.

After greeting his team, Vince replied, "To be honest I'm not exactly sure myself. For the thing to come this way, and I'm assuming that it's now residing inside the body of Ms. Moore, the only place that seems to be a reasonable destination is right over there." He pointed to the headquarters building.

As everyone began gazing in that direction I suddenly felt extremely dizzy and nauseous, to the point where I started reeling backwards. I would've fallen flat on my ass if it wouldn't have been for Sergeant Gray catching me.

Vince also quickly moved over to help support my body.

"Amy, what's wrong?" he asked in an extremely concerned voice.

I really couldn't answer right away, trying hard to shake away the waves of dizziness from my eyes. At the same time a very sharp and acute pain shot through my stomach, while my entire body suddenly became extremely hot. I quickly moved over towards a parking lot behind us and violently threw up. It was quite embarrassing to say the least since there was no grass, no garbage can, nothing but cement to let it splash all over, including my shoes. The good thing though was that I hadn't eaten in a while so there wasn't much in my stomach to spew forth. That fact unfortunately resulted in the dry heaves, something I had always hated. Something was wrong inside me though.

When I seemed to be done and the pain started to subside somewhat I slowly straightened up. Vince still held onto me which was gratifying because I did, in fact, suddenly feel extremely weak. My entire body continued to remain strangely hot.

"Hey girl, what the hell happened?" he asked. "I think you need to get home as quickly as possible and lie down. You've been through a lot lately."

At least I thought that's what he said since all sounds now seemed like they were being forced through a vacuum tube and actually had an echo to them.

"Dammit Vince, I can't leave now. We're closing in on this beast, I can feel it. I need to be here. We need every able-bodied person helping out."

"Amy, that seems to be the problem. You're not able-bodied and definitely no good to us in this condition. Maybe it's just an attack of nerves what with everything building up inside you over the last few weeks. Or, the med's you took earlier for pain are making it happen. Possibly it was something you ate this morning, but you're clearly not able to help us in this condition. Do you want us to just take you over to the headquarters building where you can rest, although it might not be safe?" he asked.

I shook my head which brought on another wave of dizziness as Vince held on tightly. "No, I think I need to just lie down somewhere so maybe I should head home although I'm not sure I can get there on my own. Plus, my car is parked back at the crime scene so I'll have to walk there to retrieve it."

Flint turned to Carrie and Tiny Tim. "Hey, do you both mind getting her home? Carrie, you can drive her car and Tim, you can follow them in your vehicle. Then both of you get back here when you feel she's okay. Do you mind doing that guys?"

What could they really say to such a request from their leader? It was obvious that he was very concerned for Amy. It was also quite apparent there was more than met the eye between them. So they both nodded yes, although Carrie did show somewhat of a disappointed look. Vince gently turned my face towards him and smiled down at me.

"Get home Amy so you can rest. When you feel up to it then get back here with us. Is that a deal? I'm worried about you."

I nodded slightly, not wanting the dizziness to return. Carrie and I started walking the few blocks back to the crime scene while Tiny Tim moved over to the parking lot at Police Headquarters to retrieve his jeep.

The entire drive home I went through periods of severe dizziness and being really sick in my stomach, to then feeling perfectly fine. Half of me wanted to have Carrie turn around and go back to the team, but then a sharp pain would stab me in the stomach while a wave of dizziness swept over me. At least I didn't throw up again, especially since I was sitting in the passenger seat of my car.

What really concerned me though was that I hadn't felt this way in many years. The sudden wave of sickness brought to the surface a terrifying period in my earlier life that I had not thought about in quite a while. I had gone to several doctors in my teen years to try and get through whatever illness it was. Plus, try to understand all the nightmares I had been experiencing nearly every night. Finally, all the therapy seemed to work and I was able to shove it into a dark room within my brain. That's where it had thankfully remained over all these years.

For some strange reason I found myself once again having terrible nightmares over the last few weeks. However, this was the first time I had really gotten this sick again. It frightened me because with these memories of my youth starting to flood back, I kept wondering why it was all resurfacing with such nightmarish clarity.

Because of traffic it took us about forty minutes to finally pull in front of my house. Carrie pulled my car into the driveway while Tim parked on the street. They both then helped me inside so I didn't fall on the ground. The auto-timers for the A/C units had not kicked in so I asked Tim to turn them on since the house was somewhat warm.

"Do you want us to stay with you Amy? At least until you start feeling a little better?" Vaughn asked.

"No thanks Carrie, I just need to lie down. I'm not really sure what came over me because I was feeling great right before it hit like a sledgehammer. You both need to get back and help Vince. He's lost without you guys," I said, cracking a thin smile

"Well okay, if you insist. I don't want him to read us the riot act if we leave you here alone and then you got worse," remarked Tim in his deep, but sincere voice. "He might hurt us really bad," he added, with a wide grin.

"Don't worry big guy, I'll be fine. Honestly, you two get moving. I'm just going to take something that hopefully will settle my stomach and then lie down back in the bedroom. Thank you both for getting me home safely. I'm just so embarrassed this had to happen because everybody is needed out in the field right now."

I removed my firearm and placed it on the stand near the front door. Anyway, I didn't believe I was going to need it now that I was safely home. Normally I would take it back to the bedroom and put it in the top drawer of the nightstand. But the way I was feeling now I figured it would just be a good idea to remove it as soon as possible. I might even end up shooting myself. Out of sight, out of mind, so to speak. I also slipped out of my shoes since my feet were aching terribly.

Carrie hugged me tight. "Just get better Amy. You'll be right out there beside us looking for this damn monster before you know it."

After they left I shuffled out to the kitchen, reached into the corner cabinet to remove some baking soda which would hopefully settle down my stomach. As I started moving back towards the living room so I could then head down the hallway I got very dizzy once again, barely making it over to the couch. There I fell heavily, one leg on the piece of furniture and one off. I then immediately passed out.

I'm not really sure how long I was unconscious. While sleeping I was thrown headlong into another terrifying nightmare. I was lying upon something very hard and flat, bright lights overtop blinding me. And it was cold, frigid in fact. I felt that several strange looking individuals stood on each side of where I lay which was extremely disconcerting. At the same time I realized that I couldn't move at all, like I was completely frozen stiff. My mouth tried to open so that I could scream, but no sound came forth. I also somehow knew that I was very young, no more than seven years old. I couldn't even move my head a fraction of an inch, like it was being held firmly in a vise. My frightened eyes flickered quickly back and forth. Several gray skinned individuals, one on each side of the table, as well as one directly behind my head, stared down at me. All three of them had these big oval looking heads and the largest black eyes I had ever seen. All I could think of was how much they each looked like a giant praying mantis.

I also began realizing that they were not really human. Hell, I didn't even know how that could be possible. The last thing I remember earlier in the evening was getting really sick after dinner and my mother putting me to bed. I slept for a period of time until I heard a loud sharp noise that brought me totally awake. Even though I felt like I was paralyzed, the sheet and blanket covering me was removed somehow. My bedroom was lit brightly. I could feel myself rising towards the ceiling and then through a big hole until I fell into a deep trance. Yet, I also knew somehow I was still awake. Frightening for anybody, but I was only seven years old and knew that my mother couldn't help me.

That was back in what I thought was the safety of my bedroom. However, now I stared up in total fear at two of these strange individuals holding extremely long needles. They both began moving them in my direction so I screamed and screamed, but no sound came from my mouth. I knew right then that I was about to die.

Heart thudding loudly in my chest I suddenly sat straight up. The very first thing I did was glance quickly around and realized that those sickly gray, insect-like creatures were not inside my living room. It apparently had just been another goddamn nightmare. As my heartbeat began to somewhat return to normal I realized that I was in my own home, safe and sound. The living room was dark because I seemed to remember Tiny Tim closing the curtains before he and Carrie had left.

I realized also that my stomach was actually feeling somewhat better. There was no more pain or dizziness inside my head either. This was really comforting because I figured that I could now just take a shower, change clothes, and get back to join Flint and the rest of the A-team. I moved my one leg, which was still stretched out on the couch, over the side until I could slowly sit up straight.

Suddenly I realized that I was not alone. Immediately I reached for the gun on my hip, but it wasn't there. Shit I thought, it was over on the stand against the wall. I looked around slowly so my eyes could adjust to the darkness. I started to make out several shadows that at least looked human. Two of them were sitting down and several were standing against the walls, one of them very, very tall. Then my gaze stopped abruptly upon a dark shadow directly across from me that appeared to be female in shape, only with red eyes that seemed to glow in the darkness.

"Who are you?" I whispered warily, trying at the same time not to display too much fear, but realizing that would've been a complete joke since I was scared shitless.

A man's somewhat deep, but gentle voice came out of the darkness to my left. "Please Detective Stephenson, do not be frightened of us. You know me. I'm General Howard Smith, we met at the hangar out on Davis-Monthan Air Force Base. Believe me my dear, you're in no danger whatsoever so please do not be alarmed."

For a moment there was a deep silence. "How did you get in here?" I asked quietly, trying to control my voice. "The door was locked when my friends left earlier. I hope you realize this is breaking and entering, total trespassing. I could just as soon arrest you all right here and now. What in God's name do you want from me?"

Smith chuckled. "I do apologize for accessing your locked house. My friend Phillip has the unique talent of being able to get inside just about anywhere. We do realize that we're invading your privacy, Detective Stephenson. Please trust me when I say that this is a matter of the utmost secrecy and highest security."

A full minute of silence swirled through the room. I was not quite sure what to do and realized that if they were here to hurt me in any way then I wasn't sure what I could do to prevent it. However, I would definitely give them one helluva' battle if they tried anything physical. I might not be big, but I am mighty.

"What do you want, General Smith? What the hell can I possibly offer you? I'm just one person, nothing more. Certainly not special in any way. And who the hell is that sitting over in the chair across from me?"

He cleared his throat. "I must disagree completely, Detective Stephenson. You are very special indeed and I'll further explain fully in a moment. However, will it be okay with you if we open the curtains a little bit?"

"Why can't you just turn on the damn lights? And again, who the hell are those guys sitting out in my dining room. Plus, that giant over there standing against the wall like a statue. Who in the world is that?" I asked, my voice rising in alarm.

"We can't turn on the lights I'm afraid because of who I have with me. I will introduce you to her in a moment. Phillip, would you please open the curtains about halfway."

The man moved quickly and did just that, allowing some light to spread into the house. Apparently I had slept for several hours because the sun was now closing in on five o'clock. I looked around and took in the very odd giant of a man standing against the far wall. Still unable to totally make out his facial features, there was something extremely predatory about him that really frightened the 'bejeezus' out of me. Especially since I had no firearm within easy reach although it would most likely be useless.

Phillip and Jeffery I had met before although we did not have any conversation since they were definitely not the talkative type. However, now I allowed my gaze to fall upon the female sitting in the chair opposite me.

"Who the hell are you?" I asked her directly, and then tilted my head towards General Smith. "Who the heck is she? I don't like any of this one little bit."

He smiled. "I need you to completely understand before I continue that what I am about to tell you is of the utmost secrecy. Anything said within this room between us must never be repeated to anyone. Do you understand and agree to that?"

"What else can I say? Are you going to kill me if I refuse?" I asked.

He shook his head and smiled. "No my dear, absolutely not. We're here to help you and assist in finding the creature that is loose in the City of Tucson. It's a very serious situation as you well know and you can be of vital assistance to us, but in ways you never would've imagined. Detective Stephenson, you need to agree to total secrecy before I can continue."

"Oh for crying out loud, yes I agree. Sweet Jesus, tell me something, anything. I'm a goddamn Tucson police detective, in law enforcement for years. So yes, you can trust me. I will not repeat a damn thing. Just jump off the alien fairy tale train and tell me what the hell is going on. You're all starting to really piss me off and you don't even want to see me when I'm angry. Trust me on that."

"Fair enough," he chuckled. "Allow me to introduce you to Aimee. She knows all about you, including your unique past. There are no secrets here between us."

I stared at her and then over towards General Smith. "What do you mean my past? How do you know anything about my past life? I only met you the other day."

"We know that you were abducted four times between the ages of seven and twelve. We are also aware of who abducted you, what tests they ran and procedures performed. Plus, how you fought so heroically to survive those terrifying episodes. So, as you can see Miss Stephenson, we know all about your life and we are very impressed."

I just sat there, totally stunned. A part of my life, over half of those early childhood years, had been a total nightmare. My parents had trouble believing tales I recited of alien abductions, little gray creatures, needles and probes, bright lights, being lifted into the heavens on spaceships. But, they did know something terrible had occurred in regards to my mental state. That's why for most of my teen years I was in constant therapy. At first I rebelled like anybody that age would have, knowing full well what had been done to me and then angry at the world since nobody truly believed my story. They all felt I was freaking crazy, although nobody would admit it to my face. Shit, teen years are hard enough and then throw in aliens and spacecraft, well you can just imagine. Having any close friends was near impossible because I was so damn paranoid.

After a while I realized that I needed to play their games so I learned as much as possible and became a very good actress. I gave the doctors, as well as my parents, what I felt they wanted to hear. It took a while for the nightmares to truly go away. I would continuously wake up in paralyzing fear and wonder if I had been abducted once again, or if it was all just inside my head. Hell, maybe I actually was crazy I began to wonder. Totally out of mind, complete fruit loops. The wounds and needle marks on my body eventually faded and nobody, not even all the doctors, could determine what they were, or why I incurred them. X-rays were taken, blood tests ran, and nothing showed up.

Now here it was flashing in front of me all over again, like it was as real as that very first evening after dinner when I was seven.

Hell, maybe I truly was crazy back then and going completely nuts this time.

I lowered my head and whispered, "What do you really want from me? What do I have to do with this creature, as well as this very strange woman sitting in my home?"

All this time the female had not uttered one single word. She just continued to look at me with those damn red eyes. I wanted to literally scream at her, but somehow I felt it would do no good. Yet, there was also a strange feeling of complete safety.

"Let me introduce you to Aimee. As you probably have deduced by now, she is not of our world. She is from an alien race that arrived on our planet over four hundred thousand years ago. She is also genetically altered to appear human and is just one of many I might add. Aimee though happens to be a very special individual with extremely rare abilities. We simply do not have the time to go deeply into it right at this moment. However, suffice it to say Amelia, she has come here at our request to help us in this critical situation. She has also brought others along with her to do battle if needed. These men are obviously very different than she is, but members of the same race, nonetheless. They are more than capable soldiers, very deadly when required to be."

General Smith suddenly stopped talking and moved his gaze towards the female. As if she was talking to him, although no sounds came from her mouth, he nodded and sat back in his seat. She moved forward a little on the chair and gazed in my direction. When she began speaking it was like listening to the most beautiful voice in the world. Both her voice and eyes were absolutely hypnotic.

"Hello Amelia, I'm so very pleased to meet you after all this time. Please accept my deepest apologies for invading your home and bringing such undue stress upon you. However, also believe me when I say that you are very special indeed. We have been monitoring your life ever since you were born. Yes, it is true that you were abducted a number of times in your early years. However, what you do not know is that your mother had also been abducted often when she was a young woman in her early teens and twenties. On that last abduction she had something implanted inside her of which she was completely unaware of. That material would be more like what you would call DNA, but it was of our race, alien to your world if you will. A year later your mother married and a year after that you were brought into this world. When you were first conceived this special DNA merged with the embryo inside your mother. You were born totally human, but very special in more ways than you could've ever imagined. Although your first memory is of being abducted when you were about seven, it actually occurred on a regular timeframe when you were still an infant. Those memories were wiped from your mind."

I just stared at her totally enrapt, listening to this extremely unbelievable story.

"Was my mother ever aware of this happening to her? Was this why she died ten years ago at such a young age?" I asked, my voice trembling, building upon anger.

"She was aware of it, but please do not blame her. She had no choice and knew that you would be well cared for which you were. After all, how could anything so precious, or fragile, ever be harmed in any way? And to answer your question, she died of natural causes, though I'm afraid the terrible guilt she had throughout her life helped her to not live a long and fruitful life. She was just as amazing as you in her own way"

Glancing down at the floor I closed my eyes. I wanted to cry. I wanted to scream. Hell, for that matter, I desired nothing more than to end my life at this very moment. Not to live another minute, another second as a freak, as an apparent human toy, nothing more than an experiment. My life never being my own and not aware of it.

Looking up at Aimee now, I did have tears falling from my eyes.

"That appears to be no thanks to your kind," I said in a hushed voice. "She never told me anything about this. In fact, all throughout my younger years she made it appear that I had a mental disorder. That something was terribly wrong with me. Does your kind even begin to have feelings in regards to how you must've ruined hundreds, if not thousands, of lives with all these abductions? I was abducted when I was seven years old, nothing more than an innocent child. And now you inform me that it started right after I was born. You stole my childhood from me for what? Some damn scientific experiment? Are we nothing more than lab specimens for your kind? I was nothing more than a goddamn lab rat, to be played and toyed with as your race desired. You ruined my mother's life and made my existence miserable even before I was born because of this DNA bullshit. All the nightmares, all the doctors, all the terrible feelings I've had my entire life. Do you have any guilt at all? Does your kind even remotely begin to realize what you've done to me and so many others?"

"I can only answer those questions for myself Amelia. Please know that I personally absolutely regret everything that happened to you and your parents," Aimee responded solemnly. "However, I was also born for only one objective, no matter how long ago it was. And that objective was to eventually meet you. My other half so to speak. For us to unite as one at some point in time. There unfortunately have been many failed experiments as you just referred to, but on my end I'm afraid. So many others like me who were born for the same purpose did not survive. I cannot speak for anyone but myself. Please know that I deeply feel every word that you just said. Nothing can be done about the past, but we can together do something about the future."

Sitting back in the couch I stared up at the ceiling. "But it wasn't only me. My father thought he was a failure because of what he felt was a mental problem that I had. You just said that my mother was aware of what happened and it was a terrible ordeal that she had to live with until she died. I can't imagine the pain they both went through."

"Unfortunately Amelia, it was part of the process. She was instructed never to say anything to you. When the time was right she knew that you would be contacted and that time has come. She was also aware that you would never be harmed in any way and that your life would be monitored. Trust me when I tell you that not a minute of your life went by that you were not protected. You have been totally human all these years."

I wanted to stand up and yell, scream, throw things, but knew it wouldn't do any good other than release my furious frustrations. Maybe that would be a good thing.

"But what the hell, I'm nothing more than a normal human female then, nothing special in any way. I have no superhuman qualities and I'm just a simple detective for God's sake. Not some damn superhero. I can't fly, or bend steel with my bare hands. What traits do I possibly possess that are so special and unique that I'm not aware of them? And, why was I never made aware of this previously?"

Aimee tried to smile. If she had any physical fault at all it was that due to the shape of her nose and mouth it came out appearing more like an evil grimace. Not very pretty to say the least, but I didn't want to tell her that.

She smiled. "I know, my smile is not very attractive I'm afraid."

I just stared at her with open mouth, realizing that she had just read my mind because I had thought that very thing and not uttered a word verbally.

"I'm so sorry. I didn't mean to be rude," I replied softly, relatively embarrassed.

"Amelia, please don't let it bother you. I was also genetically altered from before birth. However, from my true race, not from a human mother, or inside a laboratory. Thus, some of my human attributes are not perfect since they retain our natural traits. You, on the other hand, also was genetically altered from before birth, but in a very special and unique way because your mother was human. Amelia, you truly have no idea how unbelievably wonderful you are. However, I am here to tell you if you'll allow me."

"Your mother was alien then? How could you be born into the body that you're in now if your birth parent did not look human?" I inquired, obviously extremely curious, at this point, but then I realized it was all just nervous chatter on my part.

"That is correct. My parents were not human in any way. In fact, I was hatched so to speak from an actual egg. That may be startling for you to understand, but all the young in our race come from eggs. We do not have the ability to produce young any other way. However, after birth we are cared and tended for just like any newborn would be. And yes, when I was hatched I looked somewhat human in appearance."

Very slowly I sank far back into the couch. In fact, I wanted to just disappear. My gaze was now centered directly upon Aimee, who was totally captivating to say the least. But then occasionally I allowed my eyesight to flit quickly over towards General Smith and then up at the quiet giant standing completely still against the wall. He basically had not moved a fraction of an inch since I first awoke and noticed him there. Where Aimee was enthralling and captivating in a strangely magical sort of way, this particular male was alarming and frightening at the same time. It truly was like looking at a large reptilian-type figure standing erect on two very long legs. And yet, as frightening as he appeared to be, there truly was a calming and protective nature to him.

Basically though, I was nearly in a total state of shock. Not only had my current life become topsy-turvy going back to the first horrible death weeks ago related to some monstrous creature, I then had this very rugged and handsome man, Mr. Vince Flint, enter my life bringing emotional feelings that I was in no way prepared for. Through my childhood and adolescent years I had struggled so hard to forget and lock away in the deepest recesses of my mind all the nightmares. But then, they had begun tumbling back with the same horrible images I often saw as a young girl. Now I find out from this extremely bizarre group of people who had broken into my home, that I may somehow be an alien-human-hybrid. Holy shit I thought, it was like some science fiction movie.

I whispered in a very low voice, "Water please."

General Smith leaned forward, "Excuse me, Amelia?"

Looking at him, I raised my voice much louder, near a shout. "Can I have a goddamn glass of cold water if it's not too much of an effort?"

At the same time I noticed the giant twitch for the very first time. Hah, I thought, I finally scared the crap out of the big reptilian looking human.

Smith glanced over to his right which caused one of his twin puppets, Jeffery, to quickly walk into the kitchen where I heard the faucet run. He then returned and handed me the full glass. I smiled and thanked him.

I raised the glass very slowly to my mouth to drink as this scenario sped quickly through my head, 'I could toss the water at Smith, then throw the glass at lizard man, get up fast and dive through the picture window where I would do an Olympic somersault on the ground probably bleeding heavily from broken glass, race fast

towards my car parked in the driveway, grab the extra key hidden in
the left wheel well, turn on the ignition, stomp on the gas pedal, and
careen down the street to be free of their evil clutches.'

Yeah right, like that was going to happen. I drank most of the
water and then softly placed the glass on a coaster to my left on the
end table, fearful that any sudden movements might result in my
death.

"May I turn on the lamp if it's on the lowest setting?" I
requested. "It won't be very bright, I promise. I would just feel more
comfortable with a little more light. Pretty please?"

Smith turned towards Aimee and she nodded slightly. I turned
on the lamp which thankfully spread a little more glow into the
room. My strange young visitor, however, was still somewhat sitting
quietly in shadows. I almost laughed out loud when I thought '*young*
visitor' because she was probably hundreds, if not thousands, of
years old.

I cleared my throat and then reached for the throw blanket
spread on the back of the couch. My entire body had begun to
tremble and for some reason I didn't think it was because of the air
conditioner.

"Where did you come from? What is the name of your race?
Where do you live?" the questions now tumbling out of my mouth.

General Smith sat forward. "Amelia, we honestly don't have
time for those answers, but they will all be forthcoming soon."

Aimee then slowly raised her right hand again so that he
became totally silent, almost like a subject to a queen. Sitting back
he nodded in her direction. I realized then just how freaking strange
and powerful she was.

She started talking in that strangely lyrical voice. "The name of
our true race is something that cannot be verbally said very easily

in your human language, but you will know that name shortly. As a result, we adopted the name of Anunnaki and became somewhat like early God-like deities on this planet. To most of your scientists and government people, we came from a planet called Nibiru, but in actuality our journey started far beyond there. Over these hundreds of thousands of years on this planet Earth we have adapted and absorbed ourselves many different ways within your society. Our leaders do not live above ground, just we hybrids do. Their world is deep under the crust of this planet, as well as beneath the deepest oceans of your world. Plus, of course, in the sky above. Other than top secret meetings with governments around the world, they normally do not outwardly appear to human society. You will come to know them very shortly. I've lived for quite a long time in a very quiet village in far off Norway."

I just listened to her relate this science fiction type tale maybe penned by one of the great authors – Asimov, Verne, Heinlein, Wells, or Verne. I still was not in any way believing one blessed word of it. As far as I was concerned, it was total rubbish, a complete pile of nonsense. I figured they were trying to brainwash me somehow.

"So, then what you're telling me is that our government has known all about this alien stuff for years and that there really is a Book of Secrets," I stated.

General Smith replied, "No comment Amelia at this time, but you will know the total truth shortly."

"Ah, so the truth is out there. This is just really unbelievable. So my new friend Aimee, other than ripping my life apart, why are you truly here? What can this lowly human female possibly do to help put an end to what's been happening in Tucson?"

She tried to make her voice as gentle, and human sounding, as possible. Now that I knew who and what she was I could easily detect something well below her voice that was kind of disturbing in a very unsettling fashion.

"Amelia, what needs to be done will no doubt frighten you so please do not be concerned. I simply need to enhance your unique abilities further in order to complete the total transformation."

My eyes probably at that point opened as wide as they could humanly go.

"I...aaaah," and then simply started to laugh uncontrollably. "Enhance and transform me into what? Some horrible looking creature? Sorry, but some albino-looking woman like you? Am I going to be forced to look like some damn gigantic lizard like my friend against the wall? How are you going to perform this magical trick? Snap your fingers and say presto?"

Aimee smiled once more. To say the least, other than being totally strange looking, her smile was nearly hypnotic. I suddenly realized that I needed to sever that connection and look away, which I did quickly.

"This final transformation can be done right here in your home. In this very room, in fact. Amelia, both our paths have been destined to travel upon the same course until we would meet at the appropriate moment. Possibly it could've happened sooner, or even maybe at a later date, but now with the invasion of this alien creature attempting to take over your city, that special time has now arrived."

I shook my head in total disbelief. "Sweet Jesus, this just isn't happening. How are you going to do this, ah, what did you call it, a transformation?"

There was a long moment of total silence before alien-girl responded.

"I'm going to enter your body and we will then become one individual."

I stared at her, smiled broadly, and then started to laugh like a wild woman. This insane fit of amusement lasted for well over a minute. When I finally calmed down I reached for the glass of water and chugged it, while wiping away tears on my cheeks that had fallen from my eyes. I so much wanted the liquid to be ice cold beer rather than water, but my throat was suddenly extremely dry so I needed to drink anything.

"Wait just one bloody minute. You said that you're going to enter my body like how, with your mind? Through my skin? Down my mouth? Inside my ears? I know you have the ability to read minds, but what else can you do?"

"No," Aimee responded gently, "you and I will actually become one unique and extraordinary individual. My body, as you see it now, will no longer live and breathe. We will then become you. One extremely special person."

I pulled the blanket tighter. "This is the most goddamn insane thing I've ever heard of. What you're saying is that I'm going to die and become you, is that it?" I continued, my voice now starting to rise again. Oh my Lord, how I so wished that my gun was in easy reach.

"Not at all, Amelia. You will still completely retain who you are in every way, shape and form. This body that I possess will no longer be of any use. My abilities, my knowledge, my powers will then become yours. We will share everything, though trust me when I say that you will not be aware of my presence."

I just sat completely stiff on the couch although my body trembled the entire time beneath the throw blanket of an eagle soaring over a mountain. My mind was constantly trying to think of a way out of this situation, but knew that did not seem plausible.

I was, quite frankly, to become lost as I had always known my life would eventually become.

"Is this why I became so sick out on the street earlier today? I got all dizzy and nauseous, threw up in fact. Were you starting to change me then? How are you going to do this?" I asked in a very low voice, near a whisper. "Is it going to hurt? Are we going to argue back and forth like good sister/bad sister?"

Aimee smiled and chuckled softly. "So many questions and I will try to answer them all so that your mind is put at ease. Yes, I was able to enter your mind and body once I landed here in Tucson. From that point I started to sort of prepare things for the transformation. And Amelia, please trust me, it will not hurt at all. In fact, you may not even feel anything other than a heavy pressure. But there will be no pain. I just need you to lean back and close your eyes. When the process has been completed, General Smith will touch you very gently so that you can reawaken. That will be it and we will then venture forth to finally put an end to this invasion."

It seemed over the last few minutes all I had been doing was laughing or shouting. Now all I wanted to do was cry. I thought of my mother who I loved dearly and how she, at some point in her life, had gone through the same terror. I thought of my father who most likely never knew anything about all the abductions, or what was being done to both his wife and child. Only that his precious little baby girl was having serious mental issues. Or, about his very special wife who he loved dearly. My thoughts tumbled towards my fantastic partner Manny who I realized I might never see again. And then, of course, there was Vince. How could I truly have a normal relationship with any man the remainder of my life, especially not ever wanting to have a child now?

"My God," I replied, letting my head fall gently onto the back of the couch. "So let me get this straight. I'm going to sit here on the couch, close my eyes while you say *'presto chango'*, wave a magic wand, and I'm then going to become something like an alien version of *'super girl.'*"

Aimee replied quietly. "Well, I won't be raising a magic wand and waving it I'm afraid although that does sound somewhat theatrical. However," rising from the chair she had been sitting in she moved fluidly over to the couch where she then sat down beside me, "I will hold your hands in mine and we will close our eyes together. You will then as I mentioned earlier possibly feel a very strong pressure in your head. Maybe like a slight headache and stiff neck, until you awaken. It will all be over quickly, not taking more than maybe ten minutes."

"I really just want to run away right now," I said underneath my breath. "It's like I'm about to die and then be reborn as some damn human-alien creature."

Aimee smiled once more and I realized that I wish she would stop doing that.

"I'm sorry, I won't smile anymore," she replied in response to my thought.

"Damn you," I muttered. "Quit creeping inside my head although it appears that's where you're going to be very shortly. Okay," I sighed heavily, "since it seems that I have no choice in the matter, give it a rip. You'll probably kill me if I say no."

I then very nervously closed my eyes and wondered as I did so whether I would ever remember the true human person known as Amelia Stephenson when I finally opened them once again.

Chapter 32

Manny hadn't moved much at all for well over an hour. Mostly the creature was continuing to mold him into an unnatural force that was now so much more powerful than any simple human could ever be. He also sent out signals to each brood member and kept that *'call to arms'* so to speak constantly open, much like a beacon of light to home in on. The creature had decided that this location would be the true start of its invasion.

Over the last hour each of them moved quickly throughout the city so that they were now within easy striking distance. At the moment, all twenty of them were milling around outside Tucson Police Headquarters building on 270 S. Stone Avenue. The connection they had between them was strong so even though it appeared to be nothing more than humans casually strolling the sidewalks, passing through the parking lot and lounging outside the front door, they were all simply waiting for the signal to venture inside to the imminent battleground. They also recognized each other even though they hadn't really met previously in human-state after invading their new host bodies out in the desert. The strong connection they had with the parent was also constantly open to each other. It certainly led credence to that strong mother-child bond.

Robert Perkins was the closest one to the building. He was actually sitting on a bench facing the front entrance waiting for the appropriate time to go through the door. Before leaving the house he had reluctantly removed the skirt and changed into his uniform. Somewhat more presentable since he didn't need to bring attention to himself.

Three others who had been Tucson police officers were also nearby. They would enter together first and quickly commence the assault as soon as the signal was received from the parent.

Up on the third floor there was a sudden knock on the door of the office where Manny was quietly sitting. The knock was then followed by an extremely angry voice.

"Detective Corroda, I specifically instructed you to keep this damn door open and unlocked," Sergeant McCorty said loudly from out in the hallway. "You have to still be in there so get your lazy ass over here and open this door. Right now."

Manny annoyingly glanced over and then stood up from the desk. The creature inside him realized that it was time to start. He issued the order for his brood army to begin their assault and then walked over to the door as another hard rap echoed loudly.

He unlocked the door, threw it open and reached out to grab McCorty around the neck dragging him roughly inside the room. The door then slammed shut very loudly behind him. While Manny was walking over towards where the sergeant continued to make noise, the creature immediately began the outer transformation which at this point only took seconds since it previously had a good hour to perfect the entire process. Hard scales formed on every square inch of skin, both hands elongated with human fingernails stretching into sharp, ugly-looking claws. Manny's normal facial features shifted quickly to become more reptilian with both upper and lower jaws jutting out as vicious teeth became longer and curved. Black eyes bulged out forming two eyelids while the tongue grew long, flickering outwards very lizard-like. Thankfully, Manny himself was dead.

Sergeant McCorty started swinging his arms wildly, kicking out as much as possible. But he was now being easily held in the air by the creature so there was little strength behind those moves. None of the blows caused any damage. It happened so quickly that McCorty had no time to yell out in shocked surprise. Nobody in the hallway was close enough to hear, or notice anything unusual. Now he just gagged and choked, eyes bulging out because he had begun to grow feint from lack of oxygen.

Manny brought the struggling body towards him and then opened wide to bite down on the top of McCorty's head. There was a loud crunching sound as the skull split open. At this point the sergeant was still alive and somewhat cognizant of what had just happened, but that lasted only seconds more. The creature's tongue explored the open skull cavity and then leaned over to bite down into the gray matter. When it was done eating this delectable treat he used the other clawed hand to grab what was left of the sergeant's head ripping it right off. The body then fell heavily to the floor while the remainder of McCorty's skull went flying against the far wall with a sickening splat.

The creature was not really hungry for food, just domination and destruction at this point. Along with retribution for being held captive for so many years. It moved towards the door and flung it wide open to step out into the hallway.

Downstairs in the main lobby, Robert Perkins and three others dressed as Tucson cops strolled casually through the front door as if they were meant to be there. They also had plenty of time since killing their families to perfect these quick and monstrous transformations. As they entered the building the physical changes like what happened on the third floor to Detective Corroda had already been completed to their own human hosts. In addition, this process had also been accomplished by the other sixteen creatures who were now moving in a vicious predatory fashion towards this entrance to police headquarters. It was, to say the least, the ultimate monstrous army from outer space.

Once inside the front lobby Robert immediately walked up to the front desk and easily leapt over in order to take the desk sergeant down before any firearm could be drawn. The other three immediately rushed any other cops walking, standing, or sitting around. As this was all being done the other creatures moved into the building through the front door. This entire initial onslaught took less than three minutes. Several civilian workers, along with a few pedestrians who had unfortunately just entered the building, were also slain quickly in very bloody fashion. Other than when these creatures slaughtered their host families to feed and grow strong, this was the first time they experienced outright battle and it was totally exhilarating for each of them.

This small alien army then split up with a third of them remaining on the first floor to wreak havoc, while the remainder split up with half of them stalking up the stairs and the rest entering the elevator where they stopped at each floor to burst out into the hallways. Surprise, we're here! You know.....like, *"here's Johnny'*.

Back up on the third floor, the leader who once was Detective Manuel Corroda, quickly moved to slay several people walking in the hallways with their heads down, completely oblivious and unaware they were about to run smack into a hideous monster. This all happened so quickly that no firearms had been fired up to this point as over a dozen bodies quickly littered the floors.

However, that only lasted so long as screams and gunshots began to quickly ring out on all the floors. The creatures, even though they appeared physically to be male and female humans, were totally impervious to regular bullets which bounced off the hardened scale-like armor. Each alien felt the pressure of these bullets striking their bodies with the closer ones being more forceful. None of them individually was strong enough to bring any creature down with mortal wounds. In fact, they shed very little blood at all unless the bullet struck an area that was possibly not as heavily armored.

Moving with deadly determination from room to room they simply caused total destruction with slashing claws and fangs. At this point, the adrenalin had built up so much within each host body that tails had formed which became additional weapons, swinging back and forth to not only crash through walls and doors, but send flying any cop or civilian worker who got too close.

While all of this was going on, out on the corner of S. Stone Avenue across from the Headquarters Building, Flint and each commando heard the gunfire.

"What the hell is going on over there?" exclaimed Vince. "I think our creature has brought the battle to us."

"Agreed!" responded Lt. Frawley. "Sgt. Gray, notify home base as to what's happening and have the rest of the team respond to this location ASAP. The rest of us let's move."

Not even waiting for the light to change the commandos along with Flint and Prudot rushed out into moving traffic with their arms and hands raised. This action was, of course, accompanied by loud screeching of brakes and several apparent fender benders. Once across the street they all had their rifles unslung in the ready position and headed for the front entrance.

"Sir, shouldn't we wait for the remainder of the group before going in there?" asked Sergeant Gray.

Frawley looked at him with steel determination in his eyes. "GG, when have we ever waited for backup when innocent lives were at stake? There are people being slaughtered inside that building and this is what we're trained for."

He turned to his men who were all kneeling down on the sidewalk.

"Gentlemen, this is it. Let me remind you that regular ammunition does not work against these creatures so that is why we are carrying armor piercing shells. Remember also that these things are most likely inside host bodies that may appear to be human on the outside. To what extent we do not know. Since we have not seen them yet then we are somewhat at a distinct disadvantage. However, something tells me that we will be able to distinguish them easily enough. If it looks ugly and like a zombie then don't ask questions, just shoot. My suggestion would be to stay away from the trunk of their bodies and go for the legs, as well as their heads. That should bring them down. Are we ready people?"

In unison they all stated firmly, "Yes, Sir."

That included Vince and Prudot who had been supplied with extra rifles carried by Corporal's Jarvis and Storey. When they were crossing the street he had also reached out via cell phone to Carrie and Tim in order to not only see where they were, but let them know what was happening. He was advised by Vaughn that they should be arriving to that location in less than ten minutes and that Amelia was fine when they left her. He informed them to be careful once they arrived and it would be highly possible that he, along with the commando unit, would be inside the headquarters building totally involved in combat.

At Frawley's motion to proceed they all moved towards the front door, weapons at the ready. They were totally unaware of what they would be up against, or what destruction they would find once inside. However, to them it didn't matter. They had one objective and that was to rid the City of Tucson, Arizona of these alien creatures.

Chapter 33

General Smith felt his cell phone buzz inside his pocket and quickly removed it. Standing up slowly due to severe pain in both knees, he then limped to the back of the house with Phillip's assistance to where he now casually stepped out onto the patio.

"Hello Colonel McDowell, what can I help you with?" he asked.

"Where in God's name are you, General Smith? All hell is breaking loose and you're nowhere to be found when we need you the most."

"I'm in the city, but my exact location is top secret. Just please tell me what's happening."

A heavy sigh of frustration was heard on the other end of the line from McDowell before he proceeded.

"Apparently the initial attack has taken place over at Tucson Police Headquarters on 270 S. Stone Avenue. The initial group of commandos led by Lt. Frawley, along with Flint and his team, are on site and have responded accordingly. The remainder of the commando unit, along with equipment and choppers, has already departed the base and should arrive at that location shortly. We have called in all the teams who have been out in the desert searching for this damn creature since it's now here in the city. At the same time we have initiated a full scale alert here at the base. All leaves have been canceled as well. All air force personnel who were not on duty have now been assigned."

"Thank you Colonel McDowell for getting to me so quickly. We will be leaving where we currently happen to be in less than ten minutes. I will stay in touch."

"Yeah, like you've been staying in touch. General Smith, I don't need to tell you that it appears you have a separate agenda here that we are not aware of and it's highly pissing me off. Pardon me for being so blunt and rude, sir."

Smith laughed. "Colonel McDowell, I'm retired Air Force and you know full well that you don't report to me. Also, the mission I am currently on is an extremely vital one that will hopefully help put an end to this difficult situation. So please, just hold down the fort and we will stay in touch. I'll be there shortly."

With that he ended the call and turned around to look back inside the house. Well, it had finally started and thankfully they had completed the transformation here between Amelia and Aimee. He reopened the door and walked quickly back into the living room.

Kneeling down he placed his right hand gently as possible on Amy's shoulder and squeezed. At first nothing happened and he repeated the same move.

"Amelia, please wake up. We need to move quickly."

I opened my eyes slowly so that everything started to become clearer. To say the least I was somewhat dazed, but truthfully was not feeling too horrible. The last thing I remembered happening was closing my eyes with Aimee sitting beside me while we held hands. Then I began feeling a slight pressure in my head that spread quickly throughout my entire body. This intensified to a point where I apparently blacked out.

Now I stared at the smiling face of a bearded older gentleman who I slowly began realizing was General Smith. The light within the room was still pretty low and dim. Allowing my gaze to scour the room I noticed the two twin guards standing on each side of Smith, along with the six large guys who had been previously sitting in my dining room now surrounding the couch. The strange reptilian-like giant who had seemingly been holding up the left wall earlier was now standing near the front door.

I hadn't said a word yet, but felt very strongly that they all appeared to be in a defensive posture, but I was unable to figure out why since no danger was present.

Least of all little old me.

Opening my mouth slightly, I asked in a low voice, "Is there any more water? I'm really thirsty."

Smith motioned with his right arm and Phillip quickly filled the glass, then handed it to me. I drank it down completely and felt somewhat better. Looking around again I smiled and then centered my gaze directly upon the old, retired officer.

"So what really happened? Why is everybody surrounding me like I'm some type of ultimate threat?" I asked, yawning and rubbing my eyes. I still had a slight headache.

Smiling, he replied. "Well my dear, it's more for your own protection than for ours. I was not sure how you would react upon recovering from the transformation."

Then it struck me like a hammer pounding down on an anvil. I quickly looked to my right and saw the body of Aimee resting completely still with her head lying against the back of the couch, her eyes and mouth completely open. She also wasn't breathing.

"What happened to Aimee?" I asked in sudden alarm.

"She's now departed from that body. It's no longer of any use to her Amelia since her mission has been completed. She is now inside you. How do you feel?"

For some reason I was suddenly feeling dread, like the entire weight of the world was now on my shoulders. Though I must admit that I didn't feel any heavier since there was two of us now inside one body.

A slight panic attack began forming and I felt strong, heavy hands on my shoulders as my entire body began to shake uncontrollably. This lasted for about a minute until my limbs became calmer and my heart stopped pounding inside my chest.

"Are you okay Amelia?" Smith asked gently.

"How the hell would I know that since I have no idea how I should feel? What happens to Aimee's body now and what pray tell is next in line for me since my life is no longer the same?" I asked with complete trepidation.

"Aimee's body will be well taken care of, trust me. Remember though, she herself has not died, only the body that she had been born into. Her essence and powers are now inside you. They will become evident as time goes on. However, she will need to control them in the near future. The creature has apparently commenced its attack on your police headquarters building in the city. We need to respond to that location right away. Are you physically up to it?"

I looked at him with total confusion in my eyes and then cracked a thin smile. "I suppose so General. I actually feel like a puppet anyway, with you and Aimee pulling the strings. However, my instincts are that of a law enforcement person, as well as a detective, so whatever special powers I now possess will just have to shock me when they start to happen. I have many friends in that building so let's go."

Standing up I suddenly felt dizzy and fell back onto the couch which brought out some laugher on my part. Obviously I was not very strong at the moment.

"Well, it seems that I just need to learn the power of walking and regaining my strength," I said, at the same time starting to laugh.

Just then I sensed a huge shadow hover over me. Just as quickly I then felt myself rising towards the ceiling. Oh shit I thought, it was happening all over again. I was seven years old and being abducted. But then, I found myself being firmly held in the arms of our giant alien and for some strange reason unbeknownst to me, I felt safe.

We all exited my house and got into several large black vehicles that literally took up not only my front yard, but my neighbors as well. As I was being helped very gently into the back of the limo I saw Aimee's body being carried by one of the six soldier-type men and then placed into the back of a very non-descript ambulance type vehicle. A strong feeling of sadness coursed through my body as I realized I would not see her anymore even though our get together had been strangely short-lived. I also couldn't help but wonder what crazy stories would be quickly circulating in my neighborhood.

Suddenly I felt, or heard, or sensed, a strange voice inside me say, *"Amelia, please do not worry, or be concerned about that body. It more than served our purpose in order that we could become one entity. You are now so much stronger and powerful. I will be here with you always, to protect and guide you."*

I sat back in the seat while General Smith settled in across from me. It was definitely Aimee who I had just heard inside my head. I couldn't just start talking out loud because everyone would think I was freaking loony as a cuckoo bird. But now, I began to get somewhat angry.

"You said before this transformation that I would never know you're inside me and now you're talking as if I was your twisted sister. You lied to me," I thought back.

There was a moment of silence other than the outside noise of the limo starting up and then pulling away from the front of my house. As we sped quickly down the street I wondered if I would ever return to this location. Maybe it was a good thing that I hadn't gotten a dog or cat yet, as well as wasted the money on central air.

"I'm so sorry, Amelia," the voice came again forcing me to jump a little bit.

General Smith quickly looked concerned and I waved my hand back and forth, basically saying that I was okay. Wow, what a big understatement that was.

"You will definitely need my help a great deal in getting through this battle and understanding what new abilities you possess. When this is all over and things settle down I will pretty much become non-existent other than you're being aware that I'm within you. If you require my assistance then you will just need to call."

"Okay, that's fine. What do I dial – (800) Im-alien? For now, just let me relax and get used to all of this crap. So good-bye until later when I need you. I'll just give you a ring on the alien hot line," I responded, realizing that was rather curt.

Aimee didn't respond so I assume she didn't think it was funny.

As we drove off towards headquarters I shook my head since I had no idea what I had just gotten myself into, or if I would even survive at all. If I did though, then I felt strongly that my life would begin anew with a capital X, i.e. Xamelia.

Chapter 34

The creature looked back down the hallway, now littered with dead bodies. Many of them had been nearly torn in half, some with heads removed lying separately, arms and legs tossed about like broken branches from a tree. It stood before a door that read: Elliot P. Crosson, Office of the Chief of Police, Tucson, Arizona.

Screams and gunfire still echoed throughout the building. Not so much now on the third floor since nearly every human was dead. Several brood members had joined their parent in order to mainly obliterate this floor. One of them suddenly exited an office midway down the hall clutching the torn apart body of a female, her long blood-soaked hair dragging behind a nearly decapitated head. The tall lizard-like monster was gnawing on what was left of an arm that dangled from its mouth like a dog's chew toy.

There was no noise inside the room the creature now stood in front of, but it knew that at least one human was inside, possibly two. Without wasting any more time it smashed through the door and took two long steps inside the office. A cloud of dust from the shattered wall and doorway swirled in the air. It glanced around and quickly took note of a female huddled behind a chair, as well as a male half hidden behind a large brown desk against the far wall. The man held a long weapon in front of him with another smaller gun lying on the table.

It moved towards the desk, not caring about the female at all since she was obviously no threat at the moment. Chief Crosson immediately stood from behind his desk and leveled a Remington Model 870 12-gauge shotgun directly at the menacing creature stalking towards him. Without wasting any precious time, since apparently his life was about to end, he fired the first cartridge from the chamber and pumped quickly. He now had only four more bullets remaining. At least he might be able to take one of these damn monsters with him. To die with honor was always his mantra.

The first bullet from extremely close range struck the creature who somewhat still resembled Detective Corroda in the right shoulder with brutal force knocking it back two steps. It continued coming forward nonetheless towards Crosson. The chief fired again, pumped, fired once more, and continued the same action several more times until the shotgun was empty. Throwing the empty rifle aside he quickly picked up his service revolver in one motion and continued to fire at the oncoming creature until the entire clip was completely spent. Now he was totally out of ammo so all he had left was prayer.

Smoke filled his office, while he had also lost all hearing at that point. The creature had fallen to the floor from the force of the shotgun blasts, most notably in both legs and the head. Crosson moved carefully around the desk because he had no idea whether the creature was dead. A wave of sadness shot through him as he realized the body truly had been Detective Manuel Corroda, but at least it was apparent he was dead.

Crosson now stood two feet away from the creature, taking note that its head was nearly blown apart from several direct shotgun blasts. It became apparent to him that just possibly he had slain the damn monster. A quick flood of emotions coursed through his body. He had actually blown the thing away which was totally incredible to him. Maybe he would live after all to be with his lovely wife Pamela once more. He could be a hero!

He noticed that his secretary, Kathy Potter, lay flattened between his desk and a chair, her mouth open wide. She appeared to be screaming, but blasts from the shotgun and revolver at such close range had temporarily deafened him. He reached down to grab her hand which was extended up towards him, pleading for help.

"You're okay Kathy. The damn thing is dead. You can stop screaming now," he yelled, helping her to stand and then holding his secretary close, trying to calm her down.

They both took a tentative step to start going around the creature when it suddenly reached out with a clawed hand, tightly clutching the leg of Chief Crosson. It yanked hard and he fell to the floor, struggling and kicking wildly. The creature pulled Crosson closer as the chief released his terrified secretary. She scooted away like a manic crab, quickly stood and then ran screaming at the top of her lungs toward the office door only to run straight into the waiting arms of what was left of Robert Perkins.

Meanwhile, the creature instructed its precious hatchling to come over and hold Crosson tightly, which he was able to do easily enough while still holding the struggling body of the woman who was nearly passed out now from fright. Through what was left of Manny's head, the creature's original body squirmed up and out, then quickly wriggled over to Chief Crosson's face. It had needed Perkins to hold onto Crosson because when it left Corroda's body then Manny immediately died.

With clawed hands the creature opened the mouth as wide as possible so it could enter its new host. It wiggled quickly inside as the chief's eyes bulged open in terror. He gagged and choked loudly, unable to breathe. In less than a minute the creature had completed the physical transfer and then proceeded to just as fast alter the inside organs. Crosson was now in effect dead inside, but controlled by the alien. He would not see his beautiful wife again unless the creature had the opportunity to make a pit stop at their house so he could have one final, very strange kiss good-bye, plus a late snack.

The same process was being performed by the creature inside the body of Robert Perkins since he had also incurred extreme physical damage from gunfire. On the two floors below, as well as down in the basement, any brood member's host body which had suffered severe damage was also transferring to those few humans who had not up to that point been physically slaughtered and lay dead.

The creature, now firmly inside Crosson's body, stood up straight. It immediately sensed imminent danger from a new source so it sent out an alert to each of its young to vacate the building as quickly and safely as possible. Glancing over at the body of Kathy Potter which had also risen, the creature motioned for her, now controlled by the same hatchling that had been inside Robert Perkins, to move back out into the hallway. It followed closely behind.

"You need to leave, right now," the alien stated slowly, using the chief's voice that certainly didn't sound very normal. "Gather as many of your brethren as you can and we will unite again near your birth cave. Now go!"

However, right at that very moment the elevator door opened and out stepped Vince Flint, Sgt. Gray, and Corporal Jarvis. Their assault rifles still smoked from helping to clear the second floor. Apparently several of the things had escaped the building, but gunfire could also be clearly heard outside so it was evident that support had arrived.

Seeing the elevator open, Crosson moved back inside the office and slammed the door shut. The creature had not yet begun to alter the host body on the outside, thus unprepared for battle right at that moment. It was the most vulnerable now.

The three men standing inside the hallway looked left and right, immediately noticing the ghastly carnage spread about. They themselves were covered in blood, not only from innocent cops and civilians in the building who had been slaughtered, but some of it being from their own sustained wounds as well.

"You two stay here. I'm going to the end of the hallway. That's where Chief Crosson's office is. Be alert at all times," Vince instructed them.

While Flint moved down the hallway Corporal Jarvis immediately saw one of the creatures inside a female body exit an office to his right and stagger in his direction. It was kind of a nightmarish, zombie-like scene because she was dressed in a blood saturated, tailored black suit, with one high heel on and one off. This was truly the walking dead and not from any television show either. He immediately began firing a constant barrage knowing full well that even though the body appeared somewhat human it was no longer alive. The armor piercing ammunition began to tear the creature apart, protective scales not totally capable as of yet to withstand such a close frontal assault. It fell heavily to the floor, body jumping and jerking from each shot.

The corporal quickly ejected the empty clip and jammed in a fresh one. As he neared the body, suddenly from the lower ribcage erupted what seemed to be a long red worm, or slug-like body. It struggled free from the damaged host and slid onto the floor where it began wriggling towards the terrified commando

"Holy hell, GG, do you see that damn thing? It's some kind of fucking giant worm," yelled Jarvis at the top of his lungs.

Sgt. Gray was totally engrossed himself at the moment, firing nonstop at the no longer petite form of Kathy Potter which was moving directly at him from the other direction. Vince, who had gone into an office beside Chief Crosson's room, stuck his head out only to see GG firing non-stop at the horrifying female figure.

"I don't have time to look corporal, I'm kinda' busy right now. Crush the damn thing," as he continued pumping bullets into the jerking body that once was the very beautiful and single Kathy Potter. The crazy idea shot through his mind, *'what a shame, she apparently had been a very attractive woman at one point in her human life'*.

Jarvis quickly stepped back a few steps to escape the giant red slug that was continuing to squirm towards him. He was disgusted, frightened, and amazed at the same time. He raised his rifle and fired, hoping to explode the damn thing into a hundred pieces, when it shockingly leaped into the air and landed directly onto the Corporal's stomach. His rifle was knocked from his grasp as he fell back against the wall.

Quickly reaching forward he grasped the huge red worm with both hands and held it in front of him. The thing was extremely strong, flopping back and forth like some wild, out of control parasite. Its mouth, just a black hole, was filled with tiny sharp teeth.

"Hey GG, help a brother out man," Jarvis yelled.

"Throw the damn thing on the floor and jump the hell out of the way."

Jarvis did just that, tossing it against the far wall and dove to his left. At the same time covering his head.

Sergeant Gray moved forward one step and began firing non-stop from a full clip he had just inserted. The creature with no protection at all began to explode in a number of small pieces, showering the air in a nasty spray of red flesh. What was shocking to both commandos was that each piece continued to move and squirm wherever it landed, several of them on the right pant leg of Corporal Jarvis.

"Jesus Christ, it's still fucking alive," he yelled. "The damn pieces are still moving," as he reached down with his gloved hands and knocked them off his pants.

Standing up he began stomping on them hard, again and again until they were completely smashed and had stopped moving. Both he and Gray began doing the same thing together, praying that they were finding every little red speck that was still moving.

Meanwhile, since the creature inside the body of Chief Crosson had not begun any outward transformation it still appeared somewhat human. Realizing quickly that it needed to escape he turned and ran as fast as possible across the littered floor to the side window. Without even hesitating, or slowing down in the least, he dove through the window, glass shattering loudly. Sailing through the air he landed squarely on top of what appeared to be a brand new light blue Chevrolet Malibu. It would be rather funny listening to the owner explain that to his insurance carrier, *'Ah.....well, we were under attack at Police Headquarters by aliens, and our Chief had to dive out his office window where he landed squarely on top of my brand new car'.*

Rolling off the roof he landed very hard on the parking lot cement, definitely stunned and had apparently sustained a broken right arm. At least he was still alive though. Suddenly, several strong hands grabbed at his shoulders as he found himself being dragged to safety behind a large brown army assault vehicle.

"Are you okay? Can you hear me?" yelled a soldier hovering over him. "Sir, this is Sergeant Tomkins, you're safe now."

Flint heard glass crashing inside the office, going through the wrecked doorway, crouching at the same time ready to fire. Seeing nothing he quickly entered the room and was disgusted at the sight. What definitely appeared to be the body of Detective Corroda lay on the floor. Vince's first thought went out to Amy, knowing how devastated she was going to be when learning this. He then moved past the body to the wall behind the desk.

From the same third floor window the creature had just jumped through, the dirty and blood-smeared face of Vince Flint appeared. He wildly scanned the ground below searching for the Captain, but he was nowhere in sight. A sharp jab of fear shot through him. He was not actually certain whether Crosson had been compromised by one of the creatures, or had thankfully escaped without being killed. Flint then pulled back from the shattered window and walked past the destroyed body of Detective Corroda.

Back out in the hallway he glanced down at the dead body of the female who had apparently been inside Crosson's office when the creature crashed in. Something struck Vince as being very strange, but he couldn't quite put his finger on it. He nonetheless looked down the hallway and saw both Jarvis and Sgt. Gray wildly stomping away at something on the floor. It looked like a Keystone Kops episode.

"What the hell are you guys doing?" he yelled.

Sergeant Gray answered in a somewhat frazzled and high-pitched voice, "This damn freaky alien thing, like a long, fat red worm erupted from the chest of that body lying right over there, at least what's left of it anyway. The worm was going for Jarvis so I blew the damn thing to kingdom come. Then all these little chunks kept moving like they were still alive. Strangest damn thing I've ever seen in my life."

Immediately Vince knew what had bothered him. He turned quickly and stared down at the woman's destroyed body. The stomach had been torn wide open, apparently from within. Whatever monster that was inside her had escaped in that fashion and now Vince realized what was so terrifying. Immediately he became extremely alarmed.

"Hey guys, I think we're in deep shit," he yelled down the hallway.

Just at that same exact moment the door to the stairwell flew open. All three men turned in unison to point their weapons in that direction.

"Whoa, hold on. It's the good guys," yelled Tiny Tim, standing right in the doorway. "Point those rifles away because we're on your side."

"How the hell do we know that?" yelled a very frightened Corporal Jarvis, who continued to keep his rifle trained upon the door. "You could be one of these freaking creatures and we wouldn't know it."

"Flint, for God's sake, please tell them who we are dammit," came the loud nervous voice of Carrie Vaughn, who was standing behind the much larger Tim.

"It's okay guys, they're both with me. They're definitely strange and stupid, but they're not aliens. However, we have a much more serious problem," he told them all.

Vaughn and Rollins came into the blood splattered hallway, their own weapons pointed forward, shocked once again at the same sight they had been seeing ever since first entering the building.

"What now," asked Sergeant Gray, not wanting to hear any more bad news?

Flint pointed downward towards the destroyed body of Kathy Potter. "Apparently we're getting through their armor with this heavy duty ammo, but the actual alien itself inside the human body is not being killed. When it seems to be safe they appear to exit the hosts through the chest or stomach and then get away."

"How the hell would you know that?" yelled Jarvis, in a somewhat terrified voice.

"Because you just killed the thing that came out of that body. The one lying here clearly shows something also came out through the stomach. God only knows where it is right now. I don't see it anywhere around me so be careful. It could be hiding anywhere. However, what's frightening now is that we are going to have to check every single body inside this building. We were not aware of this when fighting them so it's possible that all we did was kill the host bodies, but not the aliens themselves."

Sergeant Gray crossed his chest and replied, "Sweet Jesus, I need to let Lt. Frawley know about this right away. What do I tell him they should be looking for?"

"Any part of the chest, stomach, or head that appears where something might've crawled out. Remember, there were only so many of them, maybe twenty, and lots of these bodies are just innocent cops and civilians that were killed. Hold it though, wait a minute," he said, pausing to think. "We are also going to have to check each person still alive in this building, maybe even outside. It's possible that these things could've transferred to another host body and appear to be human when they are completely not."

Sergeant Gray moved towards the back of the hallway and hit the comm-unit on his left shoulder. "Lt. Frawley, this is Gray. Sir, we have a potentially serious issue here which you are not going to believe."

Chapter 35

The black limo and van following closely behind came to a screeching halt in front of police headquarters. The streets for three blocks in each direction had been closed to traffic, both vehicular and pedestrian. Surrounding businesses in that immediate block were also evacuated. The building itself had been cordoned off, surrounded by an onslaught of law enforcement and military vehicles. All available police had been called to this location and with swat teams surrounding the building in riot gear. If there was anything dangerous still inside Tucson Police Headquarters it would be killed when trying to escape.

The window behind the front seat in the limo slid open.

"General, what would you like to do?" asked the driver. "I don't hear any weapons currently being fired so whatever battle took place here, I believe it's possibly over. At least for the moment anyway."

"If you feel that it's safe enough then we will exit the vehicle," replied Smith.

Phillip shut off the engine, got out and opened the rear door.

"Amelia, maybe you should stay inside for the moment," the general said, "while we make sure all is safe."

"You must be out of your mind, General Smith. This is where I work. These are my people. Hell, my partner Manny was in that building last I saw him so none of your goon squad soldiers could keep me inside this damn car unless you lock it and throw away the key. Now, either get out of the vehicle, or move aside," I said with conviction.

He nodded and smiled. "Please just stay with us, though. We do not know what danger still remains and you're best form of protection is right here with us."

"Yeah, yeah, well I've fought this damn thing twice already and all it did before was hit me with its tail. Besides, I'm supposed to be some super detective, right? You know, super alien girl? Me and Aimee are an unbeatable team, correct? Don't worry, I'll be a good little girl. But, I really do need to check on my partner now."

We crawled out of the limo and walked around to the other side so that we faced the headquarters building. I could easily see that a number of windows were shattered on all the floors, as well as the large main entrance doors. Four ambulances were parked right in front. There were three stretchers being carried out of the building with body bags on them. The other one had a police officer who was covered in blood and appeared to be in really bad shape. I immediately began to worry more and more about Manny.

"General, I really do need to get inside that building. You can either go with me or stay here, but I am going in there right now," I said with finality.

"You may go inside Amelia, but only with protection," he said, motioning to the group behind him.

Three of the six large soldiers started walked over to us, along with my tall reptilian looking shadow.

"So does the jolly green giant have a name?" I asked General Smith, trying to put a small bit of levity into the situation, but he didn't smile back. Guess he had begun running out of patience with me which seemed to happen a lot with people who knew me.

"He is called Zuul," he replied, "Although if you talk to him aloud he will not respond verbally."

"You mean like the word 'tool', but with a 'z' in front?" I asked.

"That would be correct. He will be near you always from this time forward."

I hesitated a few seconds before responding. "Well, I hope he won't be near me when I do everything if you know what I mean."

There was no response to my remark so I figured that I had gotten to the end of my comedy routine with the good old general.

"Okay, so then he's going to be doing the mind-speak-thing like Aimee did," I continued. "Kind of freaky I guess. He will hear me if I communicate the same way?"

"Yes," Smith responded, and then took both my shoulders and gently turned me around to face him. "Amelia, I know that levity, along with making crass and caustic remarks, is part of your unique personality. That's fine. We all deal with situations differently. But everything has its place and time. The situation we find ourselves in is more serious and deadly than you can ever imagine. We have to stop these creatures now before they multiply even more. There are times for jokes, but now isn't one of them."

He continued. "Zuul was Aimee's protector from when she was a small girl and has never left her side. Now that the two of you are united, Zuul will be your protector as well. That is to say every minute of every day. You would simply know that as 24x7. Please do not ever underestimate him because he is simply one of the best warriors of their race and it's a great honor for him to serve in this capacity."

I just nodded because there wasn't anything else to really say about that subject. However, I did turn towards the individual who now had moved closer to my right side, his long shadow hovering over me. I looked up and up and up.

"*I'm sorry Zuul,*" I thought, still muttering the words verbally. It was going to take some time to perfect this new mind-speak trick. "*Guess you're pretty old, too. You haven't seemed to age at all.*"

"*You are welcome,*" came the immediate reply. "*And yes, I am very old, both in human years and our own.*"

I surprisingly found his voice to be a much lower resonance than when Aimee communicated with me back at my house. That figured since it would be easier to distinguish between the two voices. I secretly hoped that there would only be these two voices, but then I realized I may have no secrets ever again.

"*You are correct Amelia,*" came the immediate response from Aimee. "*I am aware that it will be difficult for you, getting used to this new type of communication. However, you will be completely aware of who is communicating with you since our thought voices are different. As for secrets you refer to, you will have to explain that to me at a later date because it is a concept that I'm not familiar with.*"

I closed my eyes and slowly shook my head back and forth. "*This is just incredible, like some creepy old movie. I have a very big question for you though.*"

"*Yes, please ask it,*" came Aimee's response.

"*If I talk verbally, I mean out loud, will you know what I say?*"

"*Either way, I will know, but not Zuul. If you need him then you must request it in your mind, though he will be near you all the time in order to respond quickly. You will get used to it, but I know that will take time.*"

"*So what, he doesn't hear or speak?*" I asked, somewhat confused.

"Oh yes, he hears quite well. In fact, his hearing is more acute than any living thing on this planet. It's just that he does not speak your language. In time you will come to know how to converse with him verbally, but not yet. It's much too soon."

I realized right off that I was not going to be happy with this arrangement. "Well Aimee, I have to tell you right off that having you eaves dropping on every single word I say, or thought I compose in this crazy head of mine, will not be agreeable. You can definitely trust me on that point. I will need to have my own privacy from time to time if you know what I mean. And that's just from one girl to another. Can you understand that concept? There has to be some form of privacy."

"Yes, I do completely. Girl to girl, I mean," she answered. "I promise you Amelia, when this is all over we will work on our communication skills. Is that a deal?"

"Deal and I'm going to hold you to that, although I'm not sure how I can control it," I responded in not a very happy thought.

General Smith gently touched me on the left arm. "Are you okay Amelia?"

I still jerked in surprise. "Yes, I'm fine. Just having a woman to woman chit chat with Aimee. And also, would you please start calling me Amy if that's okay with you."

He smiled back. "I will try my dear. Just consider that I'm an old man and set in my ways. So are you ready to proceed into the building?"

"Yes, let's go. Oh crap, my weapon. I don't have it with me," I said, reaching down to my empty hip. "It's back at the house. I really need a firearm right now."

He put his arm out towards Jeffery who handed my gun to me. Thankfully I took it, smiled and slipped it into the empty holster.

When we walked through the shattered front door and entered the first floor reception area I was totally stunned. The devastation was enormous. Blood was splattered everywhere. It was pooled on the tiled floors, saturating the carpeted areas, splashed on the walls and furniture. One body still remained in the middle of the floor, covered by a sheet that had already become soaked with the victim's blood.

People were milling around, not caring in the least about contaminating the crime scene since it was pretty apparent who and what had wrought all this destruction and mayhem. It sure as hell wasn't human either. I looked around searching for anybody that I might know and didn't see anyone in particular. To be honest, everyone was just milling about with stunned looks etched upon their faces, just like on mine.

"General Smith, we need to get up to the third floor. That's where my partner Manny was the last time I saw him, along with Chief Crosson. Do we take the steps or elevator?"

"The stairs will be fine. I am going to stay down here so that I can begin contact with Colonel McDowell. You will take Zuul with you, along with Jeffery and two soldiers. Please be careful Amelia, we do not know if this area is totally safe yet."

I carefully entered the stairwell and realized that the elevator would not have been a good idea for Zuul since he had to duck down in order to just get through the doorway. Possibly that's why General Smith suggested this avenue right off. However, once through the door he was fine due to the high ceilings. We scaled the three floors fairly quickly even though we had to skirt three dead policemen. As we continued to the third floor I noticed that one of the bodies looked like his chest had been blown out from the inside. It was totally gross as I realized it was no way for anyone to die.

At the door to the third floor Zuul put his arm out in front of me. *"There seems to be humans on this floor who are still alive. We need to be very careful in case we frighten them into firing upon us."*

"Okay Zuul, thank you. Let me open the door a little crack and yell inside. Get back out of the way," I instructed him, as well as motioning with my right hand for the other guys to back up also.

I opened the door about two inches and yelled, "Hello, inside the third floor. This is Detective Amelia Stephenson. Do not shoot, we're safe. There are five of us out here. We're going to come in very slowly. Please do not shoot."

"Amy, this is Vince. Come in carefully, but please stay at that end of the hallway."

Then I heard him also tell whoever was there with him, "Lower your weapons guys. You know Detective Stephenson and if she has people with her then they are safe as well."

I opened the door slowly and stepped into the hallway. To say the least I almost threw up. Laying right beside the door as I walked in was a man's head staring with large open, terrified eyes right at me. In fact, as I walked through the doorway my right foot struck it a little by mistake causing nervous tremors to run through my leg. Beyond that was what appeared to be the headless body of a police sergeant, but I couldn't tell which one. Nor did I truly want to know at this point. Further, the hallway was just littered with dead bodies, both male and female, along with separated limbs.

Legs and arms were strewn all over the floor, like the bodies had just been torn apart with maniacal rage. Some of the limbs were intact and others displayed large pieces of open bone. In addition, huge chunks of flesh lay scattered about the floor like some crazed animal had gorged at a nightmarish feast. Not far down the hallway on the right side lay a female body with her head nearly decapitated, the top of the skull open and pieces of brain spread over her forehead, as well as what had been an attractive face.

Standing against the left wall was Corporal Jarvis, the look on his own frightened face not describable. He certainly did not resemble the brave, cock-sure soldier that I had previously been walking beside before I was driven home. His camouflaged uniform was splattered with blood and not to mention other icky-looking stuff. About five yards back from him stood a very tense Sergeant Gary Gray. His uniform was extremely blood splattered as well. It also appeared he had received a fairly serious wound on his left forearm, but he had somehow overlooked the pain like a true soldier.

"Hey, it's me guys, good old Amy Stephenson. I have four people behind me so we're all going to come in slowly, okay? Please, lower your weapons. We're safe."

"Just come in very slowly. We're a little gun happy right now," GG responded.

As I moved further into the hallway I saw Vince standing at the other end of the hall in front of Chief Crosson's office. I was suddenly fearful since I didn't see Manny anywhere.

Suddenly both Gray and Jarvis raised their weapons and yelled in unison, "Down Amy, down on the floor."

It then hit me why they were yelling in panic. Zuul had just bent down and was coming in behind me. "No, no, put your weapons down. He's with me. He's totally safe. Lower your weapons now and do not shoot. For God's sake, do not shoot."

Both the sergeant and corporal had dropped to their knees in the classic shooting position. I held my right hand back to stop Zuul from coming in any further.

"He's with us guys," I repeated. "You have nothing to worry about. Please, lower your rifles," I said in a raised voice.

"Put your guns down men," came Vince's voice. "If Amy vouches for him and the others then that's good enough for me. Shit, we have no idea what anybody looks like anymore anyway. Amy, are you okay?"

"Yes Vince, I'm fine. I'll explain everything once we're all inside the hallway."

I started walking forward, followed closely by Zuul who once inside began to stand up straight, his head only inches from the ceiling. Both Gray and Jarvis just stared with mouths agape. Jeffery, who was also over six feet and very well-built I might add, followed Zuul. Then the even taller, awesome looking human-alien figures brought up the rear. I could completely understand why GG and Jarvis would be so terrified.

"Sweet Jesus," Jarvis muttered. "He should be playing pro basketball for the Phoenix Suns. In fact, they all should be. They'd win a championship easily."

I laughed, trying to dispel the tense atmosphere. "Yeah, he might shatter all of Wilt's records for sure."

Without waiting any longer I started walking towards Flint who at the same time had begun walking in my direction. After sidestepping bodies and various limbs, not to mention large puddles of blood, we met more towards the middle of the hallway.

"Hi Vince, how are things going?" I asked him, trying to sound somewhat composed, but inside far from it.

He gave me that very disarming smile of his. "It's been kinda' interesting to say the least. Craziest damn thing I've ever been a part of. I'm glad you're okay though and back with us. I really wish it were under different circumstances though."

I nodded. "What the hell happened here, Vince?" I asked, glancing behind him.

He sighed heavily, I think to just finally release some of the tension that had built up inside his body. "After you left we decided to split up into small groups and scan the area which we did, finding nothing out of the ordinary. Then we came back together on the corner where you left us. After a few minutes of deciding what to do next we began to hear gunfire from this building and immediately rushed over. It quickly became apparent that the alien and its hellish litter converged at this location. They had begun their assault on police headquarters."

Pausing slightly, he glanced behind him and then set his worried gaze back upon me. "When we entered the reception area there was already dead bodies lying all about. We saw one of the creatures actually feeding on one of the dead cops so we opened up and blew it all to hell. We then broke up into groups and went through the first floor. When we were done with our search down there, Lt. Frawley had received notification that the rest of his commando group was outside and beginning to enter the building."

He just continued to stare directly at me then and didn't say anything for a few seconds, almost as if he did not know what to say next.

"Vince, where is Manny?" I asked, certain he was expecting that question.

"I told the guys we were coming up to the third floor so we could see what was happening up here," Vince continued, not answering my question. "Frawley and his soldiers would continue going through the first and second floors. When we arrived here and exited the elevator we found total devastation as you can imagination."

"Where is Manny? Is he okay?" I asked again, my voice rising and becoming very fearful. I got the sense that he was avoiding my question.

He took in a long breath and then reached forward to hold my shoulders very firmly. "Manny is gone, Amy. I'm very sorry."

I shook free and backed up a few steps to stare at him. "Gone? You mean, like he left the building gone? So you're saying that he's safe, just not here?"

Flint shook his head. "I'm really sorry Amy, but he's dead. Everyone up here on this floor is dead, I'm afraid. I did not find Chief Crosson's body, but I heard somebody, or something, crash through the window in his office. I didn't see him on the ground though so I can't be certain what exactly happened to him. If it was Crosson, and he had not been changed then we'll hopefully locate him once we're back outside."

Slapping at his hands I yelled loudly, "Let me go, Vince. I need to see Manny."

"Amy, no, please. You do not want to see him like that, trust me."

I then kicked him hard on the left shin and he let go of my shoulders. Regretting that I had to do that, I rushed past him nonetheless into Chief Crosson's office. Two steps inside the room I stopped suddenly and raised both hands to cover my mouth.

"Oh my God, oh my God, no. Please Lord, don't let it be Manny," I muttered like a crazy woman, tears already pouring from my eyes.

Blood was everywhere and his body lay face down on the floor. I remembered though what he had been wearing and knew for sure that it was him. My partner had been slaughtered by something monstrous. I dropped to my knees and started sobbing until I felt Vince's hands on my shoulders.

"Come on Amy, let's go. Please, there is nothing that can be done here. We'll make sure his body is well taken care of."

Spinning around I put my arms around Vince, my entire body shaking with both grief and anger. I cried against his chest as he helped me leave the office. We then moved slowly down the hallway towards the remainder of the group.

"I'm sorry Amelia, truly sorry," came the thought inside my head.

"Not now Aimee, please not now," I said aloud.

Vince looked down at me. "Not now? What do you mean Amy?"

I realized quickly that I had spoken aloud my thoughts to Aimee. "It's okay Vince. I just meant not now to have this happen, or anytime for that matter. Manny meant a great deal to me and his family is going to be crushed. Hell, I'm completely devastated right now."

He held me close again and I noticed that Zuul had begun moving towards us. I held up my hand, in effect saying that it was okay.

Vince squeezed me tight and held me at arm's length, gently wiping away tears from my cheeks. "Let's go down to the first floor. There's nothing more we can do up here."

Then he looked at Sergeant Gray. "You and Corporal Jarvis need to look at each body on this floor to see if any look like a creature might've come out from inside them. We know that it happened at least twice on this floor. One of them you guys definitely destroyed. The other we don't know where the damn thing snuck off to."

"What do you mean, Vince?" I asked with concern, still trying to recover from the devastating blow that Manny was gone.

"Our armor piercing ammo was definitely enough to get through their tough exterior so we were able to bring the bodies down. However, unless it was possibly a direct shot fatally injuring the main body of the alien inside then it appears they may not have been killed. We saw that happen twice on this floor so Lt. Frawley is having his men check all the dead on each floor to see if they show signs of something exploding from inside. Shit Amy, it's very possible that we destroyed the hosts, but not the entities themselves."

We all stood around staring at the carnage, each lost in our own nightmarish thoughts. All I could think of at that point was losing my partner, along with so many other friends in this building. I was really pissed off and now more than anything wanted vengeance.

"Amelia, you need to separate your emotions from loss and blind rage," appeared the soft voice of Aimee. *"There will be time to grieve afterwards, but for now you need to get back to General Smith. These creatures can be tracked by Zuul and the others. Trust them totally. They will not fail you."*

"How would you know about grieving? You were hatched from a damn egg and members of your race live thousands of years," I shot back, angry at her remarks.

There was a moment of silence before she responded in a surprisingly calm voice. *"It is true that I came from an egg, but once born I was raised by human parents who are long gone now. In addition, I grew to adulthood with others the same age, all of them no longer in my current existence. We may live a very long time, but we can also die in battle as both my parents did on another planet. It is true that I was not originally born into the human body of Aimee, but once they were no longer with me, and we began colonizing your world, I was changed and brought here. Once inside the human body I then lived with human parents who taught me the ways. They are long dead. Zuul has been with me the entire time and has lost much. So you see, I do know what loss is."*

I wasn't sure how to respond and realized that my remark was uncalled for, uttered in complete anger. *"I'm sorry Aimee. I'm just lost right now. Not only over losing my partner, but everything that has just happened to me. Wondering if I'll be strong enough to put an end to this nightmare and deal with my own life going forward."*

You can't really hear a smile, but somehow I felt her do that as strange it is seems.

"Amy, you need to leave the building now so that we can plan on how to end this nightmare as you call it. It is definitely apparent to both Zuul and myself that the main creature has gotten away. Your friend Vince is correct. Some of the beings inside those slain host bodies have escaped. It is only a matter of time before they invade new hosts if they have not already done so. They will unite again so we need to track them without any more loss of time. Or life, if possible."

"Okay, I got it. Again, I'm sorry Aimee. I didn't mean to hurt you."

"You're welcome and you didn't harm me in any way. We will get through this," Aimee responded. *"Now please go to General Smith and the others."*

I looked over at Flint who was actually staring at me with open mouth. Then I glanced around the group and saw both Jarvis and GG were also looking in my direction. All I could do was smile at them because I had a feeling why they were gawking at me.

"Hey guys, if we're done here then we should go down to the first floor. I need to get back with General Smith," I stated, trying to sound like nothing was wrong.

"Amy, do you realize that you were muttering under your breath, like you were talking to somebody, but not directly to us," said a somewhat concerned Vince Flint.

I laughed. "Yeah, seems I've been doing that a lot lately. Maybe when this is all over I'll need to see the departmental shrink, if I live that is. Just please overlook it. I'm not going crazy, honest guys. I've just been talking things out loud, that's all."

Jarvis responded while shaking his head. "We know that you're one tough lady Detective Stephenson and now we know you may be a little nuts, too. That's a great combination so let's go find these monsters and destroy them. We got your six!"

Sergeant Gray and Corporal Jarvis agreed to stay and finish looking around the entire floor. They would then join us outside. The rest of us, including Zuul, Jeffery, and the two large soldiers in black suits, got back into the stairway and headed down to the first floor. The entire time while ascending the steps I continued talking to Aimee in my mind, trying to get used to not verbally saying anything when I was doing so. I didn't need any additional attention brought upon myself. It was all hard enough as it was.

Chapter 36

Chief Crosson had been sitting inside the ambulance for around fifteen minutes while an EMT tech tended to the cuts, bruises, and multiple abrasions sustained when he had crashed through the window, landing on top of the car. In addition, his right arm was now in a sling as well. The technician told him to just lie down and relax, that he would be transported to the hospital as soon as possible to have x-rays and other tests taken.

The creature, however, was not about to wait. His host body needed to get out of Tucson as quickly as possible. He hoped most of the others escaped safely as well. Even though the attack on the building was a success since many humans had died, it still felt somewhat like a defeat because possibly half of his brood could've been killed and they couldn't retain this battle site as their own territory. The exact number of survivors would not be known until they all reunited again at the birth cave location.

Chief Crosson walked stiffly away from the ambulance in the direction where he had parked his vehicle. He had also gotten rid of the useless sling since pain was not much of a factor any longer so the creature didn't really care if the arm was broken.

He finally located his car and started walking in that direction while at the same time reaching inside the pocket of his torn suit coat with his good arm. Miraculously the keys were still there so he opened the door and slipped quickly inside. Not wasting any time he started the car and pulled out of his spot, turning right towards the exit. He needed to get away from this battle zone as quickly as possible.

Suddenly there was a loud shout from behind him so he glanced in the side view mirror. His mouth formed into a menacing snarl and a deep growl arose from his throat.

"Chief Crosson, wait. You need to get back inside the ambulance and go to the hospital," yelled the EMT technician.

No way was he going to slow down or stop so he just pressed down on the gas and shot forward. However, two squad cars were blocking the opening to the parking lot. As he slowed down he reached into the pocket inside his coat for identification. Pulling up to the police officer standing in front of one of the squad cars, Crosson lowered the window and held out his shield. He then came to a complete stop as the officer walked over to the window and bent down to look inside.

"Hello Stiles, would you please move your vehicle. I have to meet with the Mayor downtown right away," ordered Chief Crosson.

"I'm really sorry sir, but we have direct orders not to let anybody leave the area until everything is safe and totally contained."

"Officer Stiles, this is a very important meeting that I need to attend. I'm the one who put out the direct order that nobody was to leave. However, I need to do that at this time so I'm ordering you to remove the vehicle from the entrance."

The policeman was suddenly caught in a quandary. Here was his superior ordering him to go against what he himself had ordered everybody to do. It was either stand pat to obey the original order issued by his superior, thus possibly having the chief fire him. Or, let him leave like he was requesting now only to find that he should not have done so and then be put on report anyway for disobeying a direct order. It was a damn no-win situation.

"Are you okay, sir? Excuse me, but you really look like you're in bad shape," said Stiles, trying to basically stall for more time while deciding what to actually do.

"Thank you for asking. I'm a little banged up since I had to jump through my office window from the third floor in order to escape the claws of that damn creature. I believe that everything is now fully under control inside the building. But I repeat firmly, I need to meet with the mayor because we may have to call up the Army Reserves immediately. So I really need you to move your vehicle right this minute."

Stiles stood up stiffly and then turned towards the car, raising his hand and motioning for the cop inside to back up. Once the opening was wide enough Chief Crosson thanked him, squeezed through, and then stomped down on the accelerator, tires screeching the whole way.

Once out onto S. Stone Avenue he aimed the car in the direction to get out of Tucson as fast as possible. He used the same excuse and reason to leave the battle area with the next roadblock he ran into a few streets away. After getting through that one, then he was free and clear other than quite a bit of traffic which had been building up.

I had been sitting inside the limousine for twenty minutes with General Smith. He was still talking all hush-hush on the phone with somebody apparently of great importance from whatever ultra-secret organization he was a part of. With everything that had happened to me in just this very short amount of time, I pretty much began to believe that there definitely was a *'Book of Secrets'*

somewhere in the world. Maybe not with our government, but there sure as hell was one hidden away someplace. In fact, it was probably an entire encyclopedia *(remember those?)* that went back hundreds of thousands of years at least, with an alien dictionary and thesaurus as added volumes. I couldn't help but wonder whether I was now going to become a chapter in it as well.

On the other hand, I had been conversing with my other half, the once-albino, egg-hatched alien, Aimee. She had been giving me a brief overview of our powers. Well, my new powers anyway since she had always had them. To say the least, when she stopped talking I felt that I was kind of like Dorothy transported to the Land of Oz. Instead of having Toto by my side I now had Aimee. I supposed that Zuul could be the Scarecrow, or maybe the Tin Woodsman. Either way, he was one scary character.

I quietly closed the limo door behind me, moved towards the rear of the car and then just leaned back against the trunk. It was actually very sunny and getting steamier by the hour. Sunlight bouncing off the pavement and all the vehicles made it even hotter. Before we left the house I changed clothes and just slipped into sneakers, jeans, and one of my red Phillies tee shirts. What can I say, you can take the girl out of Philly, but not the Phillies out of the girl *(or guy, if that's what blows your skirt up)*. Not even thinking, I grabbed some of my right shirt sleeve and tried wiping away some of the sweat that had quickly beaded on my forehead. Didn't really matter anyway because most likely before this day was over I would either be dead, or covered in blood, not necessarily my own. Oh, and I also wore my hat to hide the ugly stitches.

Just then Vince walked up and leaned back against the trunk beside me. I got the impression he wanted to grab my hand, but then thought better of it considering the circumstances.

"Goddamn hot out here. Hell of a day to hunt monsters," he said, trying to be comical I suppose.

"Yeah, what ever happened to just a good old rattlesnake hunt?"

He laughed. "Too tame I suppose. I was walking around asking if anybody had seen Chief Crosson and was just about ready to give up when an ambulance drove into the lot and these two EMT guys jumped out. One of them remembered treating the chief briefly in back of his ambulance for cuts and abrasions, plus what appeared to be a broken right arm. He had left him lying on the stretcher inside the vehicle and said that they would be leaving for the hospital shortly. When he got back, his patient was not there. So he walked around a little and then thought he saw him pulling away in a car."

Vince paused, I think more for effect than anything so I just remained quiet until he decided to continue. For some reason I just seemed engrossed with other things on my mind at the moment than the whereabouts of my boss.

"I decided to check with the different exits that were being blocked and ended up talking to Officer Stiles," he continued and then chuckled a little bit. "At first it seemed he was rather hesitant to say anything. However, when I pressured him like you know I can do he blurted out that Chief Crosson had apparently pulled the big 'C' on him, thus making him worry about losing his job if he didn't move the parked vehicle. He did just that and then off he sped. I asked if he had mentioned at all where he might be going and apparently Crosson told him that he was going to visit the Mayor.

Taking a breath, he continued. "We contacted the mayor's office and apparently there was no meeting set up. In fact, his Honor is actually on his way back from Phoenix where there was some kind of get together up there. What I'm saying Amy is that it may appear the creature we have been searching for had possibly been inside Manny and then transferred itself to Chief Crosson. For whatever reason I don't know, but I think it's pretty obvious how and why Manny died. You know how sorry I am about that and I know how hard you're still taking it. We will get this monster and kill it, trust me."

Silence set in between us, but actually not over the entire area. There were vehicles moving about, horns honking, and people yelling. I just let my head fall back, closed my eyes and tried to relax. I would've at that very moment totally enjoyed Vince's strong hands massaging away the tightness in my neck and upper back. But (*heavy sigh*), all good things must wait for a more appropriate time I suppose.

Just then Lt. Frawley walked up to us. He removed his helmet and wiped at the sweat pouring down his cheeks, beading on his chin and then dripping like an open faucet. Needless to say, he looked quite uncomfortable beneath all that gear.

"I guess you two realize it's pretty damn hot out here," he said, laughing slightly for the first time since I met him.

We both nodded and smiled back since there was nothing to really say.

"We've gone through the entire building very thoroughly and looked closely at all the bodies which was distressing enough. We found at least a total of twenty bodies that showed very evident signs of something bursting out of their chests or stomachs. For six of them, the creature was killed and that was apparent because the damn worm things were blown apart and then all of the pieces were crushed because they strangely continued to move. Freakiest damn thing any of us ever saw in our lives."

He paused and took a moment to slip out of his bullet proof vest. Once that was done he seemed to feel a little more relaxed. Then he continued talking.

"It seems that fourteen of those little bastards got away. We can't be certain if they squirmed out of the building, found a new host to get away by crawling inside, or are still hiding away somewhere in there. The police are setting up stations at each access door to look closely at anybody coming out of the building, including all military and law enforcement personnel. Although quite frankly at this point we would have no way of knowing unless the person exhibited very strange mannerisms. It's also highly possible that they escaped very quickly from the building before we actually were aware of what to search for."

Vince nodded. "I have a gut feeling that they escaped. So unless we find one or two of them hiding out in the walls, ceiling, ductwork, etc. we've missed them. At least we killed six of the fuckers and that means they can be stopped."

Frawley nodded in agreement. "Well, all of my men are together just outside the front entrance and we're awaiting orders. A few of them sustained injuries, most of them minor, with only one somewhat serious. They are, or have been, getting treatment."

Vince replied, "One thing you should be made aware of Lt. Frawley. It appears at least to me that Chief Crosson's body has been used as a host, probably by the original creature that escaped from the supposedly secure air force location. You know, the one we've been hunting for weeks. Sad to say, he also used his rank to get through the roadblocks so he's gone, flew the alien coop so to speak. I've informed Captain Masters since he now seems to be the guy in charge."

Just then the rear door to the limo opened up and General Smith climbed out. Seeing our little threesome at the rear of the car he walked back and faced us. The look on his face was grim, but determined. He was definitely a man of vast experience and steel determination. It was also easy to see though that everything happening was testing his strength, as it was for everybody.

"Amelia, Lt. Frawley, Mr. Flint, I believe it would be best if we all returned to Davis-Monthan so that we can form additional search plans. I've been in contact with Colonel McDowell and they are amassing additional reinforcements, along with air power. We pretty much have come to the conclusion that these creatures, however many there may be now, have moved back out into the desert. Hopefully, they will unite and we can attack them all at once to end this nightmare."

"Sir, it appears that there may have been at least fourteen, maybe fifteen, that escaped being killed. I will get my men together and we'll head back to the base right away," Frawley said, then turned and moved off in the direction of his commando unit.

The general looked directly at me, as if I was some fragile piece of expensive glassware. "How are you holding up, Amy?"

"I'm fine physically. It's just getting used to not having my partner around anymore. Plus, adjusting to everything else as you can well imagine," I responded, not sure just how much I could actually verbalize since Vince was not aware of my own transformation. At least not yet. I was totally freaked out over how he would react.

Vince stood away from the car and tried brushing some of the dust and crud off his clothes. "I'll get my crew together and we'll meet you back at the base. I'm going to assume that we return to the hangar so we'll see you there. Amy, you coming with us?"

I glanced over at the old man who smiled slightly. "I would prefer that you come with us Amelia. However, if you go with Mr. Flint then you need to take Zuul with you."

"Zuul?" Vince asked, raising his eyebrows.

"Ah yes, well," General Smith responded. "Zuul is the very tall gentleman with us. I've assigned him to stay with Detective Stephenson at all times. So Amelia, it's your choice."

Vince looked at me with a rather shit-eating grin on his face. "Wow, you rate your own special full time body guard. Not a bad gig if you can get it."

I punched him on the left arm and he winced painfully, also falling back several steps. Then it struck me that physically my power was now even much greater than I ever thought it could be.

"Whoa Detective Stephenson, you've been eating your Wheaties it seems," Vince said, while rubbing his upper arm.

"Don't worry, it's just built up adrenalin. I think I'll go back in the limo with General Smith if you don't mind and meet up with you there. I don't believe you'd have enough headroom for Zuul to sit comfortably."

Vince shook his head, smiled and began walking away. Then he stopped and turned around to stare directly at me. "Something is definitely different about you Amy. Not sure what it is yet, but I think I'm going to find out eventually."

Without my giving him a response he just turned then and stalked off to join up with Tiny Tim, Carrie, and Prudot. A pang of guilt and sorrow struck my heart.

I turned and faced General Smith. "How am I going to pull this off? I don't even know my own strength anymore. Quite frankly, I'm scared out of my mind. One minute I'm just this normal thirty-eight year old female with all these human frailties, nothing more than a police detective who recently got out of the hospital after being knocked for a loop by that creature's tail. And now it appears I have these new strengths and abilities which I have no idea how to control. It's like I'm some damn alien wonder woman."

He took my right hand in his and we walked back to get inside the limo. "Allow Aimee to control what happens. Please remember, the two of you are one individual now and she will not allow you to fail. Depend on her and Zuul, along with the others."

I sat back in the seat and closed my eyes. Truly, I just wanted to bust out crying, as girlie as that might sound. Goddamn female emotions, I thought.

"Amelia, you'll be okay. We'll be fine, trust me. I've talked with Zuul who has an idea where they went so when we're back on the air base we will get together and make plans," Aimee said.

"How can you talk to Zuul without my knowing it? That kind of pisses me off, like I'm being left out of something vitally important," I shot back angrily.

"Amy, please remember that Zuul and myself go back a very, very long time so we have a unique connection. I do apologize and promise not to keep you out of anything going forward."

The ride back to the base was quiet other than General Smith once more talking in a hushed voice. More damn secrets I thought. I glanced over towards Zuul and found that he was staring right at me. Then strangely enough he lowered his head, something like a nod I guessed, and cracked a very thin smile. Sort of a smile nonetheless. Not sure why, but I suddenly felt a lot safer knowing the big green giant was my shadow.

Quinotoa, which was really the creature's original name from the world where he was first born, stood outside the birthing cave. It was really the body of Chief Crosson standing there. Now just a shell, a puppet whose strings were manipulated by an alien. Without a doubt, the human host looked like he had really been to hell and back. He had a multitude of cuts covering his face, along with a huge reddish/purple abrasion on the right side of his chin running down his neck to the collarbone area. The light brown suit he had been wearing was pretty much ruined, torn in a number of places and saturated with blood as well. One shoe was on and the other off. His useless broken right arm hung down at his side with the humerus bone now poking through the skin. That had not been the case when he first had leaped through the window to land on the car. But, while getting to this location he had fallen several times, thus making the arm totally useless.

There was no pain at all since Crosson himself was technically dead and the creature really could not feel anything in the way of pain. The heart still pumped blood though and the majority of the body was still physically intact, but only because the creature had immediately taken control of all the major vital organs. That way the body could still move around as a human, converse like one, react appropriately, etc.

Chief Crosson bent down and took a few steps inside the cave. He sniffed and definitely was aware that a number of humans had found the lair. That's why they knew the eggs had hatched and that others of his kind had been born. There was no reason now to stay here because it was not safe. They would definitely be coming to this location. The question was when and how many, along with what firepower.

Now Quinotoa just had to wait until the other survivors started to arrive which would be shortly since he had received signals from each one that they were free and on their way. He had discovered a larger cave higher up the mountain so that would be where they joined together. The creature knew enough now that it was certain the human army would converge on this site and try to destroy anything still alive. It was not concerned in the least because they would be prepared. The human bodies would be discarded and the true inner beings, transformed in their own image, would emerge. Their true existence and power could then be released.

The creature was not concerned about direct confrontation, or battling with the humans. Even dying which had not been an issue for a very long time. It only longed for the female to appear. She was extremely special, a feeling it had never encountered before. That transformation, when finally accomplished, would be *'out of this world'*.

Chapter 37

I asked General Smith if we could make a brief stop at Manny's house since it was technically on the way to the base. Not knowing if I would survive to see the next day, I just needed to be with his wife if only for a very brief time. I didn't want her to hear about his death from anybody else but me. Against the retired officer's better judgment he agreed, but said that I would only have five minutes. Definitely no more than ten. My life was surely on a shoestring now, even more so since the transformation.

It seemed that she knew almost right away the reason I was there, especially when she looked behind me and noticed the official type vehicle I arrived in. Tears appeared immediately. I had to reach out quickly to grab her as she started reeling backwards. General Smith had asked Phillip to come along with me so he grabbed her shoulders as well. The three of us then entered the house and quietly closed the door behind us.

We sat on the couch and held each other tightly. I tried crying with her, but for some reason found it hard for tears to actually start flowing. Ever since my teen years, especially since the abductions seemed to be over, I erected a very thick wall around me. Most of it was due to anger because nobody believed my story. Some of it also had to do with the fact I was just a more stand-offish person. Maybe that was why I could never have a sustaining relationship with anybody, especially the men I dated. I always blamed them, but in reality it was probably me. They weren't really the creeps, jerk offs, and low life scumbags in my life. That was all me. In fact, Philly guys are great, it's me that wasn't. All my life I regretted never having a happy childhood and it seemed that I just took my anger and frustration out on everybody else.

Definitely, my parents included. What they hell, they didn't understand what I had been through. They assumed there was something mentally wrong with me. Other kids looked strangely at me and I soon found myself pretty much a loner. I was shunned. Not because they didn't like me. They were just either frightened, or feared that other kids would give them the same horrible label they had placed on me. Now of course, knowing what I've found out in such a very short amount of time, it was all me. I was truly screwed up as a child, as a teen, as an early adult. Hell, for that matter, I've been screwed up all my life. I just learned how to deal with it somehow so that I could at least survive. Then I find out that my mother knew the entire story and couldn't do anything.

Manny's wife asked me how he died. Basically, I lied to her. To tell her the truth would've been impossible for anybody to fully comprehend, especially a distraught wife. It was just important that she knew he had died heroically in the line of duty. Maybe if I was to survive the upcoming turmoil, then at some point after his funeral I could return and have a more in depth talk with her. But not now. She had to have time to grieve. That sure as hell didn't mean knowing that her handsome, wonderful husband and father had been taken over by some damn alien *'freaking'* worm.

We left eight minutes later after I made sure their neighbor had come over to give support and so that she wouldn't be alone. I couldn't even begin to imagine how she was going to tell their two children, who Manny worshiped, that their father was gone.

I was completely quiet the rest of the way to the base, not even responding to thoughts from Aimee. Right then I just had to try and get my head on straight because vengeance was what I most desired now. Not only for Manny and Chief Crosson, but all the others at police headquarters who had lost their lives. At that very moment I was one very pissed off lady. Human, alien, hybrid, it didn't matter anymore. I just wanted these monsters dead, especially the original one who had started this entire nightmare.

When we finally pulled in front of the hangar it was very apparent from all the hectic, but controlled, activity that preparations were being made for war. It appeared that additional specially trained commandos had been transported in as well, maybe up to fifty now if I could count that high. That was most likely as a result of General Smith's hush-hush talks on the phone in the limo. I also noticed that Vince was standing off to the side of the building, not only with Tim, Julius, and Carrie, but now four other mean looking 'sunsabitches'. I was still kind of nervous being around Vince at the moment. I thought it best to stay away from him. He appeared to be extremely perceptive when it came to me and quite frankly, I couldn't tell him anything that had gone on at my house with Aimee. After all, I had been sworn to secrecy. Besides, he might hate me then.

Zuul stood nearby, like no more than an arm's length, which for him was at least four feet. He would've made a tremendous center for the Philadelphia 76ers, especially now since the last I read they were tanking again for another season. In fact, once known as the City of Champions back in 1980 when all four major pro teams had gotten to the finals with only the Phillies winning it all, my old town was now getting the embarrassing reputation as the City of Tankers. Maybe the rebuilding effort for all four teams would one day allow them to regain their glory days. Hopefully, I would live to see that happen.

THE REPTILIAN FACTOR

General Smith was conferring with Colonel McDowell, along with other brass. Phillip and Jeffery were near him as always, his permanent shadows. The other six guys in black stood in a circle between us and the General's group. It seemed that they never eased up, always prepared for anything in the way of confrontation and protecting us. The thought ran through my head whether they, along with Zuul, ever slept.

"*Yes Amy, they sleep. Differently than humans, of course, but they need to rest whenever possible,*" answered Aimee.

"*Dammit, there you go again, listening in on my thoughts,*" I shot back.

There was a strange sound, or a feeling I had, that she somehow laughed. I had no idea how that could happen, but since everything in my life was brand new it wasn't a total surprise.

"*So then my question to you since you're listening in on all my thoughts is,*" I continued, "*now that you and I have had a same sex marriage, will I ever sleep normally again?*"

"*Yes, of course. I needed to sleep as well when I was in the human body. Rest is important, not only physically, but mentally as well. In fact, when this is all over you will learn how to place yourself in total hibernation for as long as would be needed to get enough rest, heal any wounds, and stay strong,*" she answered.

"*Hibernation, like a grizzly or black bear?*" I asked, somewhat in shock.

"*Kind of the same, but different. Not nearly quite as long I'm afraid. There may come a time when a longer hibernation would be warranted at which time you could slow the heartbeat down to barely nothing, but still be alive. However, it's not important now. We will discuss it all later in much greater detail. After this meeting when plans have been made concerning when the military will begin their attack, General Smith will take you aside along with Zuul and the others. We will have our own plans to formulate, so for now just listen to what is being said."*

"Amy! Hey, Amelia," came a voice to my left and then I felt a hand on my elbow. I nearly jumped out of my sneakers.

"What the.....」 and I roughly swatted the hand away before I realized it was Vince.

I was immediately embarrassed. "I'm so sorry. Oh my God, I was just lost in my own thoughts and zoned out. I did the same thing with Manny a few days ago. Vince, please forgive me."

He just stared and then carefully backed up a step. "Okay, that's fine. Hey, we're all jumpy. I just have to remember not to get too close or you might rip my head off."

I smiled, but wasn't really sure how to reply so I didn't. Just then General Smith walked up to us.

"Everything okay?" he asked.

"Yes, we're fine," Vince and I said nearly in unison.

"Okay, the meeting is going to start now so if you can all follow me," he said, starting to walk away and then stopped with his hand on my arm.

When we were standing alone he gently turned me so that we were face to face.

"Amelia, this meeting will be for the military to set up plans for their assault, probably tomorrow morning. We'll find that out soon. However, when it's done and everyone breaks up, we will meet separately to discuss our own plans. I think you know what that means. I do, however, have one big question for you," he asked very solemnly.

Looking at him for a few seconds my mouth then formed into a curiosity type smile. It was all very mysterious as everything in my life had now become.

"Mmmmm, okay I guess. What could you possibly want to know from me that seems to be so secretive?"

Clearing his throat he proceeded to ask, "How much do you trust Mr. Flint?"

That certainly was an unexpected question, I thought immediately. Cocking my head slightly to the right I instantly became curious as to why he asked me that.

"Well, I've honestly only known Vince for not quite three full weeks. We met out in the desert when responding to the deaths of the two teenagers that were parked out there. He and his team had already been in the field for at least a week prior searching for this creature. However, since then I've come to know him fairly well I suppose. So, I guess you need to be a little more specific as to the reason for the question."

"In your opinion, is Mr. Flint trustworthy enough to be brought into our meeting later? Knowing full well that he will suddenly become knowledgeable about what we know and specifically about you," he stated firmly, his voice still somewhat low.

Wow, I thought. This was certainly something major to consider. A real slap in the face to wake me up. I'll admit that I was taken aback a little bit, especially since he wanted my opinion on the topic of trust and security.

"General Smith, I personally would trust Vince Flint with my life, your life, Zuul's life, anybody for that matter. His team members would follow him to Hell and back. However, I cannot vouch for any of his group in particular. For him specifically though, I absolutely believe you could trust him with anything. As for him learning about me specifically, the merging of Aimee and myself that is, I can't say for sure how he will react to that. You should know that Vince and I have had somewhat of a quick relationship of the sexual nature since we met. Unless, of course, you are already privy to that personal information since my life seems to be an open book now."

He smiled again and I wanted to ask him why he smiled so damn much. However, he was the General so I figured he could do any damn thing he wanted.

"That's good enough for me," he responded. "So my dear, let's join the others and see what the Army and Air Force have up their sleeves."

Chapter 38

Within the hour all surviving brood members had arrived at the prescribed location. Ten of them, when it was safe enough, had broken free from their original host bodies since they had been destroyed by gunfire, thus totally unusable at that point. Amid the horrific turmoil of battle they then quickly needed to find human bodies that had not been as severely injured, but still remained alive. For two of them, the human had just stopped breathing so it was still early enough that the body could be rejuvenated by the invading entity. That process needed to take place in less than five minutes after the new host body had stopped breathing. Within that very short timeframe the creature could still resurrect the heart, brain, and other vital organs before it got beyond the point of no return. They were able to escape before the army started checking on everybody.

The remaining four had been able to get away from the building, mostly through broken windows, or open doorways. Humans, totally unaware of what could happen, were then attacked by some of the remaining ten brood members once they were free from the structure. It was a simple matter of crawling inside the injured human body while it still remained alive. The brood was a unique team and able to communicate telepathically through a form of electrical vibrations, passed on to them by their parent. It was this etheric form of communication that Dr. Warring's group had somewhat discovered before the creature escaped. Developing those location devices had been a paramount project during the time the alien was still being studied. However, the creature changed those waves after it had escaped through transformations so that specific equipment was no longer of any use.

After escaping completely inside the body of Chief Crosson, their parent had communicated to each of them to get well away from the building before trying to obtain different forms of vehicular transportation. Those had included six automobiles, one taxi, and three trucks. Now they were all parked off the road near Crosson's abandoned car. Inside each of those vehicles was the driver who was dead in the back seat. Each creature did not need to transfer into another host body, but neither did they want to litter the streets around Police Headquarters which could then be noticed by law enforcement.

Anybody looking down at the desert floor from above would've been totally surprised at seeing a very strange pilgrimage in progress. A long, broken line of zombie-like human figures all traversed the same path spaced at different intervals. However, they bypassed the original cave to climb higher where the parent now patiently waited. Within several hours they were all well inside the new lair which was much deeper than the original one. Certainly the extra space was needed in more ways than one.

Chief Crosson looked upon the fourteen others with an alien form of pride. Regular emotions felt by the human population had nothing to do with the alien way of existence. The survivors had fought well, valiantly making it through the battle. With each transformation they not only got stronger, but equally more adept at quickly altering shape and adjusting to their new hosts.

Now they would need to prepare by severely altering the present host bodies. The creature instructed them on how to perform that process so for the next few hours it easily became the strangest scene ever having previously taken place on the planet Earth.

Upon first hatching from their shells they immediately retained all the structural DNA for the Gila monster that the parent had initially taken over, transforming several different times. They were now much more enhanced because it also contained the original body type of the parent going back to when it was first born on another world.

The human host bodies had immediately begun to stretch, bend, contort, and elongate, thus altering shape as if it was a bestial horror movie, becoming totally animalistic. Long, viciously sharp, extremely deadly teeth and claws grew to abnormal lengths. Grunts, growls and hisses reverberated inside the dark cave. It was an incredible sight of nightmarish shape-shifting, taking the supposedly mythical werewolf theme to ungodly proportions.

The body of Chief Crosson no longer had any substance regarding skin, bone, and organs absorbed into an entirely new bodily structure. The creature had been able to easily alter the human body so that armored scales covered the thin, non-protective skin. Some additional height could be attained with minimal growth, as well as partial facial changes occurring. Of course, there was also the additional length of nails and teeth. But for this final transformation the creature was now prepared to blend the earthbound Gila monster form with its own. The end result would be something never seen on Earth before, or possibly any other planet as well.

Now it stood on four legs just inside the cave entrance. In fact, because it was larger than the others, there was little room so it slowly lowered itself to lie on the ground. Snorting loudly, it hissed occasionally and then would make a deep growling rumble from time to time. Raising the head it sniffed, thus capturing a host of scents, whether safe or dangerous. It actually had no fear of anything so it was more of an early warning system.

Of course at this point there was nothing around that could endanger it in any way. The remaining brood as well. That danger would come soon enough and the creature would be prepared. Now primarily it tried to not become annoyed at the younger ones frolicking behind him. Being so young, they were like babies learning to move and walk, perfecting awareness of their new bodies every single minute. Like a newborn litter of puppies or kittens, they playfully fought each other with the normal sibling rivalry. Mommy had to scold them from time to time if they got out of control.

Quinotoa also selected three members of the brood, one male along with two who were more female than male because of sex organs from their human hosts. These two females would create and lay new eggs, thus expanding their growing army and replacing any that perished. It was not completely necessary for the creature to be female in order to lay eggs since the creature in raw state was asexual. But when it assumed a host body, if it was female then the reproduction organs were already in place. Whereby a male body had to go through additional transformations for the egg laying process.

The male selected was the second largest and would have the very important task of guardianship. They were, of course, not happy in the least because it meant that they would not be participating in the upcoming battle. However, they were now hidden deeply inside this larger cave where pits had been dug. They would eventually produce more young and become leaders of their own broods, so for that they were proud.

The creature allowed its yellow eyes to continue scouring the desert floor. A vital asset it had was complete and utter patience. After all, it had waited and planned for over thirty years before finally escaping. Allowing the younger ones to play, fight, and learn among themselves, Quinotoa just waited for the upcoming battle to commence. Of course, it also yearned for the human female that it so desired to eventually control.

The meeting was exactly what General Smith had said it would be. The decision was made to attack the original cave location in the desert where the creature had laid the eggs. It was determined that the aliens would unite at a place they all were familiar with. After that, it was felt they would move to a new location so striking the cave as soon as possible was absolutely necessary.

Throughout the night they would prepare, try to get some rest if at all possible, jump aboard the helicopters, and then get to the site early enough to deploy. Heavy duty equipment would be transported during the night so that it was already on location and ready to go if needed, which it most likely would be. This deployment would be made up of army and air force personnel.

On the other hand, the commandos led by Lieutenant's Frawley and Spinner were crack troops, highly trained in a very specialized form of warfare. The additional, and much larger group that had recently arrived, also came under the command of General Howard Smith. Basically, these soldiers knew their shit and I got the distinct impression they had faced similar adversity around the world. In fact, they were not officially part of any specific military branch, very top secret. They were trained by the same group that General Smith was involved with because their orders totally came from him.

I listened to everybody drone on and on about what the plans were towards preparedness and deployment, but it all eventually swirled together into one humungous fog bank. The thought flickered constantly in the back of my mind that what General

Smith was going to convey to us separately would be completely different and the military deploying at the cave location would be our backup.

Suddenly, I felt a gentle tap me on my shoulder. Breaking free from own inspired fogbank I looked around and saw Vince smiling at me.

"Hey, how are you?" he asked with concern, nervous that I might strike him.

"I'm okay I guess, and you, Mr. Flint?"

"Never better," was his response, chuckling at the same time.

We both started saying 'I'm sorry' at the same time, then stopped and laughed together. He reached forward and warmly hugged me. I would've liked it to be tighter, but at least it was an embrace which I desperately needed right about then.

"You go first," I murmured against his shoulder.

"Amy, I'm really sorry how I acted out at the headquarters building. I guess I was just confused as to why you seemed to be changing so quickly. Truthfully, I was also extremely concerned because you seemed to be so worried about something. You have seemed different in some way that I can't put my finger on. You do have to admit that."

"Thanks, I'm okay Vince. It's just that so much has happened in a very short period of time, like less than twenty four hours. Some things you are not aware of and I'm not sure when I'll be able to say anything. Please know that I truly don't mean anything by it, especially if and when I act like a jerk which is pretty easy for me to do. Just please bear with me. I still care for you a lot, I hope you know that," I responded in a very quiet voice.

"I care about you too. Hell of a time for this to happen I suppose. Find somebody you care about amid all this chaos and death. But it has and trust me when I tell you when this is all over we will pursue whatever direction it takes us. Agreed?"

"Absolutely Mr. Flint," I answered back. "In fact, I actually look forward to it."

"Another interesting thing happened. Your General Smith took me aside right before this earlier meeting occurred. In fact, it was right after he had talked to you if I'm not mistaken," he said, a twinkle in his eye.

"What did he say?" I asked, somewhat rather meekly since I knew the answer.

"Well, you know Detective Stephenson, if I tell you then I'll have to kill you."

I shook my head and started giggling. Once that started I couldn't stop so he held me even closer this time until I finally composed myself about a minute later.

"Actually, I was told that he would like me to be part of smaller meeting after this one that just broke up. He was not totally forthcoming, but he did swear me to secrecy. So I guess we've both been sworn to something you are aware of, but not me yet?"

That last part was more of a question so I looked up at him and nodded yes.

"Then you will most likely be on the inside of General Smith's unique group very soon and know everything," I stated with a somewhat more relieved voice.

I hesitated though, not sure what else to say next. "Although, you may not have the same feelings after you come to know everything about me."

Tilting my head up, he replied, "Hey girl, you let me be the judge of that. You're the most interesting woman I've ever met, not to mention the most enticing. Whatever it is then we'll face it together and that's a promise. I don't go back on my word, either."

Suddenly the voice of Zuul entered my space. *"Amelia, you and Mr. Flint have been requested to join General Smith."*

I glanced to my left and there he was, all seven-plus feet of him. Nodding in his direction, I just grabbed Vince's hand and we followed him to a smaller room in the rear of the hangar. Zuul ducked and we followed him inside. The door was closed and securely locked behind us by Jeffery. He and his twin then stood guard, very ominously.

The group consisted of me and Vince, General Smith, both Lieutenants Frawley and Spinner, Zuul, Phillip, Jeffery, Sergeant Gray and the other six men who had been with General Smith at my house. In addition, there was now a Captain DeAngelo that arrived with the larger group of commandos. One new lieutenant and several other sergeants besides GG also stood against the far wall. It was interesting to me that I did not see Colonel McDowell, or any of his staff present. Maybe they were just off doing their own thing, or possibly they were not included in these plans for a reason.

A few chairs were still open so Vince and I sat down while General Smith walked towards the front of the room.

"Good evening everyone. Nice to see you again Captain DeAngelo, glad you're here with us. Your experience is highly valued. Let me quickly go around the room to introduce everybody."

Which he did. I don't know why, but when he got to my name I got the weirdest impression that everyone stared right at me. Oh hell, I knew that I was just becoming extremely paranoid anymore. I normally had thick skin, but not so much lately.

"You all heard what went on in the earlier meeting. That's fine, we will need their assistance if we are going to be victorious, but they will be in more of a backup roll. Some of you may wonder why Colonel McDowell is not participating in this meeting. That's mainly because he and I had conferred previously. So trust me when I say that he is completely aware of what we're about to discuss here and our plans for tomorrow."

That certainly seemed to appropriately answer my own question.

"The idea that this creature and its offspring possibly went to the cave location is a valid option and definitely needs to be pursued. Especially since we have no idea exactly where it might've gone. We absolutely cannot discount that from happening. However, we are also dealing with an alien mind that will always try and be one step ahead of us. It's my distinct feeling, along with a few others, that the cave will be empty. We still need to go visit that possible option first. No stone can go unturned so to speak.

"It is now five o'clock. All you men need to eat, prepare your gear which it probably already is, and then get some much needed rest, if anybody actually can do that. You will be leaving right at midnight. I will be remaining here with Colonel McDowell. Trust me, you definitely don't need an old man like me with severe arthritis in both knees slowing you down. At least half of you will also be staying behind in a reserve capacity. I realize that will most likely disappoint those that aren't going along. You are all the best of the best and want to experience the action, I understand that. However, this enemy we are facing is highly dangerous. Probably more so than anything we've ever fought before. Just the original entity that escaped would be more than enough on its own. But now, it's a distinct possibility there could possibly be up to fourteen other creatures to be hunted down and destroyed. There is also the very obvious probability that some of you will not be returning from this confrontation. However, that tragic possibility happens for all of us each time we undertake a new mission. It's the game we all signed on for and I deeply thank you as I always do for your heroic service."

He paused then and walked back and forth, appearing to think about what he was going to say next. Then he continued, staring intently at each person in the room.

"You also need to be totally aware of everything associated with this massive endeavor. I have never been one to hold back information in case it might severely jeopardize a mission, or result in deaths. There are only a few of you in attendance that have met most everybody in this room. For those of you who are new, however, you need to be aware that you will see things happen out there that may be shocking to say the least. Several people here in attendance have very unique and specific abilities. That is why when you became part of our team you were sworn to the utmost secrecy concerning anything you saw happen, or secret information you became aware of.

"That being said, the rather tall, unique looking gentleman along the wall near the door is called Zuul. Quite frankly, he is not human. The six intimidating men in the back are also members of the same race, but different as you can see from comparison to us. Zuul would be a highly placed officer in their army, considered an elite member of their society. The other six are different in that each was highly selected from separate warrior groups. Yes, they are alien also, but vastly different than the creatures we are pursuing. Just like you they are highly trained and dangerous individuals, highly regarded soldiers in their own right. As you have been dispatched upon dangerous missions here on Earth to put down disturbances that are not truly of this world, they also have done the same thing. Not only here, but upon other worlds as well.

"Be aware that Zuul does not speak verbally. However, the other six are able to since their bodies are a form of human-hybrid. Don't expect them to be chatty type men. They are intent on only one thing and that's whatever mission is at hand. Once out in the field you will be broken up into six separate groups and they will each be assigned accordingly. That does not mean they are in charge, but I would advise you all to listen very carefully when they speak. It may very well save your lives."

He paused at that point, apparently waiting to see if murmurs erupted throughout the group. None came! Even if somebody had a comment they kept it to themselves. It didn't surprise me in the least. This group of commandos was trained to fight a different type of war so anything was possible. These people were not shocked very easily.

However, now General Smith turned and looked directly at me. He smiled as warmly as I've seen him do up to this point. I suddenly grew cold as something on the order of an earthquake-like tremble shuddered through my body. Vince quickly noticed how violently I shook and put his left arm around me tightly.

I knew exactly what he was about to say. In effect, bringing the hammer down on top of me. I breathed deeply and nodded ever so slightly, in effect telling him that it was okay. A different thought suddenly shot like a dagger through my heart. I wondered whether Vince would still have his arm draped around my shoulders when the general was finished telling everyone about this freaky female in their midst.

"It'll be okay Amelia, do not worry. Do not be ashamed. Remember that you are now, and have always been, more special than you could ever imagine. So just please sit up straight, look at General Smith with steel determination, and be proud of who you are," came the voice of Aimee inside my head, trying to assure me that all would be fine.

So I did just that as the General proceeded to inform them all about the totally screwed up Detective Amelia Stephenson. At least that's the way I considered myself to be. Listening to him talk about my life as if I wasn't even present, I couldn't blame anyone from shaking their heads in disbelief. I just prayed that Vince didn't run away screaming in horror.

Chapter 39

The room was extremely dark, exactly the way I wanted it to be. I needed silence, solitude, and sulk time – the three 'esses'. Closing my eyes I tried to sleep, but it was no use. Too much had happened and quite frankly, I was a total mess. General Smith's heavy words regarding me personally, and my transformation with Aimee in particular, continued to echo loudly inside my head. He had been concise and informative, plus surprisingly gentle and firm all at the same time. It was very apparent to me that you could literally hear the proverbial pin drop when he was through talking.

He then opened up the floor for questions. There were only a few, all about the upcoming mission. Thankfully, not one person in attendance inquired into Zuul, the six large men dressed in black, and yours truly, Miss Amelia-Aimee-alien-human-hybrid. I'm sure that they all probably wanted to start asking a zillion questions, but I actually detected a stern gaze from Captain DeAngelo leveled upon his men. Basically, he was informing them, *'Don't even go there'*. Being the good soldiers they were, they did not.

Now, however, a lonely tear began trickling down my cheek. It was apparent to me what the biggest impact had been as I sat there in the darkness feeling alone and sorry for myself. General Smith talked about my mother, as well as my own alien abductions as a child. That even though I was born human I was also enhanced with alien DNA, as close to an earthly scientific explanation as he could get. Now, after my transformation with possibly an over two hundred thousand year old female hybrid member of the Anunnaki race, I was now something resembling Super Alien Woman, able to bend paperclips with her bare hands. Thankfully, he didn't use that exact description of me.

However, the most distressing part was how Vince slowly removed his arm from around my shoulders until I was suddenly sitting in that chair, feeling completely alone, overwhelmed, and quite vulnerable. When General Smith ended our meeting I glanced towards Vince and tried to smile. He didn't even look at me. Just got up and walked out of the room. For that matter so did everybody else with the exception of Zuul, my strange protector, my huge shadow from another mother on a faraway world. So, I suppose Vince did actually go back on his word at least this one time.

I sat there alone in that empty room after the meeting for a good five minutes, not knowing whether I wanted to scream, throw things at the walls, yell out loud, or just simply disappear. Then I felt a large heavy hand upon my back. I looked up and Zuul was there, his head bent down with those piercing lizard-like eyes staring directly at me.

Then he smiled and for some reason I thought it was the most beautiful damn thing I had ever seen. That was all I needed and the flood gates opened. Tears started to flow nonstop as I stood and turned towards him. Then the big darn alien pulled me against his body and held me tight. That was exactly what I had wanted Vince Flint to do. But instead, it was an alien comforting a deeply hurt human female. Go figure!

Now I sat in the dark, twirling a pen between my fingers, and looking at the red numbers on the clock as they hypnotically changed. Then the thought struck me that I hadn't heard a peep from my alien side – the beautiful Aimee.

"Yoo-hoo, hey sis', are you asleep?" calling her inside my head.

"No," quickly came Aimee's soft response. *"Remember, I don't really need to sleep now, but I rest when you do. Amelia, there wasn't much I could say to you up to this point. I just felt it best for you to get through it all by yourself and if you needed me, then I would respond at your request, or if I felt you needed me to intervene."*

I laughed out loud in the dark and then thought, what a freaking joke. Laughing all by myself in this damn dark room like some crazy woman.

"I guess I should thank you for not bugging me," I told her, *"I imagine you've been able to hear all my inner thoughts anyway since there are no secrets between us now. It felt like I was being disrobed before the entire group, and then I just stood there naked as a jaybird, totally vulnerable to ridicule and embarrassment, thinking that I was nothing more than a freak show."*

"You know that's not true at all," Aimee replied gently. *"We certainly can't deny that you are different now. But, you also still remain the wonderful individual known as Amelia Stephenson. General Smith needed to explain everything to the people in that room because they may see unexplainable things very shortly. Like he advised them, there can be no secrets held back from such a brave contingent about to go into battle with an extremely dangerous and deadly adversary. I think what has seemed to make you so sad is how your friend reacted to the General's words."*

I smiled in the darkness. *"It's that apparent, huh? I just thought he was different and would understand. In reality, how can I now have a true and honest relationship with any man going forward? Children are definitely out because quite frankly, that baby would be more screwed up than I am now."*

There was total silence. I quickly wondered if I had thought the wrong thing. I glanced over at the clock which displayed eleven o'clock. We were to leave in exactly one hour so I needed to get ready.

After the meeting, and my mini-breakdown, I got together with Sergeant Gray who outfitted me completely with all the gear I would need when we shoved off, along with such awesome firepower. When he explained how the rifle worked I felt just like one of the guys, a badass commando. He was very nice to me though and thankfully didn't pry with any obvious alien-type questions. I really respected him for that.

"*Well, you don't have to respond to that,*" continuing my silent conversation with Aimee. "*We have much more pressing and important things to be concerned about other than my love life and potential children. Anyway, I can't sleep a wink so I'm going to go out for a walk and then gear up. Want to come along?*"

"*No, I think I'll stay here if you don't mind,*" she responded quietly. "*Oh, just so you know. I had to make Zuul promise me not to beat up your Mr. Flint.*"

"*Really? He honestly was going to do that for me?*" I asked, smiling on the outside.

"*He's become quite fond of you very quickly. Just so you know Amy, when you hurt then he hurts. But your Vince is fine, at least for the moment anyway.*"

I smiled since I detected that strangely subtle sound change in my head, appearing to me that she was laughing. Maybe some fresh air would do me some good.

As I strolled through the hangar towards the partially open door, I was actually surprised to see that a number of other people could not sleep as well, all prepping for battle. Apparently it was the adrenalin and anticipation of potential action. Police can feel it as

THE REPTILIAN FACTOR

they respond to different calls. Detectives sense it when they begin a new case, especially one of a serious nature. Military personnel from all branches can taste that adrenalin, the excitement, the worry, and the anticipation of upcoming confrontation.

Some of the guys glanced up and smiled when I walked by. A few of them said hello, but nothing else. Maybe they just didn't know what to say to me and that was fine because quite frankly yours truly wouldn't have known how to answer any of their damn questions anyway.

I walked through the doorway and stopped after about six feet. I looked up at a vividly dark sky which was dotted with a brilliant blanket of white stars. It was totally breathtaking and strangely enough, I found myself looking at the sky in a completely different way. I closed my eyes then and took in a deep breathe, letting it out slowly.

When I opened my eyes I was startled to see Vince standing in front of me. We didn't say anything and I truly felt like just turning around and stalking away. Screw him I thought, emphasized with a big fat 'F'. But I stood there like a stupid little school girl.

"Amy, I'm sorry, truly sorry. Please forgive me. What I did, how I reacted, that was completely and totally unforgivable. In fact, I wouldn't blame you one bit if you told me right this minute to fuck off and disappear forever from your life."

I didn't say a word, just stared at him for about ten extremely long seconds. Then I spun around and started to walk back towards the hangar door. But, acting like that damn stupid school girl again, I stopped and spun around to face him. He hadn't moved.

"Vince, I'm not sure what to say, or even how to react towards you at this point. When General Smith was dissecting my life in front of everyone I felt completely and totally alone except for the fact I had you sitting beside me. That made me feel somewhat safe.

Then you got up and left without saying a word, or even a glance towards me. At that point I felt truly alone. I felt like a freak. With the exception of Zuul, who comforted me with the big hug I had thought would be coming from you."

I laughed and then continued. "Kind of very strange you know that some giant alien could understand how distraught a little human female could be and extend support. Anyway, to use that age old expression, *'it is what it is'*. Now you know the truth about my life and what I am. Hell, I'll be totally honest with you and say that I really don't know what I am yet. I suppose we're going to find out soon enough."

Turning around I started to walk back inside the hangar and then felt his hand on my shoulder. I stopped and turned. He was right behind me so I looked directly into his eyes, trying to desperately read what they held.

"Amy, please give me another chance?" he asked in a gentle and pleading voice. "What I did in that room, how I reacted towards what I heard from General Smith, it was unforgivable and I completely understand that. I realized it as soon as I left, but was too embarrassed to walk back into that room. I know it was wrong and exactly what I should've done. I only ask that when this is all over you find it in your heart to give me another chance. That's all I ask. I'm not even going to continue talking right now because I'm stupid enough to possibly make matters worse. So please, when we get through this, and we will, I just would like us to talk and hopefully start all over."

Goddamn it, I felt a couple tears ready to start forming so I closed my eyes and sighed. I would not give his male ego the satisfaction of seeing me cry.

Opening my eyes, I smiled. "We'll see what happens. Right now though I think we just need to put all our attention into destroying these creatures. Or quite frankly, none of us will have to worry about starting all over."

That said, I turned this time for real and walked with purpose back into the hangar. I went right to the table where my gear was waiting and began putting it all on. GG came over to help and when we were done I really felt all weighed down. It was amazing how these soldiers could handle all of this stuff and still enter a battle.

"Ah, Detective Stephenson, I just want to say that I think you're amazing."

I looked at him and cracked a thin smile. "Thank you Sgt. Gray, I really do appreciate that. The abduction part I knew about obviously because I lived it. All the other stuff, as well as the merging, is all so new I still have not come to grips with it."

"Please Detective Stephenson, call me GG, all the guys do," he said. "I also want you to know that Corporal Jarvis thinks the same way I do, but he's just too damn shy to tell you face to face. In fact, please rest assured that all the guys are behind you one hundred percent and we have your six. You are officially part of our group, trust me."

Oh crap, I was ready to cry again, but thankfully didn't breakdown like some emotional woman. I couldn't really give him a hug because of all the damn equipment I was now wearing so I held out my arm and we shook hands. Then I saw him wince a little and realized that I squeezed too hard. Sweet Jesus, I began to wonder just how strong I really was now. Without a word we just grinned at each other and began heading out of the hangar towards the waiting helicopters.

As we did so, all the guys who were geared up joined us by falling in line. GG fell back a few feet so I quickly found myself walking ahead of everybody else, like I was in charge and group leader. We walked right past Vince and his people. He stared at me and smiled. I wanted to just flip him the bird, but thought better of it.

As we neared the first chopper Lt. Frawley looked around and started laughing.

"Well I'll be damn, it's about time somebody shaped up this sad sack outfit. Isn't that right Captain?"

Both DeAngelo and Lt. Spinner spun around and saluted me. I knew they were joking but what the hell, it made me feel good anyway since it took my mind off all the other crap in my life. I returned their salute,

"Hoorah!" yelled GG, really loudly, echoing throughout the hangar.

That was followed by more excited hoots and hollers, followed by each of the guys slapping me hard on the shoulders and back like I was a walking piñata. I glanced back towards the hangar and saw Zuul walking towards us in that very long, loping stride of his. He nodded his head towards me and I swear I saw his eyes change color.

At least it all took my mind off Vince and everything else. When I came up to the first chopper, two of the guys put their hands under my armpits and easily lifted me inside. Corporal Jarvis patted the seat next to him where I sat down.

"Feel good about this, Amy," he said, finally getting the nerve to talk to me. "It takes a helluva' lot longer for most new guys to be accepted into this outfit. It took you all but about six hours. You're one of us now girl and know that we have your back."

There wasn't anything to say so I just nodded, displayed a huge grin, and held up my hand to slap his in a commando-type high five. I glanced over at another chopper where Vince and his group were just then boarding. I felt a little pang of guilt which didn't last long. Damn it, I wanted him to feel as bad as he made me feel. I had, however, made up my mind that when this was over I would give him another chance to make it all up to me. I actually would look forward to that, but we both had to survive this upcoming battle first which was a daunting undertaking to say the least.

Chapter 40

Quinotoa heard a commotion in the distance and got the sense that humans were beginning to gather. The battle was finally near at hand. He knew that they still had time to prepare, especially since the enemy would strike the original cave first.

He rose and turned to look back inside the cave. His sight was extremely acute and being able to easily see within the darkness was not an issue. At this point after another transformation he was of immense size. No longer even remotely resembling the Gila monster that originally began as the first conversion from the snake, his true bodily structure was now more like a kimodo dragon. He was a staggering twelve feet long and nearly four feet high from ground to shoulder. His long neck and head made him seem even more gigantic. The normally thick skin was now covered completely in very hard scales as armor, kind of a dirty dark brown in color. That alone would be camouflage enough, but it still maintained the unique ability to disappear for short periods of time.

However, one issue in particular became apparent when he was in the city and had to pass through a large swimming pool when crossing a backyard. The water created a bright, sparkly effect. It went away quickly enough when he exited the water and shook its body vociferously. Still, during that short period of time there was some vulnerability.

The creature gazed at the brood which was just as anxious to taste action. They were all smaller than Quinotoa, but still massive. The males ranged between eight and ten feet long from snout to tail, while the females were slightly smaller with an average length of about seven feet. Other than getting through the attack at the building in the city, they were not what could be termed an experienced fighting force yet. They still had to prove themselves against a formidable enemy and that was definitely about to happen. It knew that the humans would not permit a surprise attack to happen again.

While resting during the night there also was a change made. Feeling that it was possible the human army would split apart and attack from different directions, Quinotoa made a decision to move the two chosen females and guardian male to an entirely new location. It had actually discovered the other cave before settling on the one it laid the eggs in. This other site was actually much further away and even better secluded because it was at the base of a narrow canyon, very well hidden. There was plenty of wild game in the area for the male to hunt and provide nourishment. And, if a few humans would be stupid and unaware enough to venture nearby then they could be added to the menu.

This alteration of plans would provide a second wave to be born and multiply in hiding. Just in case the human army was victorious in the forthcoming battle, although the creature did not believe that would happen.

Signals had been conveyed constantly to the young instructing them what to do when the attack commenced. He turned and began ambling slowly from the cave. It was still relatively dark, thus allowing some form of natural protection. Storm clouds had begun swirling across the mountain around sundown the previous evening. No rain had started falling as of yet, but the creature was a little concerned about that eventuality, hoping the battle would start before Mother Nature entered with all her might.

The new cave was well secluded and a good four hundred yards higher than the original one, as well as much further towards the north side. Quinotoa could see in the distance lights from military vehicles which were being maneuvered into battle position. At one point during the night he took note of at least three, possibly four flying vehicles with moving blades, different than their normal type aircraft. He lost sight of them and thus did not notice where they landed. He figured it might be some archaic form of transporting soldiers. It knew that more would come, but that didn't matter because it felt somewhat invincible. Their newly formed armor was even thicker than before which was now a necessity due to different ammunition the soldiers had been using. Piercing their shell now would be near impossible although direct explosions could cause physical damage.

Stopping when it was about fifty yards away from the birth cave, the creature sent out instructions for each of his brood to go forth and then hide under camouflaged conditions. Once hunkered down they would just resemble large rocks and in this mountainous terrain, that should be enough as long as they remained completely still. They had also been instructed to not move an inch even if explosions happened nearby. It had discovered humans to be somewhat totally unaware of their surroundings so it made attacking them rather easy while lying in wait, totally undetected.

Once they were all in position he settled down as well. It would not be too long before an attack would commence and they would be ready to counter react at the same time. Defeating this small army would be important because it would set them back and provide enough time for additional eggs to be safely cultivated and new young to be born.

Quinotoa would then be one more critical step closer to overall invasion.

Once we lifted off from Davis-Monthan I closed my eyes and tried to remain calm, allowing the vibrations from the chopper to relax me. Prior to this damn alien coming onto the scene, I had to pull my firearm only four times in my entire career.

I remembered back to the three times when I was still in Philly. Thankfully, I only had to fire it once and that was when we responded to a domestic disturbance where a drunken husband had been beating on his wife with a damn metal baseball bat. It was at the end of July and really hot so the front door of the house was wide open. Entering the structure after loudly announcing who we were, the crazed maniac came right at us, bat held higher than when my favorite player, Michael Jack, batted for the Phillies back in the 80's. I used to love how he wiggled his butt each time he stepped into the batter's box. The best third baseman in major league history.

There was no time to think because our lives were suddenly in jeopardy as well. I fired, hitting him in the right leg while my partner Ed fired a second later, striking the asshole in the left shoulder. He dropped like a sack of Idaho potatoes. Believe it or not, when the prick fell to the floor he started crying. The big bad he-man ended up being nothing more than a big cry baby. His wife was in bad shape, but she fortunately pulled through. Mr. Little Leaguer went up river on vacation behind bars for a nice long stretch.

The other two times it was pulled in Philadelphia I didn't have to thankfully fire it at any particular person. I didn't consider myself Annie Oakley, but if in danger I would definitely react accordingly.

The first time I pulled my gun here in Tucson was when Manny and I were following up on a ripe lead. We had to enter an empty warehouse after receiving what we perceived as a righteous tip. Believe it or not, we found the *'perp'* sound asleep, snoring away on top of some old dirty tarps. All we had to do was move in close and then yell like hell. The second time was when we had to crash through the door of a third floor apartment where we had an excellent reason to believe that a murderer was hiding out. He wasn't sleeping like the other idiot had been, but fortunately he also was not near his weapon. When he lunged for the gun I fired into the wooden coffee table where he was sitting. The bullet didn't strike him at all, but he received the gift of a few nice long splinters imbedded in his hand. Oh yeah, he also cried. Why are criminals such babies?

Now here I was flying over the vast Sonora Desert at midnight sitting inside a badass helicopter surrounded by crack commandos who would take a bullet for me. I didn't know whether to feel safe, or worry about what lay ahead of us. I figured both were good options so I felt safe and then damn worried at the same time.

"Aimee, do you think I'm ready for this? You've only talked to me about these new powers that I now possess. Plus, I've never once fired this damn big rifle I'm clutching. I'm really feeling more and more like an alien out of water," I told her.

"You'll be fine Amelia. When we land and then locate these creatures I will mostly take over so just be ready. I know that you may feel somewhat like a puppet at first, but you will also learn quickly. Also remember that Zuul will be right near you at all times, along with the others as well," she replied, trying to comfort me.

"I'm curious. Do the other six guys sitting with Zuul have names like he does?"

"They do actually. I realize they appear to look alike, but the more you're around them you will notice subtle differences. For now, looking at them starting from the left since they are all sitting across from you, their names are – Aunk, Durk, Keln, Kuhd, Tren, and Vult. They will not mind that you study their features so you have a little time to do that. They will only react to you verbally when in their human form."

"That sounds ominous. I'm not sure if I want to see them when not in human form," I inquired. "It's also interesting, do all the soldiers back on your planet have four letter names?"

"Their actual names are much longer and difficult to pronounce so no need confusing you. The names I provided are shortened versions which they respond to."

For the next ten minutes of our flight I looked from one to the other trying to remember names with faces, or unique body builds. One thing I noticed quickly though, they were all pretty damn handsome in an alien/human sort of way.

When we neared ground zero, Captain DeAngelo informed me that we were splitting up. Our chopper, and the one holding Vince's group plus a few other mean looking commandos, was going to land on one of the few wide spots along the road leading up to the top of Mount Lemon. The Catalina Highway is a very beautiful two lane ribbon of road with short straightaways and numerous hairpin turns, some of them quite severe. The scenery is absolutely stunning and the driving not for the faint of heart. It can be quite a treat though, careening around the turns, especially if you drive a shift.

The highway had already been closed to traffic in both directions. Nobody was getting up from the valley floor on the eastern side, and absolutely nobody visiting at the Ski Lodge, or living in Summerhaven at the top, was getting down. That included bicyclists, joggers, and hikers as well. This was on the east side of the mountain only.

There is a secondary route up to Mount Lemmon which is an unpaved road on the north side. It starts in Oracle, a much smaller town of around 4,000 citizens on Arizona Route 77. It is an unpaved road and is very popular with off-road 4x4's, as well as dual-purpose motorcyclists. This road ends at the Catalina Highway near Loma Linda. Before the Catalina was built it was the only road up the mountain.

Near the top of Mount Lemon on the north side is also an old mining town that I had explored on several occasions, just strolling around and allowing my imagination to go wild. I remember my Uncle Sparky telling me that he and Aunt Sis had stopped there one time because they were curious what was on the other side of Mount Lemon. The town, of course, was deserted other than an old hermit/miner who lived in an old shack with a number of feral cats at the end of the only dirt street. Apparently, he actually still was able to mine a small amount of ore which he took down to Oracle once a month and traded for supplies. My uncle said the old geezer actually reminded him of the actor Gabby Hayes from the 1930's and 40's. He sported that grayish/white beard, wore old western style clothes, and kind of waddled back and forth like a penguin when he walked. My aunt and uncle actually sat on his porch talking for about half an hour.

Sadly, there wasn't any old miner around when I visited, but I did find plenty of wild feral cats roaming about. More than a few didn't look too friendly either so I left them alone. I also discovered an old mine that me and my friend Mindy got up the nerve to explore, very carefully I might add. We didn't stay long because it also appeared to be a great haven for bees, or some other flying insect like wasps. We ran out screaming and swatting at the same time. I didn't want to stay around in order to find out what exactly they actually were because I didn't really care. Even though I was Detective Amelia Stephenson, I had no desire to get involved in any X-file drama since the last thing I wanted to discover inside there was an old skeleton with a knife blade between the ribs.

Now, here I was right smack dab in the biggest 'out of this world' drama a little old gal from Philly could find herself being a part of. I decided right then that if I jumped out of this chopper and standing there was Fox and Dana, well I was just going to breathe a heavy sigh of relief figuring this was all just a good old science fiction movie. That most likely wasn't going to happen though so I was quickly slammed back to reality.

We were aboard one of the most sophisticated choppers in the military, the MH-60M Black Hawk. At first I freaked out a little as we hovered over the open area along the roadside. First because I thought we might have to fast-slide down the rope which thankfully we did not have to do. Then I realized there was a very steep drop off the edge of the open area we landed on that fell far down into a narrow canyon. Oh, I hate heights.

I consider myself to be fairly daring, but not bravely stupid if you know what I mean. The rotors kept whirling, blowing up a storm cloud of dust as we jumped out and also unloaded some additional gear. We then hustled down the road a bit while our Black Hawk took off and the other one landed to do the exact same process. I was just in awe of the entire operation, absolutely freaking amazed. I think I was a closet commando.

Once the awesome copters majestically took off we huddled together in a group and knelt down so Captain DeAngelo could give us our orders again. We had received them once already back at the base, but they were repeated now so we were all on board.

"Okay men, and ladies (meaning Carrie, me, and Aimee – even though he couldn't see her), we are going to break up into three groups of ten. Initial surveillance of the area concluded that we are virtually right above the original cave where the creature laid the eggs. Between that location and where we are now there are three other caves that we need to check out. I can't emphasize strongly enough that the utmost stealth will be required. Any of these caves can hold the creatures hiding away."

He moved to his right a little bit, reached down and then held up a small black box with a screen.

"This is a compact thermal imaging unit that each group will carry. It should alert you to any large bodies hiding nearby. Certainly large enough to let you know there may be something dangerous around. In addition, one of you in each group will be carrying a flame thrower. We've all gone over this before so you all know what's up. Now, here is the location of each cave we're going to look at before reaching the bottom."

He knelt down in the circle and laid out what amounted to a very large photo of the mountain side with three large X's marked off with a number beside each letter.

"In our meeting before leaving the base we were all assigned groups. Looking down at this large photo of the mountainside, you will see three letter X's. I will lead X_1, Lieutenant Frawley will be in charge of X_2, and Lieutenant Spinner will lead X_3. The caves are not very far apart so we should be able to quickly come to the aid of another group easily enough. The other two choppers landed at the base of the mountain and two other groups will be coming towards us from below, but more converging on the original cave. Each team lead will also be in constant communication with those three groups from below. The last thing we need is a firefight with numerous friendly fire casualties."

He stood up with hands on his hips and grinned. "People, this is what we train so hard for. We're the best at what we do. Let's get set and break into groups. Don't forget to drop those night vision goggles into place. It's damn dark out there and we don't need anybody breaking a leg, or even worse. Gentlemen and ladies, good hunting and we'll see each other down at the bottom of this damn mountain. Let's kill these creatures and add their heads to our trophy wall so we can crack open the champagne. So people, let's lock it, cock it, and get ready to rock it."

I was in Group X1 which was comprised of me, Captain DeAngelo, Zuul, Sergeant Gray (GG), Jarvis, Aunk, Vult, and three other nasty looking commandos, their names which alluded me at that moment. Our cave was the first one that would be checked out and was just a little west of X2. Since the Catalina Highway actually curves and circles its way up to the top of the mountain like a long, festive ribbon, we all had to scale a small ridge before we could start our descent. That took about twenty minutes and thankfully allowed me to get used to the green glow of the night vision goggles. Starting down the other side we spread out a little bit in rows of five. I was smack dab in the middle of the second row feeling pretty damn safe with Zuul in front of me.

Oh, interestingly enough, Zuul, Aunk, and Vult did not need to wear goggles because their eyesight in the dark was apparently excellent since they were alien, thank you very much. It was also the same with Durk, Keln, Kuhd, and Tren. Sounded like the name of a law firm. As I was told by Aimee, my eyesight and hearing would eventually become very acute, but it was too soon for all that to have happened. I did look pretty damn cool though in my stylish night vision goggles, helmet, and bullet proof vest. I sincerely hoped that the vest was also teeth and claw proof.

The front row, besides Zuul, had both Aunk and Vult, along with GG and Jarvis. We tried our best to keep noise down to a minimum, but at night that was pretty hard to do. It was mostly small stones and gravel that we had no control over.

After we had climbed down about two hundred yards or so we stopped just above cave X1. We all knelt in unison. Using hand signals, Captain DeAngelo motioned Blake who was carrying the thermal imaging unit to come forward. They held it out in front of them, moved it back and forth, waved it in a slow circle, and shook their heads.

"There does not seem to be anything in there or around the opening," the captain whispered to the group, "but we need to check it out anyway. GG, Jarvis, and Raymond, take a look see! Be on high alert though."

Ten minutes later they returned and advised DeAngelo it was clear, no signs that anything had recently been in there. He then communicated that information to all the groups as well. We then moved towards X2 which from what I gathered was also being checked out at that very moment. It was also the group Vince and his team were part of.

I couldn't wait any longer and knew that I could communicate without talking so I did so. *"Zuul, what are you feeling? Do you think these creatures came back here?"*

There was what I perceived to be a moment of silence when he didn't answer. In actuality, it was mere seconds. It was like time had no meaning in the dark. My nerves were apparently strung tight as guitar strings and possibly breakable at any moment.

"They are here, I'm sure of it," he responded. *"But I believe lower than the three caves we are searching. They were in one of them, I believe X3. But they apparently have now moved nearer the first one. I would suggest you advise your captain of this because it's most likely a trap and they are in danger."*

I slid a few steps to my left and made a hissing sound at DeAngelo who looked around to see it was me. It sounded like he was communicating with somebody in the group approaching from below. When he was done he turned and moved closer.

"Yes Detective Stephenson?" he asked in a somewhat strained voice.

"Captain, I've been talking to Zuul and he believes that......"

But just then all hell broke loose from below. There was rapid fire and several explosions. At the same time Captain DeAngelo's comm. unit began to chatter away.

The battle had finally commenced. My stomach immediately tightened up as the darkness began to grow more illuminated with vibrant flashes from both rifle fire and grenades exploding everywhere.

"Aimee, I think it's time for you to take over and do your thing," I thought, which I felt was more of a loud shout inside my head.

"I am more than ready Amy. Just relax and follow my instructions. Also, stay near Zuul at all times so that you're safe."

I silently agreed as we started moving over to assist X2 group. I secretly hoped that Vince was okay.

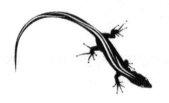

Chapter 41

Quinotoa knew that three separate groups were approaching them from above and three from below. He had only briefly noticed the four flying vehicles with the blades and then they had disappeared. That had been a major mistake because now he realized they had split up and they were caught in between. However, the error could be rectified. The fact that its hearing was so acute gave him ample warning of where they all were. At the same time, the humans had moved heavy equipment of some type closer to the base of the mountain. Those most likely would expel explosive type ammunition.

They were definitely outnumbered, but he felt assured they were fiercer and better protected. He signaled five of his brood to climb higher and attack the closest group, at the same time advising them to camouflage as much as possible. He would remain here with the rest and get prepared to attack. They were well hidden and eager to do battle.

The three groups that had been approaching slowly in the dark from below were Alpha, Echo, and Charlie. Alpha was in the middle led by Lt. Harold Silverstein. It was their sole responsibility to arrive at, and then carefully enter, the birth cave. At that exact moment the six team members of Alpha were spread out, but not that far apart. No more than three arm lengths separated each commando.

Silverstein motioned for Corporal Jose Juarez (JJ to his buddies), to approach where he was kneeling down behind a large rock. JJ was responsible for the thermal imaging unit so he moved forward until he reached his Lieutenant.

"What's that screen show, Juarez? Where are these creatures?"

"Sir, that's what seems to be really weird. The cave is just ahead of us, only about ten yards. It does seem to be empty other than some lingering images. However, as you can see from the screen, there are seven strong blips at different locations in the area surrounding the cave. If you ask me sir, there is definitely something out there and it's not friendly by any means. Seems to me to be a trap."

Harold stared at Juarez for a few seconds and then nodded in understanding. It was immediately obvious that some of the creatures were hiding in wait to attack them.

"Okay, start passing the word JJ. Instruct them to be on high alert. Let them know what you just told me. I am contacting Captain DeAngelo so they are aware of what's maybe about to happen down here."

Juarez started moving to his right. All of a sudden there was a loud roar behind him. Jose was then knocked high into the air by an immensely strong invisible force. When he struck the ground his entire upper body was quickly slit down the middle. It all happened so fast that he didn't even have time to react or yell for help. He was dead instantly.

Lt. Silverstein turned and raised his rifle, all in one motion. At the same time the air overtop Juarez that had been eerily rippling now took monstrous shape with the huge lizard starting to appear. With one enemy down it immediately spun around searching hungrily for the next victim. And that was Harold Silverstein. The creature felt totally exhilarated, eager to kill again.

Silverstein slammed his right hand against the comm. unit and yelled loudly, "Captain, we are under attack. I repeat, under goddamn attack. We need help."

He then dived out of the way as the creature lunged directly at him. All he could think of while madly scrambling away like a frightened crab was that this was the biggest fucking animal he had ever seen other than on television. Falling hard to the ground flat on his back he raised his M-16 and began firing a constant volley. The bullets were striking the creature dead on, but they seemed to have little effect other than knocking the alien off balance. At least it provided valuable time for him to squirm further away and begin trying to regain his feet. Maybe, God willing, he thought he might even get clear.

By that point the entire battleground was lit up like midnight on Bourbon Street at Mardi Gras. M16's were being rapidly fired from all the team members at anything that seemed to move, whether it was rocks, cactus, or rippling air. The staccato sound of rifle fire filled the air from all directions as it appeared everybody was heavily engaged in some form of battle. Grenades were being launched, nearby explosions both blinding and deafening. The problem was that none of the soldiers knew what the hell they were firing at because when all the creatures had begun launching their surprise attacks they were in camouflage mode. Other than the air in front of them seeming to move, they could see nothing concrete to shoot at. Only when they appeared was there a target to zero in on.

Silverstein suddenly realized he might have that one blessed moment in life that all soldiers pray for, to allude possible death. He struggled to regain his equilibrium because a grenade had very nearly struck the huge lizard directly, knocking it backwards, but primarily just stunning it. Then, as he nearly was able to stand erect, he slipped on something and fell flat on his stomach. Without hesitation, the creature was on top of him that fast. All he could think of in those last fleeting seconds of life was how much he loved his wife Maria, and that he would never get to see his soon to be born son that they were going to name Jonathan after his father. The creature hissed loudly in anger, bent down and ripped Lieutenant Silverstein's head completely off.

These two brave warriors were not the only casualties from this vicious assault. Soon there were six giant lizards right in their midst. The remaining team members fired their M16's without stopping, ejecting spent clips and jamming in new ones. They released what grenades they had from the rifles underneath barrel, but it just appeared nothing was having any effect. Due to the creatures earlier transformations where they formed even much thicker scales, the armor piercing shells being fired at them no longer were effective. The only damage being done was when a grenade, or some other explosion fired from below, made a direct or near hit. Even then, none of the creatures had been killed to that point. The humans were definitely losing this battle.

From the left appeared Charlie group, firing away at anything that moved. These were all crack commandos who were now totally in panic mode. After pretty much destroying Alpha group, the monstrous creatures immediately turned and began tearing through Charlie. At the same time, Vince's X2 group was under heavy assault as well, but only from three of the creatures. The other two brood members dispatched from Quinotoa were attacking X3.

A somewhat composed order from Captain DeAngelo went out to Echo group instructing them to fall back and find a safe position, then await further orders. He also instructed the heavier equipment at the base of the mountain to start lighting up the area around the original cave. He yelled out, "Blow these monsters to Hell."

Throughout the entire time all this chaos reigned down upon us, I was basically ducking behind a large saguaro cactus like a *'scaredy'* cat with absolutely no idea what to do, or even how I could help since Aimee was in control at the moment. It was a very frustrating situation for a law enforcement officer. Finally, I just couldn't take it anymore and stood up straight moving away from protection.

"Zuul, Aimee," I both thought, and shouted, out loud, *"what the hell can we do? Those guys are being slaughtered and we need to help them. I can't watch this happen."*

Suddenly an immense wave of power shot through my body like a thunderclap and lightning bolt hitting the ground at the same time. I tried to stand up straight, but it was as if I had just been electrocuted. If there was a mirror it would probably look like my hair was standing straight up. It wasn't actually painful, but the pressure was so intense that I screamed loudly. At least I thought it was my voice. I couldn't be sure of anything anymore since my once regimented world was now being turned upside down and inside out.

"Zuul, instruct the others to fully change," said Aimee. *"Apparently regular armor piercing ammo is not working. They must've altered their bodily protection again. We must end this fight now, right here. They must not survive."*

My hands and arms began to tremble and flutter wildly out of control. My entire body started to become extremely hot, boiling as a matter of fact, as if I had been totally submerged in a pot of scalding water atop the stove like a lobster. It felt as if I was in the midst of having an out of control fever. My eyes also began to burn intensely. I had to close them tightly because it became so painful I thought they were on fire. Plus, I swear to you, while my eyes were closed I felt my body beginning to grow larger in shocking ways that I could never have imagined, nor did I even want to know all

THE REPTILIAN FACTOR

the ramifications. For a reason that was very apparent, I just did not feel very attractive right about then.

"Amelia, open your eyes," came a strange voice before realizing it was Aimee.

I slowly opened them and was totally stunned. The entire world around me was shockingly red, like I was looking through a colored lens. I immediately realized that somehow I was no longer Amelia Stephenson, police detective or just plain old human being. My entire life, from the time of birth, had finally led to this very moment. Life as I had always known it to be would now forever change. The human who was Amelia Stephenson would never, ever be the same individual.

"You are okay Amy, do not be concerned or frightened. I will send you thoughts on what to do and how to react. It will become automatic so do not worry. Quickly get with Zuul and the others so you are not alone."

I then glanced over in Zuul's direction, just a little off to my right and was aghast that he had changed as I felt like I had been doing. Only for him, it seemed as natural as changing from a three piece suit into jeans and a tee shirt. His original bodily form that I seemed to remember wearing had been human in appearance, but now ultra-strange nonetheless. I seemed to remember it being extremely lizard-like with startling yellow eyes. Well now that's what he pretty much was, standing erect, but bent over on two gigantic legs. Surprisingly he had even grown taller and now stood well over a hulking eight feet. His human layer of skin had altered to a deep gray, his face elongated into the image of a terrifying dragon. From his mouth came a hissing screech so alarming that I wanted to cover my ears. Then I immediately wondered if I had begun altering into the same type of creature, only on a smaller scale. That was extremely frightening.

Fearfully I glanced down at the body I had previously been living in, but which now seemed to belong to somebody else. I sensed it was mine, but now outwardly different, as if I was part of a chaotic Halloween party where I wore two completely different costumes. Surprise, one moment human and the next, monstrous.

My once beautiful slim hands had elongated and the previously well-manicured fingernails were now just long, hooked claws. Skin that used to be soft and somewhat tanned from the Arizonian sun now had a totally white sheen, very albino-like, with a somewhat rough texture. Reaching down I carefully touched it and just as quickly pulled my clawed fingers back in alarm and disgust. It was freaking hard, like construction cardboard. I moved my hand up to cover my mouth and then just as quickly pulled my touch away.

Holy Mother of God, my face had changed drastically as well. Both upper and lower jaws seemed to jut out, while long teeth were sticking through my lips. Do you hear me? Sticking through my closed mouth like a damn animal you would see in a nature documentary. I tried to yell out in alarm and horror, but it came out as a strange roar. Was that really me I wondered? Holy shit, what happened to my sweet voice?

"What the hell is happening?" I shouted internally to the other person who had moved in to share space in this stranger than fiction body.

"Amy girl, you need to calm down. I told you this outward transformation was possible if the conditions warranted that it need be done. It is for our protection and defense, not to forget offense. Although quite beautiful, your earthbound body is extremely fragile, much too vulnerable," answered Aimee in that voice I was getting to despise with a deep hatred. *"When this is over you will revert back to normal."*

"Stop right there," I announced loudly. "First, don't ever call me Amy girl again, only my departed father had that right. And second, you never told me that I was going to be a combination of lizard/cardboard lady with long claws and sharp teeth. You just told me I would have new powers. Hello, this is much more than that."

"I'm sorry Amelia. You will get used to your new body, but now please move over beside Zuul and the others. It is for our protection until this is all over."

That was probably the most intelligent comment made to me in the last few hours. As I began struggling to move over to my right, and I say struggling because my freaking feet had changed as well, I glanced up and was stunned to see that not only had Zuul converted into dragon man, but Aunk and Zult had as well, but to a lesser degree in regards to height. They were not as tall, yet much bulkier in a muscle bound sort of way. They were also amazingly different than the huge alien lizards that were running amok. As I had thought earlier, the creatures we were fighting had the shape of horrible lizards, but the aliens on our side were more dragon-like with some human qualities.

"Zuul, has everybody altered shape?" asked Aimee, seemingly very calm.

I guessed that was my cue to take a back seat while she drove the vehicle.

"Yes Aimee, Aunk and Vult are with us. Durk and Keln are with X2, Kuhd and Tren part of X3 group. We need to take over completely because the human weaponry is not having any effect. Explosive devices are helping some, but only if direct hits. Each group is being attacked separately, but not as heavily as the soldiers below. Now that we've converted we will have things under control quickly and then be able to assist the others. Be aware, however, that most of the human soldiers below around the birth cave have been killed."

"I understand. Do whatever needs to be done," replied Aimee.

Zuul, Aunk, and Vult did not hesitate for one more second. I was confident they could handle themselves quite well. It was Captain DeAngelo, GG, and Jarvis that I was frightened for. The captain had moved a little higher up and stood by himself, looking down and observing the ongoing battle so that he could direct counter strikes from the base of the mountain. Sergeant Gray and Corporal Jarvis were standing back-to-back firing their M-16's nonstop and launching whatever grenades they still had available. If they were frightened their actions did not reflect it. They were true American heroes.

Suddenly, Corporal Jarvis was hit with a thick stream of spray from an immense lizard he was battling with. Jarvis immediately began screaming and contorting in pain as his body began to sizzle and burn. The liquid appeared to be some form of acid and I was becoming extremely distraught at hearing his terrified and painful cries.

I just simply could not stand by and watch this nightmare any longer so I started moving forward. The hell with being afraid. If I was wearing this freaking monstrous body now, then I sure as hell was going to use it.

"Amy, where are you going?" came a startled response from Aimee.

"Maybe you can hide behind the jolly green dragon, but I cannot. Corporal Jarvis and Sergeant Gray need our help so I'm going. What the hell is all this protection for, these claws and fangs, if we're just going to skulk around like cowards? Grow a set of balls, albino girl. You can change into everything else so be a soldier now."

With that said I moved forward and viciously struck the nearest lizard hard in the head knocking it backwards where it fell onto its side. Without waiting even one second to give it a chance to recover,

I leaped directly on top of it. Letting my own monstrous abilities take over I began slashing wildly with both hands. My new claws was like possessing the thickest, strongest steel spikes attached to the end of each finger. They were able to slice through the toughened lizard skin where the armor piercing shells from M-16's had been having little success, just harmlessly bouncing off.

I was now a crazed alien female in my own right. And you know what? It felt fucking great. I slashed away with the lizard's flesh and blood spraying in all directions. All my emotions, anger, frustrations and fears were being released in this uncivilized, wildly savage onslaught. Not everyone has the freedom to free their inner beast so that's exactly what I was doing right at that moment, as scary as it may seem. I always liked werewolves, both beast and man. Hell, now I was a creature and kind of liked it.

"Amelia, its dead so you can stop," came the voice of Zuul. *"Do not be stupid and let your guard down. You need to fight smarter. Kill quickly and move on. Please get behind me."*

I stood up and realized that I must've appeared at that precise moment like the wildest, blood-covered, savage beast in the world. However, glancing about I discovered that I was not the only beast. Zuul, Aunk, and Zult had killed the other two lizards as well. Glancing around in wild anticipation, searching for any other enemies to attack, I noticed Corporal Jarvis who was lying about twenty feet away. He was dead and it was very distressing to see that the acid-like liquid which had been spewed at him had burned mostly all the skin away from his face. His burning face and skull sent shivers of sadness throughout my body. He was a true freaking hero in my book.

My human emotions took over and I wanted to just cry, but realized that in this new body tears were not an option. I guessed that would have to wait if and when I ever appeared human again. At that point I would deeply grieve for all these brave soldiers.

"We need to help X2, that's where Vince and his team are," I said. *"Please Zuul, we need to go. I could not accept losing him."*

He nodded his huge dragon-like head and the four of us shoved off, followed by Captain DeAngelo and GG who had thankfully survived the terrible attack upon our group.

Vince and the rest of X2 were in a wild firefight of their own. When we got there. Durk and Keln had been spreading their own brand of viciousness on the three alien lizards who had been attacking them. I intensely glared through a thick veil of smoke from all the explosions, as well as fire which had been shot from flame throwers. There appeared that only four members of X2 were still alive. I suddenly panicked because I did not see him anywhere. I began worrying that maybe Vince had been killed.

Then I saw the large, hulking figure of Tiny Tim, looking like he had survived the worst fight of his life, staggering through the thick blanket of smoke carrying a blood covered Carrie Vaughn protectively in his arms. At least she was screaming in pain because it meant that she was still alive. However, it also appeared that sheer pain was coming from her lower extremities which must've taken a direct hit from the acidic liquid shot at her from one of the aliens.

Continuing to look wildly about, I prayed that Vince was okay. Not thinking at all, or heeding Zuul's warnings, I waded into the thick smoke. I was on a mission now. I needed to find Flint and make sure he was still alive. Nobody else on my watch was going to die today.

Just then I came out on top of a large rocky ledge and glanced down. Below was the entrance to the cave where X2 had been dispatched. That was where I thankfully saw Vince. He was crawling on his stomach, trying desperately to get away from one of the creatures who was after him, but also struggling somewhat since one rear leg had been blown completely away. At least they could be damaged by conventional weapons in some capacity.

There wasn't a moment to waste. I leaped down on top of the lizard with a heavy thud. Without even giving it a second thought I started slashing away with my very own claws and teeth. The lizard hissed and growled, trying to squirm out from beneath me. I wouldn't let go though. I decided to taste blood and bent down putting the lizard's neck right inside my own mouth. I crunched down with tremendous pressure and then yanked hard to the left. The entire head and shredded neck of the lizard came away and hung from my own mouth. It was my first honest to goodness trophy in battle.

It was monstrous, savage, beastly, and for some reason totally exhilarating. But, at that exact same moment it was the most horrible and monstrous because all humanity had departed my body. Now, I was nothing more than a creature not of this earth. A savage, nightmarish monster. Amelia Stephenson had died, replaced by an ugly ogre from a girl's overactive imagination. I was immediately distraught and opened my mouth, letting the remains of the lizard drop to the ground, blood dripping from my fangs. I actually wanted to be sick, but there was no time.

For some reason I then yelled, screamed, or roared, I'm not sure even what the sound was that came from my lungs and throat. Was it a wail of grief, or victory? It was clearly the sound of a savage beast that much I was certain of. I wondered just how different I was from the alien who had escaped after captivity for over thirty years and now wanted revenge. Was I now so different than the creatures we wanted to kill?

Off to my right, Vince had struggled enough to get away and was now leaning up against a rock, staring at the incredibly ugly creature standing in front of him. He raised his M-16 and pointed it in my direction. What the hell I clearly realized, he didn't see Amelia Stephenson, the woman he had quickly become so fond of. Now, he viewed nothing more than a monster that could just as easily jump upon him and rip away flesh and bones until he was dead.

I stood up straight and stared at this man who had somehow broken through my thick walls of personal protection back when I was human. The very walls I had erected in order that nobody hurt me ever again like they had in my childhood. I was fine with the fact that Vince was about to kill me. In fact, I wanted it to happen because I decided at that very moment I could not continue to go on living like a freak.

Suddenly Captain DeAngelo yelled behind me. "Flint, don't shoot man. It's Amelia, she saved your life. That is Detective Stephenson in front of you."

I turned my head and hissed menacingly at this human who dared to have the audacity to stop my execution which I desperately wanted at that moment. When I returned my gaze upon Vince he had lowered his M-16 and just stared directly at me. Through all the pain he was going through from what appeared to be multiple and severe injuries, the worst thing I saw was the terrified look of fear and disgust in his frightened eyes. He hated and feared me. I didn't blame him one bit because I was now a monster.

Hell, maybe he was shocked at hearing General Smith's description of my life, but up to this point those were just words from a rambling retired Air Force officer. Out in front of the hangar he had actually begged me to be forgiven over the very insensitive way he had acted towards me. Now, I figured that was all gone away in a puff of smoke, just blending now with all the other smoke swirling around the battlefield.

I sadly lowered my head and turned to move away when I was suddenly hit with the monstrous force of a huge tractor trailer.

Chapter 42

Quinotoa altered itself even more so that it was completely camouflaged while moving to safety. The battle was obviously over and they had lost. It was very apparent they had simply not possessed enough time to completely transform into indestructible creatures, especially the brood. In fact, it was really only a short time since the eggs had actually hatched, not long enough. His brood had been heroic and they fought valiantly. But, they were much too young and inexperienced. Not nearly enough time had been available for them to really grow and transform over and over, thus erecting nearly indestructible defenses. Plus, also become aware of all their potential powers.

The real reason they lost was it had completely not taken into consideration the possibility that earthbound aliens would come to the aid of their human pets. What was crushing in this defeat is that he and his lovable brood had lost to the very same alien beings that had originally caste him and others out of their society so very long ago as traitors. To then have to roam from planet to planet, world to world, galaxy to galaxy. Never having a home, having to fight and claw for everything. When it became rogue.

At this point there was just one final thing on his mind and that was to search out for the female it had been trailing so desperately. She was here amid all the chaos and destruction, draped in all the smoke and fire. The air rippled around him as he moved with great stealth to locate her. If he could just get inside that very unique body and then move to a safer location he would be able to produce an army that would not be defeated.

It sensed from her ethereal waves that she was only about fifty yards to the right. It was strange though because she was most definitely different than before, as if she was not alone within her own body. It was like she had grown, or even multiplied herself. The creature detected another alien being inside her and it sensed who that entity might be. That would be totally acceptable because it would make their unity even that much stronger. They actually would become invincible.

As it moved towards the female it suddenly felt drops falling from the sky. Apparently the rainstorm that had been holding off was ready to release its violence. That in itself was somewhat worrisome because the creature would lose valuable camouflage abilities since water broke through the electrical waves that rippled around his body. There was nothing to be done about that so it just proceeded forward.

It crawled to the rocky ledge where it felt the female had just been. Basically being invisible it watched with great interest at the human female who had now been converted into an alien shape. That had been the strong allure which had drawn Quinotoa to her in the first place, her apparent alien link. Now she bravely fought one of his hatchlings, basically the last one still alive. It also appeared that she had been fighting to save a human male who lay propped up against a large rock. That angered it immensely. To select a mere human life over one of its own babies was just not acceptable.

The female finally ripped the head and neck off the creature she was fighting. There was no sadness because the creature could not feel that emotion. There was only a warrior mentality filling Quinotoa so the loss of his brood was just part of war. He would reproduce again someday and all would be different at that time. Much better planned.

However, now the creature tensed and got ready to leap as the female dropped the head onto the ground and backed away. The male had been going to shoot her, but a human voice to the right yelled for him not to. Didn't matter though as he prepared to leap and finally unite with this human-alien being it had been tracking for weeks now.

I fell heavily to the right after being struck by a large, very heavy and invisible force. Immediately I realized it was the original creature, the one who had escaped and started this nightmare in the first place. The one who had killed my partner Manny.

As I struggled mightily to try and get free from its vast weight, rain started coming down in torrents. The ominous storm clouds had finally cracked open. My clawed hands were holding onto an extremely muscular body that was so much larger than my own. In fact, even though I had been surprised and frightened at how I had grown and changed, I felt like a shrimp compared to this grotesque thing atop me.

Thankfully, the rain was having a great effect on the camouflaged creature. The air around it sizzled and sparked as the creature's body steadily came more into view.

To say the least, I was completely terrified for there was no way I could even begin to defeat this monster of such immense proportions, one that was a nightmarish killer, a creature whose only purpose was to cause death and mayhem.

"Amelia, release yourself to me totally. Permit me to come forward. Please, do it now," Aimee commanded with more urgency than her voice usually reflected.

What else could I do, but exactly what she desperately requested. There was no way that I was going to defeat this hideous creature.

I felt a distinct shift in positions as I tumbled backward within my own body and Aimee moved forward. It was like watching a football team change the play on defense. As soon as that maneuver was completed I just got the strangest feeling that I was completely safe and would survive. But, did I truly want to now?

My body was being battered and thrown about the area in front of the cave like I was a ping pong ball. In the driving rain the creature's body had totally become visible. It was immense, nearly twice as big as any of the others, and so damn ugly. It roared and pounced on me again as clawed feet dug into my shoulders to hold me down.

Suddenly I felt intense pressure being released from my head. Aimee was apparently using some form of incredible mind control, reaching out from our brain to wrap around the one inside the creature's skull. The alien roared and hissed, shaking its head back and forth, trying to release Aimee's intense mind bending abilities.

Also at the same time the humongous lizard opened its mouth and a very long, thick red worm began quickly wriggling out. The head of this monstrosity, if you can call it that, started pointing directly towards mine. It forced one of its claws between my jaws and pried it open, even as valiantly as Aimee tried to keep it closed. The worm got closer and closer, brushing against my lips. The creature on top of me gagged and choked, but the worm continued to come forward, digging and prodding.

I felt both my hands holding it tight, trying to fight the wildly wriggling thing, but it was surprisingly very strong. All I could think of was watching that reality show where the idiots actually wade into a river and reach down near the bottom to grab hold of a large fish, the bigger the better. To my recollection it was called *'noodling'*. I thought it was crazy then and I realized it was totally nuts now. However, it might just save my life so I held on tightly, keeping it from getting inside me. If that happened then I knew I would most likely die. Even though Aimee was winning the fight I knew that if we lost this battle then the creature would enter our body and we might then become totally gone.

The head of the vicious worm was now trying to force itself inside my mouth so Aimee quickly reacted. Hell, we both responded. I chomped down into the worm's body as hard as I could. The creature made a loud screeching sound, as if we had actually hurt it for the very first time. I was so happy to hear that cry of pain, but the vile liquid in my mouth now was absolutely disgusting.

As we battled on the ground another huge body, that of Zuul, careened into the lizard on top of me. They both went flying and somersaulting across the open area. Zuul reached down and began ripping the lizard's body apart. He then stood, grabbed the creature's body and threw it against the mouth of the cave. Then Zuul opened his vast mouth and released a long, bright, yellowish/orange flame that set the huge lizard's body on fire.

While Zuul was fighting the lizard, Aunk appeared and grabbed the creature's worm-like body, thankfully lifting it away from my face. It was definitely getting to be quite yucky. I let go and rolled over, gagging and spitting out the parts that I had bit off the monstrous thing. Aunk tore the worm in half and threw both pieces into the already burning fire which had been the parent lizard's body.

Both pieces struck the rocky side of the cave mouth before sliding into the cave. However, when they struck the rocks they broke into numerous smaller pieces. Some of them fell into the fire while others somehow leaped to safety and crawled inside the cave itself searching for safety. None of this was noticed by myself, Zuul, or Aunk.

Now both he and Zuul released more flames in unison. All I could think of while hiding as far back inside my body as I could, was that it seemed to be a gruesome *'Game of Thrones'* episode. Instead, it was real life, a battle to the bitter end. But hopefully we had won by defeating this particular creature as I watched the body burn.

I lay on my back breathing heavily, plus continuing to gag and retch violently.

"Aimee, are we safe? Did we win?" I croaked inside my head.

A very tired and spent voice responded, *"Yes Amelia. You were totally awesome. I'm so very proud to be your sister."*

Huh, sisters. Well, Irene is my real human sista'. Now I was united even closer to my inner one. Truthfully, there are definitely strength in numbers. I realized that my family unit had now been extended by one.

Lying on my back I rolled over and found myself facing Vince. He had rolled and slid to a different location because he had definitely been too close to the action.

I tried to smile at him, but knew it must've appeared to be just a monstrous grimace. I lowered my head towards the ground to finally rest because I was so completely exhausted. Sadly, I realized that if there had been a chance we would get together when this was all over, now that possibility was no longer an option. After all, what right guy in the world wants to really have alien-lizard-woman as his main squeeze?

I closed my eyes, just wanting to sleep. In fact, I truly just wanted to disappear now. But, we had apparently been victorious although at what terrible expense I had no idea at that point. These valiant soldiers around me were the actual heroes and had given their lives to save planet Earth. That all might sound Utopian, but it was the complete truth. I was just along for this crazy, unbelievable ride and could never in an entire lifetime be as brave as the soldiers who had fought around me.

"Aimee, I'm so tired and I really hurt. Can we take a vacation now?" I asked.

There actually was a clear laugh arise inside my head that wasn't mine.

"Your wish will be granted. I would like to make a suggestion that we get away from the desert. Nowhere that is hot and sandy. Norway is very nice this time of year."

I laughed out loud, which ended up being some ghastly combination of cackle and roar at the same time.

"Hey, I think you'd really like Philly. It's actually the City of Brotherly Love you know. To my knowledge we don't get too many aliens around there unless they're illegal. The pro sports suck though right now, but there's always the Liberty Bell and the Art Museum. We could even take the Duck Tour and hope it doesn't sink."

Further off to the left Vince was getting some assistance to stand. He was in quite a bit of pain from his numerous injuries, but at least he could walk. That was more than he could say about Carrie Vaughn who had gotten sprayed with the acid. Plus, so many others had lost their lives. Maybe you could say that we won, but the human misery and death in the past month didn't make it feel much like a victory.

However, all Vince did now was stare in complete terror at the body of Amelia lying in the middle of the opening before the cave mouth. Before medical assistance had arrived he actually watched in both amazement and horror how she had fought the giant lizard, then the incredibly ugly worm that came out of the creature, and finally how he had watched her transform back into the human body of Amelia Stephenson. The very woman he had begun to have deep feelings for who could now shape shift into an alien's body. The very same woman who had once been me.

He just slowly shook his head back and forth until he was asked to lie down on a stretcher. He knew that his injuries would heal. However, he was not sure if his mind would ever be the same after seeing what had happened in front of him. He also was not sure if a broken heart could ever be repaired.

Chapter 42

I wasn't really sure how long I was unconscious. My physical injuries were vast, but nothing critical or life threatening. In fact, my entire body was actually beginning to heal itself which was quite shocking. I could easily tell that I was lying in a hospital bed. Attempting to sit up straight, the pain shot like a knife through my shoulders and back, as well as my lower right leg. Both hands were heavily bandaged, as was my entire right arm which was the one I used to shoot with. Reaching towards my face I felt bandages there also. To say the least, I was a freaking mess. I started tearing up as I remembered that Manny used to call me a big pain in the ass all the time. Now my entire body was one big pain.

Moaning a little bit I tried moving onto my right side and noticed a nurse standing there writing down numbers on a chart from a beeping unit on a pole.

"Hi there, how are things?" I asked, my voice weak and somewhat broken.

She turned and I immediately saw that it was nurse Ratchet, the one I previously had when admitted to the hospital before. Well, her name really wasn't Ratchet, it was Michelle Strong, and she turned out to be very nice.

Smiling she asked, "Well, things are okay. How are you feeling, Detective Stephenson? You appear to have had a fight with a lawn mower or something similar."

I tried to laugh, but it hurt too damn much. "You don't really want to know what it was and probably wouldn't believe me anyway. How long have I been here?"

"You have been our most important guest for five days now," she replied.

"What? Five whole days?" I exclaimed in shock. "You mean that this is the first time I've woken up in five entire days?"

"Well, not the first time. You came awake several other times, but the pain was intense and you were pretty much out of it due to pain meds. I'm glad to see that you're somewhat alert now. I'll call for Doctor Gonzalez so he can come and check you out."

I smiled in remembrance and asked. "Is that the same doctor who treated me before? He got really mad at me if it was him. Said I was a big pain in his ass if I remember correctly."

The nurse laughed. "Yes in fact, the very same. And oh, we also repaired that previously injured shoulder you would not let him work on back then. When he gets here he'll discuss everything. Now that you're awake I'll see if we can get you some broth or something else, liquids only I think for right now."

With that said she walked out of the room and I was alone with my own thoughts.

I wondered how many had perished in the battle, knowing that I was close to a few like Corporal Jarvis. Now that I was at least somewhat human again tears could appear and they did start to flow. So many who I had known were now dead.

I thought about Vince and wondered how he was doing, especially knowing that he had seen what I looked like, how viciously I had fought, and saw my body change back to the human Amelia Stephenson from what horrible figure he had almost shot.

"How are you feeling, Amy?" asked Aimee gently.

"Oh, hi sis. Well, I guess I'm feeling about as well as can be expected for a quasi-human, I suppose. I seem to be healing very nicely, but I'm definitely in pain. Cuts and abrasions will heal, but the bones and muscles need to mend, I suppose. How are you doing? It seems I've been pretty out of it for five whole days."

"Yes, it was rather crazy for a while here inside you. I was not concerned about the outward physical injuries knowing full well that you would heal, along with the help of good medical personnel. It was your mental state that I was fearful of. I know that you do not remember any of it, but believe me when I say that we had some close calls. We argued quite a lot and you certainly grieved internally which was difficult for me to help you with. But Amy, we got through it. You are an extremely tough and resilient individual and as terrible as that confrontation was, you have become even stronger."

"Thank you I guess. Has anybody been in to see me that you know of?" I inquired, hoping she would say Vince.

"You should be happy to know that Zuul, Aunk, Durk, Keln, Kuhd, Tren, and Vult have been guarding your room, inside and out, the entire time you've been here. It would take a super human being to get through them. General Smith, along with Phillip and Jeffery have also been here. I know that you were not aware, but the first few days was like this hospital had turned into a police station, there were so many law enforcement personnel here to see how you were fairing. Doing a vigil I think you call it."

"Wow, I don't know what to say. Is anybody in the room with us now?" I asked.

"Yes, in fact. Zuul is standing over in the corner wrapped inside a shadowed area. It's funny, at night I don't even think the nurses knew that he was there. Trust me when I tell you that he has been at your side nearly 24x7 for all five days."

I moved my head slowly to the right and looked inside the shadows. Yep, there he was, all seven plus freaking feet of him. I held out my hand and he moved slowly forward, taking it inside both of his massive paws. He actually smiled at me and damn it, I started to cry. At least I still retained some human emotions.

"Thank you," I whispered, both aloud and inside my head. *"Thank you very much, Zuul. You are so incredible and thanks for saving me."*

He nodded, leaned over and kissed me on the forehead. Holy crap, just maybe some of my humanity was wearing off on my giant alien friend.

Just then the door opened and in walked Dr. Gonzalez. He walked over to the edge of the bed and smiled down at me. Zuul quickly moved back into the corner.

"Does your big friend ever sit down?" he asked, with some amusement.

"You know, I've never seen him do that come to think of it," I replied.

"Well, I'm sure you won't be surprised when I say that I was really expecting you to come back at some point, just not under these circumstances. To say the least, your body was incredibly injured from head to toe. Actually, it looked as if you were just ripped apart and put back together again by something very sinister and angry.

"We were concerned with head and internal injuries, which ended up being okay. I didn't think anything could really hurt that head of yours anyway," he said, chuckling a little underneath his breath. "We did extensive x-rays which actually revealed some startling things. To be quite honest it was all beyond our normal medical experience. Maybe at some point we can do lunch and you can tell me the actual truth."

I smiled and nodded with my head lying back against the pillow.

"It's a date. So when do you think I can get out of here?"

He laughed. "Wow, that didn't take too long. You've been awake and alert for less than half an hour and you're already starting to give me problems. Here's the deal Miss Stephenson. This time around you are going to obey all my rules and instructions. You are my patient and will absolutely not get released until I feel that you are ready. Do you fully understand that? There will be no room for negotiations."

"Yes, totally. I now belong to you and actually need to rest this body. So yes, no more bugging you to get out. Oh, I do have a question if you don't mind."

"Sure, what would you like to know?" he asked with raised eyebrows.

I hesitated for a few seconds, not really sure if I wanted the answer.

"Was somebody named Vince Flint admitted here to the hospital? And if so, how is he doing?" I asked tentatively.

"In fact he was admitted here, along with a Miss Carrie Vaughn and a very, very large man with the curious name of Tiny Tim. It must've been one helluva' fight that took place wherever it was to have injured all of these people so severely."

I sighed. "You don't know the half of it, Doc. Thank you for treating me and you have my promise not to be a big pain in the ass like I was before."

He smiled, turning to leave. "We'll see about that since you don't have a good track record. You should be getting some liquids soon and the nurses will get you out of bed to start sitting up. Possibly dinner can be regular food. Tomorrow you should be able to start walking a little as well. Baby steps, Detective Stephenson, baby steps. You should definitely know about baby things. I'll bring you in a rattle if you'd like one."

Opening the door he stopped and turned. "By the way, Mr. Flint's room number is 307. From what I understand, he has been asking about you as well."

With that said the door closed and I was alone again with just Aimee and Zuul. As you can imagine it obviously became pretty quiet since neither spoke very much. All I heard was the beep of the machine to my left. I was also hooked up to an IV so I imagine they had been feeding me intravenously for the time that I was out of it.

My thoughts, however, fell upon Vince. I knew our relationship would not be the same again and that would be fine. At least, I thought so. I had gotten over my hurt feelings when he walked out of the meeting that night. Hell, looking back I would've done the same thing if he had been in my shoes and I had heard what he listened to. Anyway, I certainly could understand if he totally wished to avoid me altogether.

However, Dr. Gonzalez did actually mention that Vince had been inquiring about how I was doing so that was something positive. Right? I also wondered how Carrie was doing because I distinctly remember her legs being severely burned by that acidic spray. I made a mental note to remind myself and inquire about how she was doing.

My eyes began to get really heavy and I was trying to fight falling back to sleep. I sure as hell had enough of that, but my body was just so weak right now. I succumbed anyway, feeling in the end that rest and recuperation was what I needed to totally work on if I was going to get released any time soon. I desperately wanted that to happen.

My sleep only seemed to last no more than about thirty minutes. A different nurse brought in a tray of clear liquids. On the tray was lemon jello, chicken broth, tea, and apple juice. It actually tasted awesome because I was so darn thirsty. Especially since my stomach was starting to rumble, grumble, and roar as well, even more than my monster side had been doing out in the desert that night.

I had to drink my tea without cream and only had one pack of Splenda. Plus, it had grown warm at best, but still tasted okay because my stomach was feeling empty. It felt like I had actually lost some weight as well which is never a bad thing for the figure.

Just then the door to my room opened and in walked General Smith.

"Well, hello there Detective Stephenson, I'm so glad to see you're finally awake. How are you feeling young lady?"

I tried to sit up even straighter against the two pillows propped behind me. "I'm doing okay for being completely out of it for five days. General, did we beat them? Are the creatures dead? How many soldiers did we lose? And please, call me Amy."

Pulling over a chair and sitting down, he laughed. "So many questions Amy so I'll answer them in the order you asked. Yes, it does appear that we defeated them after an extremely harsh and deadly battle. Your second question is a little more up in the air because we counted their dead bodies at twelve and that included the parent if we want to refer to the creature as something patently so tame and wonderful. We had also counted six dead at police headquarters from that fight earlier. Units who had gone through the birth cave estimated that there could've been anywhere between seventeen and twenty eggs. If the lower number then it would appear they are all dead. However, if it was twenty or more, then where the others are could become a potential issue. Maybe they died due to other reasons, or didn't survive birth. We may have to wait on that."

He paused and took my hand in his. "The casualties I'm afraid were quite troubling for everybody involved. We lost fourteen soldiers and there are at least six in different hospitals that are still critical, but thankfully expected to recover completely for the most part. That, of course, includes you."

"Wow," I said in a very low voice. "You know, those guys are all heroes and hopefully we will treat them as such."

"Of course, without a doubt. Before I wear you out completely, let me ask something before I leave. Do you plan on staying a detective here on the Tucson PD?"

I looked at him and was curious why he asked that. "I haven't really had the time to even think about it, General Smith. Losing my partner Manny still hurts very deeply. Plus, all that happened over the last three weeks or so, both in dealing with those damn creatures, and then everything concerning myself. We also lost Chief Crosson along with so many others that I personally knew. It's just a tough question to answer at this time."

"Well, allow me to give you something to mull over while you're still here and, of course, I do not need an answer right away. You certainly know that myself, Aimee and Zuul, along with the others are part of a very secretive, worldwide organization. These people also know completely about you. They are very impressed to say the least. After all, what a special and unique young lady you truly are. We would like you to become part of our organization. I won't even begin to overload you with what we do, but you can somewhat imagine. Just think about it and if you're interested then we will discuss it at greater length when you get discharged. How does that sound my dear Amelia?"

I smiled and held out my hand. "It's a deal. I will think about it very much. And, thank you for everything General Smith. You've become an important part of my life."

"For what, almost getting you killed and changing your life forever?" he said chuckling. "You're more than welcome, Amy Stephenson. Now, your mission is to just get better and hopefully you'll be released in a few days. Talking earlier to your Dr. Gonzalez, he said that you can be a real pain in the butt when you don't get your way. I'm sorry, but I had to agree somewhat with that very astute assumption."

We both laughed at that comment, knowing it was the truth.

"Ah, General Smith, may I please ask you another question?"

He looked at me and smiled with that little twinkle he got sometimes in his eyes.

"What would you like to know?"

"Am I the only person like me? I mean are there others, either in this country or around the world that have gone through what I have? Or, am I alone now? I mean the way I am, joined at the hip with an alien so to speak?"

He stared at me for about thirty seconds, I think trying to figure out what to say.

"Well, let me respond by saying that this is something we can definitely talk about later in greater detail. But, to allay your fears and curiosity for the moment, there are indeed other people similar to you throughout the world. However, there is truly nobody exactly like you. When you're out of this hospital and totally recuperated we can talk about that further if you wish. Even if you decide not to become part of our group, we will never abandon you. Trust me on that. So my dearest Amelia, you are not alone. Nor have you ever been alone. And, you will never be alone."

With that said he turned and walked out of my room followed closely by Phillip who actually smiled and gave me a little wave. I broke into tears.

After that visit, two nurses came in and helped me maneuver into the chair. That felt great actually. I turned on the television, but ended up napping for the next four hours. Once I finished my scrumptious liquid dinner they helped me get washed up and then back into bed. Since I was completely and totally exhausted I quickly fell asleep and dreamed of all things, good and bad aliens, lots of explosions and people dying.

Sometime later that night when it was really dark in the room I was awakened suddenly by a very subtle sound. I hit the remote and raised the back of my bed a little bit so I was more in an upright sitting position. I slowly looked around, wondering where that noise had come from.

"Zuul, are you in the room with me?" I asked.

"Yes Amelia, I'm here, near the window," was his reply.

"Ah, is it just the two of us here in the room?

"No Amelia, there is one other person who has been sitting in the chair by your bed for about half an hour now."

I turned my head slowly and saw Vince sitting in the chair to my left.

"Hi, what a surprise. How are you feeling?" I asked him with the hint of a smile.

He laughed slightly. "Fine I suppose. I really had the shit kicked out of me, that's for sure. Biggest, badass beating I ever took. Broken left arm, three fractured fingers, about twenty-thirty stitches, two cracked ribs, a concussion I think. Oh, I also lost a few of my beautiful teeth in the front. See?" and he smiled. "At least I survived so that's saying something. But then, that's just me. How are you feeling, Amy?"

It was then my turn to laugh as I replied, "I'm okay also. Lots of bumps, bruises, and cuts. That can happen after being thrown around in the desert by a big freaking lizard. Seems I've been healing rather quickly though, shocking all the medical experts around here. I think I'm something of a curiosity and mystery to them."

"I can totally understand that. But, they don't even know the half of it do they?"

We both really laughed hard at that comment, true as it was.

"So Vince, you witnessed an awful lot out there and I can totally understand if you never want to see, or have anything to do with me, ever again. Hell, if I was you I'd probably run really fast in the opposite direction never looking back. Please know that I do care for you very much and at least I hope we can stay friends."

There arose a very nervous moment of silence between us that kind of lasted longer than I anticipated it might. In fact, I was sensing rather a bad feeling regarding his answer, getting the impression he was figuring out how to let me down gently.

He coughed before answering. "Amy, I also care for you a great deal. I won't deny that what I saw completely blew me away. It will take some time to understand it all. I guess what I'm saying is, if you have the time to share, then I'll have the time to listen. Then we'll see where it all leads. Sound okay with you?"

Damn tears, damn human emotions. Damn freaking human-alien female!

I whispered, "Yes Vince, absolutely. Friends to the end with maybe benefits?"

"Absolutely, as long as you remain how you look now," he replied, smiling.

He struggled a little bit to stand up. That's when I noticed he had a cane to aid getting around. Before he shuffled out of my room he leaned over the bed and kissed me which was freaking awesome. I wondered if he thought I might turn into lizard woman upon receiving his kiss. You know, the exact opposite of the frog and princess story?

"That was very sweet, Amelia. He is a very nice man, and quite handsome. I wish you luck, but prepare yourself to be let down if he can't totally accept everything."

"Thank you! Yeah, I know, but a girl can dream. It doesn't happen often that a girl has that very special Prince Charming come into her life."

But you know, it felt wonderful as his kiss lingered upon my lips. In fact, I was more than relieved. I was literally ecstatic. You can bet I slept very soundly that night and actually had dreams, not nightmares.

Chapter 42

I was released from the hospital five days later. I think Dr. Gonzalez, who was a really terrific guy and wonderful physician, couldn't wait till I got out of there. I broke our deal with him quite a few times, especially the last day because I literally bugged him to death about getting discharged. I think he actually hated coming into my room.

In fact, he personally pushed my wheelchair to the front door of the hospital. I really think he just wanted to make sure I left. Surprisingly, he gave me a little peck on the cheek, but then whispered in my ear, "I do like you Detective Stephenson, but try another hospital next time. I really need to concentrate on patients who need help."

We laughed as he closed the big rear door on the long black van and then walked back inside the hospital just shaking his head. My car was still parked back at my house so General Smith had Jeffery drive over to pick me up. I felt rather embarrassingly important since how many patients have a limo-type van waiting for them outside.

I was so relieved to get home. It felt really lonely the first few days. No Manny, no Vince, still not a cat or dog to pet, or play with. I was also on disability for at least the next two months so I certainly had plenty of time on my hands to think and ponder over things. It would've been a good time to unpack all the boxes I still had from my original move to Tucson. But then I figured what the hell, I should leave them still unopened.

Because two nights after getting home General Smith and I spoke extensively over dinner and decided that I would be submitting my termination request to the Tucson PD three months after I returned to work. That way I wouldn't be quitting just coming off disability and it would allow the department to find somebody else. Thus, I had accepted General Smith's request to become part of his secret organization of which I still knew very little about. It did sound extremely interesting, but rather creepy.

That would come in due time, being somewhat excited about the future now.

Vince was doing well and had been discharged two days later, as was Tim Rollins. Tiny Tim was quite the character because he came to my house upon getting released with a full case of beer. We laughed, cried, and got silly, all at the same time.

Carrie Vaughn was transferred to a major burn/trauma center up in Phoenix. The latest I heard she was going to be okay. Other than numerous surgeries and extensive scarring, she'd be fine. I joked with her on the phone one night that she would be back kicking ass again sooner rather than later. Plus, it held all kinds of possibilities for 'scar' stories, especially when dealing with all those macho guys she liked to hang around with. I wrote a note on my calendar, reminding me to drive up for a visit next Friday.

Alright, as for Vince, because I know you're dying to hear. We'll be going on an actual dinner date tomorrow night and I'm actually going to wear a dress. We both decided not to expect too much, but if it came along then great. If not, our connection had been set in some capacity for a long time to come. Especially since he had also been offered a position with General Smith's group so it appeared we would be working together sometime in the near future. Maybe a real life Fox and Dana, but not FBI.

Two weeks after I got home from the hospital there was a meeting out on Davis-Monthan AFB, led by none other than Colonel McDowell. It was a joke really. All he did was prance and bluster about how the mighty Air Force defeated the big bad aliens. Angry about the whole thing I stood up near the end and told him that it was their fault about keeping the crashed UFO secret, allowing the creature to escape, and then covering it up for weeks. I looked right at him and said how many people died, both civilian and military, on his watch. And, if it weren't for the commandos and a special group of soldiers, that big bad alien would not have been defeated. He was pissed to say the least.

Now, a week later, I just sat on the back deck with a cold beer on the table beside me, enjoying a really nice evening. The sun was going down, the sky atop the Catalina Mountains in the distance actually looking pink and blue. It was absolutely stunning. There was one thing about living in the desert I had come to appreciate since being here. The evenings, plus sunsets and sunrises, could actually be quite amazingly beautiful.

"Aimee, are you there?" I asked.

"Where else would I be," she asked, trying to be funny I guess.

"You know, when I sit here and look out at those damn mountains I just keep remembering all that went down out there. What a nightmare. Plus, I can't keep myself from wondering if we really did kill them all."

"I understand completely. Zuul informed me that both the Army, Air Force, and remaining commando units scoured all of that area looking closely for anything, even any little sign that one of those creatures could've survived. They found nothing so at this point we can only assume they were all killed."

Hesitating slightly I continued looking at a beautiful sunset, wondering.

"Yeah, well, I suppose so. I think I'm going to finish off this beer and go to sleep, I'm pooped. Want to come along?"

"Sounds like a plan sister Amelia," she responded.

I stood up and laughed out loud because I was definitely not a nun. All I could think about was how much my life had changed in just the last few weeks. It was absolutely incredible, totally unbelievable. Hell, I just could not help but wonder what my future would hold, with or without Vince Flint. You could no doubt place a large bet in Vegas that it would be quite interesting.

Chapter 43

A week later I walked slowly outside to pick up my Sunday edition of The Arizona Star. It was starting out to be a really nice day, warm which Arizona mornings can be most of the time. The weathercast promised a nice day, not too freaking hot.

Smiling and waving, I greeted several of my neighbors who were also out early. One thing about being on disability for any length of time, you certainly found yourself home enough to meet people. Having a crazy, full time job never gave you the freedom to do so simply because you were not around very much. In fact, I actually had become part of a Sunday morning coffee brunch in the neighborhood. Unbelievable, right?

I was a little surprised when they asked me to join because they were all wives and moms. Plus, I had really not been around much since I mostly worked the nightshift. Maybe they just needed a little perspective from the single, childless side of life. Or, maybe my being a detective and somewhat in the paper recently because of all that happened in the desert was another reason. I had to smile because very little of what actually happened out there was printed in articles, or discussed on TV and radio shows.

It was really nice. We alternated entertaining in our homes, as well as providing breakfast which varied from just good old coffee, donuts, and bagels, to full blown brunches consisting of eggs, pancakes, waffles, sausage, and bacon. Oh crap, the list got endless for some of the girls who loved to cook. Of course, I simply went with the donuts and bagels because I was still trying to get used to being somewhat domestic. We also discussed everything from books to current events to television shows to, oh hell, anything we wanted. Yeah, even men! I actually loved it and today was my day.

I walked back inside my house and tossed the unread paper on the couch. Then I took a quick shower, pulled on my usual Eagles lounge pants and Phillies tee shirt. Oh, and my cap also because of the scar on my head after the stitches had been removed and my hair was still growing in. Even though I had gone to a few Cardinal and Diamond Back games, I still bled red and green for my Phillies and Eagles. I suppose I just liked to be punished and disappointed for the most part. They would be on top again someday and I vowed to get good seats for the World Series or Super Bowl. Hey, a girl can dream, right? Well, my first dream was really for Vince to come back into my life. However, I would be just as happy with a home game seven of a world series in Philadelphia.

Oh, I forgot to mention that the date with Vince went really well. Yeah, it did!

Yesterday when I went grocery shopping I purchased a dozen assorted donuts, bagels, and muffins. Sorry, that was a dozen each. No idea why I always buy so damn much because it was just six women, all of us extremely health conscious and worried about our weight. In fact, I had decided to start jogging each evening after getting the okay from my doctor, trying to work myself up to where I might be able to eventually run a marathon someday. I have a fantastic nephew Bret who had wanted to get in shape. Even though it was really tough at first he did it every single day in all kinds of weather no matter how tired he was. I'm just so proud of him because he not only got in phenomenal shape, but also did in fact, run and complete that same Philadelphia Marathon the following year. He has always been an inspiration to me.

We decided to make the brunch anywhere between eleven and twelve which gave anyone who attended church time to do that. I had actually started attending services again myself. No, the church didn't get struck by lightning. This being my morning to entertain I decided to stay home. I had it on the television so at least that was something.

Around ten thirty I started getting everything ready. I decided it was such a beautiful morning that we could get our food from the kitchen where I had arrayed it all in a nice display on the table and then eat out back on the patio.

Rae, Gretchen, Valerie, Cecelia, and Sol all began showing up around eleven and by eleven thirty we were all sitting around the table on my patio chatting up the morning. We laughed a lot while discussing family issues, the latest music, or a book somebody might be reading at that point. I just sat back and smiled a lot, really enjoying this type of warm female companionship for the first time in my life, even going back to childhood. In fact, I could never remember being part of any group before.

Suddenly my reverie was broken by Sol talking directly to me.

"Oh, I'm really sorry. I guess I was just lost in deep thought," I said, smiling in her direction. "What did you say, Sol?"

She laughed. "I was asking whether you had read this morning's paper yet."

"Not yet. I actually just threw it on the couch and started getting everything ready. What does it say?" I inquired, curious why she would make a point of it.

She got up from the table and started walking towards the kitchen. "You sit there. Let me get the paper so you can read it."

For some reason we all smiled at each other, but I began getting a weird feeling all the same. When Sol returned, she opened the newspaper and placed it on my lap.

"Just take a look at that. Kind of creepy," she said, with an eerie sounding voice.

I pushed my chair back a little and raised the newspaper. The headlines read:

Missing People Reported
Will The Deaths Start Piling Up Again?

Glancing up from the paper I quickly noticed that all the girls were looking straight at me. Raising my eyebrows I smiled slightly, but didn't say anything.

"Creepy right?" asked Valerie. "Read a little bit of the article."

I took a sip from my coffee before picking up the paper. The first few paragraphs talked about four hikers and two cyclists who had totally disappeared while apparently enjoying the wide open outdoors up in the Catalina Mountains. The disappearances were in question because both bikes were found alongside the highway and several backpacks were discovered at different places on the side of the mountain. However, no bodies had been found as of yet even though in most of the cases foul play was apparent.

I folded the paper and cleared my throat slightly before looking up.

"Wow, I hadn't heard anything about this since I've been out on disability. It is somewhat ominous and creepy that's for sure. I guess we all have to be extra careful and stay out of those damn mountains," I said, a sinking feeling in my stomach.

After a few uneasy minutes they all forgot about the article and started chatting up a storm. When it came time for us to breakup I coerced a few of the girls to take some of the food home. I can't lie because I did keep two bagels, one large blueberry muffin, and two glazed donuts. What the hell, I do like my treats and the diet can always wait.

After they left I immediately sat down on the couch with another cup of coffee and read the article in its entirety. Then I read it once again. When I was done I folded and softly placed the paper on top of the coffee table and walked out onto the patio.

Standing there extremely still I gazed up at those damn mysterious and dangerous mountains, the very ones I had really liked a lot when I first moved to Tucson. Now, they held a completely different vibe for me and it wasn't one that I liked very much.

I knew as I scanned the article several times my inner sister was hearing the words at the same time because I made it a point to think them out loudly as I read. I didn't know what these tragic disappearances meant. Maybe there was a reasonable explanation. It was difficult getting away from one line of thinking which wasn't good.

Tomorrow morning I would call the precinct and talk to the new Captain to see if he desired that I return to work sooner. Believe me, I was more than ready anyway. Sitting around the house eating donuts and slurping hot coffee was not really my style. I also made it a point to call both General Smith and Vince later in the afternoon. Right now I just decided to discuss things with my inner sister.

"Aimee, I think it might all be happening again," I stated with trepidation.

"A-ffirm-a-tive!" she replied quietly, sounding quite worried.

Deep inside a cold, dark cave high up in the mysterious Catalina Mountains, an obscure hole in the ground extremely hidden from nosey hikers and spelunkers, along with continuing military searches that could be heard all around, there was very definite movement. Three extremely large bodies shuffled around, sharing space in somewhat cramped quarters. The sound of crunching bones and tearing of flesh was also apparent as they ate food supplied by the huge male. They were acquiring a taste for human flesh.

One of the females raised her head and listened closely, the lower part of a leg dangling from her long muzzle. Down in the two pits the cracking of egg shells had begun. The birth of newborns was always an exciting moment for any mother. And retribution for the loss of all the others from the initial brood would be avenged.

THE END OF THIS BATTLE.......
BUT WHAT DOES THE DARK FUTURE HOLD???

CPSIA information can be obtained
at www.ICGtesting.com
Printed in the USA
LVHW020724300422
717406LV00002B/3

9 781957 312583